BY VANESSA HUA

Forbidden City

A River of Stars

Deceit and Other Possibilities

FORBIDDEN CITY

BALLANTINE BOOKS   NEW YORK

F O R B I D D E N   C I T Y

A   N O V E L

V A N E S S A   H U A

Published in the United States by Ballantine Books,
an imprint of Random House, a division of
Penguin Random House LLC, New York.

BALLANTINE and the HOUSE colophon are
registered trademarks of Penguin Random House LLC.

LIBRARY OF CONGRESS CATALOGING-IN-PUBLICATION DATA
NAMES: Hua, Vanessa, author.
TITLE: Forbidden city : a novel / Vanessa Hua.
DESCRIPTION: First Edition. | New York : Ballantine Books [2022] |
IDENTIFIERS: LCCN 2021043089 (print) | LCCN 2021043090 (ebook) |
ISBN 9780399178818 (hardcover) | ISBN 9780399178832 (ebook)
CLASSIFICATION: LCC PS3608.U2245 F67 2022 (print) |
LCC PS3608.U2245 (ebook) | DDC 813/.6—dc23
LC record available at https://lccn.loc.gov/2021043089
LC ebook record available at https://lccn.loc.gov/2021043090

Printed in Canada on acid-free paper

randomhousebooks.com

9 8 7 6 5 4 3 2 1

First Edition

Title-page image from iStock

Book design by Barbara M. Bachman

To my sons

FORBIDDEN CITY

*T*HE CHAIRMAN IS DEAD.

September 9, 1976. Outside, the people of Chinatown are cheering. They light firecrackers and beat pots and pans, chanting as they march three floors below the window of my apartment in San Francisco. Their signs say, SMASH THE EMPEROR! and SMASH THE PARTY! Drips of paint spoil the sweep and curve of the characters, bleeding as if shot.

The cheering swells, the revelers giddy with rice wine and easy victory. No longer will they whisper the Chairman's name, afraid of his reach here across the ocean to America. No longer will they invoke his name to scare their children, or as a curse against their enemies.

They didn't hate the Chairman at first—none of us did. In the beginning, he *was* the beginning. He dared us to make the sun and moon shine in new skies, to end hunger and superstition in China, to end all that made us weak.

The radio crackles with another update, calling him "Father of the Chinese Revolution . . . an obscure peasant who died one of history's great revolutionary heroes. Despite criticism from other party leaders, he ordered the Great Leap Forward, ultimately causing widespread disruption and food shortages. Throughout his years in power, he toppled one rival after another in the Party. In the Cultural Revolution, he risked throwing the country into chaos . . ."

I switch off the radio, shaken each time I'm reminded how those outside of China knew more—and knew more quickly—than the people within.

Turning away from the window, I get dressed in my restaurant uniform. After smoothing down my red satin shirt, I fasten the frog closures, feeling the pinch at my neck. The Ming dynasty springs eternal at the Jade Dragon, the oldest banquet hall in the neighborhood. In the mirror, I'm hard lines everywhere but my chest. As I tie back my hair into a ponytail, my muscles pull tight, and my breasts push against my shirt. Here my awkward younger self emerges, put on display. Although I might appear strong and sure-footed, versions of me compete within: A clumsy peasant. A straight-backed revolutionary. A doubting missionary.

In Chinatown, many lies are born from necessity. Some of us arrive in America with false identities and fake papers. Others alter their ages on their paperwork: Teenagers pose as younger than they are to gain a year's advantage in school, while their parents add a year or two on their official records to move themselves that much closer to the benefits of retirement. They may change their birth date to a more auspicious and memorable date: New Year's Eve or the Fourth of July. Some invent stories about the riches they lost in China: the fine silks, the jade cups, all that the Chairman took. Far from home, in the city we call Gold Mountain, every peasant has a chance to transform into nobility, to have served as brave soldiers at the right hand of the highest commanders. Our imaginations give us what life never could.

If you saw me now, would you recognize me? The Chairman turned neighbors into strangers. No one in Chinatown knows my name. The other day, a customer told me that I looked like the girl from the movie musical *Flower Drum Song*.

"The nightclub singer?" her husband asked.

"The other one. The lead, the one who stowed away from China to San Francisco. I think her name was Mei?" She aimed her bulky camera at me. "*May* I take your photo, *Mei?*" she said, laughing at her joke, not realizing that she had hit upon my name. I ducked my head, feigning shyness to avoid the camera. Same sound, different meanings. May, for the permission I never granted. May, for possibilities that once seemed boundless. And May, for the month of green bursting and blooming that feels long gone.

Though my shift won't start until later this afternoon, I hurry out. On the narrow steep stairs, where the overhead light has burned out again, I brace my hand on the peeling wallpaper, laden with the scent of old grease.

When the throng at my doorstep surrounds me, I push back, trying not to give in to the crush, in to the heat of their breath, and their hands on my shoulders. But my legs go weak at this unexpected pleasure of the masses, so long gone.

A man with permed curls smears a kiss on my face. "My treasure, my treasure," he coos as if I'm a child or a whore. I shove him away. Entering the scent of spent firecrackers, heavy and sharp, I duck into an alley. My feet slap against the street slick with garbage, each step taking me farther from you.

I've wondered how people might treat me if they knew the truth. The curses and threats I've imagined seem more real than my life here, and sometimes, I've felt as if I were standing outside myself, watching a stranger with my face. For more than a decade, I have harbored my own secrets, trying to forget. Even you. Sometimes it feels I have entered my secrets so fully that I've lost the ability to speak them.

I hope you can forgive me.

The past always returns in the smallest reminders—in the musty scent of the yellowing newspapers stacked in my apartment, in the bitter taste of tea steeped for too long, or in the tremors of an old bachelor's liver-spotted hand. With the death of the Chairman, my memories of him are coming back stronger—in a reckoning that's long overdue.

We met the year I turned sixteen.

1965

*T*HE PARTY OFFICIAL ARRIVED IN EARLY SUMMER, THE RUMBLE of his jeep echoing along the rutted road. Vehicles didn't often travel through our narrow valley, still as remote as in the days when news of an emperor's passing arrived years afterward. I leaned on my hoe, my shoulders aching. Beside me, my two sisters had also stopped working, listening until the sound drew so close that we ran in from the fields, joining the shouts and cries of excitement.

We halted at the sight of the jeep parked in the plaza, its red flags rippling with importance on the hood. The official spoke with the headman, who pointed at a neighbor, at me, at each girl in the cultural work troupe, and gestured to a spot by the acacia tree.

"Line up. Quickly, now. Don't keep Secretary Sun waiting," the headman barked. He had a squat neck and a body powerful in its flab. He was curt as usual, but seemed apprehensive, shifting around on his feet. As I took my place, my blood jittered.

A dozen of us performed patriotic songs and skits on festival days. With few entertainments in the village, we always drew an audience, but we hardly seemed worthy of a Party official.

Secretary Sun had the look of a serpent, with high cheekbones and hooded eyes. He carried himself with a disciplined air, all tucks and polish. His thick black hair glinted gold, then red-brown in the sunlight.

I tried not to fidget. Perhaps he wanted to consider our troupe for a special performance in the city? Or maybe he was checking whether the lessons from the capital had made their way here.

My father, sitting beneath the acacia, tipped the brim of his hat at me, and I hitched up my sagging pants, hand-me-downs from my sisters that were short and threadbare.

Secretary Sun walked along the line, his steps slow and precise, pausing before each girl: the bony ones, the short ones, the village beauty renowned for her deep dimples and petal-soft skin. At last, he stopped at me.

All of us had volunteered for the troupe to get out of field work, but we hadn't practiced in months. Ten thousand hours of rehearsals wouldn't have improved our performances. Only my neighbor, who accompanied us on his bamboo flute, possessed any talent. With a nod at us, Fatty Song played an old tune, one that my grandparents had hummed as children about the long days of summer, of sunshine and dreams. The words had been changed and put into the service of the people.

As we sang about victory and freedom, we acted out each verse. We raised our arms above our heads, to imitate the sun rising from the east—the east, where the dawn, where revolution began. I stretched as high as I could, a taut line from my toes to the tips of my fingers, and set my jaw, trying to look fierce. When I glimpsed the girl beside me, though, I almost laughed out loud—her face squinched up as if she was suppressing a gigantic sneeze. Then I faltered, wondering if I might look like her.

Afterward, we lined up again. Our shuffling feet had kicked up the tickling scent of chickens, dust, and straw. Taking my place at the end, I hunched over, panting, sweat dripping down my back. I was the tallest girl, broad-shouldered and gangly, awkward as a baby calf.

Secretary Sun examined each candidate for a second time. Everyone in my village shared the same surname, Song. Our neighbors knew my parents, had known my grandparents. They recognized the inherited shape of my ears, my temper, and my fate, and had me determined while I was still in the womb.

It was 1965, a time ripe with prospect, even if in my village, the buckets of night soil still turned rank and the Party's painted slogans cracked in the heat. That year, our persimmon trees hung heavy and heady with fruit. In late autumn, we'd heap them into luminous piles, treasures rich as any robber-king's.

Cicadas droned, their song monotonous yet haunting, punctuated by the flick of their wings. Such tiny creatures, yet together, they were deafening. To my left, my neighbor sucked on the end of her braid. To my right, another tugged on her tunic and rubbed her nose, covered by a glistening mole.

My two sisters, too old to volunteer to perform for the troupe, pushed to the front of the crowd. As the official looked over us again, I prayed to the Chairman, asking him to grant me the opportunity to serve. The people's republic had been born the same year as me, and we were both still testing our limits, still ricocheting between extremes as we figured out who we would grow up to be.

Besides performing revolutionary songs, I could dig a ditch, spin wool, and demonstrate other skills that our leaders might want to review. I imagined the Chairman beaming, his hand outstretched, and mine reaching up to meet his. My looks didn't matter, only my courage.

Female heroes were few but vivid in the tales we learned at school: A teenage spy beheaded after she rallied villagers against enemy soldiers. A factory worker burned to death after she stopped a huge fire. A peasant killed when she held together a collapsing kiln. I wanted the official to pick me for this duty and to separate me from the rest of the girls in the village, from everyone here. I wanted to live like a hero.

If the official didn't select me, in a year I might get married. In time, I would have a baby, then another and another. I had to act now; it might be my only chance. Catching Headman Song's eye, I floated my hands in a gesture only he would understand. I swiveled my head over the length of the crowd as if to say, *I will tell everyone*. When his mouth twitched, I knew he understood. Headmen elsewhere in Hebei province had been beaten for lesser offenses, for the people hungered to humble the powerful. To listen to their confessions, strip their authority, force them to clean latrines and catch flies in a jar. Even if only some believed the secret I held, the headman's reputation would suffer, for such was the strength of accusation in those days.

The cicadas rose in pitch, a teeming, throbbing sound. Headman Song took the pipe from his mouth, turned to the official, and they spoke with their heads bowed.

When Secretary Sun returned and stopped in front of me, resting his hand on my shoulder, I didn't shy away.

NO ONE ELSE IN the village knew what I'd seen. Two years ago, a traveling musician had sought shelter here. Although he wore the same rough clothes as the rest of us, his pale skin glowed, and his high haunting voice silenced us in a performance fit for the Chairman. He sang of heroes, of a mischievous monkey king who rebelled against the heavens, while he plucked at a pipa, the melody spooling from his fingers. Every family volunteered to house the musician that night, for we'd never had such a remarkable visitor. Headman Song prevailed, and he moved his wife and four children to his brother's home to provide quiet for his guest.

In the middle of the night, I slipped out and crept to the headman's house in the hopes of another song. Instead I heard grunts, and through a crack in the front door, I saw their shadows on the wall come together and apart, flickering in the firelight. I moved away, but then peeked back in. The musician kneeled on all fours, the headman behind him. Their hands reached, touched, twined. As the headman let out a low moan, their rocking mesmerized me until both men had shuddered and gone still. I bumped against a stack of baskets. Though I caught them in time to keep the baskets from toppling over, the headman burst through the door, naked. His nipples, large and flat, were startling, an unblinking pair of eyes. Scowling, he gripped my wrists, and his body was heavy with a thick soapy smell. I didn't scream, and after a long moment, he released me. He must have known I would keep his secret—until today, when I floated my hands as the traveling musician once did over the strings. Over the headman.

———

THAT NIGHT, BA GAVE me the biggest portion of millet porridge, the one reserved for him. Our family sat cross-legged at the low table that rested upon the raised brick bed. When the nights chilled, we'd stoke fires in the hearth beneath the bed to keep us warm. My sisters watched, their faces pinched with hunger, with jealousy, as he plucked mushrooms drizzled with soy sauce from his own bowl and dropped them into my porridge. I inhaled the scent. Our village was famed for its soy sauce, its dark fermented flavors redeeming our bland, insubstantial meals. We fermented the sauce in giant urns, pungent proof that the simplest ingredients could be transformed with time. I pushed the mushrooms to the side of the bowl, saving them for last.

"Our Mei Xiang," he said. Fragrant Plum Blossom.

I looked up. He almost never called me by my name. In our family—like all the families in our village—we referred to one another by our titles, by our roles: Ma and Ba, First, Second, and Third Daughters.

As the stove flickered low, Ba went outside, where he fell into a fit of coughing. He might have been trying to hide it from us; all of us pushed through our illnesses. The stinking herbal brews Ma prepared never cured us completely.

My sisters whispered together. Born less than a year apart, they were always together, crows perched on a roof. First Daughter probably hoped that the official would pass over me. We three shared part of our names, Mei, to show how we lived through the same generation: Mei Tian, Mei Ling, and Mei Xiang, all of us plum blossoms that opened in late winter, pink against the snow—all that was pure, strong, and reckless. Unlike me, my sisters were both dainty, with delicate features—brushstroke brows and long-lashed eyes like my mother's. First Daughter—Mei Tian, five years older—had no patience for me. Second Daughter—Mei Ling— always tried to stop her bullying or found me after a blowup with the gift of a feather or a dried persimmon. But as much as I resented

First Daughter, I also longed for the softness she reserved for our sister.

As a baby, I might have been a doll to them, new and precious in a home with no toys and no time to play, but for as long as I could remember, they'd treated me as another task in a long day: to carry, to feed, to bathe, to silence. They stole the words I meant to say for myself, for that was the curse of the youngest child. Before I could walk, they ran. Before I could speak, they were singing. They were the first children to survive, arriving after a stillborn son and a toddler fallen to a fever. My mother loved my sisters with an intensity forged from loss, but I felt like another failed attempt at a son.

Ba had wanted an heir so much that, for a time, I'd been one for him. I carried loads twice my size and wove traps to catch fish in the river. In the evenings, I joined him and the other men in the plaza, listening to their riddles, rowdy and rousing. Then my body began to curve and swell, and I was no longer welcome.

I finished the mushrooms and set my chopsticks down on my bowl. The village disdained my family because of our misfortunes, and my family disdained me, yet the girl they'd called nothing, the girl they'd called nothing at all, had been summoned by the Party.

My neighbors already acted as though my victory had been their own. They nodded with a satisfaction that had nothing to do with me, as they might have for a sow with an exceptionally large litter, or for a baby born with the lucky ears of a Buddha—achievements that weren't theirs, but that they took credit for all the same.

"Will you serve the Party?" Secretary Sun had asked this afternoon.

I'd nodded, glinting inside.

"You'll go to Beijing."

Before I could ask him about my responsibilities, he strode away with the headman. Afterward, a few neighbors asked me to bring back a souvenir from the capital, tobacco or liquor; Fatty Song wanted a piece of candy for his sister. Behind them, Ba hung back, tall with pride.

"Maybe," I'd told them, but I owed them nothing, and I had no intention of returning anytime soon.

Now First Daughter splashed me with her cup of hot water. "Clumsy! You bumped the table!" She was the clever sister, the one whom I couldn't help but admire for her shrewd taunts and even shrewder punishments.

"What are your new duties?" she asked. Although her tone was sly, I wouldn't let her rile me. I'd been wondering the same. I tried not to worry. The Party must have its reasons for keeping it secret.

"Not yours," I said. I was leaving, and she was staying. I would see more in a day away than she would her entire life.

"Ma?" I asked.

"They'll tell you when you're supposed to know," Ma said. "The Chairman protects. The Chairman provides."

His portrait hung above us, his face stern, though with the hint of a smile.

"Maybe you're not old enough to hear such things," First Daughter said.

"Old enough to be chosen," I said. "But not old." *Not like you,* I didn't have to say.

"How can women best serve the Party?" First Daughter asked. "The same way they always have."

"Women hold up half the sky," I said.

"By lying down," she said.

At her words, I clenched between my thighs. She was trying to trick me. "You're wrong." I hated the quaver in my voice.

Ma stared into her empty bowl, her lips pinched white. Second Daughter put her hand on mine, but she didn't disagree.

When Ba came back inside to find my sister sniggering, he raised his hand as if to strike her. We all returned to slurping our porridge. No one wanted to set him off, to cower under one of his backhand slaps or shoves against the wall.

Soon after, a knock at the door rattled the gourds on the roof. Headman Song entered, ducking beneath a string of red chilies. He set down a polished wooden box, asked for a bowl of water, into which he plunged his hands, and told me to do the same. We dried our hands on a clean rag, and he opened the lid to reveal a palm-sized book, a copy of the Chairman's writings and a gift from the Party official to the village.

"I'm told his words bring blessings." The headman explained that I would study the Chairman's teachings to prepare for my duties in the capital.

"Am I joining a cultural work troupe?" I asked.

The headman frowned. "You'll do as you're told." Then he added, "You'll leave in three days."

First Daughter dropped her smirk.

Three days. Three days! Knowing when I'd leave filled me with lightness again, made the prospect real, even if I didn't have the details. It seemed the Party would only tell me what I needed to know—when I needed to know—and nothing more.

He handed the book to me. I was the only one in my family who could read, and First Daughter hated me for it. My sisters were born too soon, too old for school after the Communist victory.

Ma lit an oil lamp, setting it beside me, and Headman Song placed the book into my hands. It fit into my palm, small enough to slip into my pocket, under my pillow, just the right size, just the right weight. The cover was red, shiny, and flexible, the material like nothing I'd ever held, embedded with a portrait of the Chairman no bigger than a walnut. Here he looked to be my father's age, plump where Ba was gaunt, with full rosy cheeks and parted lips. I ran my thumb along a golden beam radiating from his head, not daring to touch his face.

I knew that as soon as he left, First Daughter would taunt me again. I flipped to a chapter entitled "Women" and looked for familiar words. " 'With the rise of the peasant . . .' " My voice sounded strange, whining as a mosquito, but when I glanced at my family and the headman, they seemed captivated.

" 'The women in many places have begun to organize . . .' " I said louder, tracing a finger along the characters printed on the rough and speckled page. " 'The opportunity has come for them to lift their heads, and the authority of the husband is getting shakier every day.' "

"Shaky men," First Daughter said. She laughed, bold and bright, the kind of reaction I wished I could have kindled in her before now.

"That's enough," Ba said. Until that day, I would have obeyed him, but from now on, I had to be brave and outspoken, a model revolutionary. I continued reading. It was as if the Chairman stood behind me, his hand at my back, urging me on his behalf, and I wanted to hold on to this moment forever. Although I didn't know the next few characters, or most of the next page, I didn't want to lose my audience. I invented what followed. "Women must take their rightful place among men."

I paused, but no one seemed to notice the difference between the Chairman's words and mine. First Daughter had been so gleeful, so sure of what awaited me in the capital. "Feudalism lulls us like an older sister," I said.

First Daughter gasped, and Second Daughter anxiously rubbed her neck. From the time we were small, we'd played games like Beat the Landlord, tackling the person clutching the ball of rags until he gave it up. We hated feudalism like we hated the dirty and scrawny, whose face, whose fate we feared could be our own. Though we didn't know the history behind feudalism, it meant someone backward, stunted, and easily led.

I went on. "Even though feudalism asks for our loyalty, an older sister is incapable of revolution. The youngest child will lead us. Bound feet lead to bound minds, while those with broad feet have broad minds."

First Daughter scowled and yearning shadowed Second Daughter's face. Did she wish for a bigger world, too? I could get away with more, much more, but I held myself back and found another passage to read.

At bedtime, I slipped the book under the blankets with me. I slept on the edge farthest from the stove, the coldest part of the bed, under the window. Sniffing the sour tang of glue, I stroked the pages across my cheek, hoping the Chairman's words would pass into me, like sunshine warming a rock, a heat that would carry me through the deepest chill.

The people of the capital would be as beguiling and talented as the traveling musician, and the buildings would be endless and grand, filled with wonders I couldn't even imagine. And somewhere in the capital, behind the walls of the Lake Palaces, the Chairman dwelled. I knew the name of where he lived and not much more.

He had united the peasants, ten villages, a hundred, a thousand, ten thousand, in the Communist revolution. With hoes and pitchforks, peasants beat back guns. With pipes and bricks, factory workers fought off bombs. Bent in unison, harvesting and threshing, we were mightier than any machine.

I ached to see him as he flicked his pen through the Little Red Book, marking up the pages and filling in my future.

AT DAWN, MA FILLED our wooden tub with hot water. She hadn't bathed me in years and wouldn't have done so again until my wedding day. A few meters away, my sisters slumbered. Later, I'd wonder if they might have been pretending, their parting gift to offer me the privacy I never had there.

Ma squatted behind me and poured ladles of water over my head, the scent of dust and sweat rising off in the steam. The drops trickled down my nape, my shoulders, my chest, every part of me cherished. I leaned into her hands. Her breathing became ragged, and I felt her trembling through my body until we were both shaking.

"Little Mei," she murmured.

When I tried to turn around, she gripped my shoulders. The water in the tub had gone lukewarm, and I shivered, the hairs raised on the back of my neck and arms.

"Ma?" I asked.

She didn't answer. She dried me in circling strokes, her hands slowed, as if to delay our parting. It was the tenderness I'd always craved from her. Though she must have heard the fear in my voice, she couldn't face me. Not then, maybe not ever again. She would no longer warn me about fox fairies, shape-shifters who roamed the twilight to lure travelers; of disappeared girls, run away or raped, kidnapped or killed.

She knew that she had no choice but to give me up, I can now see, and didn't want me thinking about the dangers ahead. In that moment, though, I hardened against her, against my fear and my anger. She couldn't help me, and I didn't need her. The picture of the Chairman seemed to nod in the flickering light. He alone would protect me on this journey.

Ma helped me step into pants and a tunic that she had patched and pounded clean in the river. She braided my hair into a coil. I gave in to the gentle tugging, in to the mesmerizing firelight, hoping that I would be transformed like the braid, intricate and beautiful and strong as a model revolutionary. Shifting my eyes, I tried to hold still, to keep from disturbing my mother's work. It was an hour spent on me alone, for what seemed like the first time in my life.

The aunties had muttered that the official would realize his error, that I'd never leave the village. Behind their words I understood they were asking, *Why not my daughter?* Yesterday, one went to the headman and presented herself to him, his for the taking if he would send her daughter in my place. He'd burst out of their meeting, calling her blackhearted, a whore. She'd been marched through the village, her arms pinned behind her back, to be dunked in the latrines. *You all might as well jump in after,* I wanted to tell everyone else, because every day here felt like drowning. I was bound for the world where the revolution quickened and I might find others like me, where my dreams might be recognized and accepted, and my worth wasn't measured only in the sons I bore.

After she tied off the braid with a red string, I reached onto the shelf for the cracked leather pouch where she kept a set of eight wooden beads carved into plum blossoms. The distinctive dowry beads were her most treasured possession. I hesitated. Though Ma couldn't look me in the eye, I wouldn't allow her fear to become mine; I would take what I deserved.

When I passed her a bead to adorn my braid, she didn't protest. Our hands lingered together. I didn't know how long I'd be gone—days or weeks or months?

Gazing at my mother's wrinkled face, I realized that she'd once been my age, leaving her family to marry a man she had never met. She didn't know she would endure beatings from her husband, endure the curse of daughters, the death of sons, and swallow suffering as often as air. If she had known, would she have left her village? That was how we survived: by not knowing what was ahead.

She pressed a wooden cup into my hands, a murky brew that gave off the smell of boiled pond scum. Sipping it, I winced, my tongue curling back on itself. She pushed it toward me again and I half-gagged. "What's this?"

Instead of answering, she handed me a pouch filled with tiny lumps the color of bone, their stench even more intense than what she'd brewed. The earthy scent reminded me of *dong quai*, the tiny white flowers and sturdy roots we gathered every autumn. A desperate neighbor had come asking for it after she'd given birth twice within a year.

It helped keep a baby from taking hold.

After I started my woman's flow, Ba warned me against walking by myself at dusk, telling me to bolt from men who got too close. Why, he never said, but I understood. The curves that made me clumsy and set my running off-kilter also invited the attentions of men who could ruin me.

"Drink this every morning," Ma said now.

I finished the brew and set down the bowl. "Every morning," I repeated, then swirled my tongue against my teeth to get rid of the sour, bitter taste.

The Party's jeep arrived with a groan and rattle. As the hens squawked, Ba climbed off the bed, ladled me a bowl of porridge, and dropped in thick slices of salted turnips. I ate while standing, holding the bowl close to my face. He did, too. My father's fingers were the finest part of him, nimble whether mending a basket or plucking a radish. As a teenager, he'd left for the provincial capital to make his fortune. Although he'd wanted to work in a textile factory, he returned a year later, missing his little finger, a failure that still defined him—and our family—in the village. I was used to the stump, but his long fingers curved around his bowl now seemed lonely, his hand missing its smallest part.

He turned away and coughed, wiping at his mouth. My family never said anything about his cough, yet another ailment among us that lingered and festered—like the sores that never quite healed, the scratch that persisted, the irritation in our eyes—that went on for so long we forgot we'd lived any other way. I stared at his hand, the smear of blood undeniable, yet when I looked up, he wordlessly ordered me to ignore it.

I set down my bowl, unable to finish more than a few bites. Difficult as this life was, it was all I had known. When Ma brushed down stray hairs at the crown of my head, my resolve disappeared and the urge to cling to my parents overwhelmed me. I wish you could have met them. Ba lifted my elbow to lead me to the door. Gentle, not rough, this gesture gave me the strength to leave.

THE PIMPLED DRIVER WASN'T MUCH OLDER THAN ME, ALTHOUGH he tried to hide his youth behind dark glasses and a scowl. After I climbed into the jeep, the driver gave me a handkerchief, instructing me to tie it around my mouth to protect against the clouds of dust and fumes.

As we left, the rearview mirror reflected Ma chasing after us. Ba held her back, her arms beating against his chest. I didn't turn around. I was already gone.

I glanced at the driver, the silence thick between us. The morning sun was searing and I wished I'd packed my straw hat. The Chairman's portrait hung from the mirror, showing him as a chiseled young soldier wearing a green uniform, his head tilted up and his arm raised in a salute. I stared at his large head and broad torso, and imagined the rest, the notches at his waist and the powerful curve of his thighs. Heat pricked my cheeks. It wasn't right to think of the Chairman this way.

Though I had tried to picture his early childhood, the exact details remained slippery as a soap bubble, shining and out of reach. Like me, the Chairman might have scattered seeds in row after tedious row and pulled weeds more bountiful than any harvest. Like me, he'd been the youngest in his family.

Corn and wheat fields ran along the northern and eastern edges of the village and a muddy river flowed along the southern half. To the west, a day's walk away, lay the county seat and the nearest medical clinic. We descended into the plain. I'd never traveled this fast or this far; the hills on the horizon had once been the edge of my world, and we now passed them by, barreling ahead toward the blur of brown and green. At this speed, I saw little up close, but gained a dizzying sense of scope.

Stomach churning, I tasted Ma's tea coming up the back of my throat. I closed my eyes, feeling queasy, my insides foamy scum. Sometimes my mother's treatments did that, brought on a suffering one had to endure before the cure.

A village whipped by. Inside each home, there had to be a straw-burning stove, blackened ceilings, and a portrait of the Chairman. Chickens pecked, to be kicked aside. Under an acacia, the men gathered at the hottest part of the day.

The ceaseless rattling of the jeep drilled into the base of my skull, and the brisk wind stung my eyes. The thick dust turned gritty against my skin. When First Daughter's sneers circled in my head, I forced down the dread that clawed in my chest. Each time we hit a pothole, the Chairman's picture swung from the mirror. I'd prove my worth to him and prove my sister wrong.

The longer our journey continued, the closer we drew to Beijing, the sturdier the homes became. The tiled roofs could ward off the strongest rain and coldest wind, the cobbled paths were level enough for a granny with bound feet to step lightly, and the whitewashed walls gleamed with pride and prosperity. The distance between the settlements shrank until early afternoon, when a continuous stretch of shops and buildings began at the outskirts of the capital.

I wondered if we'd pass the Lake Palaces. The orders that our headmen issued originated in these buildings, and it was said the walls were high and thick as a fortress, to protect the Chairman. People couldn't look directly at the Lake Palaces or their vision would turn hazy, as if they'd stared at the sun.

The air felt heavy and suffocating, wet as new laundry, as we passed a factory whose double row of shattered windows gave it a ghoul's grin. Bicycles crowded the roads, along with handcarts crammed with cabbages and chickens, alongside so many people at once, going in different directions, who looked ready to plow down anyone standing in their way. And the noise! The growl of engines, the squeak of bicycles, and honking horns so loud that the city itself seemed like a great roaring beast, bearing down on us, hot against my face. The sunshine blinded me, reflected off the paved black road, heat from above, heat from below. Even the smells were different here, the dung and straw and smoky fires of the countryside replaced by clouds of blue exhaust, dizzying as fumes coming off a still.

We passed under soaring trees arched like the clasped hands of giants, turned onto a broad boulevard and approached a massive red gate, upon which hung a portrait of the Chairman—three times my height, maybe more. I could have sat in his ear. He stared straight at me, and I fell into the curve of his full lips, his luminous gaze, and the rosy dawn of the background shading into an infinite blue. His flesh, pink and glowing, was the vitality we dreamed for ourselves. Not until the portrait fell out of sight did I feel the street's grit in my eyes and the ache from craning my neck.

"Are we almost there?" I asked.

The driver grunted.

Chilled in the sunshine, I wrapped my arms around myself. Another turn, and we cruised along the high endless walls, a deep imperial red. The Lake Palaces? I blinked and the color glowed behind my eyelids. The jeep pulled into a gate and at the sentry box, a soldier with a bayonet waved us in. Every part of me went slack with wonder as we traveled along a road that curved around a huge lake. I gasped when I spotted the first of the pavilions, the gardens, arched bridges, and pagodas, which seemed like sights from my father's fairy tales. Above a sliver of gardens, a row of golden glazed dragons perched on curved eaves. Even the sunshine seemed different in here, dappled and refreshing, and the moist air smelled honey-sweet from the deep purple flowers. Two men under straw hats watered paving stones that shimmered and steamed. The jeep tires crunched onto the gravel drive that led to a gray-brick building big as the hill behind our village, topped with a tiled roof and curved eaves. Much later, I'd come to think the clash of styles had the look of a British banker in a Chinese scholar's traditional finned hat.

A woman emerged. With a thin nose, pointy chin, and jutting elbows, she had the sharp corners of a heron, and appeared capable of bursting into flight—or rage. The driver helped me down, and after the long ride, I wobbled on my feet. My tailbone ached. Beside the woman, in her fitted sweater and flowing skirt, I felt humble and ugly, a stupid peasant girl who didn't belong here. The design of her clothing was like none I'd ever seen, foreign to my eye and intimidating as a warrior's armor.

When I met her gaze, she narrowed her eyes. She might think me less than her, but I wouldn't let her shame me.

"You're late," the woman said to the driver.

The Party official had picked me. Yet to her, I must seem as weightless and aggravating as chaff, dung to be sidestepped.

"We have to go farther and farther to find new recruits," the driver said, more than he'd spoken to me during our long ride.

The people from our province had a reputation for loyalty, for being dependable and slow as an ox at noon, not like those who dwelled in the capital, the haughty who must peer so far down at the rest of us that we seemed like ants.

"Get them here on time." She examined my greasy forehead and dusty cheeks, and the homespun clothes that hid my shape. She couldn't see the tiny plum blossoms, like the ones in my name, that Ma embroidered on the hem of my tunic, or the dowry bead, gestures that were a notch above necessity.

"We have to get her cleaned up," she added.

"I took a bath this morning!" I protested. She acted as though people here took one bath after another!

As the driver tried not to smile, I became aware of the stink on me, one that might never disappear, even if I plunged myself in boiling water. The woman stalked off toward the building without waiting to see if I followed.

INSIDE THE WINDOWLESS CONCRETE block of a bathroom, the attendant told me to take off my clothes. When I hesitated, she said,

"Now." I slipped off my shoes, my tunic, and my pants, and stood there shivering in my underwear, folding my arms across my chest.

The attendant sighed. "Take off everything," she said. "You're not getting into the bath in that, are you?"

She handled my clothes with the tips of her fingers, as if they might explode, and tossed them into a metal bin. I tried to cover my chest with one arm, and my crotch with the other. As the attendant studied my body, I could tell she found me wanting: my knobby knees and elbows, my broad feet and my chestnut skin.

She ran a bath in the white porcelain tub, the water coming straight from a pipe out of the wall and gushing with the noise and strength of a river swollen by spring rains. I'd never seen anything like it.

She motioned for me to climb into the tub and I yelped at the water, near scalding and sending up clouds of steam. But the soap she used on my hair and body was even worse, burning my eyes, with the stink of overcooked hard-boiled eggs.

I put up my hands to ward her off. "Stop—stop."

"It's to get rid of the fleas and lice you brought with you."

"I didn't—"

"You all do." She undid my mother's braids and scrubbed me so hard that I pressed my lips together to keep from crying out. She didn't stop until curls of dead skin floated around me.

AT THE DOOR OF the dance studio, I watched the other girls fly through their steps. The strange music's wild wails and thumps made me want to cover my ears. When the song faded, a few of them turned to look me up and down.

As I ventured in, my foot slid on the polished wood floor, slippery as ice. It was my first time in heels, which forced me to thrust out my rear and sway my hips to keep my balance. The tips squeezed my toes together, and the leather chafed against my wide feet. I hated feeling hobbled. If I had to, I couldn't escape.

I immediately noticed a girl standing alone, off to the side. She faced me. Gawky, she wore the same short-sleeved white blouse—itchy and tight at the neck on me—and a patterned skirt like mine, which fell just below my knees, swished from side to side and flared into a circle when I spun. I scratched my neck, and she did the same. Swiveling my head, I looked back at her. She copied me.

Was she mocking me? I blinked, and she blinked, too. She—she was me! It was the oddest sensation, watching me watch myself, as if I were standing outside of my body.

Although I'd seen my blurry, wavering reflection in the pond and glimpsed slivers of myself in the jeep's scratched mirror, I knew other faces better than mine: my family's and the Chairman's, most of all. I surveyed my broad nose and thick eyebrows, handsome in my father, but overpowering on a girl. The dimple that winked on my left cheek was the only delicate part of me. I'd never seen a mirror so big and shiny, stretching along the entire wall from floor to ceiling. I wanted to shrink my lanky limbs and clap my hands over my calves, but I also couldn't stop staring. I'd never seen myself like that, and I felt exposed—not to other people, but to myself. No one in my village would ever see themselves so clearly.

Half the girls I'd counted at first had been reflections; in total, there were about two dozen of us. The sharp-edged woman who'd met me at the back entrance was our dance instructor, Teacher Fan. "Follow along," she said. She didn't bother to introduce me to the class.

I edged over to the end of the line. "That's my spot," a girl said. When I tried the other side, that recruit wouldn't budge, either. "Make your own row," she said. Their bodies were a wall. When someone finally let me in, I stepped right when the others went left, moved forward when everyone fell back.

The music crackled. Record player, lights, electricity, stairs. I would learn their uses now, their names later. Encountering these marvels for the first time, I felt my confidence flee. It didn't matter if I'd performed in the village, or if I knew how to read. Here I knew nothing. I wouldn't even be able to find my way out of the building, the biggest I had ever entered. Despite the humiliating scrubbing, I was sweaty and stickier than when I arrived at the Lake Palaces.

A slender girl yelped when I trod on her foot. As perspiration pooled on my back and in my armpits, I tried to rearrange my feet. We didn't have to learn such complicated steps in the village. Under my breath, I asked the girls around me for help. The one to my right ignored me, and the girl on the other side told me to put my left foot forward—the wrong position, I realized too late.

"Get back in line!" Teacher Fan snapped at me. "The cadre deserve better tonight."

I looked up from the floor. The cadre—tonight?

In the mirror, the girl who'd misled me looked back at me in our reflection. She kept her face blank and didn't apologize for giving me bad directions. From the beginning, we were aware of each other, even if we didn't speak, even if we barely acknowledged each other. She glided through the steps and had a sleek, narrow-faced beauty, with phoenix eyes—a slight curve at the outside corner—that distinctive feature possessed by the beauties in the old tales. We would come to know her as Midnight Chang, because of her dark eyes and her hair, long and dark as the hours before dawn. It was also her first day, I would learn, but she'd caught on more quickly than me.

During the break, I positioned myself under the breeze from the ceiling fan. The frosted glass windows along the back wall remained closed, and the room had turned so steamy we could have been inside a teakettle. My hand grazed against the pocket of my blouse where I kept my mother's dowry bead and pouch of tea, rescued from the attendant who had taken away my clothes. After a girl clipped my heel—on purpose, I could tell from her smirk—I staggered. When I squatted between songs, resting as we did in the village, Teacher Fan grabbed my arm and jerked me up. "You'll ruin the shape of your calves!"

Hot tears pricked my eyes, and the studio went fuzzy around me. My skin itched beneath my scratchy checkered skirt and tight white blouse, but I tried to keep still. What did the Little Red Book tell us? To serve the Chinese people, heart and soul. As I tugged at the neckline and at the hem of my skirt, my terror took shape in a sudden vision of a man's rough hands and hoarse curses, everything my sister had hissed at me.

"You! Pay attention!" Teacher Fan called out.

The other girls had paired off, leaving me standing alone.

"What are you doing?" she asked. She didn't address me by my name; she might not have known it.

Feet throbbing, I swayed on my heels, the relief momentary before fiery spikes plunged back in, the kind of pain I'd heard girls with bound feet had suffered.

The others tittered. "I know five-year-olds who could follow instructions better than her," said Busy Shan, her nickname, I would learn, because of how she poked into everyone's affairs. She had a wildness about her, the feral beauty of a fox that made you aware at every moment of its bite.

"She's throwing everyone off," another muttered.

"What are you doing?" Teacher Fan repeated.

"Better that, than to run off at the mouth," I answered, glaring at the gossiping girls in the mirror. Because I had no history with them, I could be anyone—bold and confident, maybe a hero in the making.

Though I braced myself for Teacher Fan's reprimand, she took me into her arms. Up close, her skin was translucent. I kept time to the beat, gliding along a ribbon of air, as she turned my stumbles into spins and my tottering into steps. Her posture stood erect, not bent like my mother's, and her hair was coiled neat and glossy in its bun. If I followed the Party line, I might also cut through the world like her. Leaning into her arms, I stared at my feet, mesmerized by the tight circles they traveled.

"Stop that!" Teacher Fan slapped the top of my head, and the class halted. "When you're dancing, look at your partner. Looking down throws him off. Don't follow. You must anticipate." She pulled away from me and addressed the class. "When the Chairman arrives, no gaping, no staring, no crying."

The Chairman! In my village, it was said he no longer needed to shit, that he ate and drank nothing, that he was pure as jade and could grant our wishes. Though no one except the youngest among us believed he held magical powers, we repeated these tales just as we repeated legends of monks who could scale walls or bandits who could flit across the tops of trees.

No one referred to him as anything but the Chairman. To use his full name would have implied the existence of *other* chairmen, and he was our one and only. Around me, the girls twitched at this mention of him. "Every little movement he makes seems like it's for you," whispered the one known as Dolly Yu. A flush spread across her cheeks, the same heat that burned in mine.

Their murmurs turned into excited shouts. The force of this outburst frightened and thrilled me, and I wanted the dance party to start at once. A trip to the capital, being selected for the troupe—none of that mattered, now that I had a chance to meet the Chairman. No wonder the official hadn't explained my duties, which had to remain secret until I arrived. Teacher Fan clapped her hands, shouting for silence. "Do that again, and you'll be dismissed."

Dismissed? I wondered how often she sent girls away—if we'd go home or somewhere else—and how many chances she might give us. As the clamor faded, the steel in her softened into wax. "You must do your best."

Summer rain fell in heavy bursts that rattled the windows and streaked grime across the glass. The air inside felt clammy, humidity seeping into the studio. After our dance lesson, Teacher Fan led us to a classroom next door, so much bigger and brighter than our village school, which had been dark and cramped with a few wobbly tables. Here, we had individual desks in rows before a smooth black chalkboard, and in its blankness, it seemed as big as the world.

Stomach growling, I worked up saliva in my mouth and swallowed a clot of stickiness to ease my hunger. It had been hours since I'd eaten breakfast, and I'd arrived too late for lunch at the Lake Palaces.

Standing at the head of the classroom, Teacher Fan told us we had an important role to play. "You might think serving the Party means working in a field or in a factory. It is, it is. But you're just as important as a guard protecting the border. You're protecting the cadre from themselves. They'd work until they collapsed. At the dance parties, they can unwind. And when they relax, they can come up with revolutionary ideas, with ideas that serve the people. How many of you were part of a production brigade?" she asked.

We raised our hands, straight and tall as stalks of wheat shining in the sun.

"After a dance party, a cadre came up with that idea," she said. "Limber bodies lead to nimble minds."

I'd been very young when we had organized in brigades, the village divided into teams, our progress tracked and rewarded, tracked and criticized. Could I now play a part, however small, in determining how millions of people lived and worked, ate and slept?

We shouted the Chairman's words along with Teacher Fan, pride jolting through me. "Young heroes, what is work? Work is struggle. Our difficulties can be overcome because we are a new and rising force and have a bright future."

One voice, one fight!

When class ended, Teacher Fan dismissed us for a break before dinner. But then Secretary Sun strode in. I straightened my shoulders. Did he remember me? As I studied the broad strokes of his features, those deep-set eyes and high cheekbones, he announced that the Party would provide our families with two months' worth of work points because of the hardship our absence caused. Those points determined how much food we received.

You see, I was far more valuable to my family in the Lake Palaces than in the village. They had less help in the fields, but also less competition at meals and for the blankets. And they wouldn't miss what they never had. "My father will donate what he receives to the village," I said. If I shined now, I told myself, my family's reward would be greater in the future.

Though Teacher Fan seemed annoyed, she asked for more volunteers. The others looked among themselves, probably knowing they should follow my example yet unwilling to force it out. Eying me with irritation, one by one they pledged their family's allotted gift to their villages, too.

AT DINNER, WE PLUNGED our chopsticks into the serving dishes. Tender stir-fried greens, spicy chicken and bell peppers, plump pork dumplings, everything in a quality and quantity I'd never known. The slivers of chicken were the first I had eaten since the Spring Festival—the one time of year we ate meat in the village—and my mouth watered so much at first I tasted nothing.

The girls gossiped about the cadre, trading advice on who to avoid. "The one with the big ears," Busy Shan said. "He stinks of garlic."

"The one with the limp always steps on my foot," another girl said. She looked at me. "Maybe you can step on his!"

I kept eating. To the rest of the troupe, I was the latest threat, and they would try to edge me out, like piglets at their mother's swollen teats. I could already tell that if any girl wanted something, the rest of us would want it more, for the thing itself and for the satisfaction of taking it from her.

We sat at long wooden tables under bare bulbs that turned us pale and flat—a chilly kind of light like what shines from the moon. It didn't flicker with a flame and didn't smell like oil or straw burning. Candles give off a glow that softens and flatters; these lights hid nothing, every pimple, every blemish made bigger. Though the canteen could have seated my entire village, we were the only diners. I ate more chicken, its taste sweet and clean, nothing like the stringy pullets we stewed for hours in the village in honor of the new year.

The brightness I'd felt, chanting in the classroom, I wanted again—wanted for everyone. No more hunger, no more suffering, if together we persisted. I wished I could have served Ba a bite of this feast, surely greater than the meal he'd eaten on his wedding day, greater than any in his life. If he put on a few kilos, maybe his eternal cough would recede.

Ba never spoke of his youthful trip to the provincial capital, when he'd lost his little finger at the factory. He no longer seemed like a man capable of leaving his village. Sometimes I wondered if my father grieved for the man he had aspired to be, the adventurous and fortune-changing man, lost to the one he became—a drunk who beat his family, quarreled with his neighbors, and lacked a son to carry on his line.

I dropped an oily red chili on the front of my shirt, which left a stain like a raw wound.

"Rub rice on it," Midnight Chang said.

"How much?"

"A handful." She nudged the rice bucket toward me.

My shirt, made of a strange, slippery material, became a sticky mess after I followed her advice. It looked disgusting, as if little white maggots were crawling out of me.

She didn't apologize. She'd turned away, murmuring to Dolly Yu, "Let me tighten your braids."

As much as I wanted to fling the dish into her face, watch the chili sauce drip in red tears down her cheeks, I wouldn't give her the satisfaction of complaining. When I wiped off my hand on the table, a splinter drove deep into my palm.

AFTER DINNER, WE MARCHED in double rows toward the dance pavilion, a gray-brick building with thick red posts and massive curved eaves, whose size made me feel as if I were about to kowtow before the emperor. We passed through the red wooden door studded with brass circles, and inside, dazzling white lights were strung from the high rafters. The wooden floors were springy, and each of my steps vibrated back into the balls of my feet. Busy Shan shoved me, shouting at me to keep moving. Stumbling, I winced from a blister, rubbed raw by my new shoes. My shirt had dried, stiff and stained on my chest.

A dozen homes from my village would have taken up less than half the space. No one sat in the folding metal chairs that lined the walls of the windowless dance hall, whose ceilings seemed tall as poplars. No one touched the tea and snacks on the long wooden tables on the far side of the room. I counted the number of guests, but I lost track—mostly men and a handful of women, maybe a hundred in all, their conversation at a hum. The elder officials talked and smoked in clusters, blurring the air above them. A lifetime of labor and sacrifice had thickened their bodies and turned their skin to leather. Next to them, the younger officers—with their slicked short hair and stiff collars—seemed vain as roosters. Secretary Sun stood among them. His gaze swept over us, the way a shepherd might over his flock of sheep: counting us up, but not looking us in the face.

Teacher Fan had directed me to the rear, where I was supposed to observe. I clasped my hands in front of me, and then behind me, not sure where to put them or how to stand. I hunched my shoulders. The day had been long and would be longer still.

As the record player started up, the other girls invited the attentions of the men they wanted with a tilt of their heads or a toss of their hair. When someone tried to dodge a cadre, she fiddled with her sleeves or fell into conversation with another girl, pretending not to see him.

Amid the noise, news spread among the girls, who shouted into one another's ears behind cupped hands. "The Chairman's here," one said. The Chairman! I had to get a glimpse, and then I'd return to where Teacher Fan had left me.

I didn't see anyone lining up to greet him, and I wondered if he wanted to be treated like any other guest, without too much formality. Looking for him, I wedged myself into gaps, elbowing past the cadre and into the suffocating heat.

Then I spotted the gleam of a bald head in the crowd—was that him? My hand still throbbed from the splinter, the pain filling me with fight. If I'd been in a quiet room, I might have hesitated, but the buzz around me drove me on, all relentless forward motion.

The full cheeks. The fleshy ears. The mole at the center of his chin. The Chairman! I raised my hand—*Pick me*. Teacher Fan would never tolerate such disobedience, but simply seeing him no longer seemed enough. He extended his arm, as if to ask me to come forward, but when I didn't move, he motioned for others to make way for me. "Come," he said. I stepped toward him. He gripped my wrist with his leathery hand and pulled me into his arms. The shock of it felt like plunging through ice. I had seen his giant portrait hours earlier, and now he stood before me. He seemed unreal, denser than flesh, filling the space definitively.

I was a shadow beside him.

The frantic song ended and another began, the trumpets racing—following, then leading, leaping from high to low—while drums pounded. The music was loud as thunder. Inside my head, it filled my throat and echoed in the hollow space behind my nose. I couldn't have escaped the sound by covering my ears.

"What do you think of the capital?" The Chairman had to shout over the music.

"It's . . . big," I said, all but mute, surprised he kept track of the new girls.

He spun me under his arm and the room whirled around us. "You never stop feeling that way."

Reeling me toward him, we ended up side by side, rocking back and forth. The Chairman propelled me with enough force that my body understood where to go, no different than a ball set into motion.

I glimpsed a pale palm flung into the air, the blur of a twirl, a ponytail gone stiff with speed. Midnight Chang stared at me over the shoulder of her partner, unable to hide her stunned disappointment.

I clasped tighter. The longer I kept the Chairman with me, the longer no one else would have him. In unison, every couple rock-stepped, then flew into different directions before they returned to the beginning—together.

Teacher Fan must have been counting my steps as I danced with the Chairman, prepared to substitute another girl if I stumbled too much. I had fulfilled her instructions: No staring, no gaping, no crying before him. Maybe she could tell that I'd picked up enough of the basic movements, or else she didn't dare interrupt the Chairman. He was a terrible dancer, worse than me. Every few beats, our pelvises knocked together. When he stepped on my foot, crushing my toes, I forced my grimace into a smile. Scrambling to mirror his missteps, I held on when his moves jerked us apart.

I could hardly keep up, and after four songs, we were both winded.

"Let's take a rest." The Chairman's damp hand at my waist guided me to a doorway at the edge of the pavilion, opposite the main entrance. I drew back, in disbelief as much as in fear. How could I be walking beside the man who all but ruled over the sun and the stars?

I was barely aware of the cadre who nodded at him as he passed, or the girls who smiled at him. With each step, my legs became heavier with the weight of what was to come. He pushed open the door to reveal a room lit by several lamps, and a large bed that filled most of the space. In my village, we'd marveled at the tales of the landlords who had homes of many rooms. For cooking, for sleeping, for sitting, for uses I couldn't imagine.

I knew this room's use at once. I trembled. The Chairman protects, the Chairman provides.

We had nowhere to sit but on the bed. After he perched on the edge, he gestured for me to join him. "Sit, sit," he said.

I lurched toward him. "Here?"

"Anywhere you'd like," he said with a casualness that made me wish for ceremony, for a ritual that I could follow.

I gingerly sat beside him, my gut churning. He poured me a glass of lukewarm water, which I downed in one gulp. Books piled on the bed, along the wall. The bed frame dug into my thighs, and I shifted, trying to find a comfortable position. My stiff shirt scratched against my breasts. He stretched his arms above his head and tilted his neck with a crack that made us both laugh. Cupping my chin in his hand, he raised my head. Though wrinkles creased his face and sweat plastered his hair, I glimpsed the young revolutionary in him. That version of the Chairman stirred me the most: a rebel with piercing eyes and full lips, the only softness in an angular face. My breath caught. I had to find the rebel in the Chairman before me now.

He carried a scent that hinted at the dark and the bitter, like black tea, soy sauce, stagnant pond water, and night soil ripening. Although my nose twitched at the reek, I also wanted his scent to permeate me, to carry his stink in my hair and on my skin, for my tears to taste like him.

"Thirsty?" he asked. He poured me another glass of water that I drained. I noticed a pair of wooden chopsticks, stained an oily red, perched on an open crock of pickled chilies on the bedside table. He must have an iron tongue, to snack on chilies straight from the jar. When he offered me a cigarette, I shook my head. The one time I smoked a pipe in the village, I'd coughed so hard that speckles swam across my vision.

"It trains the lungs," he said. "We start to breathe from the moment we're born. But to strain them, to make them struggle, that's how you build up your strength."

He had to be teasing.

"A pipe-smoking granny must have the might of ten soldiers, then," I ventured.

He laughed, laughed at my joke! Can you imagine? I knew that faint smile and those bright eyes, the ones from the portrait hanging on the wall at home, but the laugh I didn't expect, the low chuckle that hummed through me. The sudden intimacy overwhelmed me.

"Never underestimate the grannies. Never get in the way between them and their market bargain," he said.

"Their elbows are sharp as any sword," I said.

"And maybe even faster."

I could have been back in the village plaza again, listening to my father and the other men trade quips, the quicker the better.

He inhaled again and released clouds of smoke from his nostrils like a dragon. After another puff, he tilted his head up and blew thick smoke rings, pursing his plump lips. I clapped at his performance and thrust my fist through the rings that traveled up my arm like bracelets.

He must have known such gestures would charm me; he had a way of coaxing the most tongue-tied.

In the dance pavilion, a folk opera had replaced the foreign music with the wailing song of a concubine longing for a son. Alone in her chamber, she prayed for the pains that heralded a pregnancy. Her sorrow made me shiver.

"Pitiful," I murmured. I hugged myself.

"Don't feel sorry for her," he said. "She's plotting against another concubine, the pregnant one. She'll replace that baby with a leopard cub. She'll tell everyone her rival gave birth to a monster."

"A leopard?" I'd never heard the word.

He stretched his arms wide. "A leopard, a cat, a very big cat, with babies big as a human's."

"Most babies aren't much to look at," I said.

"No matter what their mothers would have you believe." He stubbed out his cigarette into a small porcelain dish. His knuckles knobby, the skin gnarled with veins, an old man's hands, but powerful, too. The song ended, and we listened to the chatter until a harsh scratch marked the return of the foreign dance music, its beat rapid and persistent.

The Chairman swayed, snapping his fingers, offbeat, the stutter-step of my heart.

"It's not like our songs," I said.

"How does it make you feel?" he asked.

"It's like . . . I'm being chased by an ox that will trample me if I don't run fast enough," I said, then wished I'd been struck dumb for saying such nonsense.

He laughed. "Seize the reins!"

In the silence that followed, I cast about for a way to continue the conversation—trying to delay what I knew would happen next. "Like Brother Rat," I said.

At first I rushed through the story, but before long, I settled into what my mother had told and retold: Long ago, the Jade Emperor held a great race to heaven. Brother Rat and Brother Cat persuaded the ox to give them a ride across the river. Perched on the ox's back, the rat and the cat promised to watch for their rivals sneaking up from behind: the tiger struggling to swim, the rabbit hopping from boulder to boulder, the dog stopping to splash, and the pig napping in the shade. Toward the end, I slowed down, for I'd always loved this part: Within sight of shore, the rat shoved the cat into the water. "Then the rat jumped right off!" I said. Over the finish line and ahead of the ox, who lost by less than a whisker length.

He would know the legend already, but even so, his smile widened. "Enemies forever."

"Without Brother Rat, the race would have been forgotten," I said. The race determined the order of animal signs in the zodiac calendar, based on a twelve-year cycle. "No one remembers a story if they can predict everything that happens."

He studied me. He might not expect me to have an opinion besides his own, might be used to girls like me only repeating his words back to him.

"You're a rat?" he asked.

"An ox," I said. Born in 1949, the year of our country's Liberation.

He chuckled. "Don't you wish you could have trampled that rat? All that hard work—didn't the ox deserve to win?"

"Hard work is its own reward." I glanced away, shyness overtaking me again. He ought to be talking to the President or another official, and not me. He belonged on the wall of a plaza or on the cover of the Little Red Book, not beside me.

"The Party taught you well." He spoke so softly I looked at him again, straining to hear over the song playing on the other side of the door.

"And your year?" I had learned his birthday in school, and remembered the month and the day, but not the year.

"A snake," he said. His cycle had come around then this year, a year not of good fortune, but of change and uncertainty, a year in which one should take care. He wasn't twelve, twenty-four, thirty-six years old or even forty-eight—he had to be sixty. Or seventy-two. Seventy-two! Not as old as the mountains or the stars and yet he sparked the same feeling in me: how lasting they'd been, and how small and fleeting I was in comparison.

"It's your year," I said.

His gaze softened, and the hand that had penned "The world belongs to you. The country's future belongs to you" stroked my head, his touch lighter than I thought possible. After reciting the Chairman's teachings, doctors reattached a severed hand, workers raised a sinking city, and villagers harvested their crops within an hour. He inspired the people, and I, too, wanted to transform under his fingertips.

He unfastened the hair-bands and loose strands fell to my shoulders. Only little girls in my village wore their hair down. Only girls—and whores. No man but my father had seen my hair unbraided. No man but my husband was supposed to touch my hair. The women of our village crowned themselves with braids. Our beauty, our strength, our pride, now gathered in the Chairman's hands.

The floor rose up to meet me or maybe I was falling. He pushed me onto the bed, groped beneath my skirt, and ripped apart my underwear. He fumbled with the buttons of his pants, and I squeezed my eyes shut, convinced that if I saw his sex, it would curse me. I wasn't meant to see the center of his power. He pinned down my wrists, parted my legs, and pushed against me. My skirt was bunched around my waist, digging into my stomach, and his loose shirt hung like a shroud, like a veil over my face. He spat and when he rubbed the warm stickiness into me, I shuddered. He got onto his knees, wobbling, and thrust into me.

I exploded, blown apart, and then clenched together from the pain. A howl pushed up my throat. When he sounded so choked I feared he might collapse on me, I forced myself to look. He grimaced, his eyes shuttered. I never pictured the Chairman that way, because he was supposed to remain vigilant. Though I willed him to look at me, he never did.

CHAPTER 3

*T*HE CRACK IN THE CEILING STARTED RAZOR-THIN IN THE CORner, then widened as it zigzagged, the flight path of a bat that led to a missing chunk of plaster. I wanted the dance pavilion to split along that crack, for the beams to wrench apart, for the walls to fall until the earth itself ripped open. To shake like I was shaking, my teeth chattering hard enough to bite off my tongue.

I couldn't cover or hide myself. My thighs rubbed together, and I became aware of the wetness, the scent of salt and the tang of him. I could taste blood, too, from the cut inside my cheek, and felt it pumping through my chest, coursing through every part of me except between my legs, where for the moment I felt nothing.

Bile rose up my throat. I was going to throw up—I was throwing up—I retched but nothing came out. I swallowed hard.

He stood and buttoned his pants. Clothed, he became the Chairman I recognized, the shining figure who smiled on posters—except for the tremor in his right hand. He followed my gaze. He flexed his hand, his fingers stubby and the nails bitten down. Reaching up, I put mine on his, rubbing my thumb on him until the quaking stilled. I would always remember this moment, the first time I consoled him, my hand steadying his, a touch more private, more intimate than sex. Later, I'd figure out that the twitch wasn't a consequence of age, but a deeper ill—one of the earliest signs of the mysterious disease that stiffened and slowed his steps, slurred his words, and would eventually drown him in his flesh.

I've long wondered if the Chairman might have known his body was slipping out of control, compelling him to tighten his grip on the country. Those who saw him most often might have been blind to this decline, in the way they didn't notice the daylight disappearing, bent over their tasks until they looked up and realized all at once that darkness had fallen.

I waited for him to push me away, to shout at me for daring to think we shared a common flesh. The lines in his plump face seemed to deepen and lengthen, and the shadows beneath his eyes darkened. As he stood above me, his complexion mottled and gray as shed snake skin, I saw his true age.

"What's your name?" he asked. His voice sounded tinny and far-away.

I told him.

"Mei Xiang," he repeated, stroking my cheek. I held still. "Stay as you are."

Nodding, I swallowed, my mouth parched and bitter. He disappeared through the door, his body slipping into the narrow opening. Only then could I cry, shaking with silent sobs.

Wheezing, I curled up to shrink the pain, and ran my hands over my arms, my legs, my face. I am I am I am I am Mei. I clenched and unclenched my numb fingers until sensation returned. When I stroked my thighs, a dark smear of blood ran across my palms, the color of rust, of freshly turned clay. Tomorrow, bruises would bloom on my wrists and the inside of my thighs.

I drank another glass of the lukewarm water with its metallic tang. After plunging my hands into the pitcher, I cleaned myself with my torn underwear. Dumping the rest of the water into an empty porcelain chamber pot, I tried to urinate, but the knot between my legs became concentrated, consuming, and I stumbled back into bed.

Music flared in the dance pavilion. A whimper escaped my lips, and I darted my eyes around the windowless room, which had no other exit.

An edge pressed into my back and in the sheets, I found a heavy book bound in brown leather, solid and reassuring. Inside I discov-

ered foreign words, the characters swimming like tadpoles, and I
sniffed the musty pages. Aside from the Little Red Book, I'd never
touched another volume; our village teacher had read aloud from
the sole classroom textbook, a tattered one that he safeguarded like
gold. Crawling to the end of the bed, I found more stacked books
and flipped through a slim red volume, with more of the odd characters, written on pages shiny as ice-slicked fields, and containing pictures of round-eyed foreigners, their noses long and sharp. Peeking
inside a battered black book, bound in red string, I discovered translucent pages. My hands against them felt rough and of the earth, and
I couldn't make sense of any words.

I choked back another sob. All my life, the Chairman had been
the first and last face I looked upon each day, a face around which
spun the seasons. His face had turned unbearably strange tonight.

Teacher Fan entered, not a wrinkle on her blouse, not a hair loose
from her bun. Unable to face her, I turned away, twisted in the sheets
and glittering with pain.

With a firm hand on my shoulder, and another at my waist, she
eased me upright. "Slowly now." If she'd rubbed my back, I might
have crumpled again, for any softness would have confirmed I'd lost
something. But her thorough, efficient air—like a nurse, I would
think later—made it seem I had no cause for shame.

She straightened out my rumpled skirt, took a hair-band from
her wrist, and fixed my pigtails.

After steadying me, she led me back into the dance pavilion's
moist darkness. I burned between my legs, the deepest, most tender
part of me on fire. Beneath my skirt, I was exposed, no underclothes,
nothing between me and the floor. When the swirl of air hit me
there, my knees buckled. In the village, where the sound of a neighbor's fart could be mistaken for your own, we had few secrets, but
for as long as I could remember, Ma taught me and my sisters to
cover ourselves below. To protect what was most valuable in us.

Halting, I searched for the Chairman on the dance floor. If I saw
him, if he nodded at me, I would be made whole again, my sacrifice
real and worthy.

My memories from that part of the night blink in and out. Teacher Fan slipped me into the arms of a cadre who held me lightly, as if I were the kind of girl who deserved such consideration. I stared at my feet. Did he know what had just happened? He must. Did he want the same from me?

Passed from cadre to cadre in the pavilion, I caught glimpses of the Chairman's balding head. A man with sesame-seed eyes and a baby eggplant nose dragged me across the floor and cursed when our bodies slammed together. I staggered across the planks sticky with spilled fruit juice and tea, desperate to flee, but when I squirmed away, my partner's hold tightened, with the brute force of a man who punches a hole in the wall to kill a mosquito.

My mind blanked and then I was in the arms of a man who dripped with so much sweat he appeared to be melting. As we spun around, a drop of perspiration flicked into my open mouth. I swallowed it.

By the end of the night, the air had turned humid with sweat, and the other girls looked exhausted, their pigtails lank against their cheeks. Only Midnight Chang remained bright as lightning, studying me. She couldn't hide her envy. The others, though, might have pitied me. Standing on the edge of the dance floor, Busy Shan seemed to catch sight of me, then leaned in toward Dolly Yu to say something.

The dance must have ended, I must have thanked my partner and boarded the bus to our dormitory, but what I remember next was shivering in the top bunk in the dark.

I'd left home at dawn, which now seemed several lifetimes ago. Never before had I slept alone, and the bed seemed immense, the mushy mattress swallowing me and so noisy, the springs creaking like frogs in mating season. It was nothing like our family's brick bed, solid and still. Darkness pressed down and I reached up to assure myself of the limits of this endless black. For a few terrible seconds, my hand grasped at nothing until I touched the cool ceiling, and then I stretched my arms, one hand against the wall, the other on the metal bed frame. If I stayed rooted, I wouldn't disappear. I listened to the steady breathing of my roommates, but I couldn't fall asleep without Ma's soft snores, the heat of Second Daughter's back pressed against my fingers and my chin. Ba's loud farts. First Daughter, tossing and restless. Bedsprings creaked, footsteps shuffled, and someone covered me with a blanket. Settling under the folds, I dissolved into sleep.

THE NEXT MORNING, I struggled to get up. When I pulled back the blanket, I noticed a rusty stain on the sheet beneath me. Biting my lip, I tried not to heave from a pain that struck deeper than bone. Still in my clothes from the dance party, I couldn't—wouldn't—lift up my skirt. I had to be pulpy as a persimmon between my legs.

The Chairman—the Chairman's hands on me. It seemed impossible last night, impossible now if not for the proof of my body. My face felt scratched up from his stubble, like I'd tangled in brambles. How did I get here? As nausea swept over me, I gritted my teeth, snatches of memory coming back to me: the wet sloppy sound of the Chairman's breath, his pungent scent that punched deep into my nose, his fingers on my wrist, and the moment I tore open.

The rattling bed frame must have stirred Busy Shan. When a spring creaked, I peeked down to see she'd popped her head out from the bunk below to look up at me. Everyone else was still asleep.

She must have noticed my misery. "Do you need water?" she asked.

When I nodded, she got up and from a hot water bottle on a shelf, she filled an enamel mug. I took the cup warily, remembering the pouch of my mother's tea. It might prevent a baby from taking hold, if I drank it every morning. It would keep me in the revolution. I dug the tea out from my pocket and dropped a little lump into the cup. As the tea steeped, I let the steam bathe my face. I sipped, grimacing but swallowing every bitter drop. Ma's cures didn't always work—so much depended on the rainfall that year, on the length of the winter, on the cycle of the moon when you harvested the roots and flowers—but it was all I had.

"You can keep the blanket. It's an extra." She must have laid it upon me last night. "What is that?" she asked, her nose pinched. The brew smelled like wet rotting leaves.

"It's from my mother," I said.

She didn't press me. "Take off your shirt."

I flinched.

"Your button's about to fall off." She pulled out a small sewing kit with spools of thread, scissors, and a needle.

I passed the blouse to her. The other girls were waking up and shuffling out of the room, yawning and stretching. Though I sensed none of her earlier scorn, I watched suspiciously, wondering if she might snip off every button. Instead, with a few flashes of her needle, she fixed it. "They'll drop off more clothes for you today, but until then . . ."

I put on the stained blouse and climbed down the ladder. My feet, tender from yesterday's heels, ached with each step.

"When there's time, you can make what they give you yours," she said. She flipped the neckline of her loose cotton pajamas, onto which she'd embroidered a tiny bird, no bigger than a fingernail. "Add a ribbon inside the waistband or take up the hem—that sort of thing."

She was among the best seamstresses in the troupe, I would learn, nipping in her blouses at the waist and at the bust, and hemming up her skirts.

"Won't Teacher Fan notice?" I asked.

"Easier to ask for forgiveness than to get permission," she said.

At my shock, she laughed. "She knows, of course she knows. But if she gives us this . . ."

"We take it," I said. "We think we're getting away with something. Which makes us stick to the other rules."

She nodded. From under her bed, she slid out a pair of slippers. They were too small; my heels hung off the back, and my toes poked out the front.

"I'll go barefoot." I wiggled my feet against the concrete. A blister throbbed on the back of my ankle.

"Not on these floors. Your toes will rot off!"

She didn't seem to realize that I'd mucked through fields spread with what we gathered from the latrines and used to tear off leeches as easily as scabs. I kept the slippers on. She handed me a towel and led me to the bathroom, where the sound of water rushed from behind a row of curtains.

"Girls like her only bathe when they're born, and when they die," Midnight Chang said. She'd come up from behind us. As another girl exited a stall, she flounced past us. Busy Shan barked at her, "Wait your turn for the showers!"

She didn't. I suspected that she and Busy Shan were used to being the most beautiful girls in the room, used to the consideration that went along with their looks. It was only natural they'd despise each other.

Busy Shan gave me a sidelong glance. "She also tried to jump the line at the dance party, but everyone new gets a turn with the Chairman. Everyone old, too. Just remember that. The girl you replaced didn't."

"Replaced?" I rubbed my forearms, desperate to rid my body of the stickiness.

"You're in her bed. Though she wasn't a problem when she was in the bed. It was when she wasn't."

"She was with another man," I said.

She grinned. "You're a quick one. You can dance with the cadre, let them chat you up, but no more than that."

"How did she . . . how did she get together with her boyfriend?" I asked, still trying to catch up.

"She was clever, I'll give her that," she said. "To avoid the guard at the front gate, she climbed the wall behind the dormitory. Like some kind of fighting monk!" Like those from the old tales, trained to jump from roof to roof.

The girl met her lover every night until she'd been discovered missing by Secretary Sun, she said.

I leaned against the wall. "He comes by?" I asked.

"Planning to raise your hand again?" she asked slyly.

She didn't wait for me to answer. On the nights without dances, if the Chairman wanted to see you, Secretary Sun came by the dormitory. "Usually after midnight and then brings you back early the next morning," she said.

Busy Shan wasn't welcoming, not exactly, but it seemed she wanted to be the first to inform me about the ways of the troupe.

Dolly Yu cried out. Coming into the bathroom, she'd slipped in a puddle on the concrete floor.

At the village school, we'd learned about the soldier Lei Feng, who washed the feet of his comrades and darned their socks, cleaned the barracks, and served tea to his officers and his comrades. When he died, crushed by a heavy pole tall as a tree, his diary revealed his selfless deeds and his love of the Chairman. There was no limit to serving the people, he'd said.

Following his example, we'd fought over who would get to sweep the floor of the classroom or fetch the teacher hot water. Now, when I tried to throw down my towel, Busy Shan snatched it back. "That's disgusting."

"Someone could fall," I said.

"It's a low spot. Water always collects there," she said. "Everyone knows to go around it. If anyone slips, it's their own fault."

I twisted the towel in my hands.

"No one's keeping track. If you're trying to impress Teacher Fan, she's not even here," she said. "Besides, why use *your* towel?" She glanced at the one hanging over Midnight Chang's stall.

I couldn't help but laugh. She returned to gossiping about the girl I'd replaced. "I warned her, but she never listened. The attention went to her head. Men circle around a woman if they smell another man on her. And if they know it's the Chairman . . ."

I might have guessed Busy Shan had been among the longest to serve in the troupe. She seemed rubbed raw, rubbed open. Her hips swayed when she walked, to attract attention, and though the troupe wasn't her preferred audience, we would have to do. She was only two years older than me, it turned out, but at my age, that seemed a lifetime wiser.

More girls arrived in the bathroom, chattering about the day, their high voices echoing off the tiled walls. A pair came in with their arms linked together, whispering to each other, both slender and graceful as fawns.

A shower went off and water dripped in the stall. "Hurry up in there," Busy Shan called out. "At least she didn't let herself get knocked up. There was a girl who died trying to get rid of a baby." She paused, making sure she had my full attention. "She threw herself down the stairs."

The stairs I'd walked up last night? Maybe she didn't have *dong quai,* or the cure could have failed her. I palmed the damp concrete wall. Maybe she'd never heard about it. The herb might not be available in the cities, or perhaps her mother had never told her about it. "Or she stabbed herself?" she said. She watched me closely.

"Up—there?" I asked.

"That's what I heard," she said, her tone solemn and yet satisfied, too, that she'd been the first to tell me.

In the days to come, the stories would keep changing. The rumors repeated and repeated like an incantation, repeated to take away their power. It was said the ghost girl would tap you on the shoulder at night, to trick you into turning around and helping her steal back into the Lake Palaces. She didn't want to leave the only place she'd ever been significant.

Neither did I.

IN DANCE CLASS LATER that morning, I stayed ahead of Midnight Chang. She brushed her hand against me, enough to make me stumble—no accident. Then, during a polka, she slowed down in front of me. I staggered, twisting my ankle. She clipped my heel next, a scrape that opened yesterday's blister. For a few seconds, I teetered on my heels before catching myself.

If I'd tried to push her away, my fingers would have grasped air. As much as I struggled, the class kept me preoccupied, made it so I didn't have to think about the Chairman crushing me into the bed.

We galloped onward, on the verge of crashing into one another, a wild footrace going in circles. The polka would become my favorite: You didn't have to be graceful or remember many different kinds of steps; the dance let us show off our coltish strength—how high, how far we could leap on the scuffed floorboards—and the faster others twirled, the faster I went, too.

Midnight Chang stomped on my toes, then threw an elbow at Busy Shan, whose back was turned to her. Without thinking, I jabbed mine into Midnight Chang's side, to block her. Busy Shan spun around in time to see Midnight Chang jerking away, her face still a taunt. Busy Shan's eyes widened. Taking my hand, she pulled me ahead. Her fingers were warm and sticky, her grip so strong and sure that I could have followed her anywhere.

Coming between them only invited trouble, but I was used to tussling with my oldest sister. After the song ended, Busy Shan glared at Midnight Chang in the mirror.

As we caught our breath, Teacher Fan told us how class struggle had begun in Germany, more than a hundred years ago. "Workers rose up, just like the workers here. They fought for their future. They rose up like your grandparents, like your parents," she said.

Astonishing to consider how our feet answered the revolt of those workers halfway around the world. In the studio, I would move in ways I'd never even considered. It was like realizing that I could look up, instead of only straight ahead or to the side. Never before in my life, and never since, would I dwell in my body so freely, so fully as I did in those weeks just before I turned sixteen.

During a break, we milled about the studio. "When's the next dance?" I asked Busy Shan.

She gave me an appraising look. "When he's here, the dances are every other day."

Tomorrow, then?

Typically, the Chairman partnered with a few girls at each dance party and favored one in his bedchambers for a week or two at a time, she said. After several months, he might take renewed interest in a girl, she added, but in time everyone left the troupe.

"We're sent home?" I asked. The city and its wonders would vanish, and I would plunge back into the well of my village.

"Some go home, some get jobs at the Lake Palaces or in the capital. Others, no one seems to know," she said. "You look up one day, and they're gone." Lowering her voice, she told me that a girl who'd argued with the Chairman—who'd flung a cup of tea at his feet!—had disappeared. "Maybe to a labor camp? Her parents, too."

I wrapped my arms around myself. "Why her parents?" I asked.

"They raised her up, didn't they?" Busy Shan asked. "It was their fault, more than anyone else's."

Another girl who disappeared knew more than a hundred revolutionary tunes, she added. "No one could figure out why or where she'd gone."

"Who decides who stays and who goes?" I asked. "Teacher Fan? Secretary Sun? The Chairman?"

"Does it really matter?" she asked. "All of them, probably."

"Do you hear from girls who left?" I asked.

"You hear things, that's all," she said. No letters, I took that to mean, no reunions.

"You're making this up," Midnight Chang scoffed. She'd edged over to eavesdrop. "You think because we're new, we'll believe everything you say."

"Think what you like," Busy Shan said to her. She turned back to me. "You never know when your time is up. Or when he'll come and go. Sometimes he leaves for months. In the winter, he travels south. That's when we're sent home. Sometimes you get summoned back to the Lake Palaces, but never more than once. Maybe twice?"

"No more?" I asked.

"No man wants to ride an old mare," she said.

Her bluntness shocked but thrilled me, too. No one spoke like that in the village.

"What are you supposed to tell your family?" I asked Busy Shan. Motes of dust sparkled between us.

"What the Party told you," she said.

I bit my lip. "Nothing?"

"Teacher Fan says to tell them you were in a revolutionary dance troupe," she said.

"But . . ."

She smirked. "The moment you bring up political theory, they'll stop listening."

If I went home too soon, my neighbors would gloat and the head-man would punish me, force me to tote stinking night soil or order me to work in the steepest fields of stony earth. I now realized why Ma suspected what would happen to me in the capital. It was an honor I'd been selected, but she would have understood what men value most in a teenage girl. Though I'd wanted to come and wanted to stay, a sudden rage boiled up inside me. She'd warned me the only way she could, by pressing protections onto me. But she'd still let me go.

Teacher Fan clapped her hands to signal the end of our break and put on a new record. She'd said nothing about what the Chairman had done to me. She had neither time nor patience for those who needed coddling. After she told us to get into rows, I stood in front, on the far right. She turned her back to us to demonstrate the cha-cha, but she could still watch us in the mirror. When she caught my eye in the reflection, I threw back my slumped shoulders.

She stepped forward and back, and then side to side. Simple enough, I thought, until she swiveled her hips. Up and down but round and round simultaneously—no less amazing than if she'd walked on water.

I felt stiff and solid as oak, yet also as if I might go up in flames—not only because of my lack of grace, but because her moves looked like something that should only pass between lovers. Her hips swayed as if they'd been oiled. The chasm between what she demonstrated and what my own body was capable of doing seemed impossible to cross.

To my relief, the song ended.

During a pause between songs, Teacher Fan gave us another lesson. Almost three years ago, Americans had trained their missiles onto Cuba. "On our little brother!" she said. "The Cubans stood up to the Americans, and the Americans had to back down."

Capitalists were like hungry ghosts, never sated. Everyone had heard about a landlord who'd beaten a cousin to death, or an aunt blinded at a factory. They'd steal our very last breath for a handful of coins, and we'd no sooner let them return to China than turn a knife on ourselves.

"In every dance, you push each other on," Teacher Fan said. "You push your partner in ways that you couldn't if you were alone."

Anyone could repeat slogans, but I was beginning to understand that we held the revolution in our bodies, in every twirl, shimmy, and dip, the dance steps uniting socialists around the world. I wondered if the Cubans were as sinuous and sleek as their steps. If the Germans were as lively and sturdy.

"What if your partner is so clumsy she trips you?" Midnight Chang asked. She didn't look at me, yet I could tell she was making fun of me.

"If you get tripped up like that, then you're not paying enough attention," Busy Shan told her.

"Any partner of yours would end up a cripple," Midnight Chang said. "Or maybe that's the strategy. Let's pair you up with the enemy!"

The girls around us laughed, and even Teacher Fan smiled. I hated my reflection, hated myself, wanted to smash the mirror and make it disappear. How much longer would I get to stay? The dance studio—along with the classroom next door—was housed in the bottom level of an administrative building that must have been constructed after Liberation. Unlike the arches and curves elsewhere in the Lake Palaces, the building was squat as a thumb, with an ugliness that announced its power to ruin an emperor's view. The higher floors had offices, but we would never venture there, hearing more than seeing the workers who clomped in the stairwells.

After lunch, I fidgeted in the front row of the classroom, where Teacher Fan lectured on the founders of Communism. My crotch throbbed, a constant dull ache. I studied the black-and-white portraits of the very first foreigners I'd laid my eyes upon. Karl Marx, whose bushy white halo of a beard I'd learn to recognize; Joseph Stalin, with a steely gaze and a thick mustache; Vladimir Lenin, with a tiny pointed beard that made him seem pinheaded; and Friedrich Engels, his beard so huge it was as if his beard had grown its own beard. I'd never seen men so hairy, and I wondered if the fur covered their chests, their backs, and their legs.

"You've heard that saying, 'To educate a daughter is like watering another man's garden'?" Teacher Fan asked.

We nodded. A daughter would only get married, become the mother to another family's line, become the servant to another master.

"You girls have more chances now." She told us we'd been born into the most fortunate generation, born after the Party's victory over the landlords and factory owners, and into the future that the Chairman promised.

Try as I might to impress Teacher Fan, though, my attentions dragged in class like everyone else's. Nibbling on the ends of our braids, picking at our fingernails, or worrying our pimples, we peeked at the huge map of our country that hung on the wall, its thumbtacked edges curling. I tucked a foot behind the leg of my chair. A few weeks would go by before I could read a map and learn how I could see so much and so little at once, the whole of a country, the mountain reduced to a squiggle, a river into a line, and cities mere dots and our villages not there at all.

Nothing we learned in class, though, would protect us when the Cultural Revolution broke out the following year. Not even the Chairman knew that teenagers in the cities would be the first to volunteer for his campaign, the first to raise their fists against their teachers and their parents, against most anyone in authority.

And none of us knew it would begin with me.

CHAPTER 4

*I*N THE TROUPE, NO ONE CALLED ME MEI; INSTEAD I WENT BY Scholar Song, a title coined by Midnight Chang. A veiled insult, implying that I was boring and self-important—a grind, when it came to our studies—but I adopted it with pride. Even if a nickname had a teasing sting, it also set our troupe apart from the other workers at the Lake Palaces: They were our own nicknames for our own people, for the girl who only spoke in a whisper, for the one who dozed at every opportunity or sang like a lark.

The new names went along with our new lives in the capital. Our families no longer defined us; free of the names, both loving and taunting, they'd given us, we were free of the expectations that would have held us back if we'd remained home. In the villages, failures from childhood followed people until the end of their days. A greedy little boy would be forever known as Big Mouth and a smelly girl as Little Dog Fart.

As the days passed, the Chairman's absence filled me in ways he couldn't if he'd stood before me in the flesh. He swelled into the sky, itched in my scalp, and rode in my heartbeat. His mystery returned, and so did my devotion to him, a longing I knew that the other girls shared.

I drank my mother's tea, praying for blood, and one morning it arrived. I'd woken up early, planning to mop the bathroom before anyone else got up. Busy Shan was wrong; I wasn't sucking up to Teacher Fan or anyone else. I'd been feeling muddled, and a duty gave me a sense of purpose—of control.

In the bathroom, though, I doubled over with cramps and stared at the blood smeared on my underpants and at the bright streak in the squat toilet. I rested against the cracked tile wall and rubbed my fist in the small of my back, regretting yesterday's icy shower. Blood was like water, my mother had warned me when my flow started last year. If I let myself get too cold—waded in the river or sought out the breeze just before or during—the blood would thicken and slow inside me.

When Midnight Chang entered, I jerked up my pajamas and stood, waiting for her to go away. Feeling skinned raw, I didn't want to be around her or anyone else. She gasped and when I looked over, she was squatting, staring at her underpants. Was there also a blood-stain? When my sisters and their flows matched up, I felt left out. It bothered me now that Midnight Chang's body had timed itself with mine—or did mine time itself with hers?—when I didn't trust her.

"Do you need a rag?" I asked. Busy Shan had shown me where to find clean rags in the cabinet.

"A rag?" she asked in a small voice that sounded nothing like her.

If she was mocking me, I wanted none of it. "Yes, a rag," I said. "Same as in the city, same as in the country."

"Help," she said in that same small voice. She stood up.

"I'm not your mom."

Her mouth trembled. She winced, as if a cramp gripped her belly.

"Didn't your mother tell you what to do about your flow?" I asked.

"No," she said.

I looked over the squat toilets. "Haven't you seen what she did in the latrines? How she took care of it?"

"She died a week after I was born," she said tightly. In the troupe, none of us talked much about our families. The only time I'd seen softness in Midnight Chang's face was when she mentioned her father, how this meal or that piece of clothing couldn't compare to what he had given her. Had he ever denied her? Certain of his pride, she'd seemed certain in everything else.

Maybe she had no sisters, no aunts, and though her father might well have spoiled her, he didn't know how to explain that her body would betray her. Maybe she'd skipped past bad skin and other teen humiliations, but she couldn't avoid this one.

I fetched a rag from the cabinet. "Here. Fold it like this."

She took the bundle from me. She glanced at the doorway. No one was coming yet. After pulling down her pajama bottoms again, she stared at the spots of blood on her underpants.

"Now put it in the center," I said.

"Like this?" she asked, her movements tentative.

"A little farther back. That's it," I said, then explained how to attach it. "Now pull everything together."

After she finished, she stood back up. "Something isn't right," she said. She tugged at her waistband. "It feels . . ."

"No one likes how it feels," I said. Our voices echoed against the tile. "The first day or two, you'll need to change it every few hours."

She let out a long sigh. Maybe helping her would make her less spiteful toward me.

"It's not so bad. You must have seen the other women with them?" I asked. When I tried to reassure her with a smile, she must have thought I was mocking her.

She scowled. "I don't stare at other women like that. Like you do."

THE NEXT DAY, OUR bus passed a scrawny dog balancing a ball on its nose. When the dog tossed the ball in the air and caught it in his mouth, I gasped. Busy Shan leaned against me for a closer look.

"Scholar Song, don't you know, a dog can be trained to do anything?" Midnight Chang said from behind us. I turned to look at her.

"Roll over, sit up, bark on command," she said. "You can even train a dog to dance."

"Better a dog than a chicken who clucks all the way to the chopping block," I said. Sometimes she talked nonstop, scarcely taking a breath between her words. "Who runs around without its head, glad to be free of its own clucking."

She glowered at me. Teacher Fan, who sat behind the driver, didn't turn around.

Outside of our training at the Lake Palaces, we weren't allowed to leave the dormitory. Ours was among three buildings in a complex surrounded by a high concrete wall. We rarely saw our neighbors, older women who left before us and returned in the evening. Sometimes we could hear the rasp of bicycle tires and muffled conversation from the street, but otherwise my world shrank to a circumference smaller than my village: where we slept and the short bus ride to our classrooms. The route wound past warrens of homes, their tiled roofs peeping above courtyard walls.

When I first arrived at the Lake Palaces, I'd glimpsed little of the grounds, located just west of the Forbidden City, where the emperors had lived. Because the Forbidden City's dark cobblestones glittered in the sunshine—like the heat off a wok—with scant shade or greenery, emperors and their entourages used to seek relief in the gardens of the Lake Palaces next door.

After the last emperor had abdicated, his home had been thrown open to the public as a museum, but the Lake Palaces remained closed to most everyone. It seemed out of time, out of place, perfect and eternal, the view always the same whether hundreds of years ago or hundreds of years into the future.

We were now deep in July. A flock of bicycles went by. With its wide tires and sturdy black frame, the model was known as a Flying Pigeon. Such birds never soared and would never be immortalized in a painting or a poem, but they could survive the capital's dusty, pockmarked streets.

Three shirtless men in ragged shorts and rubber sandals maneuvered a cart piled high with chunks of metal, two pushing and the third pulling ropes—their bodies tilted so steeply they'd fall over if they let go. They didn't look up at the poster they passed of a bearded man in a top hat and red-striped pants, clutching a knife dripping with blood. Uncle Sam, we'd learned in class, who wanted to carve up Asia.

The stench of exhaust drifted up from a hole in the floor covered with a wooden board. There weren't many buses on the road, perhaps one trundling along every couple blocks. As we approached another giant mural, we pressed ourselves against the windows on the side closest, staring at the Chairman posed in the center beneath the slogan, LONG LIVE THE VICTORY OF THE PROLETARIAN REVOLUTIONARY LINE. Rendered in bold strokes, he was waving, surrounded by a group of men with a flurry of red flags at their feet. LONG LIVE THE CHAIRMAN FOR TEN THOUSAND YEARS!

Searching the faces on the wall, I recognized cadre who had danced with me. That one had stomped on my foot, and the man on the end had guided me with confidence. They held the nation's highest positions of power, but I'd never considered them in the village, where we had sung and prayed to the Chairman alone. We didn't know about his assistants. I would learn their names eventually, though we always referred to them by their titles: the President, the Premier, and the Defense Minister. Teacher Fan had explained that the President, who headed our country, was the Chairman's hand-picked successor. He handled daily matters, while the Chairman took a longer view, she said.

What that meant in practice, I didn't understand. Soon I'd learn that he and the Chairman wanted the country to go in opposite directions; at the moment, though, I wondered only what order would the men stand in, lined up behind the Chairman? In the mural, they looked younger than they had at the dance party; they appeared to be the same age as my father, but that was impossible. He'd been little more than a boy in the time of Yan'an.

I didn't recognize the man at the far right of the mural. Then Busy Shan exclaimed, "The Madame!" Not another man, but the Chairman's wife, with a smile broad as his, her hair tucked under a red-star cap, and a billowing jacket that hid her curves. How beautiful, how fierce she might have been when she and the Chairman first met, captivating him above all others. She seemed to transfix Midnight Chang, too. I watched her clench a fist to her heart, copying the Madame's pose on the wall.

I didn't know much about her, but in the village school, we'd heard stories about where they'd met: at Yan'an, where the Red Army, on the run during the civil war, had taken refuge. The soldiers' journey began in 1934 in Jiangxi, a province in the southern reaches of our country, hemmed in by mountains on three sides. First the soldiers fled west, and then doubled back through sodden, craggy trails, marching at night. Teacher Fan told us the soldiers had been half-starved, hollowed out by high fevers and bloody shits. Then they straggled up along the border with Tibet, along cliffs so steep that sure-footed horses tumbled to their deaths. That detail had haunted me: I'd pictured the riders caught up in the stirrups, the tangle of limbs and hooves; I'd heard their screams and the neighing terror of the horses.

They broke new trails through forests so misty and dense they got lost if they didn't keep up with the troops ahead of them. Skirted a treacherous swamp where a misstep plunged them up to their waists. If a soldier sank up to his chest, he was left for dead. At last, the soldiers staggered into Yan'an, where locals lived in its yellow hills pitted with caves like a honeycomb.

When Teacher Fan told us only one in ten who started the journey made it to the end a year later, I'd counted around the classroom, wondering which of us would have survived. Maybe none would have lived except for her.

The Long March, with its sacrifice and survival, had been the story from which our republic and we all sprang. Heroes immortalized in the poems we'd learned by heart as children. After the Communists established their base at Yan'an, they attracted aspiring revolutionaries from across the country like the Madame. Party leaders worked side by side with the peasants, I'd heard, gathering the strength for every challenge ahead. In my imagination, Yan'an seemed like the edge of the world—a place so barren, a place so wild, anything could happen. Mythical yet real.

There, the Madame had come to the Chairman's attention: She could have raised her hand in political education class, asking a clever question. She might have lingered afterward, walking him to his next meeting. Their talks could have turned into walks along the river, where their heads tilted together in a kiss.

What the troupe did—what *I'd* done—with the Chairman must hurt her. Still, she reigned just as the empress had reigned over the concubines. Perhaps she might have accepted that she couldn't satisfy his appetites, and as long as she remained his wife, people would respect her—fear her.

Midnight Chang kicked the back of my seat, jolting my jaws together.

I whirled around. "Quit it!"

"Quit what?" she asked. Her hands were folded in her lap, but her eyes were bright with mischief.

When I turned back around, she resumed kicking.

I twisted around again. "Help me," I simpered, imitating her in the bathroom.

"What kind of girl can't figure out a rag?" Busy Shan asked.

I'd told her, of course I'd told her what happened yesterday. As soon as I turned back around, my head slammed against the seat.

Midnight Chang had yanked my hair.

Busy Shan reared back, ready to strike. Up in a flash, Teacher Fan ordered us to change seats: Busy Shan had to sit with Dolly Yu in the back, and she marched me up front.

"But—" I protested.

"Now," she said.

We were getting close, only a couple blocks from the Lake Palaces. After I sat down, Teacher Fan leaned in toward me. "I'm the youngest in my family, too," she said.

I didn't expect her to confide in me, to find me worthy of comparison even after I'd tangled with Midnight Chang. I almost fell off my seat; without noticing it, I'd been teetering on the edge.

She unscrewed her drinking jar, releasing the floral scent of tea leaves, and sipped the brew, the color of dark honey. "No one expects much from the youngest," she said. "No one treats you like much of a threat."

"Unless you're Midnight Chang," I said.

She flicked her free hand, as if shooing a fly: *Don't bother*. The gesture sent me soaring.

"No one realizes you're watching, listening. No one guesses how wily the baby can be."

I felt like she'd seen clean through me. "When did you come to the capital?" I asked shyly.

"First I had to go to Yan'an."

Yan'an! I might have guessed she'd been there, too, though she couldn't have been much older than us when she arrived. I had to ask.

"Sixteen," she said.

About the same age as me. "Did you go by yourself?" I asked.

She put the lid back on. "With friends. But they turned back the next day," she said with the barest hint of a smile but a smile all the same. "They thought they had something to lose."

"Weren't you scared?" I asked. Eyes bored into the back of my head; Midnight Chang, and probably Busy Shan, too, would expect every detail of our conversation.

Teacher Fan looked out the window as we pulled into the gates of the Lake Palaces. Though I guessed that she wouldn't deign to answer such a stupid question, she turned back to me. "If you have nothing, if people where you come from think you're nothing, it's a gift, isn't it—to go where no one knows you?"

IN THE TIME OF Yan'an, if teenagers rejected their parents, if they felt lost, if they were against tradition, they found their way there, where one could also achieve greatness, or if not, the greatness of having tried.

I tell you this in the hopes it might explain who I was in the time before we met—a girl in search of her own Yan'an.

AT LUNCH, WE GOSSIPED about the Chairman: He was traveling. He was ill. We would get dismissed soon.

Dolly Yu pushed the noodles around in her bowl with her chopsticks, nothing reaching her mouth. She tore at her rosebud lips, which were chapped and bleeding; she always picked at herself. Though she was a year older than me, she seemed younger, flat-chested with a voice high as a little girl's. "I wish he'd come back."

"That's not for you to decide," Midnight Chang said. "Only the Chairman can."

Our table fell silent, our conversation replaced by the ticking of chopsticks against our bowls. But not for long.

"What did you do to make the Chairman pick you?" Midnight Chang asked me. She possessed an easy confidence, but she had failed in one respect, the most important in our new lives: The Chairman had ignored her at the last dance.

I took my time curling a bundle of noodles and slurped a mouthful of the tender and springy strands. After I looked around the table, I leaned in. She couldn't hide the eagerness in her face.

"I followed Teacher Fan's instructions," I said, my voice hushed.

Frowning, she sat back. "So did everyone else."

"I've told you what I know," I said airily.

She set down her chopsticks. "I'll help you remember."

"You were gone for a long time," she added. "What did you say to him?"

"Not much, I bet." Busy Shan shot me an apologetic glance. She never could resist a quip.

"Tell me," Midnight Chang asked.

"You'll be spoiled, if I say too much. He wants to meet us as if he were to meet us in our villages, in our factories," I said.

"Where we might as well be," she said. "If he doesn't come back soon, we'll all get sent home."

Dolly Yu picked at her noodles, her body tight with worry. We hadn't seen the Chairman in two weeks. Even though Teacher Fan had told us that the parties raised the morale of top cadre, they never took place without him.

If anyone wanted to leave the troupe, no one admitted it. From our talk, you would have thought we'd wrestle one another for a chance to sleep with the Chairman again. With everyone wanting like that, anything else sank and disappeared.

"His wife must have canceled the parties," Busy Shan said.

"You don't speak for his wife," Midnight Chang said.

Dolly Yu looked up. "Neither do you," she said, which surprised everyone—maybe Dolly Yu most of all.

Midnight Chang slapped her so hard that the timid girl hiccuped, holding back tears. Some girls gasped, and a few giggled nervously. Though Teacher Fan seemed irritated, she didn't intervene. Midnight Chang locked eyes with me.

I ignored her, but could feel her daring me to fight. I led Dolly Yu to the bathroom, Busy Shan following. I splashed water on Dolly Yu's face, the dark red mark throbbing on her cheek.

"You confront her, she hits back twice as hard," I told Dolly Yu, who examined herself in the bathroom mirror and touched her cheek. She'd gnawed at her fingernails until the tips had gone raw. Busy Shan combed her fingers through Dolly Yu's tangled hair and re-braided it.

I thought about the look Midnight Chang had given me. She'd slapped Dolly Yu to strike at me, and I had to stop her. Nothing would cut harder than if she doubted herself. How, though? I pictured her shoulders thrown back, her chest thrust forward, showing off her narrow waist. Yes. She'd panic if she thought she'd fattened up.

In addition to our dance party outfit, we each had two uniforms, a dark blue skirt, white short-sleeved blouse, and red neckerchief, each labeled with our surnames at the waistband and on our collar. We had one to wear, and one to wash that we stuffed into a basket each night and left downstairs for the laundress. Some girls complained that the clothes were rough and scratchy—and they were— but the fabric was still nicer than anything spun in my village.

After lights-out, we could dig up Midnight Chang's uniforms and Busy Shan could alter them over the course of a week, moving the button on her waist over a couple millimeters each time. She could also nip in Midnight Chang's field drill pants and pajama bottoms. Over time, she would strain to button her clothes, the waistband digging into her.

Because Dolly Yu couldn't keep a secret, I waited to tell Busy Shan until after we finished lunch and changed into our uniforms for the field drills: cotton tunics, pants, and slip-on canvas shoes with rubber soles.

Twice a week, on a patch of grass outside of our dormitory, Teacher Fan led us through military exercises. "The imperialists are relentless," she told us. "But so are we. In an attack, every one of us must take up the fight." She wore an outfit much like ours, but while we seemed like children in baggy hand-me-downs, she had an authority about her.

We touched our toes, ran in place and did jumping jacks, hurled wooden grenades and swung wooden rifles. If I squinted during the drills, I could imagine thrusting myself into battle. The grenades had heft and a purpose, even if they didn't explode, and our moves were another kind of dancing, giving order and an outlet to our restlessness. Eventually, I'd realize we would have been useless in battle, but back then, the training reminded us to be vigilant.

If people had peered over the wall, they might have ridiculed us, girls dressed all alike, playacting at war. Even still, the ferociousness of our screams might have chilled them.

That day, by the rack stacked with wooden grenades and rifles, I motioned for Busy Shan to hang back while the rest of the girls went onto the practice field. When I told her the plan, she shook with silent laughter.

Then she hesitated. "What if she catches me?"

"She won't," I said. I tossed a grenade from hand to hand. The green paint was chipping off, the wood beneath worn dark and smooth from years of handling. "She's like a rock once she falls asleep." Early one morning, Teacher Fan had surprised us with a fire drill and Midnight Chang had failed to wake up until her bunkmate shook her. "I'll sit up with you. If anyone finds us, we can say we're studying. I'll listen for anyone coming." I touched her wrist. "She jabs and she jabs, and no one stops her. We will."

I dropped the grenade, which bounced in the grass. Knotting my mouth, I sucked in my gut and pretended to struggle with the buttons. When I poked Busy Shan on her waist and tickled her, she laughed. Midnight Chang would never admit she couldn't fit into her clothes. She'd lose too much face.

"Stop dawdling!" Teacher Fan called out, waving us over. She stood where the row of girls began, in lines behind the five targets.

As Busy Shan and I trotted toward the line behind the first target, each of us clutching a handful of grenades, Teacher Fan shouted at us. "Get in different lines."

I chose the target in the middle while Busy Shan remained on the end. Though I took aim, my grenade went so far off course, it smacked the bullseye to the immediate right of mine.

"A blind granny could aim better than you," Midnight Chang shouted from the other end.

Turning away, she whispered to one of her followers. Moments later, a grenade came flying at me from that direction, ricocheted off the ground, and hit my shin.

Apologizing, the recruit trotted over, but it had been no accident. She had the best aim, with a stillness about her that you'd want in the pitched confusion of battle.

Kicking the grenade aside, I fought the urge to fire back at Midnight Chang. A shadow fell in front of me—Teacher Fan's.

"You're letting her get to you," she said quietly. "You asked about Yan'an. You wonder who lived and who didn't? It was luck, but practice, too. Practicing so many times . . ."

"You didn't have to think about it?" I asked.

"You train yourself how to shut things out," she said. "The ones who didn't, who got distracted, ended up dead."

THAT NIGHT, THE MOON rose, golden and unblinking as a cat's eye. Within a day or two it would be full. Tomorrow was our day off, when we swept and cleaned the dormitory, and gossiped under the scholar trees, which grew all over the capital, their slim branches curled like twirling ribbons against the high white walls.

Snores started up around me. In the bunk beneath me, Busy Shan was so motionless I wondered if she'd fallen asleep. If I didn't wake her up, we could drop the plan; maybe I shouldn't make more trouble. Seconds later she was on her feet, and I pulled out the dirty uniform I'd balled up in my sheets.

Downstairs in the empty common room, as we settled onto the sofa, I glanced at the door, harboring the secret hope that Secretary Sun might come to fetch me. What the Chairman had done to me, I wasn't certain I wanted again, but I also yearned to see him, more intensely than anything I'd ever felt.

Busy Shan snipped off the button. "When she tries on the skirt, she'll panic! Can you imagine the look on her face?"

"Do you think it's true?" I asked. "That we're all about to go home?" My family, the entire village would know at a glance that I'd lain under a man. Teacher Fan, glad to be rid of me, would never invite me back.

She threaded her needle. "The only thing true is that Midnight Chang can spread a rumor. He'll be back," she added with a certainty that could only have been bluster.

"In time for the Mid-Autumn Moon Festival?" I asked. On that holiday, everyone in my village would hike up the hill to eat cakes stamped with the design of flowers, pray for blessings, and recite the legends about Chang'e, the woman who lived on the moon. Sometimes she was tragic, sometimes brave, depending on who told the story. I held on to these tales, an accidental gift at my birth. None of them were true, and all of them were.

"That's my birthday." I used to pretend the celebrations that day were for me, but it seemed too childish to admit now.

"Birthday! How old?" she asked.

"Sixteen."

"A young lady," she said, as if she were a matron and not two years older than me. "Shall we bake our little scholar a moon cake?" She always teased me for reading ahead in our lessons.

In the village, we'd spend weeks preparing moon cakes stamped with worn wooden molds, with simple blurred outlines of flower petals. Soaking, boiling, then grinding the lotus seeds and mixing them with oil and honey, and making the dough from sweet syrup, flour, egg, and lye water made from ashes. We wrapped dough around a lump of filling big as the palm of our hands, pressed it into the mold, painted it with egg yolks, and baked it in a clay oven. We made scores upon scores of cakes until we went cross-eyed keeping track.

"I hope we'll get some in the canteen," I said.

She puckered her mouth. "I can't stand them. One bite sinks like a brick! The festival is so boring—the day feels like it never ends."

Was she insulting me? "I liked staying up late." I tried not to sound defensive. It could be that way with girls. Even the ones who were supposed to be your friends could have knives in their smiles.

"Listening to the same stories every year," she said dismissively.

"It depends on who's telling them." I remembered our picnics on the night of the festival. Under the silvery moon, I would nestle behind Ma and my sisters, warming myself on the hearth of their backs, as Ba began his story.

"Long ago," he would say, "ten suns rose into the sky." I repeated his words. The people rejoiced at this new dawn, until the extra suns scorched the earth, withering grasses and shriveling animals. Chang'e's husband, Hou Yi, an archer, raised his bow and shot down nine suns.

I hopped off the sofa to demonstrate. Ba always pulled back his arm at this point in the story, flicking his forefinger to imitate the archer, and now I did the same to entertain Busy Shan.

To reward Hou Yi, the Queen Mother of the West gave him two doses of an elixir of immortality. Though Ba called him a man blessed by the gods, others said Hou Yi had come from the heavens to save us.

He wanted to surprise Chang'e, and he hid the bottle of elixir before he left to hunt for their dinner. Finding the bottle, she un-corked the stopper and inhaled the heavy scent of peaches. She floated off the ground. With a shriek, she held on to a chair, then a table, which both tipped over, but then the wind gusted through the window and she drifted to the moon. The gods punished a woman for her cunning.

Stumbling around, I imitated Chang'e trying to keep herself from going out the window.

Though Busy Shan must have known this tale, she nodded with approval. I bowed. She didn't hide when she lost interest; she didn't care if she seemed rude. But when I caught her attention, it pooled like sunshine that felt intended for me and me alone.

When she held up the skirt to show me her handiwork, I traced my finger on the stitches. "No one could tell the difference!"

The light went off in her face. "My mother made sure of that," she said flatly. "I used to sew for hours every day."

"Since you were small?" I asked. Busy Shan had grown up some-where in the capital.

"Since she started losing her eyesight."

I could tell she didn't want to talk about it, but her family must have suffered without Busy Shan at home.

"Did she know what would happen here? Did you?" I asked.

"No one told me, if that's what you're asking," she said. "It didn't matter. I might have guessed if I'd thought about it long enough."

I nodded. She didn't want to feel like she'd come in blind to the Lake Palaces, and neither did I.

"Who could say no? I wanted to go, though," she quickly added, before her face snapped shut again. She started altering the waist-band of Midnight Chang's pants. After a moment, she shook her head. "You act like the Lake Palaces are some kind of labor camp."

I didn't know what went on in labor camps, only that such places seemed as close to hell as one might find. "I never said that."

"My neighbor returned so wrinkled, so shrunken that people mistook him for a ghost," she said. She stared into her lap. "People thought he was the ghost of his father, who'd died ten years before.

He used to help us—moving heavy things, sweeping the walk for us when it snowed. After he returned, he jumped at every sound. The whine he'd make! Worse than a dog beaten every day of its life. He always smelled like piss, like piss and fear."

"I didn't . . . I'm sorry."

"Can you pass me the scissors?" she asked. She still wasn't looking at me.

I fumbled with the scissors. "You want to hear my mother's version?" I asked after a long silence. It was what she told us after we came home from the festival and were all tucked into bed. Though Busy Shan didn't answer, I began. Instead of a bold hero, Hou Yi was a tyrannical king, desperate to discover the secret of immortality. He ate crane eggs, tortoise soup, and elixirs of cypress and pine, drank the blood of newborns and nursed from their mothers. He traded jade, gold, and rubies for lilies picked in a double-moon month, the tail feather of a phoenix, and the squeak of a mountain monkey—fool's cures that drained the imperial treasury. When his wife begged him to stop, he slapped her mouth shut. One day his runners arrived with a magical peach, plucked from a tree that ripened every two millennia. Despite its long journey, the peach remained fragrant and golden with fuzz, Ma said. By then, I was usually sleepy, warm and cozy against my family. She would sit up, pale moonlight shining on her face through the window, and cup both hands to convey its size. I'd dream of peaches all night long.

Ma. I'd gone through more than half of my mother's tea. Did she believe I'd return to the village by the time I finished the pouch? She'd instructed me to drink it every day; her cures built up over time.

Busy Shan studied me. I'd paused for too long, and she could tell my thoughts had gone elsewhere.

Upstairs, someone cried out. Busy Shan set down her sewing and I tilted my head toward the sound, ready to crack open the Little Red Book if we heard footsteps. But the girl, whoever she was, didn't wake from her nightmare.

"I know the ending. Don't bother," she said, but I finished telling it anyway.

Hou Yi sent for his advisors to admire the peach. Chang'e poured them cup after cup of liquor, her smile enticing them to drink until they were near senseless. She scooped up the peach and consumed it in three bites, the juice dripping down her chin. When Hou Yi lunged at her, she jumped out the window and floated to the moon.

"Everyone acts like Chang'e must be so lonely up there," Busy Shan said so fiercely that my throat caught. "She got away, though. She got away."

LATER THAT WEEK, AFTER dinner, we perched in our bunks, listening to the radio debut of the latest revolutionary hero. Selfless and brave, this one had run into a fire, sacrificing herself to save dozens in peril. Their lives always *did* end, the heroes vowing to give their all for the people and for their country. No one so perfect could last in this world.

What thrilled me most wasn't each new hero, but the unseen crowd, murmuring and cheering in the background. To win an audience was to win a hero's legacy.

The first time I'd heard the thin, flat voice from the radio, I had asked, "Is someone hiding in the room next door?"

"No," Busy Shan had said. "They're not in there, either!"

The radio was black, with silver numbers, made of a material I'd never encountered: not wood, not metal, not woven, not pottery, but something hard and shiny as a beetle. I didn't believe there were fairies inside, and yet I didn't know quite what to think. Maybe it was like an echo, the sound bouncing off and carried on the wind, though farther and louder. There were so many differences between the capital and the village that it seemed to me that we were in another country, yet I wouldn't let on how much the radio amazed me.

Maybe if I'd been the age of my mother or even my sisters, I would have forever been uneasy around the radio, but I was still adaptable. What might have been explained in the village as the work of ghosts and spirits I came to understand as the creation of inventors—men, not gods.

Midnight Chang was prone in her bunk. She'd been quieter ever since we altered her clothes, and didn't eat much. The tight waistband must dig into her sides, making it difficult to bend or to breathe.

After the broadcast ended, everyone reached for their Little Red Book; we always read it before turning in. Fumbling with hers, Dolly Yu caught the edge of a page, which tore in half as the book tumbled to the ground.

Midnight Chang jumped up from her bunk. "You ripped out a page to blow your nose!" she said. She rubbed her side, trying not to wince from the tight waistband.

Dolly Yu cowered. "No."

"You were going to use the pages to wipe yourself!" she shouted.

"I wasn't." She shook her head. "It was an accident."

Midnight Chang grabbed a broom from the corner. "You're so sloppy. Clean up the floor around your bed."

As Dolly Yu stood up, she gave me a pleading look. I nodded at her, wordlessly telling her she could get through it.

Midnight Chang saw what passed between us. Rather than give the broom to Dolly Yu, she raised it in the air, gripping with both hands. "Our comrades' minds and our Party's work collect dust, and also need sweeping and washing!"

She swung it against Dolly Yu's back. The girl gasped, too stunned to scream. None of us moved. Raising the broom, Midnight Chang looked around the room, daring us to stop her. A button popped off her skirt, bouncing once on the floor. Dolly Yu backed away, and got tripped up, tottering. She crouched down, shielding her face with her hands.

I bolted upright, the springs jangling beneath me, and jumped down to the floor. The frames squeaked around the room as Busy Shan and a few other girls sprang to their feet, too. Together, we could have easily taken away the broom.

"What you did is like spitting on the Chairman," Midnight Chang shouted. "Like shitting on him!"

We fell silent for a moment, and then broke loose: Our rage over his disappearance, building for weeks, landed on Dolly Yu.

A girl kicked her in the butt. "Stupid melon-headed girl!"

Dolly Yu wobbled, then fell onto her hands and knees.

Midnight Chang raised the broom again.

"At least a melon stays still!" another girl shouted as she yanked on Dolly Yu's hair.

"I'm sorry," Dolly Yu said. "I never . . . I'm sorry."

And me? Me—I wish I could tell you that I helped her up, that I shoved everyone back.

I screamed at Dolly Yu. "Shut up, shut up!"

With a final swing, the broomstick snapped in half, and Midnight Chang tossed aside the broken remains. We were flushed, dazed as though we'd just stepped off the dance floor. As though we'd just left the Chairman.

"You strayed," Midnight Chang said softly.

"I strayed." Dolly Yu winced. Her hair had slipped free of its ponytail, revealing a bald patch near the crown of her head. She'd been pulling out her hair, or maybe it had been falling out in clumps. "I'll never stray again."

"Louder," Midnight Chang ordered.

"I strayed!" Dolly Yu shouted.

"Again!"

"I strayed!" she shrieked.

Please believe me: I wish one of us had stopped Midnight Chang or run for help. It could have been that our self-criticism sessions were so frequent, held several times a week, and so long, sometimes several hours, that we didn't think this one would be any different. A girl would start the accusations, and we would all join in or else risk the same fury. Damaging a book, taking showers for too long, or leaving food uneaten: Nothing was too small for our collective scrutiny, our collective fury.

Such struggles had long been a part of the country's revolution. When my parents were children, a local landlord was paraded naked, forced to crawl through several villages until his hands and knees were shredded bloody. During my childhood, there were more denunciations, and the guilty—a corrupt headman, a thieving miller—were spat and cursed at for years.

When the Cultural Revolution boiled over, I would come to understand how much the Party depended on scapegoats. Not because we punished the guilty on their behalf, but because we could let loose every frustration that might lead to revolt. We turned on one another instead of the Party.

I'm grateful you were spared this violence. If you'd seen it, you would have thought us mad. None of us were born this way, I hope you would understand. That capacity for it, to endure it, to welcome it, we learned over time—and maybe that would frighten you most of all.

TOSSING ALL NIGHT, I kept thinking about Dolly Yu, her arms raised to ward off our blows. I must have known we'd gone too far, although I didn't admit it then. Near dawn, I climbed out of bed. I wanted to go outside and feel the damp earth beneath my feet once more, take in the familiar loamy scent, even if I ventured not much past the front door.

In the common room, Midnight Chang was reciting a passage from our lessons in revolutionary thought. Her back was turned to me. Every time she forgot, she slapped her own cheek. Rubbing her eyes, she started over. I stood in the doorway, watching as she slapped herself again, alone and terrified, same as the rest of us. I could have helped her practice, apologized for my prank, and sworn an oath that we would help each other—forged a bond like the one my sisters had, born from the youth, fears, and dreams they shared. Instead I crept back upstairs.

CHAPTER 5

NOT LONG AFTER, AS WE FILED ONTO THE BUS TO GO TO CLASS, the screams began. "No, no, no!" Craning my neck, I glimpsed a blur of motion through the branches of the poplar trees, something falling from the top floor. Then a thud that silenced the birds.

I sank onto the asphalt, pebbles digging into my knees. Busy Shan stumbled out of the dormitory, grimacing, her eyes averted from the heap. The driver climbed out of the bus, cursing, and ordered us to get on board. Teacher Fan hadn't yet emerged from her cottage. No one moved, all of us struck still and dumb. He bolted, taking off his jacket as he ran, and when he reached the heap, he kneeled down and flapped it over the body. Even as I looked over the troupe, I already knew who would be missing: Dolly Yu, the girl we'd attacked, the girl who'd stopped eating, who'd stopped talking, and whom we all suspected would soon go home.

Busy Shan gasped out what she'd seen: Rushing to leave, she'd noticed Dolly Yu standing before an open window. She called out her name, but the girl said nothing as she hoisted herself onto the ledge and pitched herself into the air. She didn't hesitate, didn't turn around, her arms spread open to embrace the empty air. She left no note, only a copy of her Little Red Book on top of her pillow.

"If I'd been quicker—" Busy Shan passed her hand over her eyes.

The ghost girl had struck again, others murmured. We'd been cursed, for how else to explain the struggle session gone wrong? I dug my fist into my mouth. If only I'd drawn the beating away from

Dolly Yu, if only I had turned it onto myself. I could have withstood the troupe's blows. But she'd been on the edge of madness, and that was why we'd wanted her gone. She reminded us of the weakness we all carried within ourselves.

In the troupe, we were finely tuned to one another's moods, sensing hurts and desires sometimes before we'd admitted that we felt them, too. Like perceiving the first rumble of an earthquake before anyone else could feel it. For me, it was like that most of all with Midnight Chang. Even when I kept my expression blank, somehow, she knew if I roiled inside. Her eyes would fall upon me, just as mine went straight to hers now.

She tightened her arms around herself, her head bowed. Did she regret beating Dolly Yu with a broom? If we hadn't altered her clothes, maybe she wouldn't have been so ill-tempered, maybe the beating wouldn't have gone on for so long. Maybe Dolly Yu would still be alive.

THE TIP OF THE pencil snapped off in my skin, like a tick, burrowing in ever deeper. I'd been tracing the Chairman's name into my wrist, going over each stroke again and again. The lead itself left no mark, but each pass scratched faint white lines, my skin puffing up in the shape of the characters. A brand, a talisman I didn't know I'd wanted until it appeared.

My wrist throbbed. Hours had passed since Teacher Fan had left with Busy Shan and the rest of us had been shuttled off to class, where a dour official ordered us to read the Little Red Book. Glancing around, I caught Midnight Chang digging her thumbnail into her forearm, half-moons rising up in ridges. Her skin was splotched red and white.

It was the sort of picking, plucking that Dolly Yu did to herself—that many of us did in the troupe, secretly and not so secretly. Our eyes met, and something flickered on her face. Shame. Apology. Sorrow. Could she see that in mine, too? She dropped her hands into her lap.

The door creaked open. Teacher Fan and Busy Shan had returned.

"The Party no longer requires Comrade Yu's services," Teacher Fan announced, her face impassive and her tone brisk. To take your own life was to resist the Party, to betray us all. If only she'd believed. Why couldn't she believe in the revolution? That heap on the ground had been still and silent, dark blood pooling around her head. I tried to catch Busy Shan's attention, but she was back in her seat, dull-eyed, dazed.

Turning to the chalkboard, Teacher Fan faltered, her shoulders jerking once as she started the lesson. I needed more of a reaction from her, from all of us. I wanted to flip my desk, to smash the windows, to howl until I turned myself inside out.

AFTER DINNER THAT NIGHT, Teacher Fan brought us back to the classroom. She might have suspected that we feared returning to the dormitory, where someone might be tempted to follow Dolly Yu out the window. Maybe she didn't want to be alone, either.

A boxy black machine sat in the rear, with two wheels connected by a shiny plastic thread. She explained that we would see *The East is Red*, a musical about the struggles of the people and our savior, the Chairman. The movie, inspired by a patriotic peasant's song, had premiered the previous year to celebrate the fifteenth anniversary of the republic.

When she turned off the lights, I didn't know what to expect. Like magic, dancers appeared on a screen, clad in sky blue outfits, waving fans golden as the sun. I turned around to look at the machine, at the tiny images repeated upside down in the round glass hole, passing through the beam of light—like Ba's shadow puppets. A solitary horn began, followed by drums and other swelling instruments.

Ma would have loved such a wonder, the lights and music dropped into her lap. My sisters, too. Ba would have whistled along to the songs. I pictured them at home. After finishing their chores and dinner, my family had the best part of the day ahead of them: sleep.

Dolly Yu's family would never see her again.

A keening ache started inside of me, and I restlessly tugged at my ponytail until it came loose. I ran my fingers through the knots in my hair. With each tangle came a burst of pain I welcomed, that I deserved. At the click of heels, I looked up. Teacher Fan held out a brush, which I stared at until I realized she was offering it to me. I dropped my hands from my hair. Without a word, she set it on my desk and returned to her seat.

With each stroke of the brush, the throb in my temples faded. When I turned to look at Teacher Fan, she frowned and pointed to the screen.

None of us had ever been inside her cottage, and I couldn't imagine her anywhere except in the classroom or the Lake Palaces, not pedaling her bike through an alley nor placing an order at the market, nothing so mundane. She never mentioned children, a husband, or a life outside the troupe.

I ran the brush once more through my hair, now free of snarls, glossy and smooth. Busy Shan stared at her hands, clenched on top of her desk. As the song ended, I scooted my chair behind her. "Lean back," I said. After she complied, I undid her braid and brushed her hair. She sighed, giving in to the tug of bristles against her scalp, releasing her earthy scent, like the first rain of the season.

I missed my family's unthinking touch, how First Daughter's body pressed against mine, how Second Daughter's feet twined between my legs on the coldest nights.

"Where were you this morning?" I asked.

She said nothing for so long I regretted my question. After I finished brushing her hair, she turned to look at me. "They asked what I'd seen," she said. "Over and over again. As if Dolly Yu wouldn't have jumped if I could answer differently."

I rubbed her shoulder, letting her shudders pass through me.

"I'm on next," Midnight Chang suddenly whispered. "That's me, in the back." The kick of another dancer obscured her face, but that could have been the glint of her hair.

The others started whispering. "There, there!" someone shouted. Was that her, off to the side, twirling? To me, the girl seemed indistinguishable from the other performers dressed in identical uniforms, each with rouged cheeks and braided hair. From anyone else, such boasts would have seemed absurd, plain lies. With Midnight Chang, we listened.

"The one with the mole—he was having an affair with the woman playing his *mother*," she said. "That one? She had stinky feet and a terrible temper."

Even if she was lying, I admired her boldness, her inventiveness in bending the truth to her will.

ABOUT A MONTH AFTER I'd arrived in the capital, Teacher Fan announced that we would perform for troops around the country.

The gloom we'd sunk into over Dolly Yu had hung on, but excitement now rippled through us. As the other girls murmured around me, I thought only of the Chairman, and how such shows meant we probably wouldn't see him for a while longer. Busy Shan had cocked her head, intent for the first time in days.

"You'll all put on a play that one of you will write, about a revolutionary hero," Teacher Fan said. "It's a contest. One of the Madame's ideas."

After the success of *The East is Red*, the Chairman's wife wanted to discover new talents, she said. We were still absorbing the significance of the Madame's interest in our work when Teacher Fan added that the recruit whose play was selected would be given a trip to the Party's seaside retreat. I had never seen the ocean. Busy Shan had described it as a plain of the saltiest water, waves rippling across the surface like wind over grain.

Midnight Chang spoke up a moment before me. "I need no reward."

The rest of us nodded along, the mindless bobbing of poppies in a field. Everyone had acted in cultural work troupes in our hometowns, but I worried the girls from bigger, fancier places had received better training in schools affiliated with their provincial government, the railway, or the artillery corps.

"Seize the reins of the ox," Teacher Fan said. "Don't be trampled."

My words—mine!—from my conversation with the Chairman, coming out of her mouth. He could have mentioned me to her, the night of the dance party or sometime later. He'd remembered me and what I'd said about Brother Rat and the great race to heaven, and repeated my words to others at the Lake Palaces.

We got to work at once. In her play, Busy Shan retold the story of Rebel Li, who'd rallied her neighbors to join one of the earliest peasant uprisings, led by the Chairman against the landlords of Hunan. Rebel Li had jumped off a cliff rather than get taken alive, and landed in a pine tree. Battered, bleeding, she'd survived and gone on to become the army's first female general. From the beginning, the Chairman had believed in us, believed in the power and rage of a teenage girl.

I doodled in my notebook, tracing spirals in the margins, my mind blank and at the same time bursting with stories of heroes. As a child, I'd wanted to be Sister Yu, who herded her commune's escaped sheep during a blizzard. She crouched against the wind, straining to hear their frightened bleats, shepherded the last one to safety, and then collapsed, her heart stopped. After tying rags around my ears and eyes, I had tried feeling my way home from the edge of the village. I'd dipped my hands into the icy river until they went numb.

Later on, I'd obsessed over Iron Girl, who grabbed the reins of a stampeding ox to save three terrified elders. She died when the cart ran over her. I had flicked stones at an exhausted ox, willing it to run and rage at me. It didn't raise its head. My neighbors called me muddleheaded, a stupid egg. I never explained that although heroes died, they lived forever in me.

I decided to write about a hero we'd needed, that I wished I could have been: a peasant girl who foraged for bamboo shoots to feed her village, stricken by famine, during the Great Leap Forward.

I was nine when the Chairman's plan began. None of us had noticed the new point of light winking above, the Sputnik satellite that had launched the space race between our big brother Russia and America. All we knew was that we didn't want to be left behind. The effort to surpass and smash our enemies united our country, not only the workers in the cities, but the peasants most especially, most importantly.

We pledged to outmatch their output in steel, agriculture, poetry, and song with the power of the collective. Instead of spending our days farming, we followed orders to stoke the fires with our wooden bowls and melted my father's hoe and my mother's pot. Yet the iron we smelted was useless, as dull and cracked as dried clay. Row after row of homemade furnaces had lit up the night like torches, like hope.

The headman urged couples to have children early and often, for in the future, our country needed as many hands as possible. In a mural painted in the village plaza, babies perched on bountiful cabbages. We broke apart our brick stoves, to get at the dirt below to fertilize our fields, sang songs about bumper harvests, about sesame seeds the size of corn kernels, peanuts as big as sweet potatoes, and beat drums night and day, until my hands blistered and throbbed, to keep the swallows from stealing our grain—all decrees under the Great Leap Forward.

I remembered the strange pelting sound, the birds terrified by the endless drumming, and falling exhausted from the skies and trees. The puff of dust as they hit the ground. The seeds we planted close together sprouted, but never grew. We starved, hollow and unable to stand against the wind, and the years that should have been the heart of my childhood became the end.

I don't know what it was like in the cities, but in our village, half my neighbors died, most by starvation, in their beds if they were fortunate, or else collapsed outside, in search of food. We ate chaff steamed into buns, and gathered scattered animal bones and scraps of leather, boiling them into a broth that smelled like rotting flesh.

First Daughter had slapped me after I licked the faintest grease from a bowl. Second Daughter had dug into the ground with her fingers, searching for grubs until her hands had bled. Ba had shivered in the noonday sun, his eyes huge and sunken. Hunger had been as inseparable from us as our shadows.

During that time, a former landlord's grandson—dreamy and quiet and slouching—got caught stealing a handful of corn. My next-door neighbor and his son beat him with boards spiked with nails. I returned empty-handed from foraging and discovered a patch of bloodstained earth by the granary, the scent rusty. The boy died two days later. Nature itself had turned against us, the headman said, though we knew the ultimate fault lay in our imperfect hands. If only we'd worked harder, we could have willed enough out of the ground and plucked enough from the skies.

Three harvest seasons had gone by since those days. The weather had turned in our favor again, and with food in our bellies, we'd returned to walking upright. We'd shown our true faces, though: every family, every person out for themselves. If only we'd had a hero then.

AT THE CHALKBOARD, TEACHER Fan clapped together erasers. I rubbed my nose, sneezy from the chalk dust.

"Stop copying me," Midnight Chang hissed. She'd been peeking at my page, and I noticed she was writing about a famine, too, about villains who stole from the communal kitchen.

"You're copying *me*," I said.

Midnight Chang hailed from Shanghai, but I thought only our county and the surrounding ones had suffered such shortages.

I didn't yet know the truth.

"My father told me," she insisted. "He saw the thieves with his own eyes."

"You didn't starve," I spit out. I wouldn't let her steal my idea.

Teacher Fan picked up the rod that she rapped against our knuckles when we gave the wrong answer or spoke out of turn. Standing over us, she said, "Find another story."

Midnight Chang seemed irritated, but held her tongue. If I couldn't tell the story, no one should. Only later would I piece together what happened during the famine and the Great Leap Forward. None of us knew that the hunger had spread, and that no commune could keep up with the Chairman's impossible production goals. When officials in the countryside reported fake yields, the cities took more and more food. Meanwhile, families like mine had starved. Bad weather didn't cause the famine—the Chairman's ambitions did. But to understand the scope of the hunger would have required us to understand the scope of the lies—to understand there had been lies at all.

HERE IN SAN FRANCISCO, my customers at the restaurant joke about getting hungry again an hour after eating Chinese food. All of them so plump and rosy, stuffing themselves until they push their bowls away, saying they can't eat another bite, until they do, nibbling at the crispy skin of an egg roll, or slurping down another noodle, their mouths ringed with grease. They scrutinize the other tables, as though wondering if they should have ordered differently.

If only you and I could have shared such plenty.

Our diners have enough money in their pockets to feast ten more times that night. They loosen their belts, and break open the fortune cookies, because they always have room for something sweet. The starvation in my childhood drove some mothers to eat their own. Despite everything, at least that's a hunger you've never known.

THOUGH NO SUBSTITUTE FOR the Chairman, the play gave me purpose. In my next attempt at a story, a fever struck down a village. My heroine walked for a week through snowy mountains to reach a doctor, and died upon her return, collapsing beneath a spreading acacia tree, like the one in my village plaza. In her fists, she clutched the medicine that would save everyone's lives.

The force of my pencil rattled my desk. As I kneaded my cramped hand, smeared gray from pencil dust, I noticed Teacher Fan reading a book, a thin volume whose pages had the brittle look of a wasp's nest, like the ones I'd seen on the Chairman's bed. When she caught me looking at her, she tapped her desk, signaling I should get back to work.

I raised my hand. "What's the best role you ever had?" I asked. The kind I could write into my script, one that she'd want to pick. She'd mentioned her time in cultural work troupes over the years, though never in much detail.

Teacher Fan closed the book. "My parts at Yan'an were so small, I never had a name. In the chorus, I played a peasant, worker, or soldier, whatever the Party needed," she said.

"Did you die?" I asked.

She smiled wryly. "Over and over again. It's easy—you'll see."

She turned expansive about her time at Yan'an, and we all stopped to listen: A bugle woke them daily at six A.M., she told us, and they attended lectures all morning, sitting in rows in the open dirt fields. In the afternoons, they tilled their vegetable plots and cut wood to make charcoal.

From 1935, at the end of the Long March, until 1947, Yan'an had been at the center of the revolution. The history we'd learned seemed distant until she told us her stories: In caves lined up like swallows' nests along the river, you studied under the blurry glow of soybean oil candles, the air so dry and dusty that you were always thirsty, she said, your lips cracked and numb, and your hands and feet tough as jerky. Wolves howled deep into the night.

"When did you meet the Chairman?" I asked.

"A few weeks after I arrived," she said. At a performance on market day in the nearby village, she and a handful of actors had launched into a revolutionary song. "Then he showed up."

As she told the story, her expression turned wistful. I tried to picture her as the girl she'd once been, wide-eyed and watchful.

"We tried not to let it distract us from our duties," she said. I yearned to come into my own like that, too.

His gaze would have followed the length of her long legs, the graceful arch of her neck, and the sweep of her sinewy arms that I admired in her still.

"His visit would have been memorable enough," she said. "But then bombs started falling."

She spoke casually, as if remarking upon a passing rainstorm. It made her seem all the more courageous. Glamorous, even. Everyone gasped at once. We couldn't help it, even though we must have seemed naïve. We'd learned of war, we'd heard of war, but none of us had ever been bombed. We'd been born too late.

"We took cover in an abandoned church," she said. "He led us there. That's where the dance parties were usually held, with records the foreigners left behind. While we waited for the planes to finish flying over, the Chairman put on a song."

She'd faced down death with the Chairman! I wished I could have been there. I couldn't forget she'd been at war, and that we were still at war with the imperialists who wanted to invade, with the secret capitalists who rotted us from the inside. Looking back down at the page, I wrote my way into the future I deserved.

CHAPTER 6

*M*IDNIGHT CHANG WON. SITTING IN THE CLASSROOM AND listening to her script read aloud, I realized that she had copied whole lines from *The East is Red*: "The poor used to stand shorter than the rich, but today their heads touch the sky." I kept quiet. If I complained, it would show that she'd fooled Teacher Fan.

Because I guessed that she would cast Midnight Chang as the star, I auditioned to play the older brother, who had lines second only to the lead and spoke the final words of the play.

"That's perfect! You walk like a boy," Midnight Chang said.

"We need an actor who can carry someone as big as you," I retorted. I was strong, much more than a girl from the city like her, who would have crumpled after working a single day in the fields.

She tossed her chin at me.

Teacher Fan added more characters, including a landlord, bandits, and a sniper who wounds the heroine, until just an echo of Midnight Chang's play remained.

For the next week before each rehearsal, we warmed up our voices, which were high and thin and wouldn't carry across the stage unless we put our whole breath, our whole body behind it. We swayed back and forth, our arms above our heads, and folded ourselves in half, bent at the waist, inhaling then blowing out, the air loud and steady coming up through our bodies and out our mouths. Midnight Chang moved effortlessly as a willow tree in the wind, while others, like me, jerked our limbs. In the back row, I struggled along, wishing for ordered steps, wishing I could be as confident as her.

"You have to keep the throat open, because it so easily closes in on itself," Teacher Fan called out.

Busy Shan nudged me, and I smirked, though I wasn't in on the joke like she was. Was she referring to something people did together, something the Chairman enjoyed?

Last night, I'd brushed my hand between my legs, the sort of exploration I'd begun back home after my family fell asleep. I'd expected to feel dead, desiccated, but a tingle began. Raising my hips, I stroked at the flicker—a straining that I was scared to set free. I didn't want to ask Busy Shan about it, for her worldliness intimidated and attracted me in equal measure. As little as she might think I understood about such matters, I knew even less.

We hummed together, our chests vibrating like the radio in our dorm. "Think about the sound going *out,* going off the stage. Think of it landing in a seat out there," Teacher Fan exhorted as she walked between our rows.

She was behind us now. As she approached, I hurled my voice like a grenade through the dark. She squeezed my shoulder and moved on, so quickly I almost thought I'd imagined it.

The exercises made us bigger than the slender girls we were, and wasn't that revolutionary? What the Chairman's rebels had lacked in size and strength, they'd made up for in their ability to enlarge themselves, swelling in the skies above the countryside and into the nightmares of their enemies.

WITH A SWEEP OF the brush, I blackened my eyebrows and studied myself in a hand mirror. The bushiness looked ridiculous up close, but without makeup, my features would wash out under the stage lights.

For the dress rehearsal, I'd slipped on my costume, a green jacket tied at the waist with a red sash, with pants that tucked into leather boots. No peasant had ever worn an outfit in such vibrant colors, nothing like the faded hues of plant dyes we used in the village.

Teacher Fan examined my makeup. "You're not much of a man." Wielding a tiny brush, she stippled stubble onto my jaw.

At Yan'an, women were rare, and men often took their parts in plays, she said, as she worked on my face. "Boys who sounded like girls. They didn't shave, didn't yet have hair in their armpits. Their fans were mad to death when they discovered what hung between their legs!"

She put down the brush. "Cut out those old ways. Spring, don't slouch. You're not a wisp; you'll never be a wisp. Don't make yourself into one. You're built to take up room," Teacher Fan said; her tone was brusque but not unkind.

A few girls giggled until she silenced them with a look. "Beauty isn't as important as will and power," she said. More quietly, as though confiding in me—but loud enough for everyone to hear—she added, "The quickness of your thinking brought you to the troupe. You're quick enough to realize that beauty won't keep you here; it won't keep anyone at the Lake Palaces."

A worker knocked on the door, asking for Teacher Fan's help with the stage lights.

After she left, Midnight Chang said, "That's what you say to someone whose looks are quick to shatter a mirror."

More laughter. I could have wished for Midnight Chang's curves and glowing skin, for Busy Shan's big bright eyes, or the glossy hair of my sisters. A part of me *had,* and always would.

Busy Shan wanted to fix my eye makeup. "It smeared."

She wiped and dotted and traced my eyes, and then ran brushes all over my face with sure strokes. In the mirror, I saw that she'd made me fierce enough to sear the back row of the audience. When I bared my teeth at her, she threw up her hands, pretending to ward me off. The air was thick with the waxy smell of our makeup.

She'd also given me cheekbones sharp enough to cut glass, and warmed up the colors in my skin, as if I'd just come in from the cold. "Where did you learn this?" I asked.

She shrugged. "I figured it out. I did everyone's makeup in my troupe back home."

"You should keep doing it," I said.

We'd both had trouble sleeping after Dolly Yu's suicide, moving blunted through the days. She straightened the brushes on the table. "Remember not to rub your eyes."

"She's got her nose so far up Teacher Fan's ass, no wonder it smeared," Midnight Chang cracked. A few girls laughed in a way that made me think that they'd been talking about me behind my back.

"You know how to do a black eye?" I asked Busy Shan.

She leaned in. "A few ways."

Smiling uneasily, Midnight Chang said no more as everyone finished getting ready.

MIDWAY THROUGH THE REHEARSAL, the door to the auditorium banged open, blinding us with sunshine. The Madame had arrived.

"Granny's here," Busy Shan whispered. We peeked out from the wings.

"Great-Granny," I added. The danger of such rude talk made it irresistible—a dare.

The heavy frames of her glasses and hair dyed boot-polish black gave her a severe air, though a widow's peak softened her face.

Our words were bolder than I felt. Still, the Madame was at the age when men stop noticing or listening to women; the age when they're no longer young enough to grope or to bear children. The buzz of a fly would have garnered more attention in a room than this woman—if she hadn't been the Chairman's wife.

She and Teacher Fan sat in the front row, holding hands like my sisters did. Side by side, their differences were stark: Teacher Fan had preserved her beauty; she hadn't hidden it in a baggy gray pantsuit like the Chairman's wife. She seemed younger than the Madame, though back then, I knew only that she was older than me, older than my sisters, somewhere in that wide span between maiden and crone. Teacher Fan was probably in her forties, like our mothers, but unlike her, they were spent and sucked dry.

The Madame nodded as each girl walked onstage. She jotted in her notebook, and chuckled, deep and throaty, when the landlord tripped and fell into a pigpen. Her laugh surprised me, for I had imagined her grim and determined, a statue, a symbol. Teacher Fan laughed out loud, too, which she hadn't done during any rehearsal. The Madame was red-faced, bent over, and Teacher Fan gasping. When they looked at each other, they burst into laughter, the sound of long association, of younger, finer selves.

The landlord rose to her knees, uncertain. She'd never played the scene for laughs; she was a serious girl, of few words and even fewer smiles. If I'd been in her place, I might have improvised, wobbled, slipped around with my arms flailing.

"Continue," Teacher Fan said.

The Madame resembled a beetle, I thought, her belly straining against her pants, with her thin arms and legs. She met my eyes and I ducked behind the curtain, where the air smelled like greasepaint, dust, and hot lights.

Midnight Chang pushed me. "You missed your entrance," she said, probably loud enough for the Madame and Teacher Fan to hear. I crossed the stage to where Busy Shan, who played my mother, waited for me. For this performance, I needed to impress our audience of two. Sometimes at night, First Daughter would take on the strut, the twitch, and the growl of one of the village men, choosing a distinctive gesture to imitate, to jeer at. Or she'd hunch her back and twist the left corner of her mouth like one of our aunties. I now sank into my neighbor Fatty Song, into his loose, confident gait. Disappearing into him, I no longer worried about tripping over my feet or forgetting what to say. Busy Shan placed a bowl of noodles before me, her son, which I refused. "We'll eat together," I said.

Women no longer dined after men, on the scraps gone cold. I twirled strands around my chopsticks and deposited them into her bowl, a filial offering, a gesture the script didn't call for but one which kept the attention on me.

After we finished, Teacher Fan asked for the houselights to be raised and for the troupe to assemble onstage. I felt suddenly slack, a puppet with its strings cut.

The Madame stood. "Fighting off oppression, that's the message the audience should remember," she said. "Every time the word 'oppress' comes up, shout it! *Hurl* it."

She folded her arms across her chest. "Young friends, whose performance did you believe most?"

Busy Shan glanced at me.

"Who's the playwright?" the Madame asked.

Midnight Chang raised her hand.

"You acted with such passion, I should have known you'd also written the play," the Madame said. "I came here today because I want you to understand you're carrying on an important tradition."

Midnight Chang flicked her hair over her shoulder. More than her looks, her blithe self-assurance drew your eye, a jewel catching the light. Thinking back, I see that she had none of the humility that my parents would have expected; she didn't call her play garbage or say, "It's nothing—*I'm* nothing."

She was American that way.

The Madame continued. For decades, the Party used plays to inspire the people, she said. I'd heard she'd been an actress before joining the revolution. Plays and operas had once been amusements for the rich, a reflection of their decadent life, and now the arts served a higher cause, for the good of the people.

She climbed up the stairs onto the stage and paced in front of us.

"You've set off sirens to warn about approaching bombers?" she asked. I wasn't sure what she was talking about, if she was comparing us to soldiers in battle.

She neared me. "Some art tries to bombard our minds with capitalism, and we need to fight back with the kind that corrects our thinking."

Her voice booming, she no longer seemed pitiful. The ash in her had been relit. "You are continuing the revolution that the Chairman began!"

Without warning, the Madame poked me in the chest, just below my collarbone. "Don't slouch," she said. Around me, the other girls cringed. The jab didn't hurt, but her message was clear: She had her eye on me, on all of us, and if she wanted to cuff us around like wayward toddlers, she could.

OUR FIRST PERFORMANCE BEGAN with a blunder. The girl who played the landlord forgot her lines. We—the cast, the audience— stared until I finally answered for her. "Where are we going? To the hills," I said.

The sound of my voice, fed back to me through the speakers, startled me. And yet amplified, I sounded confident, and that was enough to keep going.

We'd traveled to an army base two hours south of the capital, set amid villages that seemed as ramshackle as mine. We were performing for the soldiers, for Teacher Fan, but most of all, for the Chairman. Every movement, every line was for him, though he wasn't there. None of us knew his whereabouts.

The landlord chased after Midnight Chang, the rough planks rattling beneath their feet. While Midnight Chang pled for more time to pay our taxes, the landlord stared into the stage lights, her face washed out in the glare.

She groped Midnight Chang with an uncertain touch. Troops appreciated only the crudest humor, we'd heard, and they would talk through our monologues. When the soldiers booed, the landlord dropped her hand.

I rushed onstage to save Midnight Chang. Though I didn't look at the soldiers, I felt them. When I shoved the landlord, the soldiers gasped and muttered.

She stumbled, for I had never pushed her this hard in rehearsals. When I came at her again, departing from the script, her annoyance turned into alarm.

The landlord's thugs arrived. "Come with us!" one shouted.

Another reached for me and I raised my fists, filled with an exhilarating fight. They circled me, unsure what to do until Midnight Chang hissed at me to exit. I dashed offstage.

The performance sped to the final scene. Midnight Chang fell to the ground and crawled to me, in the throes of a hero's death.

Her gestures were suitable for drama, for roles blazing with strength and sacrifice. She projected all the way to the back row. I couldn't stop watching her, yet at every moment I was aware of *her*, the character she was playing an afterthought.

The soldiers clapped, and when I picked her up, mourning my sister's death, their stomps thundered through us. Individually— like snowflakes, like feathers, like dust—the viewers were nothing, but together they were a storm. Their excitement became mine.

"We shall never forget you! We shall be our own masters now!" I cried. The stage directions called for me to stand under the red sun, cradling my sister high as the curtain fell. Though I had no more lines, I found myself shouting that I would carry on the fight my sister began. All eyes, all hearts fixed upon me, the adulation the Chairman must feel when he stood above the cheering masses of Tiananmen Square. The crew waited to draw the curtain closed, but I didn't leave. I dug in my fingers beneath Midnight Chang's rib cage until she winced. The claps and whistles grew louder, and the soldiers jumped to their feet. I was the heroine's brother, their brother. I was them, they were me. Heroes of the motherland.

Midnight Chang raised her head, but Teacher Fan called out from the wings, ordering her to stay dead. She went limp, her anger pulsing beneath my fingers like venom pouring from a snake's fangs.

We played the show at eight bases that August, each crowd greater than the last, always to huge applause. For me.

CHAPTER 7

*A*S WE WALKED INTO CLASS, THE GIRLS AROUND ME SLOWED down. A few trailed in my wake, and I wondered if they could have been waiting to choose where they would sit, to see what I did first. The desk in the center of the front row remained empty—Midnight Chang's usually, but mine if I wanted, it seemed.

When she hooked her arm through my elbow, I flinched.

"The other girls will go soon enough," she whispered in my ear. We'd returned to the capital late last night. "Us, though. The both of us together, the Chairman would never tire of us."

When I stared at her, she held my gaze. The ripple of the other girls wasn't my imagination, then. Midnight Chang may have sensed a shift in the order of things, an order that she wanted to rearrange. What was she proposing—a special performance, with the two of us starring? Or something else unnatural in his bed-chambers, the sort of coupling that went on between an emperor and his concubines?

"Don't think you can sway the Chairman," I said. When I jerked my arm away, she clamped down with her elbow. Lurching off, I sat beside Busy Shan, who gave me a quizzical look.

I couldn't deny that I was flattered. Out of all the girls in the troupe, she wanted me as her partner. I suspected her ultimate goal: If she could, she'd take down every girl in the troupe. Then she'd go after me—unless I could put an end to her first.

———

SECRETARY SUN KNOCKED ON the classroom door, interrupting
our political-thought lesson, and asked Teacher Fan to join him in
the hallway.

She told us to read the next passage. He nodded at us. "Comrades, continue."

As they conferred, we strained to listen, hoping his presence that
afternoon meant that the dance parties would resume. More than
two months had passed since I'd first arrived at the Lake Palaces, and
despite all our fears, so far, none of us had been sent home. I willed
Teacher Fan to summon me. I tried not to fidget as she approached
me. Although I wanted to believe that the Chairman had asked for
me at last, what if she sent me away from here?

"Remember what you've learned," she added, with a tenderness
that frightened me. Midnight Chang's snicker unnerved me until I
reminded myself that she knew no more than I did about my fate.

I followed Secretary Sun, who was as brisk as he'd been on selection day. His purposeful stride gave me hope that he wasn't getting
rid of me; we had to hurry somewhere, to someone. We cut through
a courtyard with a tiny pagoda capped with a green tile roof, perched
on a mossy rock and surrounded by white pebbles. Until now, I
hadn't seen much of the Lake Palaces beyond what could be glimpsed
along the troupe's daily route, and the blunt modern buildings had
given me no hint of the grounds, which were even more magnificent
than I had imagined. I wanted to remember everything on what
might be my last walk here. Emperors had once strolled these paths,
their concubines mincing behind on their bound feet no bigger than
a child's fist. Princelings would have played hide-and-seek behind
the whitewashed walls, peeping their heads through octagonal windows, and throwing pebbles into the ponds.

The trees here must have been saplings in the last dynasty. As a
stand of towering bamboo clicked and swayed in the breeze, I turned
my attentions back to Secretary Sun. He was shorter than I remem-

bered, but the power he carried with him on selection day had turned him into a giant in my memory.

We passed an armed guard, standing at attention. Walking through a marble archway, I trailed my fingers over a carving of lotus flowers, pressing its memory into my skin. Bent cypress trees shed a medicinal smell. Much of our work in the village disappeared, was worn away, planted under, or eaten after a season, but here, the craggy broken rock had become a monument for the ages.

Our steps churned through the gravel. "Do you miss your family?" he asked.

"Not anymore," I said, hoping I sounded committed to my duties.

He nodded with approval. "You have no say in your family. They were once your fate. But we left our families to serve the Party."

We.

"We will never give up the fight!" I thumped my fist against my chest. Secretary Sun said nothing. Almost at once, I felt silly rather than patriotic. Such gestures were meant for a crowd. Studying him as we walked side by side, I realized he was younger than I'd thought, his cheeks smooth and eyes unlined. He tried to make up for his youth with his crisp shirt, slacks, and a formal bearing.

A pebble lodged in my shoe, and I flicked it out. After we turned a corner in the corridor, waters stretched before us, the blue-green of a swallow's wings, glimmering in the late afternoon light. I'd glimpsed it on my first day, but not since. Our classroom was elsewhere in the complex, away from the waters that must have given the Lake Palaces their name.

I pointed at a tower on the far side. "What is that?"

"A pavilion," Secretary Sun said. "Emperors needed a place to rest when out on a stroll."

"They decided to build the palace here because of the lakes?" I asked.

"They dug up the two lakes for the palaces."

I surveyed the shoreline. "When?"

"A few hundred years ago."

"An emperor ordered lakes like he might order his favorite dish?" I asked. "Just . . . like that?"

Secretary Sun nodded. "They were expanded a few times since then."

I pictured the emperor saying, "Make them bigger!" Big enough to show he mastered land and sea.

Each lake was several times the size of our village and fields. Willow trees fringed the inlets, thick with pink lotus blossoms, dotting lily pads big enough for a child to float upon. I couldn't stop thinking about the workers shoveling the rock and dirt, then carting off the load. Farther down the shoreline, past the bridge that spanned the lakes at their narrowest point, squat concrete buildings poked above the trees. We passed a long pool covered in dead leaves, giving off the faint scent of decay, the water murky and tea-colored, too deep to be a fountain. Beside it, steam billowed from a vent on a long, tin-roofed building we approached. A kitchen? Guards flanked the heavy door we entered.

Inside, my cheeks flushed at the heat. Another guard allowed us to pass, and our footsteps echoed as we walked by a row of curtained booths and shelves piled with towels. The air was thick with a strange, bitter smell that stung my eyes and my lungs. Alarmed, I breathed through my mouth.

Then I saw him. The Chairman was floating on his back, in a pool that could have fit dozens of him. His belly protruded above the water, a pale island, his nipples brown dots lost on his massive barrel chest. His striped trunks were tight enough to reveal the bulge of his crotch.

My gaze moved from his lumpy toes, up his legs, his thighs—to there, to what had torn me apart. I clenched deep within, holding back everything from that night, everything I couldn't name.

The Chairman righted himself and waved to us before swimming to the broad stairs. When he emerged from the water, two female attendants rushed at him with towels and dried him off. He hung a towel around his neck, tied another around his waist, and sank onto a slatted wooden bench. He beckoned me. I felt as if I were on the edge of a cliff, fearful of falling yet drawn to the chasm all the same.

"Have you eaten?" The Chairman's voice sounded nasal and soothing as honeybees.

I shook my head. When he motioned for me to join him, I sat down. His thigh pressed against mine, and I moved a hand's breadth away from him, not enough distance for him to notice, but enough for me to breathe. The bitter smell grew fainter as I got used to it.

A stocky attendant rolled over a cart piled with beef jerky, pastries, and unfamiliar delicacies. She poured us tea. The attendant seemed a few years older than me, about the age of my eldest sister, and had a bowlegged walk, her feet splayed like a duck's. A former recruit? Her floppy pants and tunic hid her shape and snuffed out her youth. I stuffed a roll into my mouth. It was filled with potatoes and savory ground beef, and I stashed another in my skirt pocket to save for later. The attendants shook their heads in evident disgust, but I didn't put it back. The Chairman hadn't noticed, too busy cramming in crackers, the crumbs clinging to his lips.

His appetite inspired me. I hoarded for tomorrow, but maybe he had suffered enough deprivation to know he should eat it all now. Better to carry it on you than to store an apple that will shrink and become pitted with worms.

The Chairman gestured toward the cart, but Secretary Sun declined. He remained standing. After the Chairman bit into a steamed bun and tossed it onto the floor, frowning as if displeased by the flavor, I resisted the urge to pocket it. The meals in the canteen seemed like scraps compared to this feast, enough food here to feed my family for days.

He gobbled away as if he barely tasted the food. As he reached for a dish of peanuts, his elbow bumped my waist. At his touch, I remembered his knee, forcing apart my legs, his hands pinning down my wrists, and his tobacco gasps against my cheek. I'd wanted more than anything to see him again and now that he sat before me, I felt like I was choking.

All at once, the flavors mingling in my mouth—sweet and savory and sour—nauseated me. I dropped a tea egg and it bounced toward the pool, rolling toward the water, placid and perfect. Corralling it with my foot, I tried to hide the wayward egg, but bits of yolk and the whites flew out from my shoe, along with any grace I'd learned from Teacher Fan.

Another look passed between the attendants, who must have thought me backward, a peasant with no manners. With a sigh, one squatted down to clean the mess. Secretary Sun handed me a cup of tea. I sipped, grateful.

The Chairman had splashed the bench when he sat down, and the drops had soaked through my skirt. Like I'd wet myself. As an attendant poured us more tea, a fan kicked on. He patted my shoulder, a gesture that was faintly affectionate, almost toothless and elderly. " 'We can learn what we didn't know . . .' "

He looked at Secretary Sun, as if expecting him to finish the sentence. I recognized the quotation, one that I'd read so often that I remembered its placement on the page, high on the left side, near the center of his Little Red Book.

"I can't remember the exact wording, but the thrust of it, it's . . ." Secretary Sun said.

The Chairman held up a palm, cutting him off, and looked at me expectantly. I had studied the passage last night, last week, and every week since I had arrived at the Lake Palaces.

" 'We are not only good at destroying the Old World, we are also good at building the new,' " I said. " 'If we have a correct theory but merely prate about it, pigeonhole it, and do not put it into practice . . .' "

I offered the Chairman a turn.

"Put it into practice . . ." he repeated slowly, as if the words were unfamiliar. A slow smile broke over his face, like honey oozing from the comb.

He must be testing me. " 'Then that theory, however good, is of no significance,' " I said.

Secretary Sun edged closer, until he was almost standing over us.

"We have a disagreement," the Chairman said. "He says he can predict what the recruits will be like before he arrives at their village. There's nothing for him to learn."

"That's not what I meant," Secretary Sun said. A bead of sweat, or steam, trickled down his forehead. In my village on selection day, he'd seemed confident and powerful. It scared me now, to see him so reduced.

Though I pitied him, I also wanted him humbled. We girls were identical to him, peasants rolled like balls of dough on a tray, endless red chilies drying on a roof, tin pots from the same mold.

Secretary Sun turned to me. "Did your father beat you?" he asked.

I shrank down, small as when I used to crouch in the corner of our home, my arms shielding myself against Ba's fists. Hating him and myself. Reluctantly, I nodded.

"Did your family huddle together for warmth in a single bed?" he asked. In early spring, did we stretch the last of the cornmeal, the porridge becoming thin as cloudy water?

Yes, yes, yes. Squirming, I slid my foot over a gap left by a missing tile.

"You see," he told the Chairman. "Maybe some details are different—how many siblings, a widowed mother—but these peasants lead the same life. It is the stamp of their class. The revolution is not yet finished." He turned to me. "Someday, you, your sisters, and your mother will lift your heads together."

"Could you have predicted me?" the Chairman roared. He lurched to his feet, and I braced myself with both hands to keep from falling off the bench. He was taller than his advisor, half-naked, twice as wide—and loud. Secretary Sun stepped back and clasped his hands behind him. Though he kept his face blank, I could tell that he was shaken.

Settling back onto the bench, the Chairman launched into the legend about an old man who lived by a mountain so high that darkness fell an hour after noon and the peaks snagged rain clouds that flooded the valley below. I knew it well, and everyone else did, too, but listening to the Chairman was like hearing it for the first time.

"The old man toiled, like his father, his grandfather, and great-grandfather, on their land, but after heavy rains carried away their pigs and chickens and their roof collapsed for the second time that year, he'd had enough, and he vowed to get rid of the mountain. He led his sons and daughters to the mountain, where they dug, one spoonful at a time. Mocked by their neighbors, the old man said, 'When I die, my sons will carry on; when they die, my grandsons will carry on, and their sons and grandsons. High as the mountains are, they cannot grow any higher and with every bit we dig, the mountains will fall.' "

He added flourishes and asides, the bench inching backward from the force of his gestures. His face took on the cast of the old man, his jaw jutting, and became the wife, signified with a simpering flick of his hand. The attendants went slack-jawed, like elders no longer able to chew. Secretary Sun lowered his eyes in concentration. Even if the Chairman's hand had trembled in front of their faces, they would have been unable to see it.

His towel fell open as he spoke, revealing his thighs, pale and heavy as dough, but he didn't seem to care. The moisture in the air kept him slick as a newborn, and his hairless arms and legs gleamed, as though rubbed in oil. Inside the building that housed the swimming pool, everything seemed brighter, louder, distilled, a different world altogether.

"The old man, he knew that he'd need workers. Lots of them. That's what he told his young wife each night he visited her." When the Chairman laughed, we joined in.

A traveling tailor, a god in disguise, was impressed by the old man's determination. The Chairman drained his cup of tea with a sharp suck through his teeth. "He moved the mountains the next day."

"Waaaah!" cried the skinny attendant, her mouth wide and revealing missing teeth in the back. The stocky one clenched her fists, as if to hold on to his wisdom.

Every time I'd listened to the story, I had always wondered why the old man didn't just move his family somewhere else.

"In Dazhai, they moved mountains, too," the Chairman said. He was referring to a new model village.

I'd heard about it from the headman. " 'Change the sky and change the land!' " I said, Dazhai's slogan we'd chanted in the fields.

He nodded. We'd learned how they made big fields out of little ones, digging up rocky hills to fill gullies and ravines. Everyone— from the youngest child who'd just learned to walk, to the grannies on their last steps—had pitched in.

"Now the mountain to be moved is you," the Chairman told me. A drop of water trickled from his scalp and clung to his eyebrow.

I didn't know what he meant. Would he make me disappear, dig up dirt and rock to reveal the treasure I was meant to be? He put his hand on my knee. I braced myself, picturing him pushing me down and forcing my legs apart.

"Girls like her get treated as if they stink of the dung heap," the Chairman told Secretary Sun. "But with enough tutoring, this one could pass as a student intellectual who could hold forth with any cadre on National Day."

He slid his hand off my knee. *"We shall be our own masters now,"* the Chairman said.

It was the line I shouted in Midnight Chang's play, the line that always brought the soldiers to their feet.

"I'm told that you're quite convincing," he added.

As his praise sank in, I blushed.

"Teacher Fan says she has a good ear and a quick tongue," the Chairman said to Secretary Sun. "And she can act, too."

"She recommended me?" I asked. I was surprised he knew anything about my role in the play.

"She promised with our training, we can take you anywhere and pass you off as anything!" he said.

"Who's to judge, though?" I blurted. "Who would challenge you, if you introduced me as one of those students?"

I shouldn't have spoken up, but the Chairman didn't chide me.

"Quick on her feet, too," he said to Secretary Sun. He turned back to me. "We need to present you to someone who doesn't know we've trained you. Someone who holds himself in high regard, higher than his regard for his own country."

He leveled his gaze at me. "The President."

The President? I tried to remember what he looked like from the mural our bus had passed by, but I couldn't picture him. Soon I would learn that he didn't often attend the dance parties, perhaps once or twice a year.

I had assumed high officials spoke with one voice, united with the Chairman's. From the time we were young, we'd learned how our leaders had been forged together on the Long March and at Yan'an. But hadn't Teacher Fan, in our lessons, talked about those who wouldn't listen?

For years, I would learn, the Chairman had suspected the President's disloyalty, almost as soon as he'd picked him as his successor. He was second only to the Chairman, which I would come to understand was a blessing and a curse. If the President considered himself an equal, the Chairman would never stand for it.

"You're to trick the President into believing you're a university student," the Chairman said.

"Not just any university: Peking University," Secretary Sun added.

I'd never heard of it, but I could tell it was prestigious. Located in the capital, it had to be among the best in the country.

"Why would he care about students?" I asked.

"Again and again, students have helped stir up revolution in this country," Secretary Sun said. "What they lack in cannons, they make up for in ideas. No leader wants the students against him." He glanced at the Chairman. "The President included."

"He'll get duped by a girl, a peasant girl!" the Chairman said. He chuckled. "He needs to remember where he comes from. He worships intellectuals. He adopts their backward ideas and claims they're his own, as if any of them know what's best for the villages. They've never been or haven't visited in years! They don't believe peasants can move mountains. Did your headman expand household production?"

I didn't know how to answer.

"Does your family get to keep anything extra?" Secretary Sun said. "Or sell it?"

There had been a time, toward the end of the famine, when Ba prodded us awake before dawn. When all my neighbors rose earlier, too, tending to our crops with greater care, and our bowls filled again.

Secretary Sun looked at me, his eyes a warning I didn't understand until the Chairman muttered, "Selfish nonsense, a waste of time."

I didn't dare say anything about that time that might sound like praise. If I could make an army of myself to defend the Chairman against the President, I would do it. Then I realized one might already exist.

"What if the students turned against him?" I asked.

The Chairman studied me. "How?"

"What if he got in their way?"

"Go on."

"Maybe I could give him bad advice." My voice cracked. "Never mind."

The Chairman grinned. "*Maybe?* That's exactly what I want you to do."

He glanced at Secretary Sun. "You doubted my plan, but she's already caught on!"

He turned back to me. "You'll tell him he needs to go into the schools. Convince him that he needs to get a grip on them. First you'll make him think you're a university student. Then you'll send him astray."

"Won't he . . . guess what will happen if he meddles with the students?" I asked.

"The President will think he knows students better than they know themselves," Secretary Sun said. "Students, peasants, factory workers, cadre, anyone and everyone. He'll think students will buy anything he says."

"When?" I asked.

"He's scheduled to return for National Day," Secretary Sun said.

Six weeks from now. The Party would mark its victory in the

civil war on October 1, when the Chairman and other top officials would take in the spectacle from Tiananmen, the imperial gate high above the vast square. This morning, the troupe had begun preparing for our dance performance.

Six weeks! The turn of the moon and a half—the midpoint of a season. In the village, we measured the monotony of our days against the height of the corn, against the accumulating pile of fallen autumn leaves. The Chairman and his aide would be assessing me, too. Panic gripped me so completely that I couldn't utter a sound.

It didn't seem like enough time to make a transformation, and yet, hadn't I already started? I was no longer the squatting, spitting peasant girl who had arrived at the Lake Palaces at the start of summer; Teacher Fan had seen to that.

My performance in the play had brought me back to the Chairman's attention. He needed an actor, unpolished and unknown— a shape-shifter, just like in the old tales, when a fox-spirit turned into a beautiful girl who beguiled travelers off the road, or a snake became a young bride. In their human forms, the spirits tested us, our devotion to our homes, to love, and to our country. It would be a strange duty, but no stranger than the other duties I had taken on since coming here: the dance parties, acting for the soldiers, and my services to the Chairman—all roles I had learned to play.

The Chairman nodded to Secretary Sun, the plan coming together. "On National Day, he'll be trying to convince officials to follow his lead."

"We can say that she won an essay contest," Secretary Sun said. "Meeting you is the prize."

"Yes—that's it!" The Chairman took my hand and traced out a character on my palm, I couldn't tell what, but it had the feel of new lines and new fortunes. Inside, I vibrated like a plucked pipa string.

"We will make you a hero," he said.

"I will follow you," I said with a fearlessness I didn't feel.

"All the way to the President." The Chairman dropped his towel and with a splash, he dove into the pool, a streak rippling along the bottom.

CHAPTER *8*

*A*T THE DORMITORY, SECRETARY SUN TOLD ME TO GET DRESSED for the dance party and to gather my belongings. I started for the stairs that led from the common room, then halted. "How will I know if I'm good enough? If I'm making progress?" I asked.

"I don't think he knows," he said.

I stared at him.

"He doesn't know—yet. He wanted us to train you, and had the President in mind, but hasn't worked out the details. He's not the sort who plots ten steps ahead. He taught me that there's so much you can never predict. How the best-laid plans go off course because of a rainstorm without end, or a rumor that stirs up your men. With him, the only certainty is uncertainty. You just have to keep up.

"You'll get used to it," he added. "Sooner than you think."

I would learn that the Chairman's frustrations had driven him down this path, to see where it—and where I—led. For years, the President had been getting the better of him, and the Chairman wanted this victory to be the first of more reversals to come.

There were larger forces at work that I didn't understand, on the scale that dictated the phases of the moon, that turned the sun in the sky. I might as well ask to go home now, before I failed.

Secretary Sun must have seen the worry in my face. "The Chairman already took a shine to your spirit. Teacher Fan says you keep up with your lessons and that you can act. I expect we'll go through a list of books and speeches, on history and political thought. Poems, too—everything that a first-year college student should know. We can't read everything, but we'll draw out one or two important lessons for you, enough to make conversation with the President."

With a nod, I went upstairs to pack. The other girls were in class, and alone in the dorm, I felt like the last pea rattling around in the pod. Glancing into the empty courtyard, I fingered the bars that had gone up on the windows, installed after Dolly Yu jumped. My weeks in the troupe had been the most vivid of my life. Everything was about to change all over again, and the speed of starting and stopping made me feel as if I might get jerked out of my body.

As my heels clicked against the concrete floor, I glanced at Midnight Chang's bed, its sheets pulled tight. Remembering her snicker as I left class, I wanted to rumple her covers. Flip over her mattress. Leave a bloody rag balled up under her pillow.

I folded up the blanket that Busy Shan had given me on my first night in the capital and set it on the bunk below mine. My limbs went heavy, and I lay down there, staring at the underside of my mattress. Every time either of us moved, we'd felt the same vibrations, heard the same squawk of the springs. Turning my face into her pillow, I inhaled the familiar scent of her hair. A spot on the wall was nearly level with the mattress. No one else would look here.

From the bottom of the stairs, Secretary Sun called to me to finish up. Grabbing a pencil, I sketched a plum flower. When my pencil snagged on a bump in the concrete, I pressed harder into the paint, until five wobbly petals emerged. I'd told no one else in the troupe about the plum flower of my name, Mei Xiang. Busy Shan would understand I'd been thinking of her. I was saying goodbye, even if I didn't know it then.

AT THE DANCE PARTY, I tugged the Chairman back for song after song to tire him out. When Busy Shan spotted me, she couldn't hide her relief—or her hurt, when I looked past her. I'd talk to her later, I told myself; I couldn't turn away from the Chairman that night.

We didn't stay for long. He led me from the pavilion, slipping down a covered corridor with carved stone posts and red and gold stripes of paint glimmering on the beams overhead. As we approached a courtyard, the guards flicked on harsh lights that revealed patches of sweat blooming on the Chairman's back and at his armpits.

The thrum of music had faded and it felt like we'd taken a path into one of those wooden puzzle boxes made by a neighbor in my village: a ball rattled inside that I had to figure out, to determine where to go. One wrong move and I'd get turned around and never find my way out.

After passing through a moon gate, we entered a garden, where gravel crackled beneath our feet on paths that wound around arched bridges, ponds, and statues. "You could take a different path each time. It's never the same garden twice," the Chairman said.

High on a wall hung a wooden carving of calligraphy, the sweeping strokes traced in gold. Awe descended over me. Emperors used to idle in these pleasure grounds, and the Lake Palaces seemed a fitting home for the Chairman, who deserved every star in the sky for his sacrifices.

He pointed at the sign. "It says, 'In here happiness lies.' " He probably had said the same to those who came before me—to those who would come after me—but the words were still a gift.

We strolled by a grotto of boulders with the look of hunched deities, beautiful, strange, and everything I had wished for at the Lake Palaces, a place that expanded the possibilities of the world.

The lady on the moon, Chang'e, loomed above us, alone in her pale palace. At night, did she regret stealing the elixir of immortality when she saw people below? The Chairman noticed the moon had drawn my attentions.

"You stare at something long enough, you can convince yourself you're seeing something, even when there's nothing there," he said. "Everyone's always looking for the legends, for Chang'e and her pet rabbit, but they're not there. They never were."

He stroked my cheek with his thumb. "You can get so distracted by what's high above, you don't pay attention to what's in front of you," he said. "You want to look at the moon? I'll tell you a story about the moon."

Centuries ago, General Zhu had launched a sneak attack against Mongol invaders on the first day of the Mid-Autumn Moon Festival, he said. His most trusted deputy, disguised as a priest, entered a city under enemy control. "His robes held many folds, but his secrets were hidden elsewhere—in the cart he led, filled with hundreds of moon cakes," the Chairman said. "A holiday tradition, but he also presented it as a special blessing for the Mongol emperor. A master-stroke! Appeal to the vanity of your enemy."

We walked on. I'd heard versions of this story from my parents, but what seemed to excite the Chairman most was the theatrical deceit—the sort he wanted me to carry out with the President. I wondered if the Mongols had also considered the cakes women's work, kitchen business, trivial and harmless.

Whatever the reason, the guards had waved the rebel through the city gate without bothering to sample the moon cakes. The Mongols didn't have a taste for the sticky filling, the Chairman said.

"A people of meat and milk," I said. He laughed.

Mongols were barbarians from the north, I'd been told, hairy and red-eyed and vicious as demons, who'd ruled over China hundreds of years ago.

Chinese families sliced open the cakes to admire the whole salted duck egg yolks, round and orange as the moon, embedded in the lotus paste. They also discovered a call to action: "Rise up! Rise up at midnight!"

HIS QUARTERS WERE SHADOWY except for a frosted lamp on a bedside table. As the Chairman moved ahead of me, I tried not to trip. The floor resembled a field besieged by gophers: A blue-and-white-striped bathrobe puddled on the threadbare rug, surrounded by cigarette butts and mounds of books, a mess so great it looked irreversible. Wooden cabinets packed with books lined the walls, adding to the scent of sweat, old paper, and black tea.

Even before the Chairman touched me, I ached between my legs. My resistance: my glance away. I didn't fight him. I kept my eyes fixed to the ceiling and my body rigid, hoping he would soon finish.

This time, the Chairman demanded a different response. He flipped me onto my back, and took my nipple into his mouth. My body arched up, yielding to the pull—a current I didn't know I had in me, threatening to knock me over and carry me along. I didn't expect it, didn't know how to stop what was unfurling in me. He didn't linger, though. He crawled down my body, hooked an arm under each leg, and buried his face into me. Stunned, I choked on my screams.

The groans he coaxed from me were the sounds of someone I didn't know, a wail of mourning. Of pleasure. My breath clicked in the back of my throat. Shuddering as lights exploded in my head and I was falling, breaking, tumbling. He rolled off of me, settling beside me. Our panting slowed. I slid along his body, flesh against flesh, and pressed close to his head for a glimpse of his sparse eyelashes, the spiraling cave of his ear, and the sunburst of lines radiating from his eyes. I preferred him in fragments. Whole, he overwhelmed me.

His eyes distant, he swallowed a handful of golden pills from a bottle on the bedside table. In each of our conversations so far, he'd told me a story. And he'd listened to mine.

"The moon cake story . . . Who baked the moon cakes?" I asked cautiously. "It had to be someone General Zhu trusted."

"Go on," he said.

"Someone who could keep the secret at home, who could read, who ran the kitchen. His wife," I said, the story coming together in my head. The secret code, it could have been Lady Zhu's idea, too, for who but she would have considered the filling as closely? In Ma's version, recipients found a slip of paper inside, while Ba claimed that the different patterns on cakes placed side by side revealed the secret message. That victory led to many more, until the Mongols were overthrown and the Ming dynasty emerged in their place. The history of our country went so far back, and long after emperors rose and fell, only a story or two from each reign remained in our memories.

"General Zhu thought of it only on his tongue, but never of its making," I said. The most trusted rebel wives would have baked for weeks, I added. "They're heroes, too! As much as General Zhu."

But they'd been lost to history, I thought, falling outside the official record.

He propped himself up on his elbow. "Some things you look at so often, for so long, you miss them. You're opening our eyes to things that we've stopped seeing." He rubbed my thigh, smiling with a bubble of pleasure I would come to recognize as a side effect of the pills that put him to sleep. Within moments of turning off the lights, he was snoring, sprawled on his back, his arms and legs splayed, a man no longer accustomed to sharing his bed. Wondering if I could fall asleep beside him, I edged toward the wall, as far as I could go, up against stacks of books.

When I undid my hair, my scalp throbbed in relief. Licking my cracked lips, I tasted blood, salty and sacrificial. I'd been spared from getting pregnant tonight, but I'd run out of my mother's tea, and I'd have to find more. *Dong quai* grew in the hills above the village, in the moldering damp beneath the forest canopy. The gardens at the Lake Palaces were vast, though, and such treatments might have been passed down from dynasty to dynasty. An imperial doctor could have secretly cultivated it for the empress and the other court ladies, and maybe it still grew here, the gardeners tending it as they would any other ornamental flower.

Women had other ways to keep a baby from taking hold. Busy Shan once explained that you were most likely to get pregnant a couple weeks after your monthly flow. "Think of when sows are bred, how long after they go into heat," she'd said. If you washed yourself with vinegar afterward, rinsing as far up as you could go, you could protect yourself, too. "You have to wash immediately after."

We'd been whispering after lights-out in the dorm.

"Can't Teacher Fan help?" I asked.

"You say one word to her, you're gone," Busy Shan said.

To avoid getting sent away, the girls tried to take care of it on their own.

"Is there anything else?" Dolly Yu had asked shyly.

"You could offer him a dish of tofu!" Busy Shan said. "Some men love to eat tofu! They want nothing else!"

Her talk set off shocked giggles. I hadn't understood the joke then, but now all at once I did. Tofu: soft and wet as a woman. What the Chairman had done to me tonight, I might persuade him to again. I could do the same to him—which disgusted me so much I could hardly stand to think it—but such an act would keep me from getting pregnant.

None of us asked how Busy Shan possessed such knowledge, the sort of wisdom we taught one another, girl to girl, without the help of our mothers, who didn't want us contemplating such matters. When they were our age, they might have whispered about such secrets: Swallow a jar of tea steeped for two days, choke down a mouthful of cold ash, jump from a tree, jump a thousand times a day for a week. We didn't expect any man to concern himself with how to prevent a pregnancy or how to end one.

Although I'd never slipped into the fields or down by the river, others in my village must have: the newlywed bride who gave birth not so many months after she married or the sprite of a classmate sent to live with an ailing aunt. When she returned, people said they could smell the milk on her, the milk meant for the baby she'd given up to another family. In her time away, her waist had thickened, her legs turned stocky and veined, and her high sweet voice had coarsened. Her parents matched her up with a sickly old man.

The widow haunted me most. She hid her pregnancy until she collapsed in the fields and gave birth to a baby boy, raw and red as a skinned rabbit. He died a day later. How broken she was afterward, her arms and legs shambling, and her hair matted. A worn-out shoe, a whore.

She might have been raped and raped again, every man a suspect. She'd been someone's mistress, every wife made vulnerable. She had wronged us all, and in return we despised her: She had to empty the latrines and tote water to the hilliest fields, stuck with the worst chores, until one day she disappeared.

Wind rustled in the trees, their branches tapping against the windows. The Chairman shifted, kicking me in my calf. I held still, and he didn't wake up. Back home, my family would curl together on our brick bed. In the dormitory, Midnight Chang would turn her wrath on another girl, doing to her what she couldn't to me.

I alone had the Chairman that night.

CHAPTER 9

*W*HEN I WOKE UP, THE CHAIRMAN WAS CLEARING A CORNER of his desk, big as our family's bed. He wore a pair of red swimming trunks, topped by a wrinkled robe. I leaned over to pick up my outfit crumpled on the floor. When he noticed me, I stammered out a "good morning," and he wished me one in return.

I wondered how late I'd slept. Because heavy velvet curtains draped the windows, it seemed like twilight in his bedchamber. The room was almost as large as the dance pavilion, with stacks of books everywhere, stacks that seemed to reach halfway up to the high ceiling, more books than bricks in my village. I didn't yet know he'd gotten up earlier than usual, eager to start our lessons. His days typically began in early afternoon or later, and at night, he was active as a bat on the hunt.

My mouth tasted gummy and stale, and I longed to rinse off the stickiness between my legs. Barefoot, I felt like a rough country girl. Hurrying, I tied back my messy hair into a ponytail. The troupe would already be awake, too, gossiping about last night. I'd spent my every waking moment with them, and my every sleeping one, too, and I wondered what they would make of me—and my belongings—suddenly gone. I wasn't sure if I'd stay in the Chairman's quarters during my training, or if he'd send me elsewhere.

Beside a fat jar of brushes, he set down a sheet of paper, so translucent it glowed in the dim light on his desk. White rings spiraled across the wood where he must have spilled tea and left his cups sitting.

While I dressed, I heard him on the phone, summoning Secretary Sun. I went to the bathroom to splash my face and rinse my mouth. As soon as I emerged, the Chairman called me over and told me to write my name.

I stared at the sheet, unsure how calligraphy would help me pass as an intellectual. The President wouldn't ask to see me write, would he? The Chairman could be establishing what I knew, and how I responded to lessons.

Secretary Sun arrived then, and the Chairman explained what he'd asked me to do. Both men flanked me, and I fidgeted, uneasy that Secretary Sun might smell the sourness of our bodies in the rumpled sheets nearby. My hand hovered over the brushes. With their porcelain handles and billowing bristles, dark brown or grayish white, they were finer than anything I had ever used, finer than my bones.

"Maybe she doesn't know how," Secretary Sun said.

I whirled to face him. "You think I know nothing. I know how to write my name!"

He and the Chairman exchanged a look.

"The Party did much to improve our country's literacy rates . . ." Secretary Sun trailed off, as though realizing how foolish he sounded, presenting the history that I'd lived.

Heat still in my cheeks, I returned to examining the brushes. The Chairman handed me one about the length of a chopstick, with soft white hairs—from the belly of a goat, he said.

He poured water from a pitcher onto an inkstone in the shape of a dragon, its fanged mouth open in a hiss. He rubbed a rectangular stick into the water, making ink that was blacker than black, the sort of black that blotted out the stars, that sucked in all available light, and had the bitter, oily smell of soot.

"You can't rush through this," he said. "If your ink is too watery, or thick as soybean paste, everything that follows will be spoiled."

At his nod, I dipped the tip of the brush into the ink.

"Relax your shoulders," the Chairman ordered.

"Stand with your legs apart, planted firmly on the ground," Secretary Sun said.

Holding still, I could have been a mare up for sale, assessed by the height of my flank and the wear on my teeth.

"Everything's connected." Secretary Sun seemed like the kind of person who might have taken apart a radio to learn how to put it back together, a man methodical and orderly. "Steady body, steady characters. Now, move your hand up the brush. Not too far—then you won't have control. Too close, and your characters will smudge."

Moving my fingers up the brush, I didn't know where to position them until Secretary Sun nodded almost imperceptibly. I finished rolling the brush in the ink until it turned glossy and heavy.

"Start with horizontal strokes. Then vertical," Secretary Sun said.

"That's like taking off your pants to fart," the Chairman said. "Just write your name." He lit a cigarette from a gold-and-navy pack.

A hint of how they would teach me: Secretary Sun wanted me to start from the beginning, plunging me into tedium with no seeming end. The Chairman urged me to see the whole, to inspire me to achieve everything at once.

The village schoolteacher had praised the curve and sweep of my characters, asking me to demonstrate for the class on the pitted, crumbling chalkboard. With a rabbit's beady eyes and twitchy manner, he'd been little more educated than his students. My characters were wobbly but recognizable, better than the crooked attempts by my classmates. The first, simplest words I learned became the basis of more characters. "Woman" and "son" combined to mean "good": 好, *hao*. "Sun," "moon," and "sky" joined together meant "tomorrow": 明天, *ming tian*. Three women together, 姦, *jian*, became "evil." These characters were like messages from ghosts, revealing the thinking of our ancestors.

Compared to most of the girls in the troupe, I wrote with the hand of a court calligrapher. I told myself this would be no different, even though I'd never wielded a brush, only chalk and pencils. Clenching my fingers around the brush, I began, but ink soon blotted and I lifted my arm to start over again. My name emerged, messy as animal tracks through mud.

I set down the brush, wanting the characters to vanish—wanting to disappear from the room.

"Song Mei Xiang," the Chairman muttered, his mouth twisted in irritation, as though I'd smeared shit instead of ink on the page.

"She's not to blame," Secretary Sun said. "You can't reverse the old ways overnight."

The old ways. As if he'd joined the Long March and hadn't been a schoolboy at the time of Liberation. Though I fumed, how could I dispute what we could all see before us? The Chairman deserved the gift of my ignorance, but not him.

"It has been crushing us, the old ways of thinking. Made us weak. What do we sacrifice: our inheritance or ourselves?" the Chairman asked.

When he spoke like this, he seemed to see history all at once, thousands of years of oppression and failed revolts, millions upon millions of lives wasted until revolution arrived. I strained to understand what seemed just beyond the limits of my perception.

An attendant arrived, wheeling in a cart of tea and snacks. I'd come to know her as Servant Ping.

When I raised the brush again, I knocked the dish of inky water off the desk, which exploded on the stone floor in a splash. Stains spread across a stack of papers piled on the ground. I snatched it up, desperate to blot the top page clean and noticed it was from the President. Horrified, I tried to fan it dry.

Taking it from me, the Chairman crumpled the page and tossed it into the puddle. "It reads better covered in ink."

Kneeling to clean, Servant Ping couldn't hide her scorn for me. She flicked the puddle with her rag and a dark drop flew onto my leg.

The Chairman rolled up the sleeves of his robe, selected a brush that he swept over the inkstone, and in an explosion of motion, he conjured the characters on the page. The ink sparkled, the lines broad and strong and flexible as bamboo. After watching how his shoulder connected to his arm, his arm to his hand, his hand to the brush, the brush to the page, I drew a line beside his, sweeping and bold. This I could follow, this I could learn.

"Excellent!" the Chairman exclaimed. "Now this."

From his brush flowed the character for "look," 看. *Kan*. Not to see, but to look. To pay attention. A single character, shaped like an eye, a square with two horizontal lines, a simple concept for a simple girl. His command, his lesson; he'd demonstrate, and I'd copy. All my life I'd repeated after my teachers, but I no longer wanted only to echo.

One character paired with another became a third word, and so I added the character for "difficult," 難. *Nan*. Difficult to look at: ugly.

The Chairman grinned.

"The movement starts at the shoulder," Secretary Sun chimed in. "Not just in the wrist."

We ignored him; he had no part in the game I'd started, which became all the more fun because we excluded him.

I dashed out "little," 小. *Xiao*. Little sister, little daughter, the last and least. Turning toward him, I gestured at the page, an invitation to combine it with other characters. 小聪明, *xiao cong ming*, clever but petty? 小孩, *xiao hai*, child. 小姐, *xiao jie*, young miss? Would he play along?

He traced out "heart," 心. *Xin*. Together, the words meant "careful." *Xiao xin*. I should consider the phrase in its sum and in its parts. Keep your heart small: a lesson in survival at the Lake Palaces.

MY SCHOOLING HAD BEGUN, and though I had far to go, I'd made it through the morning.

Servant Ping brought in lunch, steamed spare ribs, cured ham with pickled beans, fish heads in chili sauce, and a heap of rice, which she set on the other side of the desk. I sipped my tea, smoky on my tongue. The brew served at the canteen was harsh compared to this one, with its lingering fragrance that rose up my throat and into my nose before the warmth spread through my body. Dipping my chopsticks into the fish head, I dug out a morsel from the hollow between its eye and its gills—so tender the flesh almost melted against my tongue, with the sweetness of the clear waters through which it had once swum.

I bit into a translucent spring roll, which crackled and shattered between my lips. Ma wasn't here to stop me from devouring the greasy foods that were said to stir up your body's fires, causing nosebleeds, chapped lips, aching throats, or sores around your mouth. According to my mother, a greedy granny in our village once used up her family's weekly oil ration in a meal for herself. She bled to death, drained like a pig on a hook.

As I gobbled the spring roll, Secretary Sun looked away, probably repelled by a girl who ate as much as the Chairman. During the famine, he'd been somewhere comfortable and well fed, for I sensed he'd never been crooked with hunger, his head too heavy to lift, his body consuming itself. I would never give up a chance to feast on plenty.

The Chairman dismissed his aide, sending him away with a sheaf of reports to summarize.

"Little Beijing!" the Chairman called out after him.

Secretary Sun turned, and for all his seeming reserve, he couldn't hide his pleasure at the Chairman's nickname for him, an endearment based on his birthplace.

"Go slowly," the Chairman told him. "For the sake of everyone else. No one can keep up!"

Secretary Sun left. As much as his appraisals had pricked me, I couldn't disregard the things he'd said—they'd hit me squarely—and it seemed clear the Chairman relied on him.

If I wanted him to rely on me like that, I had to study him more than any other subject. The jar of calligraphy brushes caught my eye, and I wondered which one the Chairman used most often. Which one he'd used to write the poems that children like me learned in school. "What's your favorite?" I asked.

He tilted his head, encouraging me to guess. Not the one with the tiny brush, its bristles stiff and new, but maybe the thick one, that could make big strokes that would swoop like swallows from a cliff. When I pointed at it, he shook his head.

"You won't find it," he said. "No one can. It's the brush that fed me for a summer!"

Traveling tailors, weavers, musicians, and others earned their way around the countryside, and so too a student with a brush and ink?

"You wrote what others couldn't," I guessed. I'd never heard about this part of his life.

He seemed pleased I'd figured it out. On summer break from school, he and a friend had roamed the countryside in Hunan, writing wedding couplets, signs for businesses, and other announcements. "We bathed in the sun and in the wind," he said. In the heat, they slipped off their shirts, ducked their heads into gusts, and slept in open fields beneath the moon and the stars. He stood bare-chested in the rain. "We meant to toughen ourselves up," he said. "Too many books turn you soft, twist you around."

A dreamer, I thought, imitating those legendary bandits with names like Blue Faced Brute and Horned Dragon, masters of crossbows and cudgels, who raided the rich and gave to the poor.

He'd carried a bedroll, his journal, ink and brush, and not much else. The people provided the rest, and those with the least had been the most generous. One family wove him a pair of straw sandals when his fell apart, and a granny fed him a soft-boiled egg, tender and rich, the first that her hen had laid in weeks. "When I returned home, I knew the people deserved more," he said. "They were nothing like the intellectuals who ignored me when I worked as a library clerk at Peking University. Or else winced when I talked, as if I was poking chopsticks into their ears. Later, they were begging for a chance to meet me. They wouldn't listen to me, just like they wouldn't listen to you, because of how you're dressed, because of how you sound."

Yawning, he climbed into bed and motioned for me to join him. I approached, cautious, wondering if he wanted to nap, or something else. I sat on the edge. He didn't reach for me, and the tightness in me eased.

"It's not just the intellectuals, though," he said. "Even those who are redder than red, even those who should know better, get swayed by fancy talk."

"Like the President?" I got under the covers. Back home, we used to nap every day after lunch, and I realized I'd missed giving in to sleepiness in the afternoon. The servants had changed the sheets with soft, smooth ones that smelled freshly laundered.

He turned onto his side. "Like the President! He licks the boots of the bourgeoisie, and takes us down the capitalist road."

It didn't matter if I couldn't picture the bourgeoisie or a capitalist; the feeling that gathered around the words meant more than the meaning. If the Chairman despised the President, so did I.

THAT AFTERNOON, RETURNING FROM my lessons with Secretary Sun, I searched along the garden path for clusters of *dong quai*. Fresh, it might lack the potency of my mother's tea to bring on my flow, but it was better than nothing.

Secretary Sun noticed me straggling. "Sitting for so long, it's tiring," he said.

I let myself feel the exhaustion of the last day: the dance party, the late night with the Chairman, the hours of lessons. "My stomach is sour," I said. It was too embarrassing to admit the real reason I wanted herbs, but if he took me to a medicinal garden, I might find *dong quai*'s white flowers and dig up its stringy, yellow-brown roots, or feathery white *sheng ma*, yellow balls of *hou hui*, or the purple blooms of *bai tou weng*, all the bitter herbs that Ma kept out of reach from me and my sisters. She provided them to the women who came to our door late at night, pretending they'd gone to the latrines, who had only a moment before their husbands caught them.

A squirrel darted across the path and raced up the tree. The troupe would be in field training right now. When Midnight Chang hurled her wooden grenade at the target, would she picture my face?

Bees hummed around a bush. I could tell the gardeners had been by here, the air musky with fertilizer and turned earth in the summer heat.

"All the new foods you're trying can give you a stomachache," Secretary Sun said. "And if you're feeling nervous, too . . ." He'd ask the kitchen to bring me millet porridge for dinner—a bland and soothing dish, and an unexpected kindness.

His voice reminded me of polished wood, of refinement, a scholar of the sort who memorized poems almost as soon as he could talk. His slacks and button-down shirt stayed tidy, and compared to him, I always felt disheveled and shrill.

In the library, we'd studied a scholar-official who'd conspired against the Hongwu Emperor, scheming, flattering, sabotaging. He'd been executed. Emperors wanted the brightest in their service and not their enemy's, and yet again and again, faithful servants turned on their masters. The President was the latest example, but surely not the last.

I knew so little about him, even though I was supposed to deceive him. "How old is the President?" I asked. "What province is he from?"

Secretary Sun gave me a wary look. "It doesn't matter."

"How did he become a slave to the bourgeoisie?" I asked, fumbling the words.

"Don't repeat things you don't understand," he said.

I stared at him. "Aren't you supposed to teach me?"

"The Chairman believes capitalist infiltrators are everywhere," he said in a low voice.

In our classroom, we had learned how America had invaded Vietnam. They were coming. They were here.

"At every level of government, in every part of society, from the President on down, someone is trying to destroy everything the Chairman—and the people—have achieved," he said.

At the time, I must have assumed Secretary Sun felt the same, unable to conceive of any situation in which he—in which I—might question the Chairman. How could the President overthrow the Chairman? It made as much sense as if I'd been told the sun was a candle or that the moon was a silver coin.

"Yesterday, you asked if my family got to keep anything extra after the harvest," I said.

"Toward the end of the Great Leap Forward, the President

pushed for peasants to be able to sell some of their crops," he said. "If you had anything left after putting in your share to the village, then you could keep it for yourself. Or sell it. Yes?"

I nodded slowly.

"The President claimed it could end the famine, but the Chairman knew what the President was really after: for capitalism to take root."

The Great Leap Forward was supposed to make the Chairman legendary, but instead we'd plunged into disaster.

"Now they're both circling around Dazhai," Secretary Sun said.

The model village.

"The Chairman wants that collective spirit to spread everywhere," he said. "But the President wants families to farm their own plots, too."

Plots that weren't communal, plots that the Chairman had made clear that he hated.

"The President wants to turn the model villagers into model capitalists," I said.

Secretary Sun nodded.

Only later would I realize that the Chairman would turn the country upside down to get rid of the President and his allies.

"The Chairman is biding his time," Secretary Sun said. "He opens the way, and lets the snakes come out of their holes. The President is wily. Publicly, he claims he's putting an end to capitalist activities. He made a big show of it and even sent his wife to the countryside to investigate corruption: headmen who favored their friends when passing out work assignments, when giving out food, that sort of thing."

"But secretly . . . ?" I trailed off.

"It's not so secret he wants to make a name for himself. He's trying to get out of the Chairman's shadow. If it were up to the President, we'd turn capitalist tomorrow. Why should anyone leech off your labors? During the famine, shouldn't intellectuals have worked alongside you in the fields? Students and their teachers?"

"Yes," I said.

He shifted on his feet. "Instead, they ate better than you! And why? Because they spent their days in classrooms?" he asked.

"Like you?" I asked.

His mouth twitched. "Your training will prove how a peasant is every bit an intellectual's equal. And only socialism treats us all as equals."

"Do you think I can convince the President to meddle with the students?" I asked. If I failed, I might return disgraced to the village, or worse. Busy Shan had told me about the girl sent to a labor camp, and about her neighbor, who'd returned from one a ghost.

Secretary Sun nodded. "The Chairman thinks so. If you study. If you do nothing else but prepare for the next six weeks."

We continued through the lush garden. Though Secretary Sun might consider my request a distraction from my studies, I needed the *dong quai*. "There must be herbs grown here?" I asked.

"There aren't." He quickened his pace. "Not that I've heard of."

He'd heard of most things at the Lake Palaces, his clipped tone implied.

"Do you even know what they look like?" I asked.

A guard passed us, the first person we'd encountered on the grounds, which seemed tranquil as burial mounds. High white walls sectioned off a garden nook, with a round doorway that framed the willow trees inside, its leaves as delicate as embroidery. In the distance, the silver tones of a water fountain trickled. I felt like I was trespassing until I spotted a familiar plant, the same here as in the hills above our village. Squatting down, I pulled a bunch of soft green leaves.

"Hey, hey, hey—stop!" he said. "What are you doing?"

I held it up to him. "It smells like lemons."

He drew back, but then inhaled. "You'd never know."

"*I* knew," I said. "My mother knows, and she taught me."

When Ma gathered herbs, she moved in a way she never did inside our home. Alert, not downcast, and her steps swift and sure, not cowering, discovering possibilities where others only found weeds.

I popped a leaf into my mouth, and offered him one, which he chewed.

"The taste—I can feel it in my nose," he said.

"It helps you sleep, and with any aches," I said.

"Just from a leaf?" he asked. He examined the waist-high bush from which I'd plucked the leaves.

"Just from a leaf." I ran my hand over the bush. "Now that you've seen it, you won't be able to stop noticing it."

He glanced at the sun, low in the sky, and then at his watch. "Probably not." Too busy—too important, he didn't have to say.

I rolled the leaves in my palm, releasing their bright scent. "It clears and calms the body. Though it turns your skin green."

Secretary Sun spit it out.

"Not actually!" I added. I couldn't needle him like he was one of my sisters. If he'd rebuked me or reported me, I would have deserved it. But Secretary Sun surprised me.

"Too bad," he said. He smiled. "It might have improved my coloring."

Something between us eased.

"There's another one that turns your skin yellow," I teased.

"Another time." He hurried ahead. "Come! The Chairman is waiting."

THE MORE I TELL you, the more I remember. It haunts me, all that remained unsaid between us, and going over these stories makes me feel closer to you. Everything I never told you is coming out now.

CHAPTER 10

Just beyond the door to the chairman's bedchambers, a silk privacy screen—four golden panels embroidered with cranes—blocked the view inside. Through a gap, we glimpsed him in bed with the Madame. He slouched in his robe, and she wore a khaki pantsuit, her shoes off and her legs curled under her. Her jasmine scent hung heavy in the room. So engrossed in their reading, their heads bent together over a page, they didn't seem to hear us. Though they weren't touching, I could see they had an easy familiarity with each other, the kind held by my parents between the bickering and the beatings. When his robe slipped off his shoulder, exposing the sagging pears of his chest, she pushed it back up. The gesture seemed absentminded, born from repetition, as if for years she'd adjusted his collar or run a comb through his hair.

Secretary Sun tugged on my elbow, and we backed out of the room. Her perfume lingered in my nose, cloying and thick, gagging me. In the entryway, Bodyguard Wei straightened. He wasn't as fierce and stoic as I imagined someone charged with protecting the Chairman might be, even if he had to be an expert marksman, and trained to take down an assailant with his hands. He was one of two dozen guards who worked in teams of four on shifts to protect the Chairman in and around his quarters.

"The Chairman is occupied," Secretary Sun told him, and led me into a courtyard with two intertwined cypress trees at its center, their trunks twisted in an embrace. I sank onto a stone bench beneath a grape trellis.

Secretary Sun remained standing. The Madame might have come through the back entrance, through the dining room that connected their bedchambers, he said. Come at the Chairman's invitation, he didn't need to add.

In my imagination, their heads dipped closer and closer together until they slid into the sheets that still held the outline of my body. His hand on her cheek, hers on his chest.

"She's loyal," Secretary Sun said. "Loyal as a dog."

His frankness surprised me.

"He tells her to bark, she barks."

"Does she whine at the door when he's not there?" I asked, and then wished I'd held my tongue. I wedged my restless hands under my thighs. The Chairman had warned me to remain *xiao xin*, to keep my heart small. Midnight Chang, Busy Shan, any of the girls would step into my place if they could. At the Lake Palaces, I had to master the turbulence that swirled within me, that left me clumsy and off balance one minute, and sent me soaring in the next, all the extremes and in-betweens.

"He tells her to bite, she bites," he warned.

"But—" I knotted my hands together, dusty and grimy. Nothing would get me banished from here faster than my jealousy. But I had to pry out more about her, about them.

"Why doesn't he send *her* after the President?" I asked.

"She's tried, but hasn't yet hit her mark," Secretary Sun said. "She complains that the President treats her like a bored wife who meddles in cultural affairs."

"What do you think?" I asked.

"She's at her best when she's busy," he said. "Don't give her cause to look your way."

"Have you ever seen any of her movies?" I asked.

"According to the Chairman, onstage, no one was her equal. Strong as a general, but in her eyes, you could see the pain, the sacrifice. You felt it," he said. "She didn't cry on command, not like those actresses who wail with fat, fake tears. She understood if she cried too loudly, she took that release away from the audience. She brought herself to the brink, but let them cry."

I wished the Chairman could have seen me perform in our play. And yet, what if I came up short and always would when compared to the Madame?

"I doubt she's here to talk about cultural affairs, or even about the President," he said. "Their daughter is coming to lunch tomorrow." He explained that she'd recently graduated from Peking University, the school I'd first heard about yesterday.

The Chairman had worked as a young clerk in the library there. At lunch, in the stories he'd told me, his class resentments seemed to have grown with each patron's snub.

He had a daughter only a few years older than me? A prickly seed ball from a sycamore tree had fallen on the bench, and I flicked it aside. "She takes after the Chairman?" I asked. Huge alert eyes, broad nose, full lips, or the Madame's pinched nose and appraising gaze?

"Her mother." He couldn't hide his faint irritation. "The Chairman summons her to ask about what she's heard from classmates, but none of what she tells him is much use. As if she might flush out spies! The Chairman said she wasn't to receive special treatment, but it couldn't be helped. Her professors used to give her their class notes, and the school's president would send her back to the Lake Palaces if she so much as sneezed!"

He leaned back on his heels. His last year in college, he'd been her tutor, he said.

I wasn't sure how old he'd been when he went off to college— Eighteen? Nineteen? Twenty? If he'd first met her during his last year of school, and she'd recently graduated, then he was somewhere in his mid-twenties, about a decade older than me. "Was she much of a student?" I asked.

"She was as much of a student as she was a spy," he said, his tone so dry I wanted to laugh.

"Is that what you'll say about me later?" I asked.

He glanced at me. "From what I can tell so far—no."

I tried not to smile. "But you were such a good tutor, the Chairman wanted to meet you?"

"She was full of complaints about me. She told her parents that I was lazy. That I wanted her to come up with her own answers!"

"She was used to people telling her what to write down," I said.

He nodded. "Her grumbling got the Chairman's attention. Everyone else had given in. Easier for everyone to do so, except that she wasn't learning a thing."

A magpie squeaked and burbled on a branch high above us, its feathers flashing black and white.

"He asked me to come visit," he said, the wonder at that invitation plain in his face, years later.

"You never left?" I asked.

"I never even went back to class," he said. "Which his daughter didn't mind. She found another tutor more to her liking."

"Sounds like you didn't mind, either," I said. "Does she visit often?"

"If she comes by, she usually eats from the canteen, not from his kitchen. Not with him," Secretary Sun said. "The Chairman doesn't play favorites with his family."

I felt stupid for not knowing, for not assuming the Chairman had a family, even though he was married to the Madame. We never discussed his children, not in my village nor in our classes with Teacher Fan. We didn't gossip about that part of his life. The Chairman was a peasant turned revolutionary, and if the notion of family arose in our lessons, all we had to know was that he'd given his up. He was the Chairman—timeless as the sun, sprung full-born into the present, no history, no duty other than to serve the people—and not someone's father, not someone's brother or son.

To become a hero, your life had to be worn away, worn smooth, until you were blank, the barest of outlines. Only then could you become a light leading the people of this generation, the next, and the next. That is how people preferred their heroes—at a remove.

I chewed on my lower lip. The Madame wasn't his only wife. Before her, the Chairman had other wives whose patriotism we'd learned about in school—Martyr Yang, who'd been executed by a warlord, and Comrade He, who joined him on the Long March. After something happened to her—I couldn't remember if she'd been wounded or had fallen ill, or if she'd gone away for treatment. Maybe she'd died. Sometime later in Yan'an, the Chairman met the Madame.

"Is Yan'an when she started giving him advice?" I asked.

He looked up at the trellis, shadows dancing across his face in the breeze. "When she started working on revolutionary plays?" I asked. "Because she was an actress?"

"Her fame preceded her," he said.

The officials could have deemed a movie star an improper partner for the leader of the revolution, I guessed. "The other cadre didn't like her."

He didn't confirm or deny it, but something in his expression made me think I'd hit upon the truth. Though he wouldn't know firsthand, maybe he'd heard rumors.

Why, then, would the cadre have changed their minds in Yan'an? Then I remembered the lunch tomorrow with their daughter.

"The Madame got pregnant," I said. Maybe she didn't know the tricks to stop a pregnancy, the ones that Busy Shan taught us. Or she let it happen, to bind the Chairman to her.

He dipped his head. He didn't want to discuss it, but perhaps the scholar in him—the one I'd seen emerge in our lesson at the library—admired how I could piece it together.

"After that they accepted her?" I asked.

"Not exactly," he said. "She got their blessing, if she looked after him. And kept out of public life. No politics, for at least thirty years."

Long enough, the officials might have thought, to silence her for the rest of her life, for who would pay attention to a woman who'd lost her bloom?

I kicked at the gravel, puffs of dust rising around my feet. "How many children does the Chairman have?" I asked.

Elsewhere on the grounds, the whine of a motor and a metallic ping started up. "One with the Madame," he said. "And another daughter with Comrade He, and a son he had with Martyr Yang. That I've met. That I know of."

We'd both learned about the revolution through stories, and that put us in the same generation: earnest latecomers, never as brave, never as daring, both nostalgic for what neither of us had lived through.

"How many children did the Chairman lose?" I asked.

He pressed his lips together. "It's not so clear."

"The history of the Chairman is our history, the people's history," I said, louder now. "I have two sisters. And two brothers, too—one died at birth, and another when he was a toddler."

He reached out his arm but stopped short of touching me. "I'm sorry."

A pill bug crept across the path. "I never knew them." My family never talked about them, the ones we'd lost. But we didn't have to. Their absence was in what might have been, brothers who could have eased our burdens, who could have carried on the line that would die with my father. The lost who'd shaped me as much as those who lived.

"What were their names?" he asked.

"My parents never told me," I said. I struggled to get out the words. "To have a big brother. If just one of them had lived . . ."

His mouth twitched. "The Chairman had three sons with Martyr Yang," he said. "But only one has survived. After she was killed, the children lived on the streets in Shanghai. The toddler died."

My brothers. Why was I swiping at my eyes? My brothers were strangers.

Secretary Sun reached into his pockets, as if in search of a handkerchief, but I waved him off. "What about the other one who died?" I asked.

"He was a soldier," he said. "Killed in an air strike in Korea."

The Americans waged war across Asia, first Korea, and now Vietnam, drawing ever closer to China. Though Teacher Fan's lessons about the imperialists had been hard to grasp, the Chairman's losses made them real. I wondered if his sons looked like him, if they'd inherited his wide mouth, his temper, or his quickness.

"What about Comrade He's?"

"Two were . . . left behind, during the Long March," he said. "As soon as they were born, they were taken in by local families."

I shivered, shot through with a chill. Comrade He would have spent her pregnancies knowing she'd have to give up her baby soon. The Chairman must have mourned his babies, too, but the pain couldn't have been the same.

"The Party went looking for the Chairman's children, after the war, but couldn't find the families where they'd been placed. There may have been other children, too." He clasped his hands behind his back. "Ones I've heard mentioned but I've never asked about."

At least my parents knew where I'd gone. By the time the Chairman married the Madame, he would have understood that no earthly bonds could hold—not between lovers, not a parent and a child.

I couldn't imagine such a loss. Not yet.

CHAPTER 11

*T*HE CHAIRMAN STROKED MY HAIR. AS HIS FINGERS TRACED my ear, I sank deeper into his lap. Though his swim trunks scratched against my cheek, his scent musty, I didn't turn away from the movie playing on a screen hung against the wall.

We were studying the enemy.

A week into my training, he wanted me to see the films from the West that portrayed the perils our country might suffer if we fell back into capitalism, into greed. I couldn't tell if I was moving any closer toward what he wanted for me or wanted *of* me, though. More than anything, I craved his praise, a nod, smile, or laugh, but I sensed that keeping up with my lessons, repeating after him, and serving him weren't enough to hold his interest.

The couch squeaked under us. His shoulders jerked, and I reached up into his robe to scratch his back, his skin tight and dry after our time at the pool. He settled into my hand, and I scratched harder. A spring dug into my side. As I withdrew my hand, he told me to scratch higher. He sighed. "That's it, there."

It astonished me, how quickly we had settled into a routine. Mornings, while he slept, I slipped out to take dance and private voice lessons with Teacher Fan, who worked with me to smooth out my peasant accent, my peasant ways. She taught me how to make polite conversation, to laugh delicately, not openmouthed; how to hold my teacup, fingers poised like dragonflies instead of grasping it in my fist; how to leave two bites on my plate for every one I took. She'd refrained from teaching the troupe these lessons because the

Chairman wanted to meet us as if we'd come straight from the village. He considered us spoiled, she said, if we put on too many airs.

By the time I returned to his quarters, the Chairman was usually reading the newspaper, the latest headline about the war in Vietnam, the increased production of tanks, or a large watermelon grown in the south, big as an ox. After lunch in mid-afternoon, we napped before swimming or walking in the gardens until I left to study with Secretary Sun, who taught me history, politics, proverbs, and other references that I might weave into my conversation with the President. He and the Chairman had drawn up a long list of books. Secretary Sun read aloud passages, which we discussed. If intellectuals worked on such assignments all day long, they were lucky, I thought. Not only because they stayed out of the sun, not only because their labor consisted of turning the pages, but because of how much further they could see.

Aside from the dance parties—held every other day or so, which went on until after midnight—I never dealt with the troupe. At the pavilion, the other girls had studied me with the bold curiosity of dogs but gave me a wide berth, as if by ignoring me the Chairman might, too. More than once, though, I'd sensed someone lurking near me and discovered Busy Shan a few meters away, the air between us grown woolly, prickly, impassable.

After the dances, the Chairman and I watched movies until dawn. At first, I'd had trouble following what was happening, too caught up in the bizarre settings: the narrow buildings tall as cliffs that poked through the clouds, cars sleek as arrows and yet big as haystacks, so numerous I could have crossed the street by walking on top of their hoods, and the foreigners, who seemed alien and ancient, their eyes so pale I thought they'd gone blind. The men clad in skinny suits and ties, and women in knee-high boots, under skirts so short they couldn't dare bend over. It was my introduction to rock music, with its insistent beats that surged through me. At the dance parties, we never listened to the Rolling Stones, the Beatles, the Beach Boys, or anything else popular at the time.

Secretary Sun attended to the roaring projector, changing the huge reels and fixing the film if it blew apart, pasting together the loose strips. Even though he remained silent in the shadows, his presence gave me somewhere—someone—else to look at. With him around, I felt freer, less shy, three turned into two against one, an equation I preferred at times to the intensity of being alone with the Chairman.

One night, the musical was the oddest yet. It was set in America, in San Francisco, though I forgot the city's name almost as soon as Secretary Sun told me. I never dreamed that I'd walk its streets myself one day. The actors had Chinese faces, but spoke perfect English, a feat that seemed as impossible as breathing underwater. The sound of Chinese sparkled, a shower, whereas English sounded flat, a line of water dribbling across a tilted table.

"The subtitles aren't correct," Secretary Sun said. "He's not an 'old codger.' She's calling him a bastard."

He'd learned English at the university, and some French and Spanish, too. It made him seem worldly, even if he'd never been to those countries.

"How do you say it?" I asked, curious if the word sounded as harsh in English as it did in Chinese.

He said the word in English and I repeated it eagerly. *Bastard.* The Chairman did, too.

"*You* only ever want to learn the curse words," Secretary Sun said to him.

The Chairman smiled. "What else do you need to know?" He moved his fingers in slow circles on my thigh, under my skirt. My face burned. I couldn't look at Secretary Sun, who must know what happened between me and the Chairman. I wanted the Chairman to stop, and yet I wanted him to continue, until the world fell away and only we remained.

"You can only speak one language at a time. It's just showing off," he said. Pointing at the screen, he let out a sharp hiss, as if spitting out watermelon seeds. "Look at how they degrade their women!" he muttered. A curvy actress shimmied half-naked before the shocked old man.

"Feudal as landlords," I murmured. Secretly, though, I admired the bounce in her step and the sinewy ripple of muscle across her shoulders. If she'd been a ghost that lured travelers off the road, I would have gone astray, too. The soaring songs and the world lit gold filled me with yearning.

The Chairman must have sensed my fascination with the woman. "Don't be dazzled," he said. He ashed his cigarette, the flakes drifting in the light. "An actress streaks across the sky. Her youth, her beauty are soon gone—no matter how much she tries to hold on to them."

Like his wife? The Chairman hadn't mentioned what they'd discussed at lunch, or that they'd had lunch at all. He never spoke of her. Walking to and from my lessons at the Lake Palaces, I'd felt I was being watched: by her, her spies, or someone else. I glanced at the door that led to the dining room, and beyond that, to her quarters. Though I'd been tempted to peek, the Chairman never used that door; it might as well have been a wall. I had yet to hear any sounds from that direction, which I hoped meant she was too far away to hear us.

Secretary Sun had told me how she'd occupied herself over the years, combing through newspapers and magazines for what might interest the Chairman, evaluating movie projects at the Ministry of Culture, and redecorating villas. He didn't have to explain that none of these pastimes held the political power she clearly wanted.

Leaning against the Chairman, I nibbled on dried persimmons from a wooden bowl. The fruit softened and expanded in my mouth, salty and achingly sweet. Hunger dug at me, different than the hollowness of my childhood—this appetite was born from plenty, after I had grown used to full bowls at every meal. We snacked idly to occupy our mouths, and the more I ate, the hungrier I felt.

We spent most of our waking hours by ourselves, or in the company of his bodyguards, who often asked for his advice on love while we played mahjong. Sometimes the chief of security would drop by to discuss arrangements related to National Day, or the scholarly doctor to discuss naval battles and other bits of history, but the

Chairman had far fewer meetings than I would have guessed. Aside from the dance parties, he never met with his fellow old revolutionaries. I didn't know if that was typical, or only during my training. After living what must have felt like ten lifetimes together during the war, it seemed they'd had enough of one another.

Instead, they traded stacks of letters and reports in boxes delivered twice a day, or else an occasional phone call from the Defense Minister or Premier or another high official. How little we'd understood in the village, how a distant stroke of the pen by men in the capital determined our fate.

These top officials must have once been like bandit blood brothers to the Chairman, swearing oaths while hiding in bamboo groves, but running a country seemed mostly bureaucratic. I was disappointed, just a little, that the Chairman didn't have to burn the paperwork after reading it to keep it from falling into the wrong hands and that it wasn't written in code.

At the time, I was oblivious to the Chairman's loneliness. How could any of us, the Chairman included, admit that a man so beloved lived in such isolation?

LATER, AFTER WE CLIMBED into bed, he read aloud from *Jin Ping Mei*, a book that held every coupling possible between a merchant and his six wives, his maids, and various singsong girls: a woman kneeling to offer the flower of her bottom; the lovers used rings and balls between their legs, and dabs of a powder that enabled the merchant to have sex with ten women in a night; and another woman groaned as he tossed iced plums rhythmically between her thighs. Her legs spread, her ankles tied to a trellis with foot-binding ribbons.

Then he fed her the plum, the Chairman said.

"Was one plum enough? I don't think she would have her fill," I asked.

He grinned. "None of them ever had their fill. Officials drank, they gambled, they had their pick of girls—so lazy, so decadent!

Peasants had to sell their children to survive. They had to choose: die in poverty, or rebel."

I crept my fingers on his thigh. When he reached for me, I pushed aside books and got onto my hands and knees, crouched beside him on the bed. He'd posed me once before in this position. It had taken him a long time that night, and I hadn't known where to look or if I should close my eyes. Toward the end, I'd been rising, expanding, and I grasped at that sensation again.

He got onto his knees. As we rocked, my left arm buckled and I lurched forward, off of him. He groaned. Something cracked—His back? His knee? When I tried to turn around, he pushed back into me. I learned then that the delay intensified everything for him and for me. I refused to remain a body that he pushed around, pushed apart, and soon might replace. Throughout, I kept him waiting.

As we sprawled on the knotted sheets, I supposed that the force of his will could also keep me from becoming pregnant. The force of mine, too. Ma had struggled to conceive and keep children in her, and if I was the same, the curse would protect me.

"What's the name of the author again?" I asked.

He smirked. "I doubt it will come up with the President." He reached for the book, which had fallen to the floor. "Did I ever tell you about what happened to one of its readers?"

Seeking revenge for his father's death, the author of *Jin Ping Mei* had dissolved tiny grains of poison into ink, copied his book while wearing gloves, and given it to his enemy, who licked a finger to turn the pages quickly, never quickly enough. Before reaching the end, he'd collapsed and died with an erection that didn't disappear, forcing the family to hide it under layers of silk funeral gowns. "They buried a tent pole!" the Chairman said.

"Send it to the President," I said.

"His gingerroot is too gnarled to raise its head!" He laughed.

I wondered if the Chairman wanted me to lure the President to bed, to pry out his secrets or to blackmail him. No—he would have told me. Or maybe he still could, but first the training would determine if he could trust me. I pushed the thought away.

"Not that he wouldn't try," the Chairman added. "He claims he's such a family man, but he's been married five times."

Though the Chairman had been married at least three times, I didn't remind him.

"Each wife more of an intellectual than the last," he said. "As if that might erase the stink of where he came from."

Pulling on a robe, he went to his record player, weaving around the piles of paper strewn on the floor. He could have built a bonfire that lasted for days with the correspondence around his bedchamber. More than once, I'd seen him dig through papers on his desk, irritated if he couldn't find what he was looking for. If I could help him keep track, I'd become indispensable.

Where to begin? I drew a sheet around myself and got up. On his desk, I found a letter from the Defense Minister, who complained about a military official who "sang a different libretto!" A libretto? I didn't recognize the word, but if there was singing, it might have something to do with music. What an odd insult, yet one that he could have thought compelled the Chairman. While the Chairman searched through his albums, his back turned to me, I read on.

The Defense Minister must agree with the Chairman that corruption within the Party had to be rooted out, and it seemed he had enemies of his own that he wanted to purge. In time, I would notice that—unlike the letters from other top cadre—the President's correspondence never hinted at dark plots against the Party. What he didn't say expressed even more than what he did. I could only guess, but maybe the President wanted to preserve the order that kept him in power.

When scratchy, languorous music drifted from the record player, I startled, worried the Chairman had caught me snooping. He was studying an album cover and didn't seem to notice me. Maybe he would have considered the correspondence a part of my education, or else he doubted how much I understood. And he'd be right. Most of the letters and reports ran up against the limits of the characters I could read.

As the song began to play, the Chairman held out his arms, the sleeves of his robe casting huge bat-like shadows. "Come."

I dropped the sheet, found my robe, and made my way through the mess to which I'd become accustomed; it made the grand room cozier. Without the piles of books, we would have been like pebbles rattling around in a basket. He drew me close, and we danced alone and barefoot in his bedchambers for the first time.

I stifled a yawn. In his insomnia, the Chairman seemed to achieve a kind of immortality, awake for twice as long as everyone else. In a day, he lived a week. In a week, a year. I'd come to understand the intimacy shared by two people awake while others slept. In the village, I awoke at sunrise, and slept at sunset. I never knew the night until the Lake Palaces, when my life reversed. In these tranquil hours, the Moon Cake Ladies had plotted revolution. In these hidden hours, Chang'e, the immortal on the moon, ruled.

I looked up at him. "Do you ever think we might need *new* stories about model revolutionaries? Stories that people won't forget, that they can't stop talking about?"

He tightened his hands on my waist. "Go on."

"Who doesn't want to hear about the powerful getting humbled?" I asked. I had loved Sister Yu and Iron Girl, but their stories— first announced in the cities, then trickling into the countryside months, sometimes years, later—were out of date by the time they reached the village, I said. "What if I traveled around the country, talking about how I tricked the President?" I asked. "Wouldn't it excite young people? Promote your calls for revolution?"

I wouldn't admit to my other fantasies: How my shining portrait could get reprinted in posters and hung in classrooms and homes. How the people might think of me before they fell asleep and when they awoke. My father would carve my name into the ancestral tablets, among the men's, and future generations would sing my legend.

"Think of all my training," I said. "I want to keep serving the Party."

"You're an eager one!" The Chairman smiled. "Get past the President first. Then we'll see."

After the song ended and another one began with brassy horns, I asked him about the origins of this music. "Paris," he said. "When I was a student, I had a chance to study there." To learn how to build factories all over China. "I turned it down. Couldn't pay for the ticket." The disappointment still caught like a burr in his throat.

I nestled my head into his chest, his sparse white hairs tickling my ear.

"My mother was dying. If I'd left, I never would have seen her again." He nuzzled the top of my head, and I imagined him my age, his features unformed, not yet swollen and imposing. Playful one day, serious the next, dreamy or pragmatic, his character not yet set. I likely wouldn't have drawn his attention. He might not have attracted mine.

The record kept skipping and he guided us to the player, where he flicked something off the disc. He spun me beneath his arm, and we resumed swaying. I traced my finger on the nubby mole on his chin until he swatted my hand away.

The span of my life was so short, compared to the Chairman's. Four of me could have lived and died in his many years. I wished I had known him then—in the decades before he became the Chairman, in the decades that made him the Chairman.

He studied my face. "You're always asking questions about the old times. Maybe Yan'an is just the place for you!"

I faltered. "I haven't learned everything I can here."

He smiled, mischievous or malicious or maybe both. "You could live here ten lifetimes and still wouldn't."

"Would you go there now?" I asked, trying to change the subject. "To Paris or Yan'an?"

"The river never turns back," he said. A moment later, he broke apart from me. Back at his desk, he wrote quickly, tapping his pen in a staccato on the pages. Sleepy, I tucked myself back into bed, wondering if our conversation had inspired him. Turning onto my side, I chided myself for daring to think I could matter like that.

The horns lulled me. I dozed, my thoughts flickering in and out. The dance parties commemorated the life that the Chairman didn't take. A part of him still might long to hear live songs rather than his jazz records. If he had left for Paris, he might still be there, strolling with a lover. If he had left for Paris, capitalists might rule over our people, building mansions out of our bones and drinking our blood. Perhaps I might have died, enslaved and starved, or I might never have existed. I owed my life to him. We all did.

WE HAD SO LITTLE time together. In person, I might hold back from telling you about my quiet moments with the Chairman, but the distance between us makes me bold. I'll reveal anything, everything that would have helped you inch closer to the mystery of who I am, that might explain who I was when we met, and why I had to leave you. Every question you might have asked, I suppose, must answer that final question most of all.

CHAPTER 12

WHEN BUSY SHAN APPROACHED ME AT THE DANCE PARTY, my stomach twisted. Not because I'd been thinking of her, but because I hadn't. The Chairman had crowded out everything, everyone else in the two weeks that had gone by, and seeing her reminded me I couldn't ignore what was happening elsewhere at the Lake Palaces.

That night, each girl wore her hair in two braids, just like me. Even Midnight Chang. It felt as if I'd gone walking in the twilight and stumbled upon a village populated with my doubles. Did the Chairman feel the same way, when he first appeared on buttons and pins and posters, discovering himself endlessly replicated?

"Happy birthday," she said. "Almost."

White lights above her, strung on the rafters, glowed like hovering fireflies. Sometimes, just before my birthday, they descended upon the village. They didn't live for long, flaring before disappearing. It was early September, and the harvest moon was waxing. In three days it would be full, and I'd turn sixteen.

"You remembered." Over her shoulder, I noticed Midnight Chang beelining toward the Chairman. "What's she up to?" I asked.

Hurt and anger flashed across her face.

"Did she do something to you?" I asked.

She glared at me, probably because I hadn't bothered to ask how she was doing, because of everything I had now that she didn't.

Guilt twinged in my chest. "Midnight Chang's like a dog after a bone," I said. Couldn't we go back to making fun of our common enemy?

Her expression soured, a cherry puckered in vinegar.

She wasn't going to play along. "You're his favorite now," she said. "But it will pass. It always does."

Not this time, I wanted to say. *I'm not like you, not like the rest.*

"If it weren't for me, you would have gone running home after the first day." Turning on her heel, she disappeared into the crowd. I imagined the rumors she'd spread in the troupe: I had schemed against them all.

I searched for Midnight Chang and discovered another cadre had intercepted her before she'd reached the Chairman. But she'd already danced with the Chairman, and eventually—soon?—he'd bed her.

The air was thick with the scent of sweat and mildew. Across the pavilion, a girl started talking to Secretary Sun. She fiddled with one of her braids, twirling it. Teacher Fan had instructed us to draw out the ones who didn't often dance. "Those who stick to the walls need a turn, too," she'd said. He never danced, though, and he flagged down another official who led her away. Then he fetched cups of tea and joined me.

I pointed at the girl he'd rejected. "You couldn't give her one dance?" I asked, trying to keep my tone light, still shaken by my encounter with Busy Shan.

He shook his head.

"You'd be quicker on the dance floor than the Defense Minister," I said.

No one in the troupe much liked the man, with his limp, damp hands. I remembered how his sweat had flicked into my open mouth the night of my first dance. Slight and bespectacled, he was now holding forth in the corner with a group of cadre.

"He's known as the Chairman's pupil," Secretary Sun said.

Jealousy cut through me, a bright knife. They'd been forged in the same fire decades ago, on the Long March and in Yan'an, and I would never know him as well as his old comrades did.

"He created the Little Red Book," he said.

In the troupe, we'd studied the book of the Chairman's writings every day. It was a book so important we'd attacked Dolly Yu when she ripped one of its pages. A book, none of us yet realized, that millions of Red Guard would wave in the air at rallies next year as proof of their devotion. I'd never thought about who'd been behind it; it was like discovering a man who'd manufactured rain clouds to end a drought. "He must be loyal. The most loyal one of all," I said.

"So loyal, he wants everyone to know," he said.

I looked at him in surprise.

"What does he think of the President?" I asked. "Is he trying to replace him?" I remembered the piles of mail from the Defense Minister on the Chairman's desk. "He sends several letters a week."

"You'll find no correspondent more faithful," Secretary Sun said.

At the center of the pavilion, the Premier danced with Busy Shan. He ran the government, Secretary Sun had explained. "The Premier plans the budget. Makes sure all the parts work together and keeps the lights on."

I'd shrugged off the details; I only had to understand the Chairman trusted him. The girls had all agreed that the Premier had the lightest touch among the cadre. You wanted to partner with him at the end of the night, when your steps were at their sloppiest, because he kept you upright. He seemed attuned in ways that the other top cadre didn't, anticipating where you might go, what you might want, and what suited your abilities, turning every step effortless. "Where did he learn how to dance like that?" I asked.

In his youth, the Premier had studied in Japan and France. "He even taught Teacher Fan at Yan'an," Secretary Sun said.

But he couldn't help Busy Shan that night. As we watched, she arched back, jerking him forward. She wasn't usually clumsy, and knew the steps better than I did, but our talk must have thrown her off. They halted, and she rushed away, with Teacher Fan in grim pursuit.

Nearby, the girl who'd asked Secretary Sun to dance struggled, too. When the cadre stomped on her foot, she grimaced.

I squeezed my hands around the teacup, watching the dregs vibrate from the music.

"Aren't you more graceful than him?"

"Not necessarily," he said.

"Can't you give her one dance?" I said.

"It's not for me," he said. "I don't dance."

"It's not for *you*? This song makes me feel like I could do anything." I flung open my arms, the drums pulsing through me. A few drops spilled from the cup. I set it down on the table. "Like I could dance all night. Like I could set off on the Long March. You don't feel a thing?"

"Only that it's time to sleep," he said, with the slightest suggestion of a smile.

"If you don't dance, then how do you select us?" I asked. "How can you tell from our performance if we can dance?"

"It's not important." He looked onto the dance floor, where couples whirled and rocked, faster and faster as the tempo sped up.

I folded my arms across my chest. "You're saying we're not important?"

He turned back to me. "It's not that. Several factors go into the selection process."

"What is it, then?" I said.

He exhaled. "Every situation is different. You each have your talents," he said.

I shook my head. "I didn't even know these dances before I arrived!"

He couldn't hide his pity, and with a jolt, I realized what he was too discreet to say: Our dancing abilities didn't much matter in the course of our duties.

As thumping drums launched the next song, Midnight Chang darted toward the Chairman. They twirled like the spinning gears of an ornate clock—separate yet together, their movements inevitable.

I jumped to my feet and in a few strides, Secretary Sun closed the distance between us.

He shielded me, his body radiating the smell of steamed buns, of soap and clean laundry. I moved closer, until our shadows merged together, undulating.

"She has no claim over the Chairman," he said. "Neither do you. None of us do."

"You can't deny her talent," I said, unable to tear my eyes from them.

"Or her connections," he said.

"Connected—how?"

He opened his mouth, catching himself. He wavered until I asked again. "The dance studio where she trained in Shanghai is led by a former recruit," he said. "After her time here, she married a vice mayor's son and opened a studio."

I had to repeat the words to myself to understand. "Did you arrange the marriage?" I asked.

He shook his head. "Teacher Fan. The troupe has quite a reputation, among those who know about it."

"Reputation for what?" I asked. "For beauty? For grace?"

He didn't answer.

For our talents in bed? My skin crawled. I wanted to rinse off in the shower and disappear down the drain.

The heat of the pavilion and the noise of the music made my head throb. I thought about the former recruit's groom: a vice mayor's son. If Teacher Fan supplied girls to the most powerful and well connected, she had eyes and ears everywhere. No wonder she'd been able to keep her position at the Lake Palaces for years. No wonder the Madame valued her; Teacher Fan could have made matches for the girls the Madame found most troublesome, sending them away from the Lake Palaces.

"Why didn't Teacher Fan tell us?" Though I shouldn't have expected her to; neither she nor anyone else at the Lake Palaces explained anything unless—until—necessary.

"Not everyone is selected for a match," he said. The song reached its frantic peak. "Do you want to get matched up?"

"No!"

He leaned in. "Teacher Fan wants to give recruits a chance," he said. "Every chance you wouldn't have otherwise for a different kind of life."

"Just like a farmer gives a chance to the cow it leads to market," I snapped.

Teacher Fan was talking to a stoop-shouldered official wearing a uniform so tight you could see his every cascading stomach roll. He had mottled skin, dark and wrinkled as fatty sausage. After he gestured at someone on the dance floor, she escorted him to Busy Shan.

When he clamped down his hand high on her waist, grazing her breasts, Busy Shan gritted a fake smile. The privilege of these elders was to flatter young women, their gropes disguised in a fatherly embrace.

"With him?" I asked Secretary Sun. His mouth hardened.

"She doesn't want model revolutionaries. She wants model brides!" I said. "If I fail to pass as a student intellectual, will I get led off like that, too?"

"No," he said tersely. He sounded angry—at me for asking, or at the matchmaking, I didn't know.

It seemed a fate not much different than my parents marrying me off to someone from a neighboring village. The clear-eyed part of me understood the opportunity, and yet I also seethed. Our cause was supposed to be patriotic, not matrimonial, and I now questioned Teacher Fan's every claim that we served the country.

"Does the Chairman know?" I asked.

Of course he knew. He might consider us in his service long after we'd left the troupe. It could please him that he'd been with us first. Though I wanted to run from girl to girl here to warn them, most probably would welcome becoming a prize at a powerful man's side. Maybe even Busy Shan.

For now, I couldn't dwell on it. Midnight Chang was leading the Chairman off the floor, across the pavilion, toward the room that held his bed. I wanted to fly up out of my shoes and attack her, even though I knew I couldn't expect his sole attention. As soon as she slept with him, she'd find a way to take my place. When I lunged toward them, Secretary Sun grabbed my wrist. I broke free, though instead of chasing them, I lurched toward the record player. The album had finished, and as the attendant reached for another, I pushed aside records in the stack—waltzes and foxtrots and rumbas—my hands shaking until I found a Chinese opera.

"Stop!" the attendant shouted. "Don't touch that!"

Ballroom dancing didn't pair with such music, which the attendant only played to give the troupe a rest. I'd never touched the turntable, or any records, which spun like a riddle. My hands hovered. What happened to girls who meddled?

Secretary Sun took the record out of my hands, putting it on for me. At the opera soloist's first wail, the Chairman halted, causing Midnight Chang to stumble. Her hands fluttered around him, never quite touching him, frantic as oil poured on a hot wok. He clapped a hand on her back, as if he were sending off an ox. She teetered on her heels before she found her smile, and glided away. She'd slap herself a hundred times tonight for letting the Chairman slip from her grasp.

As the opera's gongs started clanging, Secretary Sun turned down the volume on the record player. When I tried to thank him, he looked away. "All songs come to an end."

The Chairman strode toward us, trailed by a clutch of cadre.

"Have you taken into account the drought in the northwest?" one asked.

"The drought may break this year," the other said.

"You can't count on rain!"

They were trying to impress the Chairman, but his expression seemed resigned. Did he want to escape the boring talk? Then I realized his hand had begun to tremble at his side. I wondered if the tremors that I'd witnessed the night I'd met him had returned, if they came on when he was tired. He'd been dancing hard all night. The more he tried to control his hand, the wilder it might turn, like a fish thrashing in the grass.

Taking the Chairman's hand, I raised ours high together. "To the peasants!" I shouted. It startled the cadre into silence. How odd I might have seemed, but I didn't care, so long as I drew attention to myself.

I held his hand until it went still.

YEARS LATER, I WOULD recognize that a customer at the restaurant suffered the latter stages of what plagued the Chairman. Every Saturday, while his wife and daughter chattered over dim sum, he sat in silence in his wheelchair, his eyes hungry for the spareribs and dumplings that passed him by.

CHAPTER 13

*T*EACHER FAN ROLLED HER EYES BACK TO IMITATE ME. WHEN I was concentrating, I gazed so far up my eyelids, it must have looked like I was on the brink of a seizure. It was a habit she'd tried to break in me.

"Say it again. Slowly this time," she ordered. In the dance studio, we sat facing each other as she led me through the tongue twisters once more to improve my pronunciation: *Mama qi ma. Ma man, mama ma ma.* Mother rides a horse. The horse is slow. Mother scolds the horse.

The syllables turned nonsensical in my mouth. Just as the smallest gesture might offend or please, mark me as a peasant or an intellectual, so, too, would my accent. Though halfway into my training, I felt far from ready to face the President.

"Your words are mashed together again," she said. "Like your mouth is full of porridge. You have to remember to work your tongue. Make a tiny circle with the tip of your tongue. Both directions. Work the root of the tongue, without moving your chin."

I'd woken up feeling out of sorts, every subtle irritation leaving me on the verge of tears: the scratch of my wool skirt against my legs, the tea that burned my tongue. Nerves, I told myself, with three weeks to go until National Day. I felt frayed after the endless hours of studying. If I failed, the Chairman would punish me. Send me to a labor camp, and maybe my family, too. Or Teacher Fan could have other plans for me—ones I didn't want to contemplate.

Even if she claimed the girls had a choice, that we could say no to a match, I had my doubts.

The studio's floor-to-ceiling mirror reflected how my flesh had responded to the bounty of the Lake Palaces: My curves and hips filled out, and my skin glowed and my hair turned glossy. In the village, I might have withered before I blossomed, but here I had a new body, for a new life.

I'd never studied as much as I did now, never had teachers pay this much attention to me. Even as I struggled, sometimes hours would fly by during our lessons. In the fields, every minute ground us down. But maybe I belonged there instead of here. Each time I attempted the tongue twister, my mouth grew wet with slobber. Teacher Fan held up her hand to stop me and opened her mouth wide to reveal the placement of her tongue, arched like a leaping fish, the tip touching the roof of her mouth. I attempted to match the shape of her lips and tongue, my muscles pulling tight in my jaw.

"Pay attention! Stop pushing your tongue out. It makes you look like you're choking!" she said.

I exhaled. If I couldn't get rid of my accent, I'd never deceive the President.

"Again. Slowly this time," she ordered. I repeated the words sluggishly until they mangled, until I sounded like my neighbor Fatty Song's younger sister, the one who had never learned how to speak, who pointed at her mouth if she was hungry.

Teacher Fan rested her fingers on my jaw, intent on my mouth, guiding me with light pressure. I was too surprised to move. Pulling away, I tried the tongue twister again. She nodded in approval as I spoke, but then slapped me in between my shoulder blades. "Sit up! Stop slouching!"

I was forgetting how to act. Hadn't I convinced the soldiers? For them, though, I'd been playing the part of a rough peasant with the crude valor of a man who would take revenge with his bare hands, who would sooner light a fire with a book than read it.

How could I pass as a university student? I had yet to meet one, and the paces Teacher Fan put me through made me feel I needed lifetimes to prepare. "I can't—I can't."

"You must!" she commanded.

My stomach writhed like a den of vipers. At my political-thought lesson yesterday with Secretary Sun, my eyes had been heavy, head foggy. We'd studied the Chairman's speech about how contradiction gave rise to transformation. Capitalism was contradictory because different social classes had different goals, which led to class conflict and revolution. I agreed, of course I agreed! But I'd also yawned so much that Secretary Sun made me stand up and walk around the library before cutting the class short.

I'd been caught up in the maelstrom of the Chairman's insomnia, which had intensified: the twitch of his legs, tossing and turning until he rose to fetch another book to carry him through the night. He thrummed like a beehive—talking nonstop, moving from desk to bed and bookshelf and back in his chambers. His hours at the pool didn't settle him down. A deep unease tinged him like woodsmoke, a scent you couldn't get out of your fingers or your hair, out of your mouth.

The weakness in his right hand had also returned, with a tremor that shook his teacup and blurred the ink when he wrote. He had to be exhausted. If only he could sleep. If only I could, too.

"Again," Teacher Fan said. "Say it again."

"I—I need a break." I rocked back on my heels.

She wagged a finger. "We've just begun!"

Retching, I brushed the back of my hand across my mouth. Teacher Fan nudged me toward the garbage can, asking if I was going to throw up.

I pulled away. "It's nothing." Everyone took great care not to sicken the Chairman; at the first sneeze or cough, attendants and bodyguards would retreat.

Teacher Fan scrutinized my stomach before returning to my face. "How long have you felt like this? Just now, or for a while?" she asked.

"Just now." I wrapped my arms around myself.

"You're not sleeping," she said.

My mind twitched. I'd tried to hide it, but could she see it?

"Did you throw up this morning?" she asked.

"No," I said, squirming under her gaze. "I'm not hungry."

She nodded to herself. "Are you feeling sore?"

"Just tired." A weariness I'd never known, as if I'd been kneeling and weeding for a hundred years.

When she studied my belly again, it dawned on me what she might suspect: pregnancy. I hadn't been able to find any *dong quai* in the gardens. I'd gotten my flow only twice since I'd arrived at the Lake Palaces, which wasn't unusual. Months might pass between them, especially in lean seasons.

My skin went clammy. "My flow's coming on, that's all," I said. "It's always like this, before."

After I'd been with the Chairman, I cleaned myself up, when I remembered, when I could. Sometimes we swam, which could protect a girl, according to the troupe, but more often than not, I fell asleep. Sometimes he ended with a silver slick across my belly. Now I resisted the urge to touch my stomach, gritting my teeth until my nausea passed.

Teacher Fan declared we'd return to my accent after we practiced dancing. "Sitting still will only make it worse. The room will keep spinning."

Her hand slid between my shoulder blades, holding us in balance, and I leaned back, giving in to the press of our bodies.

"I've never been to the part of the province where you're from," Teacher Fan said.

"There's not much reason for anyone to visit." I tried to picture her stepping past the pigsty and the garbage heap.

As the music wailed, she spun me. I flew out, twirling under her arm. "Next time I'll go with Secretary Sun, to find more recruits like you," she said.

She'd complimented me, but she also meant to replace me someday. Stumbling, I apologized for losing track of my feet. Teacher Fan counted to eight and I willed myself to let the steps overtake me.

Another cramp swept through me. When the needle crackled at the end of the record, I asked, "Can my mother visit?" Ma might know why I'd summoned her. Why a girl with my duties might need her mother, or maybe I could come up with a message that only she would understand.

Teacher Fan pursed her lips. "Without fail, you girls are always asking for your mothers."

"It's not like that!" I wasn't homesick, pining after Ma. Not really. Not entirely.

Tomorrow was my birthday, the first night of the Mid-Autumn Moon Festival. My family would hike to the top of the hill to peer into the heavens and tell stories—without me.

Even if my parents could read and write, we weren't allowed to send or get letters from home. Ever since I'd arrived at the Lake Palaces, I'd watched the progress of a patch of sunlight, which had started in the middle of the floor in the dance studio. Each day it moved closer to the window, and now it never crept inside at all. Like the sunlight, my family had faded away a little more each day.

My neck prickled and at the corner of my eye, something moved. I spotted Midnight Chang in the mirror, her smile tight as stitching. At the last dance party, the Chairman had paired off with her for most of the night. Even though he'd taken me back to his bedchambers, I couldn't sleep much afterward.

"You're early," Teacher Fan said to her.

"I didn't get a chance to tell you," Midnight Chang said to me. "I'm worried about Busy Shan."

Had she seen us arguing at the dance?

"She can take care of herself," I said.

"She feels guilty," Midnight Chang said.

I said nothing.

"She's worried about her mother," she said.

Busy Shan would never confide in her. She'd told me about her seamstress mother going blind, but wouldn't share that with Midnight Chang. Would she?

"I caught her by the window the other day," she said. "She was wiggling the bars. Like she was trying to get them loose."

"You're lying," I said.

I glanced at Teacher Fan. Her face appeared taut with worry, as if she was hearing it for the first time. She pointed at the door. "Out, now."

"I don't know why I thought you would care," Midnight Chang said. "You don't care about anyone but yourself. You're a whore. A stinking, oily-mouthed whore."

I'd told myself in serving the Chairman, I had no higher cause. Yet what I accepted in darkness shamed me to hear out loud now.

"Enough!" Teacher Fan said.

When I slapped Midnight Chang, her head snapped back. I almost cried out, surprised by the loud crack and the tingle of my hand. I had never slapped anyone, and I didn't expect this shocking intimacy, skin on bone against skin on bone.

"You wish you had my duties," I said.

She touched her cheek but didn't wince. "Watch yourself."

Teacher Fan barked at her to wait in the hallway, and then put on another record, a waltz, and turned up the player to its maximum volume, even higher than before, until my ears buzzed and the strings vibrated in my throat. She took me into her arms.

I felt shakier on my feet than when we'd begun. If I was pregnant, I could hide it; I couldn't falter in my training now. It would be months before the curve of my belly betrayed me, and by then, I would have tricked the President.

If I was pregnant—but I wasn't.

"Maybe Busy Shan should go home," I said. She'd entered the troupe last fall, and wasn't her term ending? "Or . . . she could get married?"

Teacher Fan shook her head. "Leaving the troupe could throw her off," she said. "It sometimes does." Other troubled girls, other suicides, she didn't have to say. "I've told the recruits to watch each other carefully."

"You can't leave it up to us," I said.

Teacher Fan looked away. Maybe I could convince the Chairman to keep Busy Shan at the Lake Palaces—not in the troupe, but in his quarters as an attendant. Then I could keep an eye on her.

She'd hate serving the Chairman. Hate me.

We resumed our lesson, swaying, rising, and falling. The door remained closed, and I pictured Midnight Chang pressing her ear against it and hearing only music, her eyes closed as she willed herself back inside the room.

Telling Midnight Chang about the Chairman's plans for me could have shut her up, but few knew about my training. The attendants and bodyguards knew better than to let the secret get out; any slip could get traced back to them.

To everyone else, though, I was merely the Chairman's latest entertainment.

"Why is Midnight Chang here?" I asked Teacher Fan.

We spun. The song intensified, to the point where I'd always pictured myself at the top of a hill on the verge of tumbling down.

"She's getting private lessons," she said.

"Why?" I tripped and she tightened her grip on me.

"You've made an enemy," she said.

"I've done nothing!" I said.

If she let go, I might drop to the floor. Did the Chairman want a backup if I couldn't pass as a student intellectual? Or was it someone who wanted to pit Midnight Chang against me, who'd already identified her as promising? Someone who wanted me gone.

"Are the lessons the Madame's doing?" I asked. Our heels clicked and clicked against the floor like woodpeckers gone mad.

"You've kept the Chairman's interest for the last three weeks," she said. "I'll give you that."

"What does he say about me?" I tried to make myself heard over the song, coming to an end.

The record crackled, but she didn't change it. "Not a word! Not a fart!" she said in hushed tones. "But no recruit has ever occupied him so completely. And that's the problem. The Madame puts up with these arrangements—"

"Because she has to."

She looked at me sharply. "She puts up with it as long as his attentions are divided. You want the Madame to stop meddling? You'll need to send him off with other girls."

I jerked to a stop. "I won't. If Midnight Chang gets in with him, she'll never leave."

Teacher Fan shook her head. "She'd bother him; she sets off too many tongues. Too many rumors about them, and soon she'd be gone."

I didn't know if I could trust her. She would have claimed she acted on behalf of the Chairman, but she could be helping the Madame, too. Maybe she played them off each other, with me in the middle.

"He'll still take you back to his quarters. I'll make sure of that," she said.

"*You* send someone, then," I said.

"Best if it comes from you," she said. "Best if he believes you encourage such arrangements."

"You arrange everything else that happens at the dances. You arrange the rest of our lives!"

Teacher Fan didn't deny it. "You girls. You don't understand, no one else looks ahead. No one else cares what will become of you."

"The Chairman—"

Pulling me close, she told me about when the Madame had first arrived in Yan'an. She'd sought out advice from the Chairman himself. She claimed that she had a delicate constitution: Too much wind gave her a sore throat, and cold water brought out boils on her skin. She asked him what to do about her long hair, turned dry, tangled, and lice infested.

"He thought her vain and decided to play a trick on her. He told her to rub her hair in mud," she said. "He called it a local secret."

She would have rubbed fistfuls into her hair, the drying clay like many little fingers, yanking. My own scalp ached. She must have been horrified, furious—all of which she'd had to swallow with a smile.

The prank had been anything but a game to him. He wanted to teach her a lesson, just as he wanted to teach the President a lesson now. "She had to cut her hair, even shorter than any of us," Teacher Fan said. "The knots wouldn't come out."

If he'd do such a thing to someone he loved, to someone he'd marry, how would he punish those who failed him? Though the story frightened me, back then, I was young enough to think he reserved his cruelty for those who deserved it.

For decades the Madame had suffered every humiliation, waiting for a chance to lead alongside her husband. The world now knows her for her petty ruthlessness, for long-held grudges against those she would punish during the Cultural Revolution, but I've come to understand that such a muzzle would have driven anyone with her ambitions crazy.

THAT AFTERNOON, IN THE changing room at the pool, I got into my bathing suit and studied myself in the tiny round mirror. My belly didn't seem any bigger. The tightness of my suit made me feel sleek, slippery as water. Though I craved that constraint, that feeling that the fabric held me together, it might also reveal every new bump and curve if my body betrayed me. I had to hide my worries from the Chairman until I figured out what to do.

I got in, floating on my back, arched like a bow, with my arms above my head. A mural spanned the ceiling, filled with golden wheat sheaves, glorious blue skies, and smiling peasant women with bulging forearms and calves. Heroes and martyrs of the revolution— not a pregnant woman or mother among them, as far as I could tell. No child underfoot, no baby strapped to her back.

When the Chairman swam, he became calligraphy, a poem as stunning in its twirling curves as in its meaning. He glided toward me, the bubbles trailing in a veil behind him.

"Let's see how long we can last underwater," he said after he surfaced beside me.

If I shied away, he'd get suspicious. After filling our lungs, we dropped to the bottom. I sat with my knees up, my arms wrapped around my legs, while the Chairman dangled and hovered. He strained against himself, his cheeks puffing, his entire body shaking and bubbles trickling from his mouth. I sank deeper into myself. When the Chairman tickled me, digging his fingers into my waist and my armpits, I held steady, letting only a single air bubble escape to tease him. He watched my face, but I allowed nothing more.

The water pressed down on me, pushing me to the bottom of the pool, plugging up my ears—could it explode what might be growing inside of me? Like a grape, squashed underfoot. The Chairman kicked to the surface, breaking through and roiling the water behind him. After waiting underwater a while longer, I surfaced. Unsnapping my cap, I climbed out of the pool and draped a towel around myself. Though the pool was warm as a bath, by the end of our swims I felt chilled, and my skin turned wrinkled and pale. The Chairman, sulking at his loss, fiddled with the edge of his towel. He draped it over his head and reclined in his wooden lounge chair.

I sat beside him. My skin prickled, despite the steamy heat of the pool, and I felt as if I might come apart with a tug. I needed the *dong quai,* and I needed Ma.

The Chairman didn't notice. The attendants rolled him into a pool of sunlight, the wheels of the lounge chair squeaking like mice caught in a trap.

Drawing the towel off his face, they bathed him, dipping towels into a basin of warm water, wringing out the excess before wiping him down. He never showered or bathed, considering it pointless when he swam almost every day. He gave a shake of delight, like a cat stretching in the sunshine. The attendants progressed down his body, wiping his legs, the bottoms of his feet—he laughed, ever ticklish—and behind his ears, then laid a fresh hot towel over his face.

Their tenderness reminded me of how Ma had bathed me the day I left home, and how she'd blessed me with a final touch as we parted.

Drops trickled down my neck, my body, and pooled at my feet. I sat down on the deck chair by his feet and tugged on his big toe. "My mother?"

He didn't answer.

"I want to see her." She could come in time for my birthday.

The Chairman tossed the towel onto the bench. Sitting up, he blew through his teeth. "You say you want to be a model revolutionary. But you're not putting the revolution first."

He draped the towel back over his face.

"My parents can help you."

He didn't move.

"You're always saying you can't trust reports about peasants. My parents can tell us firsthand what's happening, with no one getting in between."

The Chairman whipped off the towel and threw it at me. I caught it one-handed. He got to his feet. "Your parents! They taught you to worship them, to put them before your country," he said.

Footsteps approached, echoing off the concrete floors. When Secretary Sun entered the pool deck, it seemed he could tell that he'd walked into an argument. "I brought the report," he told the Chairman, and handed him a folder.

Secretary Sun turned to me. "Let's go."

But the Chairman wasn't finished with me. "When's the last time you saw your family?" he asked his aide. A few meters away, standing along the wall, the two attendants and bodyguard on duty watched.

Secretary Sun hesitated. "Last year. A year and a half ago? Before Lunar New Year."

"And they only live fifteen minutes away!" the Chairman said. He tried to pour a cup of tea. When nothing came out, Servant Ping bolted over, apologizing. The servants hovered over the Chairman's every breath and burp, but didn't know what to make of me. She bent over to retrieve the pot, thrusting her bottom into his face. His eyes lingered, out of instinct. Habit. Desire.

"Do you want to see your family?" he asked her.

He played off everyone around him against one another, praising one and criticizing the other, and then doing the reverse the following week. Now it was my turn.

"I have no family but the revolution," she cried, fist to her chest.

He asked Servant Ting the question. Shouting the same reply, she stepped away from the wall and struck an identical pose. Sparrows, now fierce as hawks, both shining in his attentions.

I wanted to smack them.

" '*I have no family but the revolution*,' " I said. "Listen to them! They don't even know what they're saying, they're just repeating something they once heard. You need someone quick, like Busy Shan."

I needed her at my side more than ever, and she needed me. Unable to sit still, I started to pace.

"Her pronunciation is good, her grammar, too," the Chairman told Secretary Sun. "But the way she still walks, it's like she's hauling a bale of hay on her back!"

I halted. "I'm not a donkey!" I said. "*Qu ni de.*"

The rudest words that passed between the men in my village, that I'd never before dared utter.

The Chairman shook his head. "And *what* she says. How do we stop that?"

"I'd need to stop listening to you," I said, then wished I could take it back.

He snorted with laughter. Even he couldn't deny that he often uttered those very words himself.

"A visit from my parents isn't for me. It's for you. It's for the revolution," I said. "Servant Ping, Servant Ting don't have any reason to see their families. They don't have my duties."

"They did."

I couldn't move, I couldn't breathe. No one spoke. When I grazed my knuckles against the Chairman's, he withdrew from my touch, receding, flattening, once again becoming the giant portrait in the plaza. I felt tiny and hollow. I shouldn't have argued with him, asked to see my parents, and made him think I was stupid and backward, a waste of his time.

"Let's go," Secretary Sun said to me.

I walked away, trying to collect myself. Without a word, the Chairman lunged to his feet and shoved me into the deep end.

As soon as I hit the water, I forgot how to swim. Thrashing, I inhaled water. I coughed and coughed, sinking to the bottom. Nose stinging, eyes burning, I swam to the side. I hoisted myself out, draped over the concrete, half in, half out of the pool.

The Chairman stood over me. Secretary Sun took a few steps toward me, but stopped short of reaching in.

"You wanted a life preserver?" the Chairman asked. A few years ago, he had invited Khrushchev, the Soviet premier, to this very pool. He'd told me that Khrushchev, who didn't know how to swim, had bobbed around in a life ring while the bodyguards waded in, standing within arm's reach. After Stalin died, his successor, Khrushchev, had denounced him—the kind of betrayal I understood later that the Chairman feared at the hands of the President.

"You have to be prepared," the Chairman said to me. "You rescued yourself. Not your father. Not your mother. You."

I PRESSED MY MOUTH TO THE CHAIRMAN'S EAR. "WHY DON'T you take a rest? With her?"

We looked across the dance pavilion to a girl, a quiet one. All day, he'd been in a surly mood. But now he grinned and a pit yawned inside of me.

"Why not?" he asked.

Although I didn't want him with other girls, if it was only in the bedroom off the dance pavilion and not in his quarters, not where we slept, I could stand it—I could learn to stand it. He led her straight to the pavilion's bedroom. I stared at the doorway, feeling squashed flat, overwhelmed at the thought of his mouth all over her, their bodies moving together. For the first time, Secretary Sun wasn't at the party, away on an errand for the Chairman, and I felt like a turtle that had lost its shell. A song or two or a dozen had played when I sensed the others watching me.

"Tired?" Midnight Chang had come up from behind, Busy Shan close on her heels.

"The night's just started," I said breezily.

Could Busy Shan tell I was faking my ease? I looked from her to Midnight Chang. Their friendship felt like a betrayal.

I wasn't sure how much time had gone by since the Chairman disappeared with the other girl. A half hour? He emerged from his bedroom, followed by the girl, who was knotting her hair back into a ponytail, the faintest smile at her lips—pleasure in what had happened, or in being chosen. Inside me, something flipped over and crashed into shards.

As a cadre elbowed his way over to them, Midnight Chang darted in their direction.

"What did she promise you?" I asked Busy Shan. I felt like I was breathing through a rag. "She'll turn on you the first chance she can."

"She never pretended she wouldn't," she said.

I could have apologized; maybe then she would have listened. "There are plots everywhere at the Lake Palaces," I said. "The Madame has her fingers in everything. In everyone, including Midnight Chang."

She said nothing. She probably knew more about it, but she'd never tell me. "You don't want to get caught up in that," I said.

She folded her arms across her chest. "I've eaten more salt than you've eaten rice."

Teacher Fan took the Chairman aside while Midnight Chang lingered nearby.

Busy Shan nodded toward our teacher. "She's the one who plots most of all."

"You knew she was a matchmaker?"

She laughed meanly—the kind of laugh she used to reserve for when we talked about Midnight Chang. "That's the least of it."

I don't know what Teacher Fan said to the Chairman, but he headed straight toward me, not stopping when Midnight Chang called out after him.

Busy Shan's smile faltered as he squeezed my shoulder. He didn't look at her. As we exited the dance pavilion, he clasped my hand. It took everything in me not to pull away and wipe my fingers on my skirt. Where had his hands been?

We entered the gardens, where the moonless sky was clear and the stars bright in the deep black. The cool air felt like relief, like possibility.

"The tall girl?" he asked. "What does she go by?"

"Midnight Chang."

"She never stops talking." Gravel crunched under our feet.

He didn't recognize how alike the two of them were, both accustomed to dominating the conversation and the people around them. "She has a lot to learn," I said.

"So do you." Scowling, the Chairman hurried ahead with a speed I didn't know he possessed. How quickly he could turn! Scrambling to catch up, I reached him as he flung open the door to his bedchambers, its hinges squeaking. Servant Ping, waiting in the duty area, jumped to her feet in alarm, and gave me a look of such pity that I wanted to cling to her.

He didn't stay angry for long. As he changed into his robe, he asked if I was hungry.

I nodded though I felt like I might throw up.

"Should we get noodles? Or dumplings?" he asked.

I nodded again, unable to speak.

"Which one?" he asked. "Or should we try something new?"

"Whatever you please," I said.

"Some men—most men—have a type," the Chairman said as he lit a cigarette from the pack on his desk. "They marry their mothers or keep chasing after the younger version of their wives." He took a puff. "I never understood it. If you have to end things, there's so much fighting, only to wind up with more of the same? I say that old dishes can have a new taste, the longer you go in between trying them."

He was talking about the girl he'd slept with; it was probably a test, to see if I'd get jealous. I stroked his arm. "Depends on how hungry you are."

LATER THAT WEEK, TEACHER Fan presented me with an outfit for National Day: a pair of dark blue slacks, a checkered jacket, a white button-down shirt, and sturdy black leather shoes. "These should fit." She placed everything into a cloth bag. "Tell me if they don't."

I shouldered the bag, wanting desperately to ask her about Midnight Chang's schemes. "Is it enough?"

"Is it enough?" she asked.

"Is it enough of a disguise? Won't I get recognized from the dance parties?" I asked.

"You girls are interchangeable to the cadre," she said crisply. "Always another coming or going."

I fingered the straps. She touched the ends of my braids, and then moved her finger up to my ears. "We'll bob it here and get you a pair of glasses."

"But—"

"You've only just met the cadre, but I know them. What they see and what they don't.

"Most of the officials from the dance parties won't be at the reception," she said. "The President hasn't met you, won't have met you."

"Hasn't there been talk, though?" I asked.

"Of course everyone knows the Chairman's shared his bed with you," Teacher Fan said. "But very few are aware of these lessons, about the time we've spent on you."

"Why bother with someone like me?" I said. "Why not Midnight Chang? She wouldn't have as far to go in her training."

"She wouldn't," Teacher Fan agreed.

It felt like she'd slapped me. It was the truth, though.

"But the Chairman's interest isn't in girls born ahead, girls who would have their pick wherever they lived. And neither is mine," she said.

"A girl like Midnight Chang would find her way to cadre even without you," I said.

She eyed me, but didn't disagree.

Eventually, I'd understand she played matchmaker not only to please the Chairman, not only to hold on to her position at the Lake Palaces, but also as a matter of pride. She could raise a flower from mud, turn the lowest to the highest. A girl from the countryside could keep company with the highest officials in the land. In a year, a girl like me would see more than generations of my family ever could.

BACK IN HIS QUARTERS, I found the Chairman playing his records at full volume, the booming drums and blaring horns rattling the windows. He paced his bedchambers, ignoring me as I put away the outfit. I made myself as small as I could until his mood passed; I didn't want him shoving me again. The Chairman ground out his cigarette and lit another. Later, I would think of him as a wooden top, spinning out of control, twirling fastest before it wobbles and falls.

Something lingered in the air—his wife's jasmine scent? There were two teacups on his desk, and I wondered if she'd been here.

When Secretary Sun arrived for our lesson, I could tell from his taut expression that he sensed the Chairman's ill temper, and we hustled out. The library was a short walk away, in a courtyard that adjoined the Chairman's quarters. With its cabinets brimming with leather-bound hardbacks and ancient, fragile scrolls, it was my haven at the Lake Palaces. Usually, I sank into my lessons, forgetting that my future and my family's rested on me.

Today, though, the windowless library felt airless and still, the scent of leather and yellowing pages pressing in on me.

"Let's visit Peking University," I said. If I was to fool the President, I'd need to venture into the capital for a closer look. On National Day, I was supposed to borrow Secretary Sun's life for my own, a university student, born into a family of leftist professors.

"No time to make the arrangements," Secretary Sun said. "No point. You didn't need to visit rebels to play one in the troupe, did you?"

"We're not cramming for the imperial exam," I said. If I had to read another paragraph, if Secretary Sun quizzed me again about a long-dead court official, I'd hurl the book. Rip out the pages, set the whole library on fire. "Don't you think he might ask me about school? About where I'm from?"

"It's not practical. You might be seen," Secretary Sun said.

"No one knows who I am."

"Let's keep it that way."

I hadn't left the Lake Palaces in weeks, and even a trip to the concrete block of the troupe's dormitory would have been an escape. "These books aren't enough. I should see it, I need to see it."

"It won't matter what you see if you can't carry on a conversation," he said. "We have to finish going over what the President might bring up."

"We can do that in the car," I said. "We don't even have to get out." I was shocked when he nodded.

RUNNING MY HANDS OVER the sedan's soft black leather seats, I marveled at the tiny stitches. I couldn't believe that Secretary Sun had relented; maybe the walls of the Lake Palaces closed in on him, too.

The sedan skirted the edge of the former imperial city that was synonymous with our country. The Lake Palaces had become the new Forbidden City, with its power, secrecy, and isolation from the world unchanged.

We turned into a neighborhood, passing a granny who paused inspecting a bamboo cage of crickets hung from a tree and turned to stare at our car. A group of five men squatted by the side of the road, sipping from mugs as they watched us go by.

I tried to absorb everything a student who'd grown up in the capital might have seen. "Everyone's looking at us," I said.

"It can be overwhelming," Secretary Sun said. "The first time I went out in an official car, it scared me, to realize how much was expected of me. All those people depending on me."

He tapped on his window. "Peking University."

The university's crimson gate had three portals, edged with an ornate design of interlocking squares. No locks, no doors, but the elegant brick buildings, the smooth walkways, the order and symmetry were as intimidating as any guard dog.

Secretary Sun told the driver to stop in front of another university gate and pointed at a young woman. She cut through the world with the confidence of someone who never stepped aside. "Look at the way she carries herself," he said. Straight-backed, she held a stack of books under one arm and slung a satchel across her chest. She glided to a stop beside two other students on the sidewalk. They studied the sedan with evident curiosity, but then returned to their conversation. It wasn't unusual for an official vehicle to drop by the university, Secretary Sun said, unlike in other parts of the capital where pedestrians might follow a car like this one for blocks.

He rolled down the window, wide enough for us to listen in, but not for the students to see us through the tinted glass. The breeze crept in, ruffling a cowlick on the back of his head. His hair was unruly in a way that he wasn't, and I fought the urge to smooth it down. I'd never been in such close quarters with him.

"Listen to how they talk," he said.

They spoke quickly, swallowing the hard sounds in their words, which gave their conversation a forceful air. Their tongues rolling as if their mouths were full of rocks, the accent of the capital, adding an "aaar" at the end of their words, a sound that reminded me of gargling.

"You finished the assignment already?" asked the boy in glasses.

"Last week," the girl said.

"Gou pi!" he replied. Dog fart—nonsense. The same kind of crude talk that the Chairman claimed I should wipe from my vocabulary.

"The professor didn't assign it until last Thursday," he added.

"I finished it that night," she said.

"Pai ma pi," he said. Suck-up.

"You're the suck-up," the other boy said.

"Ni pian wo," the boy with glasses said. Liar!

Laughing, they parted ways.

"Gou pi," I said, imitating them. *"Gou pi. Gou pi!"*

"Who knew that university students these days sounded like factory workers after they'd guzzled a jug of home brew?" Secretary Sun asked.

I tried out the phrase. "Should I talk faster?" I asked, jamming the words together.

Was it pity, or laughter at the corners of his mouth? "It's not just the sound of your accent, or even what you say," he said. "It's about their conviction that everything they have to say matters, has always mattered. Even their jokes demand your full attention. If you learn that, then you could fill your conversation with curses, and you'd still convince the President you were one of these students."

"Ni pian wo," I said, bold as the student the teacher always calls upon first.

When he nodded, I flickered with hope.

"Everything you've been studying, it's a lot. I don't want you to leave today thinking you have to copy all you see and hear," Secretary Sun said. "Have you been up late studying?"

I looked away.

"You may think, 'I'll read just another page, just another chapter,' " he said. "Do you know the story about the scholar who tied his long hair to a roof beam to keep from dozing off? Or the one who jabbed himself with an awl to stay awake?"

I nodded. Folktales.

"But how much do you think they remembered the next day? How much do you remember?" he asked.

I picked at a hangnail. "I remember everything," I said sullenly.

"What the students are saying doesn't really matter," he said. "Say what the President expects a student to say. If you can play along with that, he'll never question you."

"Who cares what they say?" I said. "They don't know how soft everything is for them."

I'd aimed the remark at Secretary Sun as much as the students.

"Don't count them out," he said.

"So you've said. They'll attack me with a pencil?" I asked. "Get it really sharp?"

Instead of answering, he directed the driver toward his neighborhood. A man skidded to a stop in front of us, ringing his bell, the bald tires of his bicycle squealing. The driver honked at him and we continued.

Beijing seemed flat and sprawling. As we drove down a street lined with shops, I noticed a sign for an herbalist. My flow still hadn't arrived, and my fear that I was pregnant—or could get pregnant—never left me.

I asked if we could stop by, but Secretary Sun told me that we didn't have time.

"Could we go on the way back?" I said.

"Why?"

When I'd asked about an herb garden at the Lake Palaces, he'd brushed off my concerns. If I explained, maybe he'd understand the urgency, but it still humiliated me to bring up such matters. I looked out the window. "I need something . . . for my flow. To bring it on."

His eyes met mine in the reflection. "It's taken care of already."

"Taken care of? How?" I asked. Sprinkled in my food, steeped in my tea? Impossible. The Chairman ate everything I did.

"You don't need to worry," he said. "None of you girls need to worry."

He was telling me not to concern myself with the one thing that I might control. "How did it get taken care of?" I asked.

He said nothing. Yet another secret of the Lake Palaces, yet another decision taken out of my hands. No more, no longer. I thumped my fist against the driver's headrest. "Stop!"

The driver hit the brakes and turned around. "Crazy," he spat. "Get ahold of her," he told Secretary Sun.

Trapped. As if at the bottom of a frozen pond, beneath a layer of dark, rippled ice. I panicked, not just from this moment, but from the months spent under minute examination, my every moment tracked and judged. After jerking the locked door handle, I pounded on the window with my fists until they went numb. The people outside couldn't hear me screaming. I could burn to death in the sedan and they would know nothing.

Secretary Sun clamped his hands over mine and pulled me away from the window. The driver started up the car again and we passed across the intersection, waved through by an officer blowing on his whistle.

I edged as close as I could to the door, aching to get away from Secretary Sun, from everyone. Ever since I'd begun my training, I hadn't had a moment alone. Even in my crowded life in the village, I could escape into the fields or down by the river.

The silence between us lengthened until we entered a broad boulevard lined with poplars and Secretary Sun cracked the window on his side. "Do you smell it? The air's fresher where I grew up than in other parts of the capital."

I sniffed. Dust and gasoline. Then deeper—the same.

"It's not any different," I said. Bicycles whirred by. I could tell he wanted me to share his excitement about his neighborhood, reminders of a life, however inconsequential, before he came to the Lake Palaces. My teachers would have me deny my family, Ba and Ma and my sisters whom I missed with a sudden ferocity. First Daughter, raising the blanket to make room for me. Second Daughter's cupped hand, filled with daisies. Ba, dropping tender fish cheeks into my bowl. Ma, pressing a sweater on me.

I belonged to no one here.

We turned down a smaller street, wide enough only for a single car, in a neighborhood of walled courtyard homes that gave off an air of permanence and privilege. Secretary Sun told the driver to park across the street from a house with a red door, flanked by two stone lions. Tiled eaves topped the high gray-brick walls.

Three generations of his neighbors, the Pangs, lived there, he said. The door opened and a withered man came out and lit a pipe, smoke curling around his face. He glanced at the car, but didn't linger. Like the university students, the residents of this neighborhood might be used to visits from government officials.

"That's Grandfather Pang!" Secretary Sun said. "He may not look it now, but he was quick with his reed cane." He pressed a hand against the glass, fingers spread, Grandfather Pang's head captured between his thumb and forefinger. Secretary Sun had claimed he left behind his family and friends to serve the people, but when he saw them, he wavered.

A woman, slender and bright as a candle, stepped out of the red door after him. She turned, calling to someone inside, a toddler who followed her for a few steps before reaching for a fallen leaf. He might have been three years old, his hair mussed from a nap. Secretary Sun placed both hands against the glass, as if willing himself to pass through it.

"Who's that?" I wondered if she could have been special to him, once or still. Even if he didn't visit her, he might have someone else he spoke with in low tones, someone whose curves he stroked, someone whose head tucked into his chest.

"Is that Grandfather Pang's wife?" I asked nastily. "His mistress?"

He dropped his hands from the window. "The President will probably ask what you're studying," he said stiffly.

My taunt had hit its mark, but I felt bruised all over, as if my hurt had spilled like ink across my skin.

"What else will he ask me? And what about him? What's the gossip about him?" I'd been preparing to meet him and yet he remained a mystery. The Chairman had said he didn't want me knowing too much about the President. The details could trip me up: what I might forget, what I was supposed to know, and what I couldn't as a college student.

Though the President had been born a peasant, he'd forgotten where he'd come from, his head turned by intellectuals, by capitalists in disguise. Like the other enemies I'd been warned against— the counter-revolutionaries, the running dogs, paper tigers, cow monsters, and snake demons—the President seemed limitless and menacing and yet also not quite human, either, easy to hate and easy to fear. No different, really, than the fox-spirits and demons that my mother had warned me about when I was a child.

"You don't have any gossip?" I asked.

Secretary Sun looked at the driver, and then at me, as if to tell me, *Not now.*

Back at the Lake Palaces, on our walk to the Chairman's quarters, Secretary Sun murmured, "The President has spies everywhere. Don't ask too many questions about him. A bodyguard was shipped off to the border after I noticed him silently mouthing the Chairman's words to himself, over and over."

"To memorize them?"

Secretary Sun nodded.

"Like memorizing the Little Red Book?" I asked.

"Or maybe to tell someone," Secretary Sun said. "The Chairman didn't trust him after that."

Shaken, I wondered what the driver, what anyone else at the Lake Palaces, might have overheard.

THOUGH THE MUSIC HAD stopped in the Chairman's quarters, the air was still charged. Sitting at his desk, he asked what I'd seen that afternoon. He must have been notified after we'd left the Lake Palaces. "Where did you get out?" he asked.

"We stayed in the car." I slipped off my shoes.

He got up so quickly he swayed on his feet, almost losing his balance. He steadied himself on his desk. "Then you didn't see a thing!"

"Secretary Sun said we couldn't."

His face darkened. Until now, he hadn't concerned himself with the finer details of my training, and this oversight irked him. Anything could have set him off, though, even if I'd answered differently.

"We overheard some students," I added.

"What did you make of them?" he asked.

"*Xiao cong ming,*" I said. Clever, but only in the most trivial matters.

He touched my arm. "You weren't intimidated. You weren't blinded."

I remembered what Secretary Sun had said: Silly as the students seemed to me, the highest leaders counted on their support. With the Chairman in such a mood, wouldn't he want that reminder?

"They're loyal to you, though," I said. But not to the President, if our plan succeeded.

At the knock at the door, the Chairman barked, "Come in."

Busy Shan entered, squirming in her uniform and pushing a cart with a fresh pot of tea and snacks.

Flustered, I sat down on the edge of the bed. Her eyes were swollen, as though she'd been crying.

I reached for the tea she poured. As I figured out what I'd say to her, she looked at me with such hatred that I inhaled tea, coughing. I set down my cup with a clatter, and when I looked up, she was gone.

The Chairman studied me. "Something caught in your throat?"

"She . . . we used to share a bunk."

"You thought you'd have an ally, didn't you?" The Chairman leaned both arms on his desk, which wobbled on its wheels. "Someone you could talk to about me?"

Someone I'd worried about and wanted to protect, but he'd never understand. I stared at my feet, knobby with calluses.

"It's those closest to you who can turn on you the quickest," he said.

"Isn't she wanted elsewhere?" I looked up at the Chairman.

"Not until you've learned you should never drop your guard," he said. "You may think you know everything, but don't let that be your downfall."

He drained his cup. After I served him more tea, he tapped three fingers on the table.

I'd already poured it to the brim. "More?"

He tapped again, and I set down the teapot and copied him in return.

"It's how to say thank you without saying anything at all," he said. "It comes from the Qianlong Emperor, who wanted to see how the common people lived."

"What happened?" I asked.

In school, we'd learned about the emperor, one of the country's longest-reigning and longest-living rulers, who'd doubled the expanse of our borders. I'd never heard the story that the Chairman now shared. One day, he told me, the emperor decided to travel the country dressed as the servant of a high official, who was played by his most trusted advisor.

Did this tale inspire the Chairman to disguise me as a student intellectual? Soon I would understand he must have also yearned for the freedom of anonymity. At the moment, I just hoped that if I encouraged his storytelling, it would turn his foul mood. He acted out the scene: At a teahouse, the emperor had served everyone. In the palace, protocol would have demanded that the advisor kowtow, throw himself to his knees, stretch out his arms, and press his forehead against the ground in gratitude. The quick-witted advisor, unable to acknowledge this great honor, mimicked the gesture instead by tapping his three fingers on the table—the middle finger the head and body, the fingers around it the arms.

He tapped his fingers again on the desk and swished the sip of tea around his mouth before swallowing. "If I'd been the advisor, I would have had a little fun. Told the emperor to wait outside—just a minute—before inviting him in for a drink. Or had a word with the local beauty that the emperor had been eying for himself!"

"And the people?" I asked. "What did the emperor learn from them?"

He pressed his lips together, irritated. He didn't have to tell me: The peasants weren't the point of this story. They never were.

"The emperor had to see the country for himself," he said. "He took six tours of the south in all. He couldn't trust the reports from his advisors. Every word was a lie."

He went to his record collection and ran his finger along the spines. "The other night, Midnight Chang told me the troupe misses you," he said, baiting me. "Do you want to go back for a visit?"

"I haven't thought about it." I led him to the bed, where I pushed back the sleeves of his robe and nuzzled the soft flesh in the crook of his arm, salty with sweat, where the skin remained supple and young. There, he was my age. I had to distract him, to make him forget Midnight Chang. My lips danced on his arm, to his shoulder and his neck, where his pulse fluttered. My hair, set loose from its ponytail, trailed over his arm. He moved his hands onto my hips, and tried to flip me over, but if I weren't already pregnant, I might be entering my most fertile time. Even though Secretary Sun had claimed I didn't need to worry, I couldn't let the Chairman empty himself inside me.

Crawling down his body, I pulled down his trunks and then took him into my mouth, his sex soft and slippery. It was the first time I'd tasted him there and the scent was familiar yet fermented. Gagging, I forced myself to go on. He hardened, though not entirely. I rocked back and forth until he grimaced, and the hot, bitter spill of him twitched weakly in my mouth.

I slid off him, but instead of pulling me into his arms, he back-handed me. White lights flashed in my eyes, and my cheeks writhed with wasps.

"Who taught you that?" he asked.

"No one." I blinked, still senseless.

The Chairman pushed me off the bed and I landed in a heap, smacking my forehead and my ribs against the floor.

"There's been no one. No one but you," I said.

He loomed over me, the moon, his face pale and wide. "Whore!"

I huddled on the threadbare rug, which scratched my knees. He'd never been this brutal to me, not in his words, not in his fists.

The Chairman jerked on his swimming trunks and stalked off, slamming the door. He'd never left me alone in his bedchambers, and I didn't know if I should follow him to the pool. I hung my head, ragged inside. When I looked up, I noticed his sleeping pills. He'd never offered any to me, but the pills eased his nerves night after night. Weighing the bottle in my hand, I listened to the pills rattle and clink against the glass. I popped the lid and sprang back at the poisonous stink.

Was he going to exile me, force me into a labor camp, where I'd carry rocks on my back until I crippled? Where I'd get trapped in a cell, dank as a weasel's den? Everything felt murky and muddy. Swallowing a handful of pills, I prayed for sleep, silence, or whatever else might overtake me.

*T*HE CHAIRMAN PULLED BACK THE DRAPES, LETTING IN WATERY morning sunshine. I watched with sticky eyes, dazed, my tongue thick in my mouth. He or someone else had put me in bed and stripped me down to my underwear. I pulled on my robe and came up beside him.

"Falling out of bed like that," he said affectionately.

I couldn't hide my bewilderment. He'd pushed me, hadn't he?

"You like to tumble about, but you have to take care," he said.

When I opened my mouth, something passed across his face. He wouldn't stay playful, the look told me, and I swallowed whatever I might have questioned, so deeply I couldn't see what I saw, couldn't hear what I heard.

I know it sounds like I'm making excuses. I don't expect you to understand. I hardly understand it myself.

"You have been studying too many things. Too many books are harmful, leading you this way and that. You don't know what to follow," he said. I could smell the sharp scent of the pool. He must have gone there while I'd slept.

"I'm canceling your lessons," he said. "From now on, I'll teach you." As that sank in, he told me Dr. Li would examine me.

Because I'd taken the pills? He seemed in no mood to elaborate, taking a seat at his desk to page through the newspaper. I lingered by the window, gazing at a maple tree, its delicate leaves a deep red, edged in gold. They hadn't started falling yet, but soon would.

The doctor arrived not long after. "It's the first time I've examined you?" Dr. Li asked, more of a question to himself than to me.

I nodded.

He was a thin and nervous man with an oversized head like a tomcat's. After sliding on rubber gloves, he told me to undress below my waist, cover myself with the sheet, and lie down on the bed.

When I didn't move, he repeated himself and the Chairman nodded at me. I had no choice. After the doctor turned his back to give me privacy, I slowly did as he requested.

Staring up at the carved wooden panels on the ceiling, I pressed my thighs together. He told me to bend my knees, and to rest my feet at the edge of the bed. He tented the sheet over my legs. He folded it back and before I could protest, he inserted something cold and hard inside me. It began to turn. I yelped and then went quiet as black speckles swam before me. I wasn't here, I wasn't here, I wasn't anywhere.

"If I'd told you what I was about to do, you'd clench up." The doctor's voice sounded far away. "This won't take long."

He snapped off his gloves, folding them inside out, and stuffed them into his bag. I would never forget the powdery smell of the rubber, of disinterest and detachment.

"She doesn't appear to be pregnant," he told the Chairman.

He turned his back on me again and told me I could get dressed. I awkwardly pulled on my underwear and smoothed my skirt, not sure where—if—I should sit or remain standing by the bed.

The Chairman passed his hand across his face. "I'm a eunuch."

Eunuch? Much later, I'd understand what he meant, but at that moment, I was still groggy from the pills, and thought he was saying that he felt like less of a man.

"You're not," Dr. Li said. "Your function is normal, it's just that . . ."

"Has she been with anyone else?" the Chairman asked.

Could he uncover such information through an examination? The Chairman would be angry at the doctor for not having a ready answer, even if finding out wasn't possible.

"No, there's been no one else," the doctor said.

I was surprised—relieved—that the Chairman didn't argue. Maybe he trusted the doctor more than I realized. Then his shoulders jerked. Was he weeping . . . or had the shaking returned and spread?

"Chairman?" Dr. Li asked. "How did you sleep?"

The Chairman glared at him. "Go away."

Dr. Li fetched his satchel. He rubbed the brass clasp of his bag, anxious as I was, performing but doubting the rituals of a cure. As he walked off, I followed him. "Can't you give him something?" I whispered, his touch still throbbing between my legs. He could cure the Chairman's sickness with his bag full of pills and medical instruments.

We stepped behind the silk screen by the door. The doctor shook his head. "This isn't a cold or stomachache. It's unpredictable—it could be a few days, or a few weeks. Has he been asking if he looks sick?"

"*Looks* sick?" My head was starting to clear.

"Did he . . . rehearse?" he asked. "Cough one way, then another? Make his voice raspier?"

The questions baffled me. What was he talking about?

The doctor must have sensed my doubt. "I have served him for more than a decade," he said loftily.

"Then cure him!" I said.

He waved his hand dismissively. "You don't know anything."

"You can go now," the Chairman said.

We stepped out from behind the screen. "Who do you mean?" the doctor asked.

"Don't be stupid," the Chairman snapped, his face reddening with a frightening exertion. He thumped his fists on his desk.

"I—" Dr. Li said.

"I told you what to do," the Chairman said. "You're still here, doing nothing." He climbed into bed.

"Summon me at once if there's any fever," the doctor told me softly.

After he left, I called out to the Chairman. He didn't reply. I wasn't sure how to soothe him—not with my touch; I might disgust him. Not with my words; he didn't seem to have any patience for conversation.

Lifting the stylus off the record player, I held the delicate arm between my thumb and forefinger, fearful I might snap it off as I would a cricket's leg. After placing it gently at the edge, I pressed a silver button—the most worn one on the console—and music played. The Chairman didn't move. The warped record rose and fell as it spun, the stylus moving toward the center, an orange circle bright as the sun.

The next song was brassy and bright, with a sinuous melody, the plucked strings and playful drums calling us to dance. I picked up the record sleeve, the cover featuring a black-and-white photo of musicians in a dark club. The stiff paper smelled musty, its edges rounded and frayed white. Small round tables topped with candles ran along the border, with shadows indicating the audience. If we were seated at one of the tables, the Chairman would listen, bobbing his head. He'd take my hand; our heads would come together and his whisper—one I couldn't make out over the music—would tickle my ear. We would be in Paris.

The record crackled, startling me. The Chairman remained sprawled on his back, his eyes open and unblinking, dull and black as buttons. The vision of us in the club together was more vivid than the lumpy form in bed. That was how I wanted to think of the Chairman, not like this, never like this.

The air was so stale, thick with unwashed bodies and the tang of leftover food, that I wanted to throw open every window. "Can you play it again?" he asked. I moved the stylus to the outer edge and when it drew to the end again, I reset it.

I touched the bright sleeves of his collection—the spine of an enormous beast—and pulled records out at random, with covers that peeked into different worlds: a dark-skinned singer in a shiny blue jacket and tight pants, his knees bent. A castle in the mist, men and women in pointed green hats and short leather overalls. A black lace fan, hiding most of a lady's face, except for her dark eyes. I balanced records on my fingertips, staring into the glossy black, into the pattern of scratches, arching like rainbows.

Like the Moon Cake Ladies, I had to send my messages to him in secret. They, through the cakes; me, through the songs: Rise up and fight. Where did he drift: To his life unled in Europe? To his time at Yan'an? His greatest victories turned to regret. His comrades now traitors—the President and his allies. If he didn't like the music, I noticed, he turned on his side away from me. Otherwise, he remained on his back, a vast city whose walls I circled, trying to find a way in.

I flipped the record between sides, with a touch so light that the pause in music seemed shorter than a sigh. Such deftness came naturally, the fine gesture returning to me as a memory of flipping corn cakes to keep them from burning, a movement quick yet delicate.

That is how we got through the morning.

A SHEAF OF PAPERS rustled under the door. Gathering the pile of incoming mail, I brought it to his desk. Three days had gone by since his melancholy began, but it felt like a month.

Aside from brief daily visits from his doctor, the Chairman refused to see anyone but me. Not Teacher Fan, Secretary Sun, or his wife, who sent gifts, herbal brews he didn't drink and volumes of poetry he didn't read.

I reviewed what I could in case I found anything that needed his immediate attention: the boxes of reports on cultural, agricultural, and economic policies, with columns of numbers and indecipherable terms. Briefs on the expansion of U.S. troops in Vietnam, and the tensions over India's border. I emptied myself into this task and the others. If I'd had time to consider my responsibilities, terror would have overcome me. Ill, the Chairman consumed me, maybe even more than when he was well. He'd been sleeping ten, twelve hours at a time. He spoke little; I spoke less. He didn't tell me if he suspected plots against him—if his weeks of insomnia and his tremors had drowned him at last. He refused to eat, and no matter how much I begged him, his chapped lips pressed tight against the spoon when I tried to feed him.

While playing records for hours at a time, I cradled him, my arm going numb beneath him. I stroked his cheek with the kind of tenderness, pity, and caution that I might have for the smallest chick in a litter, who wouldn't survive the night, who might die in my hands if I squeezed too hard. Each night I made the bed over him, the billowing sheet a shadow winging from an enormous bird that would carry him wherever he wished. Then I would slip in beside him, willing him to fall asleep, for his breathing to ease and slow.

Much later I'd understand he'd trusted me enough to show his throat to me. Beyond my cleverness, beyond my stories and our couplings—or maybe at the heart of them—he found a harbor in me.

I sorted through the mail. On Dr. Li's latest visit, something in his manner—his agitation, his desperation—made me understand how much the Chairman's sickness worried him. If only I had my mother and her cures. I tried to picture him vivid once again, wisecracking about the movies, shuffling tiles at mahjong, or dancing in the pavilion. I missed being in the pool with him, where he was graceful, determined, and strong.

The stack of mail slipping out of my hands jolted me from my daydream. Retrieving it, I found a large stiff square, light and flexible, wrapped in brown paper, addressed to me, but with no indication of the sender. I ran my fingers along the edges and inside I found a record with foreigners on the cover, in jackets and bow ties, their hair slicked back, trumpets tilted high up, their shadows in sharp relief against the wall. After placing the record on the turntable, I set the volume low. I'd listened to the first song with Secretary Sun; though the music had stirred me, he'd joked he couldn't stand it.

He'd remembered.

Closing my eyes, I wrapped my arms around myself and swayed to the music. Cut off from everything I knew, I hadn't realized I'd been disappearing, too. With each beat, my outline filled in. When the Chairman sat up, I hurried over to him. He reached his hand toward my face. He stopped before he touched me. Until now, I couldn't grasp his mortality. I couldn't believe it until he'd fallen under this spell of sadness.

"I've ruined you, Mei," he said, his face old and awful. "How old are you?"

"Sixteen." He had never asked until now.

When I rubbed his hand, his bones shifted like a bundle of twigs. I felt like I was trespassing. Despite our weeks together, he was a stranger to me.

He gripped my thumb. "I'm sorry," he said, his voice hoarse. He seemed like a broken kite, sadder for having soared.

It was the only time he ever apologized to me.

ONE MORNING, A WEEK and a half after he'd taken to his bed, no mail arrived. None came the next day or the next, either, nothing from the President or the Premier, and not even the Defense Minister or the Madame, the Chairman's most faithful correspondents. It wasn't long before National Day. I said nothing to him, but I startled at every creak and footstep, hoping for something. Gossip could be spreading at the Lake Palaces: A kitchen worker could have let slip the menu of sickbed foods. A clerk could have noticed that the Chairman had stopped replying to correspondence. Maybe a few high-level officials suspected what was happening and gathered behind the President, who must soon be arriving in the capital. I might never meet him. Because I'd fallen so far behind in my studies, I'd all but given up trying to deceive him. Every time I finished a paragraph, I forgot how it began, my mind a fishing net that didn't catch much of anything.

I churned with shame when I thought about how I'd dared to believe I could become a model revolutionary. All my dreams seemed foolish now: a tour across the country; teenagers imitating me, mothers praying for daughters like me, fathers urging their sons to find a wife like me. I'd even fantasized about asking for improvements: paved roads and factories, electricity in each home, and swimming pools for factory workers.

During the summer, the Chairman had stopped holding dance parties. I wondered if he'd sunk then, as now, into this sadness. If he didn't recover in time, he would miss this year's festivities. I didn't dare admit what I feared most: If he went missing from National Day, wouldn't it sow doubts about whether he could still lead?

In the stacks of old newspapers, I found photos of the President grinning at a commune, another of him posed with Ho Chi Minh. The Chairman's photo appeared more often, but always in the same official portraits. Seeing the President out and about made him seem more vital compared to the Chairman.

According to Ma, in the time before the Chairman, villagers worshipped at the temple for help. The gods never replied. Bandits stole our chickens, officials beat villagers who couldn't pay their taxes, and landlords stripped the strongest men naked, shot them, and lit them on fire. An uncle, beaten to death. A cousin, raped by enemy deserters.

If the President let the capitalists overrun us, that devastation would descend upon us again.

CHAPTER 16

THE NEXT DAY, I SLID BEHIND THE CURTAINS, HEAVY AGAINST my back, and pressed my hand against the cobwebbed window, wanting to pass into the autumn. In the gardens, workers raked the gravel paths, crossed by no footsteps. No one but me admired the broad leaves of the jade-ribbon plant and the bright pink camellia. In late afternoon, the air felt dusty and still, a burlap sack yanked over my head. I rolled Ma's bead around in my hand, its raised ridges pressed into my palm.

At the Lake Palaces, we never heard the clamor of the capital, the chatter and the shouts, the squeak and hiss and rumble. In the moments after the music ended and before the sleeping pills took effect, in his dark and musty bedchambers, the Chairman would have found the sound of his own breath suffocating. The higher he ascended, the farther he must have found himself from the everyday, from the sighs and the murmurs of people living on top of one another.

Emerging from the curtains, I noticed the door at the far end of the Chairman's quarters. It led to the dining room and to the Madame's wing. If he'd had these spells for years, maybe she could talk me through a cure?

In the dining room, the air was stuffier, and the chairs were stacked off to the side of the big round table, a sign they weren't often in use. The room was twice as big as the dance studio, with a brown carpet that dampened my footsteps. It smelled stale in here, though with no trace of past meals. Behind the door to the Madame's room, I could hear music playing softly. I slowly twisted the knob, which seemed unlocked, but I stopped myself. I shouldn't go in un-announced; maybe I shouldn't go in at all.

There was a knock—not at the Chairman's door, but from the main entrance to the Madame's quarters. Somewhere in the distance, the door creaked open to a flurry of greetings. There were footsteps, the music turned off, and the muffled conversation became distinct: the Madame and Teacher Fan. I pressed my ear against the door, straining to listen.

"He's hardly eating," the Madame was saying.

She must have a spy in the kitchen, or maybe Busy Shan reported to her in secret. I wondered if I should hide what he left in his bowl, toss it out the window or flush it down the toilet so that he might seem to have a heartier appetite. She ordered her attendant to fetch broth and hot washcloths so they could freshen up.

"His appetite always returns, twice what it was before," Teacher Fan said.

"I don't like it," the Madame said. "Not when the only one watching over him is that fox-spirit."

Those demons lured travelers off the road, the men who feasted and frolicked with a beautiful young woman, only to wake up in a cemetery the next morning.

"She'll be gone soon enough," Teacher Fan said. She'd said the same to me about Midnight Chang. True, all of it, but her words flayed me.

An attendant called out a greeting and what sounded like a cart rumbled in, followed by the clink of bowls as she served them.

"It tastes like a hundred chickens were boiled down for this cup," Teacher Fan said. They must be sipping broth.

"I drink this every day," the Madame said. "I can have it sent to you, too."

I heard a thump, as though she'd set down her bowl onto the table. "I sent it to him, but it went back untouched! I don't trust that girl. Maybe she kept it from him."

He'd taken a whiff of the broth and pushed it away, but I couldn't defend myself from her and from everyone else she might have been poisoning against me at the Lake Palaces."

She sighed. "I shouldn't have told him to keep an eye on her."

On me?

"I pointed out how well she and Secretary Sun served together," the Madame added.

"I doubt that was it," Teacher Fan said. "There's never one thing that causes these moods."

I realized then his wife had hinted that I was carrying on with Secretary Sun. Maybe he'd been suspicious, maybe he'd had us watched for days. There was nothing to see between me and Secretary Sun; there would never be anything to see, a thought that made me go oddly hollow.

"She's not like those recruits who fall for any man who pays the least attention," Teacher Fan said. "Goodness knows Secretary Sun has had many opportunities! He's never taken up a single one."

"As far as you know," the Madame said.

"I know," Teacher Fan said testily.

Anywhere but the Lake Palaces, girls might have chased after Secretary Sun, drawn to his sinewy build and his straight-backed certainty. But would I? It felt dangerous to consider the question too closely.

"What's Secretary Sun been teaching her anyway?" the Madame asked.

"This and that," Teacher Fan said. "Lessons from books."

"Books?" the Madame asked. "Books?" She sounded satisfied; she probably didn't think such lessons much of a threat.

Neither of them spoke for a long moment, until Teacher Fan said, "He'll pull through. He always does."

"To disappear now, though," the Madame said. "Right before National Day." Three days from now. "There will be talk, if there isn't already. Maybe it's better if the President thinks the Chairman is holed up with a silly whore. Otherwise, he might guess what's come over the Chairman again. The doctor should force his way in . . . How could he leave it up to her?"

"He doesn't want visitors. Don't worry! She's not as brainless as some," Teacher Fan said.

A backhanded compliment, but one I clutched onto all the same. I missed her firm hand at my back, the order and discipline of our lessons, how everything shrank down to the eight-count.

"And at least she doesn't fancy herself a poet," Teacher Fan said. I'd heard how difficult the Madame could be, arguing with the servants, her aides, anyone who had the misfortune of crossing her path. Teacher Fan knew how to handle her, how to steady the nerves of her high-strung friend. "Remember the one who wrote that poem? In honor of the Chairman? *Sheltering oak / Birds nesting in its branches / Squirrels darting up its trunk / Acorns falling to the ground / It is never alone.*"

More laughter.

"How did you even remember?" the Madame asked.

"It is never alone, " Teacher Fan intoned.

They chuckled again. "You never did forget a thing," the Madame said.

My ear ached from being pressed against the door and I stepped back, wondering if I should keep listening. If I risked it, I might hear important gossip.

"Have you been outside today?" Teacher Fan asked. "How about yesterday?"

No, the Madame said.

"Let's go for a walk in the gardens," Teacher Fan said. It sounded like she was pushing her chair back from the table.

"It's too windy," the Madame said.

"Everything feels worse the longer you stay inside."

"I'm tired. Maybe tomorrow," the Madame said. Back and forth they went until at last she agreed. Heels clicked, and what could have been a closet creaked open and closed.

When a door slammed shut, I sank to the floor, realizing how tightly wound I'd been. I should have assumed that Teacher Fan and the Madame met, and yet hearing them together still bothered me.

I knocked. No answer, no movement. I knocked again and called out, "Hello?" I cautiously pushed the door open. Though half the size of the Chairman's, her rooms were spacious, golden with soft and warm lighting. I took a few steps inside, my heart thrumming. If the Madame or the attendants caught me in here, I'd get expelled from the Lake Palaces.

The teapot and empty cups of broth still sat on the table, and the attendant might be back at any moment to clear them. I looked around, wondering if I'd find a photo of the Madame and the Chairman in their younger days. But she had no pictures of people, no photos of her daughter with the Chairman, only a dozen black-and-white framed landscapes that hung on the wall. In the biggest print, a lone cypress perched on a cliff. I stepped deeper into her room. Her desk was bare except for glossy magazines and a report.

I kept glancing at the front door and also listened for the Chairman, for any sound of him stirring awake. Skimming the report, I discovered information about every girl in the troupe: our ages, where we were from, and the political reliability of our families. It detailed when my father had challenged the headman a few years ago: Why dig up the graveyard and change the course of a river, Ba had asked. Even though the river flooded every few years, it made our fields richer. The land where our families had lived for generations was beyond change. The headman triumphed, Ba lost, and the river straightened where it once curved. An icy pebble lodged in my stomach. Would the Madame use the information against him, against us?

I shakily turned to Midnight Chang's entry and learned her father was a drunk who brawled with his neighbors. He wasn't the model factory worker she'd led us to believe. What else had she lied about? I remembered how she'd slapped herself, how she'd gone after Dolly Yu. Maybe he used to beat her.

I flipped to Busy Shan's page. Last month, on her way to a

political-thought meeting, her mother had fallen down a flight of stairs.

ALMOST AS SOON AS I darted back into the dining room, I heard the Madame return, grumbling to her attendant that she had dust in her eyes and that she wanted a bath. There was no sound from Teacher Fan, who must have already left.

Knowing they'd gone outside made me yearn for it, too. If I could feel the sunshine and breeze against my cheek, I might calm down. As I slipped out of the bedchambers, the Chairman slept on.

In the duty area, Busy Shan and Servant Ping giggled, shelling walnuts with a small hammer, bits littering the floor. When I interrupted, Busy Shan stared as though I'd burst out of a coffin. Her mother, her mother. I'd have to find a way to tell her without revealing how I'd come across the information. Or should I tell her at all? There was nothing she could do. I combed my hair with my fingers; I'd been too exhausted to bathe, and my skirt was crumpled and my blouse stained.

"The Chairman told me he's not to be disturbed," I said.

No one followed me as I stumbled out the door. Blinking in the sunlight, I passed through the courtyard and nodded at a bodyguard at the entrance. Through the smoke trees, I glimpsed the vast Central and North Seas, whose grandly named waters today seemed green as an old copper coin. The Chairman's compound was at the heart of the palaces, on the fan-shaped spit of land between these two lakes.

I took a few strides down the cobbled lane until I realized I had nowhere to go. Home? The Chairman had forbidden me to see my family, but if I found my way to one of the gates, couldn't I flee?

I wouldn't have to take care of him any longer, wouldn't have to worry if I could disguise myself as a student intellectual. I wouldn't have a chance to become a model revolutionary, but I'd be free. The Lake Palaces would be glad to be rid of me, the girl who had taken up too much of the Chairman's attentions—the girl the Madame blamed for his sickness.

I might have guessed the Madame's wrath, but Teacher Fan—the way she'd talked made me feel like something pink and hairless, helpless as a newborn mouse.

Her allegiance was not to me.

The wind picked up, swirling dust around my feet, and from the trees above came the furious cheer of birdsong. I wheeled around, taking in my surroundings. The Lake Palaces were even bigger than I supposed, and the spaciousness stunned me anew. The luxury resided not in its imperial treasures but in its emptiness, its walls that shut out the density of the city and the countryside. Everywhere else, all available land had been terraced for fields, every bench crammed with yet another person.

The Chairman had taken me on daily walks on these grounds and sometimes we skirted the southern shoreline, past the towering gate in the vermilion walls, and gazed at Yingtai Island, where the Qianlong Emperor used to have his solitary breakfasts in a pavilion. Or we'd visit the northern part, with its marble bridge that reminded me of a caterpillar. He'd always led the way, and now nothing seemed familiar in the courtyards, covered walkways, and gardens.

Up ahead, I spotted a sentry who was facing another direction. I'd forgotten that they were posted around the Lake Palaces, checking passes, restricting access to most other areas. He'd deny me entry. Doubling back sharply, I almost tripped.

I wasn't ready to return to the Chairman's quarters, though. Stepping into a pine grove, I inhaled the air sticky with their scent and emerged by a pavilion gone rickety with loose boards and missing tiles, spattered with sap and bird shit, and a round bridge missing slats that no one had seemingly tended since Liberation. I tried to imagine Secretary Sun, waiting for me beyond the next bend. I couldn't deny that I wanted to see him, a longing that had no name. The sun, hanging low in the sky, told me that I didn't have much time left. The Chairman would call for me, and when I didn't answer, he would force himself to sit up. When he noticed me gone, he would wail.

As I rounded the corner, I ran into Secretary Sun. We both sprang back.

He looked over my shoulder, as if checking whether anyone had followed me. "What happened? Does the Chairman need Dr. Li?"

"Were you coming to talk about the Chairman's mail? Do you know why it's stopped?" I asked. "Is there someone else officials are asking for favors now?"

"You've been reading the Chairman's mail?" he asked.

The accusation in his question made me flush, but my shame turned to indignation, and then defiance. He'd sent me the record, hadn't he? He expected me to sort what came, but not read the rest of the mail?

"The Chairman isn't reading or replying to anything. Nothing at all," I said.

"It's a delicate time." He told me that the Chairman's rumored ailments helped him identify whom he could trust. If certain officials seemed too eager to turn to his successors, or to make plans without consulting him, it was one way to find out.

A few years ago, the Chairman had tested how the Russians might react to his death. He'd slumped under a blanket, groaning in front of his aides and attendants, before asking them if he seemed ill. When they'd agreed, he'd called the envoy to his bedside and pretended to be so weak he could no longer read. "The Soviet seemed very worried, which reassured the Chairman. He was back on his feet the next day," he added. "Maybe he's testing us again."

"It's not like that," I said. This malaise didn't seem calculated; it seemed like a culmination. "Who knows the Chairman can't get out of bed?" I asked. "Does . . . the President?"

He nodded grimly. "He's trying to get control of Dazhai. There have been reports of secret meetings, secret deals. If the President can't convince the Chairman, he'll go around him. He'll finish marshaling support on National Day. If he has his way, he'll put a model village in every province."

"A model village of model capitalists," I said.

He nodded.

A branch cracked and we fell silent. I listened for footsteps, for breathing. When I remembered the Madame hinting I'd fallen for Secretary Sun, I blushed. Had he heard the rumor, too?

A minute passed, and Secretary Sun exhaled. "I received word about your family. About your mother."

Ma? "What about her?"

He rubbed the back of his neck. "She's very ill. With a fever. It spread through the village."

I stared at him, not understanding. Ma was never sick, had no time to be sick. He'd mixed me up with another girl. Busy Shan's mother was frail, wasn't she?

He held my gaze. "One of your sisters died."

The sky tipped up. He grabbed my arm to keep me from falling and eased me onto a marble bench as a great wind started up inside my head. "Which one?"

"I don't know," he said.

"Why didn't they receive any treatment?" I beat my fists against the bench.

"We didn't know about the fever," he said.

"Summon Dr. Li," I said. I would order him to give my family the same injections and pills that he offered the Chairman. We would both go; Secretary Sun would drive us in the jeep. We would arrive after midnight and the doctor would cure my mother—not just her, the entire village.

"He is the Chairman's doctor," he said.

I covered my face. Couldn't he understand I wanted the best for them? Wouldn't he want the same for his own family?

"No one at the Lake Palaces would ask for such a favor," Secretary Sun said. "Not even his children are allowed to see his doctor."

"Your parents aren't dying!" I said.

"We can't give your family special treatment. It causes problems. It was decided that they should receive the same treatment as others in the village."

No treatment at all, then. I looked up at him. "Who decided?" I asked. His stricken face confirmed my suspicions. "Not the Chairman. It was you. It was you!"

CHAPTER 17

*W*HEN THE CHAIRMAN SPOKE, AFTER ALMOST TWO WEEKS of near silence—two weeks that could have been a year—his voice sounded like something giving way, like ice cracking on a river. I had to step lightly, or risk being swept away.

"Do you have any news?" he asked, rubbing his fists in his eyes. He coughed and I brought him a cup of lukewarm tea.

"No," I said, too numb to talk about my family. Later, I would understand that I was also protecting myself from his indifference. One of my sisters was dead—which one? First Daughter, Mei Tian, with her thunderous laugh, never afraid to take up the space she deserved, with a gift for cursing? Now I could curse like that, too. Second Daughter, Mei Ling, who scratched my back in wide circles to help me fall asleep, who knit our family's mittens and socks?

If one died, the other would soon follow.

"No news?" he asked again.

I shook my head.

"All this time—nothing?" he asked. He'd been asleep when I returned from the garden yesterday, but if I told him about meeting Secretary Sun, he'd have questions I wasn't ready to answer. He'd want to hear the gossip, to know what I said and to confirm we weren't plotting against him. I would have to tell him eventually—soon—but couldn't bear to now.

My mother had already lost one daughter to the revolution. She didn't deserve to lose another. Maybe I would never see Ma again; maybe I'd never see any of them again. I grieved for what had been lost, for the perfection my family would never have, after so much was promised to us all.

Swinging his legs around, he climbed out of bed and made his way to his desk. His robe flapped around him, exposing his sagging belly, the skin gone loose from the weight he'd lost. He turned on the fan and searched through his papers for a moment. Then he asked me to order red-cooked pork belly, one of his favorites, braised until tender and glossy amber, steeped in rock sugar, soy sauce, and star anise—the savory taste of his childhood, of autumn abundance. The Chairman had an appetite again. For food and for all else, I hoped, in time for National Day, the day after tomorrow. In time for the President.

In the hallway, in the duty area a few meters away, Busy Shan and Servant Ting were unraveling an orange sweater to reuse the yarn. When I called out to them, they hurried toward me. After I ordered the red-cooked pork, Servant Ting nodded, but then ventured a few steps inside. I followed her, the both of us peeking around the privacy screen to see the Chairman lighting a cigarette. Only then did she turn and bolt, her skinny arms pumping, in a journey to the kitchen that would signal to the Lake Palaces that he had reemerged.

Busy Shan lingered by the doorway. I stepped back into the hallway.

"Where did you go yesterday?" she asked.

"On an errand for the Chairman," I said, wondering if he could hear us over the noise of the fan.

"With Secretary Sun?" she said. She could have been guessing or maybe she'd followed me into the garden. If she'd been hoping to catch us in each other's arms, she would have been disappointed. I'd fled as soon as he told me about my family.

"We met at the Chairman's request," I said.

She shoved past me, but when our bodies brushed together, we both went still. The touch reminded me of how close we'd once been in the troupe, our hands clasped, paired in dance class. Giggling over Midnight Chang. Her scent swept over me, earthy and familiar, like bricks warmed in the sun. Did I smell the same to her? For a moment, I thought she might cry, and that I might, too.

Then she scowled. She had little status now, no longer part of the troupe because of me, because I'd told the Chairman to make her a servant. When she tried to push past me again, I blocked her. "What do you want?" I asked.

"Spill his lunch down the front of your shirt."

I gasped. She wanted to humiliate me, to let me know she could see me for who I was, an awkward peasant girl.

"Do it," she said. "Or I'll tell him Dolly Yu killed herself because of you."

She'd said it out loud, said what I didn't want to believe, said what I'd tried to forget: Our prank on Midnight Chang turned her mean, turned her against Dolly Yu.

"It wasn't just me." Everyone had joined in beating her.

"But it started with you."

AT HIS DESK, the Chairman paged through his correspondence. With National Day almost upon us, his preparations had to be urgent. He smoked greedily, drawing down in big puffs before stubbing out the cigarette.

Lost in thought, he toyed with his chop, a stick of green jade so dark it was almost black. His name was carved at the tip so he could stamp official documents with his signature. I could tell how much pleasure the chop gave him, with each satisfying thump. No one but the Chairman ever touched it, and the hand that held that chop ruled the country.

When I reached for the chop, the Chairman resisted but then let go. Taking his hand, I traced the top of the chop against his cupped palm. His eyes went heavy with pleasure as the jade warmed with the heat of our hands. "Jade gets darker, you know. The more you touch it," he said. "A part of you gets into it." He took back the chop and stroked his fingers along the back of my hand.

When the dish arrived, still bubbling, the look Busy Shan gave dared me to ignore her threat. In truth, it wasn't much of one; the Chairman wouldn't concern himself with Dolly Yu's suicide. But spilling on myself seemed like just punishment for what I'd done to the girl—or more what I'd failed to do—before she died.

I'd been too hollowed out to eat anything since hearing about the death of my sister. Now the greasy smell made me nauseous. After lifting the scorching dish from the cart, I let it slip from my fingers and onto me. As the dish bounced onto the floor, cracking into shards and spattering sauce, I swallowed my scream and tugged at the neck of my shirt, trying to pull the fabric away from where it had scalded me.

"Be careful," the Chairman said irritably. He turned back to the page, not bothering to check if I was okay.

The pain was nothing compared to what Dolly Yu must have experienced in her final days, in her final moments. It's hard to explain, but shaming myself in front of the Chairman felt like an apology long overdue.

Busy Shan hurried inside the chambers to clean the mess, but he didn't thank her. He didn't even notice her. Her face clouded with disappointment, she kneeled down to wipe the floor. When she got to her feet, we stared at each other. I'd done exactly as she'd asked, but it wasn't enough, would never be enough until one of us was gone.

THE SHIRT I'D CHANGED into brushed against a patch of skin—red and tight and pulsing—just above my breasts, where I'd spilled on myself. I'd moved to the couch. Wincing, I tried reading one of the Chairman's speeches, but I kept thinking about my family.

If I asked him to go to my village, he would refuse me. Though I was supposed to present myself to the President two days from now, I couldn't wait, not while Ma still tossed with fever. In another day, she might die. In the next hour. If I left just after dawn, when the Chairman fell asleep, I could make my way to the Central Garrison and convince a driver to take me home with crates of medicine and food from the Lake Palaces' abundant supplies. By the time the Chairman woke up in early afternoon and realized I was gone, I would be on my way back.

Except no one was allowed around the Chairman if they so much as coughed or sneezed. If I went to the village plagued by fever, the doctors would consider me tainted. I'd never get to come back here.

I should have, could have gone. That was my mistake. Sometimes still I picture it, how I would have prepared lunch for my family, held a wet cloth to my mother's forehead, and lit incense at my sister's grave. Wanting it so much now it almost seems like a memory.

At his desk, the Chairman shook out a crick in his neck and glanced over at me. "What are you reading?" he asked.

I held up a book.

"What a diligent student," he teased. Then he noticed it was a collection of his speeches.

"Everyone treats me like a dead ancestor," he grumbled.

He felt respected but never consulted, I knew. He'd had enough of adulation, enough to last ten generations; he didn't want to be treated like a fragile porcelain vase on a pedestal. I dove at him. He dodged me, then pushed me on the bed and pinned me down. Arching, I thrashed against him, and he tightened his grip on my wrists. He grinned. He never suspected that I held back my strength, mindful that his rickety bones could break, that his thin, spotted skin could tear.

When I brought up a leg, as if to shove him off, he pushed down my thighs with his knees, the knobby joint grinding into my flesh.

"My brothers and I used to sneak up on each other like that," he said. "No one dares now but you."

If he saw himself as old and weak, he might come to resent me and the future he would never see. I protected the Chairman not only from others but from himself. Understanding this secret saved my life.

The moment I forgot it, you were fated to lose yours.

He rubbed his thumb along the inside of my wrist. He undressed me, and as he blew gently across the burn on my chest, I shivered. His hands leafed through my hair and roamed at my waist.

Mad with grief, with fear, I'd been taut as a bowstring. As he stroked lower, lower, lower down, I remained stiff as a wooden doll under his stubby fingers, light and circling. Here he was tender— not blustering; here he was solicitous—not bullying. We slid beneath the fresh sheets, smooth and soothing as a dip in the pool.

CHAPTER 18

*A*BODYGUARD CLOMPED IN AND TOOK OFF A SHINY NEW SET of leather shoes that he presented to the Chairman, who shoved in his broad, pale feet. Almost always barefoot or in slippers, he relied on his bodyguards to break in his shoes. His new dark brown suit, with a high collar and four large pockets at the chest, seemed both Western and Chinese, touches of a solemn scholar paired with the crisp cut that foreigners favored.

Last night, my thoughts had circled endlessly around what I had to do today until gray light seeped through a crack in the curtains. The Chairman hadn't slept much, either. Now he had to leave in a hurry, at an hour when he sometimes went to bed.

"How do I look?" he asked.

"Like the portrait that hangs above the square."

He playfully assumed the same pose, that direct gaze and dignified set of his lips.

I straightened the red-star cap on his head. "I wore this on my first National Day. It almost blew off!" he said, but he'd caught it with his fingertips, rescuing it from getting crushed under the wheels of a tank. Nothing much had survived those days, nothing much had survived in his life, and I could tell how much the hat delighted him.

I smoothed the shoulders of his uniform, a duty which felt odd—wifely. The Madame had to be getting ready in her quarters, too. He rested the back of his hand on my cheek. Slowed down, the gesture was a caress; speeded up, a blow. I leaned into his hand. He had survived the loss of child after child, wife after wife, life after life so that the revolution might take hold in this country and across the world.

He circled my wrist with his fingers. "Bring us victory."

I felt like a rock skipped across the water, fleet and light.

After he left, I got dressed, everything a perfect fit, nothing that drooped or pinched, the second skin I hadn't known I'd needed. When I dug my hands into my pants pockets, testing them out, my fingers brushed against something small and hard, slipped into a tiny inner flap. Turning it inside out, I discovered another one of my mother's dowry beads. I held it up, running my thumb over the carving. Ma—Ma! Her face contorted, the blankets soaked in sweat, under our portrait of the Chairman. In her fever dreams, he promised to deliver her.

Teacher Fan had given me the outfit shortly before the Chairman sank into seclusion, before the fever swept through my village. Maybe she'd obtained the bead while gathering information for the Madame's report. When I'd listened in on their conversation, maybe Teacher Fan hadn't been insulting me. She'd deflected the Madame's attention, protected me by making me seem typical and insignificant.

I didn't know then what it would cost her.

When she arrived, I slipped the bead back into my pocket. She helped me finish dressing, tightening a belt around my waist and tugging out a wrinkle on my pants. After she attached a row of enamel pins to my chest, badges of the revolution, I reached into my pocket.

In a cupped palm, I showed Teacher Fan my mother's dowry bead. She closed her hand around mine, folding my fingers into a fist around it. That pressure steadied me, our secret at its core.

"How is my family?" I asked.

"Secretary Sun got a call this morning," she said. "The medicine he sent arrived in your village."

"I don't understand."

"He made arrangements the other day. Right after you met."

I shuddered, so tightly wound it pained me to exhale. "What's to become of me?" I asked. "Of them?"

Which sister? Which sister died? If it was Mei Tian, First Daughter, she'd never again tug the tightest braids into my hair—so tight my eyes watered—that held fast all day. If it was Mei Ling, Second Daughter, she'd never pluck a honeysuckle for me, the both of us tasting the nectar golden as sunshine.

"It depends on how you perform," Teacher Fan said. "No different than on the dance floor or on the stage." She glanced at the door. For the moment, we were alone. "You could stay on."

I stared at her.

"Not with the Chairman, but with me." She adjusted the cap on my head.

"You don't want to marry me off?" I asked. "No takers?"

"I need you to keep an eye on the girls."

"What's the point?" I said. "If anyone disobeys, you'll get another the next day."

Sorrow shadowed her face. "What happened to Dolly Yu—it can't happen again."

No new girls had arrived since she'd jumped out the window. My throat went tight. More than anything, I wanted her to say that she also wanted me with her.

Busy Shan bustled in then. Teacher Fan stepped away from me, her expression instantly unperturbed, unflappable, which made me doubt her words—doubt her. As she cleared the breakfast dishes, Busy Shan's eyes were hard with resentment. She looked at Teacher Fan and then back at me, probably blaming us for her misfortune. It had been a while since she'd seen our teacher, who barely acknowledged her, treating her as she would any other servant.

Busy Shan would stay behind at the Lake Palaces today. If she'd remained in the troupe, she would have had a chance to perform, instead of being shut up in these musty quarters.

All at once, I felt like I was suffocating and my hands flew to my neck, scrambling at the buttons. My fate could be hers, if I failed at my duties. My fate could be hers, if I was fortunate.

Teacher Fan searched through her bag, pursing her lips. "I forgot your glasses. I'll be right back."

After she left, Busy Shan rolled away the cart piled with dirty dishes. If it had been me, wouldn't I want her to tell me about my family? "I don't know if you heard. Your ma fell down some stairs," I said.

She squinted at me.

"I saw it in a report."

"You're lying!"

I bit my lower lip. "She was going to a political-thought class. At the local school."

"They always hold the meetings there . . ." she trailed off and glanced at the mess on the Chairman's desk, perhaps wondering if she'd find the report there. She took a few steps toward me. If we'd still been friends, I might have sat her down. Instead, my arms dangled at my sides.

"You're lying," she repeated, but sounded less certain this time.

I listened for the click of Teacher Fan's footsteps. She'd return at any moment. "Listen, everyone will be at National Day. You could slip out of the Lake Palaces and return before anyone finds out."

She bit her lip. "Why didn't anyone tell me?" she asked.

My chest ached. "No one tells us anything. Until it's too late. Yesterday, I found out that one of my sisters died. That my mother's half-dead from a fever. I can't get to my family, but you can go to her," I said. Saying it out loud made me want to scream all over again.

Her eyes turned glossy with tears. "I—they'll never let me out." She blinked. "I can't even get past the inner ring of guards without a pass."

Then I noticed the Chairman's chop sat on top of the container of red ink paste. He used the chop for official documents and his paintings, a signature that could not be forged. If I wrote a pass and used the chop, it would carry an authority that could not be disobeyed. I reached for the chop, my hand hovering, and picked it up gingerly, expecting a jolt through my body.

"Don't!" Busy Shan cried.

I tightened my fist around the seal, slid off the lid of the paste, and bore down to coat every crevice. The smell of the ink was heady, heedless, and it felt as if his hand went on mine: Go. His mark bloomed on the paper, bright red characters.

MY FIRST DAY IN the capital, I'd passed by Tiananmen, the entrance to the Forbidden City. Located at the northern edge of the enormous square that shared its name, the massive red gate held five archways that led into the former imperial grounds. For generations, only emperors had been allowed to pass through the largest archway, in the center, and now the Chairman's huge portrait hung above it.

The gate was so large and imposing that a long balcony and adjoining reception hall could perch on top of it. Just before we stepped onto the balcony, where scores of guests had gathered, I checked my costume. My family would no longer recognize me in my schoolgirl's checkered jacket, white blouse, and dark blue pants; I hardly recognized myself. I pictured Ma, curled on the brick bed, shivering despite being heaped with blankets. Ba, turned inside out with helpless exhaustion. And my sisters: Mei Tian, fierce and first. Mei Ling, second in birth, but first in my heart.

Secretary Sun looked around the crowd, probably in search of the Chairman. "What have you heard about my family?" I quickly asked.

He turned toward me. "Everyone in the village is getting treated." He would never apologize for not acting any sooner, for he believed he'd done nothing wrong.

"Which sister was it?" I asked.

He went still as stone. "The courier we sent didn't tell me."

"Then send another!" My pulse skittered.

"Passing the test today is the best way for you to help your family."

And yet, in the look he gave me, I understood he would still help them if I no longer could.

If I found out anything more about my family, I might forget everything I'd learned. I stepped outside, where red blazed on the flags that rippled against deep blue skies, on the giant paper lanterns, bobbing and swaying, dangling from the double row of eaves, and on the pillars, thick as tree trunks, that held up the roof.

We moved toward the railing. When you faced south, looking at the square, you couldn't see the Forbidden City or the Lake Palaces, since they were located behind us. I peeked down at the seven white bridges, dragons and guardian lions that served as ceremonial protections in front of the gate, outlasting the emperors they were supposed to defend.

Seeing such grandeur had once been like falling, as if I were a drop of rain overwhelmed in a storm. Now it felt like drowning. We spotted the Chairman: As he walked along the railing, taking off his cap to wave at the crowd, the shouting from the square grew so loud it could have been coming from inside my head.

The clapping and stomping turned to thunder. I clapped, too, until my hands ached with a thrilling pain—the ache of patriotism and purpose and passion. Of overwhelming want, of a lust that somewhere else might have led to kisses and caresses in a meadow on a moonless night or in a dark doorway, but consumed the crowd gathered here. The Chairman didn't have a deep powerful voice, and he wasn't handsome like the stars in the movie musicals. It didn't matter. The people in the square would never have a chance to hear or see the Chairman up close, so they could find whatever they wanted in him: Father. Liberator. Helmsman.

Pausing by the podium, he spoke into a microphone. "How are you, young comrades? How are you?" When he spoke, the slogans didn't sound like slogans, but words from his heart, a personal message for each of us. "Dare to think, dare to act!"

He would live forever and reign a thousand years.

EVEN NOW, I TELL you, I miss it sometimes, the certainty—I'll never be that certain of anything again.

CHAPTER 19

As we approached the Chairman, I tucked a strand of hair behind my ear. My hair, which used to fall to the middle of my back, had been chopped into a bob—its severe lines replacing the crown of braids my mother had sent me off in. My head felt lighter, but my neck was exposed and vulnerable, bare as bone.

I had anticipated and dreaded this moment for weeks: Perfection was still possible before I began, before being spoiled by a forgotten line or a stupid answer. I pushed back the heavy black frames of my new glasses, an irritating prop that kept slipping down my nose.

As the crowd jostled around us, I went over the plan in my head: After small talk, I'd get the President curious about university students. I had to convince him we needed his guidance and the strong hand of the Party. His attentions would inspire our loyalty, I'd say.

But if he meddled—if he gave instructions on how to behave or clamped down on their meetings at the university—the Chairman knew it would backfire. The students would resent the President and his allies, and turn against them.

The Chairman's chuckle roiled through the noise. I'd almost forgotten what his laughter sounded like; he hadn't been that loud and boisterous in a long time. When an official stepped in front of me, I elbowed past him to get to the Chairman, who stood under the shade of the eaves, surrounded by four officials.

"That's him," Secretary Sun murmured, even though I recognized the President at once—the man with the bushy eyebrows, slicked-back hair, and an efficient, watchful air. I hated him on sight, a hate primal and essential. Before my training, I'd rarely thought of him, but for weeks, the Chairman had built him up as his enemy, as the gravest threat to our people. He stood in the way of everything I wanted. Now I hated the President for how ordinary he seemed. *This* man had afflicted the Chairman? The most fearsome demons never have fangs and red eyes, I knew that, but the fact of him before me made no sense. I'd prepared to deceive a man who looked as harmless as Secretary Sun's stooped neighbor.

The Chairman caught sight of me. He opened his mouth as if to speak, but said nothing. Everything went intense as the noonday sun. Had I shocked him—dazzled him? Impossible.

My teachers had trained me well and dressed me for the part. Like steam blowing the lid off a boiling pot, I had risen up to meet the contours of this disguise.

"Happy National Day!" Secretary Sun said, his tone serious and purposeful, with a ceremonial flourish I wasn't used to from him.

The men nodded in greeting. "Welcome!" the Chairman said.

"This is Dong Feng, a first-year agricultural student." Secretary Sun touched my shoulder, nudging me toward them.

Dong Feng, the East Wind, bold and blatant as the deep red in our country's flag. I might as well have been named Daughter of the Revolution. Not my family's name, and not the generational name I shared with my sisters, not something out of a sentimental country folktale.

My skin went clammy. I tried to hide my apprehension, but didn't know where to put my hands; they were ridiculous, useless at my sides. Clasping them behind me felt strange, too.

"She won a university essay contest, making a case for continuous revolution. A visit here was her prize," Secretary Sun said.

The sun in my eyes, I squinted up at the Chairman.

"I had to cross China on foot and defeat army after army before I climbed Tiananmen," he said with a grin.

The pause that followed went on for too long, a sticky gear caught, and then everything slid into motion for me. As if I were in a play, once I started, I had to go on. "I'm lucky, then," I said, surprised at the sound of my own voice. I hoped that my accent wasn't creeping in.

"Lucky and bright," the Chairman said.

I stepped back to escape the glare of sunshine.

"Not like those students so busy with their gossip," the President said. The quip seemed for the Chairman's amusement, not mine.

The Chairman smirked.

"So busy talking, they wouldn't look up if a bomb went off," the President added.

"Not students that I know," I said. "We pay more attention than you might think."

I couldn't tell if he was always this dismissive of students, but when the President glanced at me, his interest leapt, suddenly visible.

The Chairman laughed. "You're a spirited one!"

"*Some* students," the President conceded. "Nothing gets past my daughter. But some of her friends . . ."

We'd decided I'd portray myself as confident, outspoken, and modern, but I'd never been so bold when we practiced.

"Sounds like she needs new friends," I said.

The men laughed again and the Chairman nodded appreciatively.

The sudden entrance of soldiers—rows and rows of them marching in formation—interrupted our conversation. Just when I'd gotten their attention! Soon, though, my annoyance gave way to awe. As bands played revolutionary music that pulsed in my veins, I lost myself in everything before me. I felt as mighty as the tanks rolling down the broad boulevard, as the warplanes now soaring overhead. The imperialist threats against us were relentless but so, too, was our defense: A couple weeks ago, we'd shot down an American spy plane over Hainan Island, off our southern coast. If we betrayed any weakness, the Americans would invade us, like they'd invaded Vietnam.

The Chairman believed that the President was just as much of a threat, but coming from within.

On the western side of our view, the Great Hall of the People loomed, and to the east, a museum of revolutionary history—both hulking, with long lines and broad surfaces, and yet still not even half the length of Tiananmen Square, the biggest in the world. And the crowds! Since dawn, people had been roaring with pride, "Long live the People's Republic of China" and "Long live the Party!" I'd never seen so many at once, waving red banners, twirling paper streamers in green and pink and purple, and knocking together bamboo clappers in a clacking cacophony.

They pressed against the stage, where performers sang and danced, kicked and spun and swung their swords. Was Busy Shan pushing through the crowds streaming in the opposite direction? Marchers poured in from the horizon: a group lifting hoops adorned with paper flowers, another waving red kerchiefs, men beating small drums tied to their waists, and dancers prancing in pink silks.

Turning away from the spectacle, the Chairman drew out a pack of cigarettes and offered me one. I shook my head. I didn't want to make a fool of myself coughing.

"Aren't young women smoking these days?" he asked, addressing his question to the others as much as to me.

"I don't—I don't have time," I said. The Chairman and the officials laughed, but not the President and Secretary Sun. I hunched my shoulders, suddenly doubting if I could convince the President of anything.

The President took a cigarette and drew down hard. "She's reminding us of our own bad habits." He spoke with a kindness that confused me, that I rejected as condescension. He had a quiet intensity about him; he was the sort who was early to bed, early to rise, in a way that the Chairman would have considered a drudgery but also a threat.

The Chairman stubbed out his cigarette under his shoe. Butts littered the floor. He never smoked to the end, preferring the flare of pleasure inherent in the first drag.

"Where are you from?" the President asked me. "I can't quite place your accent."

Sweat pooled in my armpits. Teacher Fan had told me to speak slowly and clearly. "I . . ." In the story that the Chairman had invented for me, I lived at home, near Peking University, and I had a brother in the army, and a married older sister. The details escaped me now. I tugged at the sleeves of my new jacket—a little too short, I suddenly realized, exposing my wrists.

He must know that I was a fraud. Blinking up at him, I pushed on my glasses, whose heavy frames gave me a headache. "From here," I said finally.

The Chairman pressed his lips into a thin line, and Secretary Sun frowned. You could sink a coin in the groove between his eyebrows.

"Where?" the President said.

"Not far," I said. I felt like kindling, brittle and flammable. "Near the university."

The President looked toward the balcony. "Are your parents in the square? They must be proud of you."

When I gaped, Secretary Sun stepped in. "We grew up down the street from each other. Her older brother and I went to school together."

It was the sort of background that would impress the President, the Chairman had pronounced—what the President wanted for himself and his children. "Just look at his wife!" the Chairman had said. His fifth wife, who'd been born into wealth, spoke French, Russian, and English, and held a science degree. They'd met in Yan'an, where she'd served as an interpreter, when the President had been nearly twice her age. The President cocked his head at me, with what might be new respect. As another official pulled him away, I shot a grateful look at Secretary Sun. When the Chairman shook his head, I inched toward the President, wondering how I might get his attention again.

A great cheer interrupted. On the wooden stage below, schoolchildren with red neckerchiefs danced, fists to their chests, twirling and leaping with a military precision all the more impressive because of how young they looked. After they finished, they bowed so deeply, the tops of their heads nearly brushed against the floorboards. The smallest girl stepped forward, carrying a huge bouquet of flowers almost as big as she was. She shyly took a step and then halted.

A woman—their teacher?—urged her forward and the girl raised the bouquet high in a tribute for the Chairman. He saluted them and the children jumped up and down in excitement until the woman ushered them down the stairs of the stage. When the woman turned back for a final look up at the Chairman, I gasped. Even from many meters above, I recognized her taut bearing and elegant profile: Midnight Chang.

So poised, she could have balanced a cup of tea on her head at the height of a storm. The Chairman whistled, piercing as an air-raid alarm, a sound that drilled deep into my skull.

Secretary Sun ducked his head toward me. "They're all from the Shanghai dance studio." The one led by a former recruit, the one where Midnight Chang had trained. "The Madame has plans for Midnight Chang."

An empress couldn't quarrel with every concubine, I knew. It would be to the Madame's advantage to take a recruit under her protection, if only to keep watch on the man they might someday share.

"What kind of plans?" I asked, afraid to hear his answer.

"Don't let it rattle you," he said gently. "The Madame prefers a devotee to a student, but even they never last for long."

The sky filled with red balloons, blotting out the sunshine for a few seconds. A group of marchers had released them in unison when they reached Tiananmen Gate. Higher and higher the balloons rose, carried on the smoky autumn wind. I wanted to watch them sail away until they were only pinpricks in the blue.

The Chairman gestured at us to follow him into the gate's reception hall, big enough to host a village wedding or two. In one of several seating areas, we sank into carved wooden chairs with cushions thick and soft enough to protect an egg dropped from high above. The Chairman sat at one end of a low table that came up to his knees. I flanked him on one side, and the President and Secretary Sun on the other.

"You're still here?" the President asked me.

"We can't send her off without refreshments," the Chairman said with a laugh.

"I'd like to hear more from our young comrade," the President said. He smiled.

I didn't smile back.

"Tell me more about the essay," he said. "It was on continuous revolution? What about it?"

I took a deep breath. "We can't let the revolutionary spirit die. People my age, we only know about it through stories. Stories about you, about the Chairman. But we want a part, too."

"Be glad for what you have," the President said. "Revolution takes many forms. You can't follow in our footsteps. We didn't follow in anyone else's, either. You have to break your own path."

The Chairman flagged down a hovering attendant, who pushed over a tinkling cart loaded with teapots, stubby porcelain bottles and glass snifters, and dishes of snacks. She placed three glasses on the table—one for each man.

"For her, too," the Chairman said.

She fetched me a glass, poured, and left the bottle on the table— the Chairman's favorite brand, with the red-and-white label.

The President raised his eyebrows. "You'll have a drink, but not a smoke?"

"Young women having a drink is the new fashion at the university," the Chairman said. "We have to get accustomed to the new ways." He sounded jovial, though I heard the edge in his voice.

"I want to toast to the health of the Chairman," I said nervously. From the President's expression, I could tell I had chosen what he'd wished to say.

"We'll drink together." The Chairman poured the oily liquor, filling the glass cup until it splashed onto the table.

"A long, long life to the Chairman!" I said. The glass clinked against my teeth, and in my hand, the stem seemed frail as a baby bird's leg. Maybe I'd only wet my lips. Maybe I'd only taste it. Its heady bitter scent burned my nose, and then my throat as I swallowed the liquor, fire cascading into my stomach. Once I'd started drinking it, I couldn't stop without spitting it out.

I coughed, a damp and dark sound. As I stroked the rim of the glass, the taste began to mellow in my mouth. If this was what being drunk felt like, maybe I didn't have much to fear.

The President poured a second round. "Only under the brilliant leadership of the Chairman can the revolution blow from the east," he said, flattering the Chairman and me, with this echo of my fake name.

We drank again, this shot burning a little less. Then the Chairman toasted me. "The future belongs to you."

His was the final toast. I peeked at the beams painted with stripes in the deepest reds and blues, and the golden lanterns hung with red tassels between the polished columns that dwarfed us all, the colors hot enough to burn. The silk cushion beneath was slippery, and I braced my thick-soled shoes on the rug.

"The last empress drank maotai every day to keep her young and beautiful," the Chairman said.

We nodded, but the conversation lulled.

He yawned. "This day never ends. Should we play a game? How about Truth or Challenge? Or Two Falsehoods and a Truth?"

"No one could ever beat you at those games," the President said. He smiled, a smile that the Chairman shared in earnest. It could have been the last of the warmth born in Yan'an and on the Long March, those days scored in the lines on their faces.

My father and the other men in the village plaza had played those games, too. "Are the young people still amusing themselves that way?" the President asked. He glanced at the Chairman. "You're trying to impress her, by showing we used to have fun, but people her age are probably playing games we've never heard of." He turned to me. "Let me guess: You don't have time."

Secretary Sun cut in again. "We played the same games back when I was in school. People probably played them long before you and will long after any of us."

"What are you studying when you're not playing games?" the President asked me. He smelled like cigarettes, like smoldering.

"Bacteria. Nitrogen compounds." I'd memorized the terms, even though I didn't know their meaning. I repeated the words in my head, and bit my lip, struck by a wave of hilarity. The words made no sense at all! I fanned myself, the reception hall suffocatingly hot.

Secretary Sun eyed me. The maotai was seeping into me, stronger than I'd realized. Time flattened and I wondered how long I'd stay muddled, if I could hold my posture. I sat up straight, straining in the way I'd later realize was the way of a drunk who thought—hoped—that no one would notice and in doing so, called the attention she wanted to avoid. I hoped the liquor was making the men around me as slippery inside their heads.

"How funny!" the Chairman said. He scratched his crotch. "My family never used such words when we planted. We didn't know them. We just did what had always been done before us." He poured more maotai.

Without thinking, I gulped my drink. It gave me more time to think. Secretary Sun inhaled sharply. If he could have, he would have knocked the glass from my hand.

"Why are you studying agriculture?" the President asked me. "Students from the capital aren't usually interested in the plight of the peasant."

My head thrummed. "It's my belief that peasants should no longer go hungry. Feeding the people feeds our future." I let the words, heavy and solemn as a funeral gong, fill my mouth. "Consider the Sui dynasty, which lasted only thirty-eight years, because leaders didn't take heed of that lesson."

The emperor had forced millions to build a second capital. Because people toiled on buildings instead of in their fields, the crops were stunted from neglect. The famine sparked a rebellion that led to his downfall. After rebel forces captured the imperial granary, the peasants ate their fill again.

The Chairman smiled, his eyes dark slits above the buns of his cheeks. He was pleased with me—and himself. It was a smile of recognition and possession.

Hunger gnawed at me. I'd picked at my breakfast, and if I had food in my belly, maybe it would settle me. I wolfed down a flaky pastry filled with curried ground beef in three bites.

"What an appetite! I'm always after my daughter to eat more," the President said.

Though I wanted another, I didn't take it. An intellectual gorged on ideas and nibbled on food. My fingers were greasy, but I resisted the urge to wipe them on my sleeve or on the silk cushions. "How old is she?" I asked. "She's in college?"

"Not that one!" the President said. "She's thirteen."

Perhaps that was why he didn't attend the dances. It could have alarmed him, to see the cadre pairing off with girls not much older than his.

Blood pounded in my ears, so loud I didn't realize I'd tilted toward the Chairman, nearly falling into his lap. As I sat up, the rug bunched under my feet. Clenching the arms of the chair, I stared at my fingers, gone white around the knuckles. If I let go, I'd slide onto the floor. Catching a whiff of the liquor oozing from my skin, I feared I might go up in flames.

Secretary Sun summoned the attendant, asking for tea. When it arrived, I drank it quickly, grateful to wash out the cloying taste of the maotai. I tightened my hands around the teacup, studying its decorations, dragons traced out against the deep imperial yellow, a color born from the sun. I was far from clearheaded, but I could see the possibility in the distance.

The President studied me with the depthless, lidless stare of a lizard, as if to pinpoint what didn't fit. "Her name is too plain," he told the Chairman. "It doesn't suit her."

"You meet her for the first time, and you insult her?" The Chairman couldn't contain his smile. "You don't like her name?"

"It's patriotic but there's no music," the President said. "The sound is heavy in my mouth, plopping like mud. Dong Feng, Dong Feng, Dong Feng," he said.

"What kind of name would you expect?" Secretary Sun asked. "Expectations have a way of getting overturned by the younger generation."

"What about a name like Mei Xiang?" the Chairman asked, unable to hide the mischief in his voice.

The name my parents had given me.

The President shook his head. "Old-fashioned."

I sat on my hands to stop them from trembling.

"Mei Xiang, Dong Feng—neither of them fit her. Her parents would know better," the President insisted. "Or did you come up with Dong Feng?" he asked me. "You students have been renaming yourselves patriotically, 'Revolution' this and 'Red' that."

I glared at him.

"Either way, you and your parents would have picked a name as sophisticated as you are." He was making an elaborate backhanded compliment, of the sort I've come to recognize that men often use on women: to undermine our confidence and make us seek their approval.

The liquor made me reckless, made me mistake being heedless for confidence. Maybe my sister's death had also put me past caring. So what if I'd talked back to the second most powerful man in the country? If the President knew that I was a peasant, he would expect only simple accomplishments from me, like chanting slogans and refraining from wiping my nose on my sleeve. It was insulting, to understand how little the President would expect from a Mei Xiang, even though he was from the countryside, too.

"What makes her seem sophisticated?" the Chairman asked. "The way she looks? Or is it the way she acts?" He paused. "The way she talks?"

The President gestured with his hands as if to say *yes, yes, yes*. He turned back to me. "Did you learn to read almost as soon as you could walk?"

"Yes," I said. I'd stick to a one-word answer.

"Do you have so many books they stack double on your shelves?" he asked.

I nodded.

"She seems like a peasant to me," the Chairman said.

"Nonsense!" the President said.

"How sure are you?" the Chairman asked.

"I'd swear on the revolution," the President said. "On my mother's grave."

I blinked, settling back into my body, my tongue thick and disgusting from the liquor. The President had known the Chairman for so long, couldn't he tell he was laying a trap? Maybe he thought he'd play along.

"If you were wrong, you'd take a dare?" the Chairman asked. "You'd bark like a dog?"

"I'll never forget the look on Comrade Wu's face when he howled at the moon!" the President said. It was probably a prank the Chairman pulled on someone years ago.

"You'd kiss her feet?" the Chairman pressed.

"You always came up with the most ingenious challenges! I think Comrade Tang tasted mud for days." The President smirked, a man thinking he's in on the joke when the joke's on him.

Then I realized even if the President suspected the Chairman was trying to trick him, he thought he knew better, thought he could outwit the Chairman—and that was why the Chairman wanted him gone. He gave the Chairman a sidelong glance. "And if you're wrong, then you'll give me Dazhai?"

The Chairman nodded.

"You'll think about it?" the President asked.

"If I'm wrong, it's yours."

The President couldn't hide his delight. He could have believed he'd forced the Chairman's hand. "Her upbringing is in her face!"

Judging by the Chairman's amusement, he had no doubt that I'd deceived his rival, so much that I now had to convince the President of the truth.

"In my face?" I grabbed the President's hand and flipped our palms over. Mine were dark and hard; his, white and soft. His eyes went wide. Mine did, too.

In touching him, I'd gone too far. He yanked back his hand.

The Chairman moved to the edge of his seat. "Six weeks ago, Secretary Sun and I decided we'd try to pass off a peasant as a student intellectual. Everyone knows peasants have no greater friend than in you," he told the President.

The President offered a thin smile. "You never could resist a prank."

"Aren't you going to kiss her feet?" the Chairman asked.

The President stared at him.

"Come now," the Chairman cajoled. "Shouldn't she get rewarded? You can thank a peasant for her services to the revolution." He put a hand on my thigh, and I rested mine on top of his, his sweaty heat oozing into my skin.

The President tightened his jaw. At last, he understood I was the Chairman's mistress. At last, he understood he had to play along until the end. He reluctantly looked around the reception hall before kneeling down and brushing his lips against the tips of my shoes. His hair thinned on the top of his head, and his scalp beneath was papery and liver-spotted. He smelled stale, musty. The President—a father, a husband—kowtowed to me. It made me squeamish, realizing that with a shove, I could knock him over.

The Chairman swept the teapot off the table, which shattered on the stone floor. He must have wanted everyone to look at us, drawn to the sound of the irreplaceable breaking, the sound of no turning back. Chatter dipped, like a candle snuffed out, and every head turned in the reception hall. The Chairman grinned at me.

Struggling to get up from his crouch, the President braced himself on the low table and a chair, the furniture heavy enough not to wobble. He swayed, his face turned dark and red as a pig's liver. A few officials, among the dozens clustered inside, were nudging one another now. They'd seen something; maybe they'd seen everything and soon word would get out: The Chairman would do the same to anyone who supported the President.

"Lei Feng washed the feet of his comrades," the President said loudly, grandly. That model soldier. "But this will have to do. Who's next?"

He'd try to laugh it off. In truth, his humiliation couldn't have been more complete. The Chairman had explained it might spur on the President. Wounded like that, wouldn't he convince himself he deserved students who worshipped him? Whom he deserved to control?

The Chairman gestured for him to sit down. "I could always count on you to play along!"

The President smiled, but he'd balled his hands into fists. As attendants rushed up to wipe the shards of porcelain and spilled black tea leaves, conversation buzzed again, louder than before—people no doubt gossiping about what had happened.

"It turns out that training her taught us as much as it did her," the Chairman said to him. "It was a way into the schools. The time she spent on campus—you wouldn't believe what she's seen. I've been away too long. We both have."

"I could see what students couldn't see about themselves," I said.

"It takes an outsider to recognize it," the Chairman said.

"They dream of being revolutionaries," I said. "But they don't know how."

Though a vein pulsed on his temple, the President spoke evenly. "I've found students are the same, no matter when or where you are. Caught up in the same quarrels we found ourselves in. Thinking they are the first to reinvent the world."

"They need a model," I said. "A model like you."

"And how should I tell them?" the President asked. "Who's to say they'll listen to me any more than my daughters do?"

"You could have someone from the Party who goes on behalf of you—someone closer to their age," I said. "Someone from the Party, not much older than us."

The President nodded slowly.

"We need someone students can look up to," I added. "It's easier for us to picture ourselves where we might be in five years than in twenty. Maybe a whole group of cadre could go." If many officials showed up on campus, students might resent them even more. "To show how much you want to hear what the students have to say."

The President leaned back. "I'll think about it."

"If you're not going to take her up on her idea, maybe I will," the Chairman said. He gave the President a sidelong glance.

After falling for the prank, the President had to be twice as wary. I wondered why he was even listening to my advice; though of course, he couldn't help but see himself as smarter than me. And smarter than the Chairman; that had been and would always be his undoing.

"You have a point," I told him. "Who could possibly sway the students?"

Not you.

His expression hardened. "It must be easy to teach a clever girl," he told the Chairman.

Easy? He had imagined the masses reaching up for help, but could never see me pulling him down so that I could climb up. He didn't believe that people like me deserved to control their destinies, decisions best left to him and his allies.

A clever person turns great troubles into little ones and little ones into none, and perhaps I wasn't so clever after all, because I couldn't leave the President's praise alone.

He set down his cup with a thump.

"Maybe after the trip to the university, you could go to my village." I rolled the empty teacup in my hand, absorbing the last traces of warmth. "Maybe you'd learn something from us. If you just looked long enough. If you looked at all."

It was too noisy in the reception hall for the other guests to hear us; if they could, they would have surely found me rude—brazen as the teenage Red Guard who would rise up against the establishment in half a year.

None of them knew I'd lost a sister and none of them would have cared. "What are you doing to keep the revolution alive?" I asked him.

The President couldn't hide his irritation. He'd put up with the

Chairman and his eccentricities—he might well have preferred the Chairman being caught up in such antics while leaving the country for him to run—but he'd had enough of me.

"Yes, what?" the Chairman asked him.

The President sagged in his chair.

"Away from the countryside, people turn weak," the Chairman said. "They forget the sweat, the toil of peasants. They turn selfish, looking only after themselves and not the collective. You must take care of the communal fields before you take care of your own! If intellectuals never learn to eat bitterness, they'll never carry on the revolution. They can learn from the ways of peasants, *must* learn from the ways of peasants."

Looking back, I'd realize this command was his opening call to action in the Cultural Revolution, even if none of us—the Chairman included—knew it then, with a campaign that would begin in the schools and in the cities, before moving to the countryside.

WITHIN WEEKS OF NATIONAL DAY, the President recruited cadre to go on his behalf to universities. Nothing public, not yet, but word of it reached the Chairman.

Our arrow had found its mark.

"Who volunteered first?" the Chairman asked Secretary Sun. He'd arrived just as we were about to get into the pool.

At night, temperatures fell to near freezing, but in here, it felt humid as summer. Drops of sweat beaded above Secretary Sun's lip. After he listed a few names of cadre I didn't recognize, the Chairman smacked the table with the palm of his hand. His robe flapped open, and our empty teacups jumped with a clatter. I smacked the table, too. Laughing, he clasped his hands around mine.

"The way he talks about the idea, you'd never know he doubted it at first," Secretary Sun said.

I lifted my chin, riding, gliding on the wind. The President had lost face because of the prank—and in his desperation, he would turn to, then turn on, the students.

"He's always been like that," the Chairman said. "Quick to question, quick to take credit."

Secretary Sun's eyes met mine. I was proud of the Chairman's excitement, proud of what I'd set into motion. There was something else in his expression, too, a hint of worry that I chose to ignore. Couldn't he let me relish this moment?

The winds were turning. I didn't yet know they would carry me to you.

As the Chairman knotted his robe, the new attendant rushed over to refill our cups. She'd replaced Busy Shan. Though I knew better than to ask about her disappearance, I pieced together what happened from scraps of hushed conversation between the servants: After Busy Shan had returned from visiting her mother, a suspicious guard detained her at the gates of the Lake Palaces.

Only later would I realize we'd both been too young to understand that my plan for her escape had been doomed. She could still blame me for it. Maybe she thought I'd wanted her to get in trouble. And did I, some cold-eyed, calculating part of me that had emerged at the Lake Palaces? I didn't want to believe it.

Though the chop always remained in view on the Chairman's desk, never put away, I could tell the servants were nervous around it, giving it a wide berth. Clearly, they'd been warned and I suspected that Busy Shan had been punished, not only for leaving the Lake Palaces, but for forging the letter, for the crime of daring to use the Chairman's chop. She must have ended up in a labor camp. Digging my fingernails into my palms, I tried not to think about it.

If the Chairman hadn't been so giddy about National Day, he might have questioned me. But he didn't mention her again, a lesson more chilling than anything he could have said.

I didn't tell Secretary Sun, either. I never should have urged her to go, and she never should have listened to me. I couldn't have saved her, though. At the Lake Palaces, you could only save yourself, she would have been the first to tell me.

After the Chairman sent Secretary Sun in search of a movie we could watch later, we got into the water. Through the high windows, a crack of brilliant blue opened up in the dark clouds.

We paddled around, and then returned to the steps. I sat lower down, to keep myself submerged. When the Chairman squeezed my shoulder, I hooked my arm around his ropy legs, and leaned my head against his knee. His hands smoothed over me, polishing me, his heat passing through my body.

Steam rose, dancing on the water. We clung to each other, our bodies dissolving into one flesh. Minutes, hours, or days could have passed. The pool seemed outside of time, and as long as we stayed in here, we would be eternal, too.

"Enough of this cold," he said. His voice rippled through me and lapped against the tiled walls. "It's time to go."

1966

CHAPTER *20*

*T*O STAY OUT OF THE FRAY, WE LEFT THE CAPITAL. FOR MORE than half a year, we would travel to villas on the coast and along the Yangtze River basin, the lush landscape where the Chairman had grown up. The train carried us, his armored sedan, and even his wooden bed from the Lake Palaces, as we called upon Tianjin, Jinan, Xuzhou, Benfu, Nanjing, Changsha, Guangzhou, Nanchang, Nanning, and the other places he felt most at home, places I would have wanted to explore more thoroughly if we'd had a chance to leave our villas.

For the most part—aside from visits with local cadre and a few officials who flew in from the capital—we were alone. When I think of those months, I remember the quiet, how the plush carpets, built-in couches, four-poster beds hung with mosquito nets, and velvet cushions dampened sound like new-fallen snow. We never stayed for more than a few days in each place. Though he'd left the capital in high spirits, he soon turned restless.

I was restless, too. I missed the purpose and deadlines that had shaped my time at the Lake Palaces, and sometimes I wondered if the Chairman felt the same. I'd trained hard to get through National Day, and I'd duped the President! All that had revived my childhood dreams, and I'd never burned brighter for the Party.

Though he promised he would make me a model revolutionary, it would have to wait until we returned to Beijing. Until then, I had to keep his boredom and loneliness at bay. As long as the Chairman still viewed me as his student, his apprentice, he might someday

trust me on a larger stage. I'd travel the country on his behalf, finding ways to inspire the people.

One afternoon, on our way to Shanghai, the Chairman advised
one of his bodyguards on how to win over a woman close to her
family: kick around a shuttlecock with her little sister, join them on
an errand, or bring a perfect peach for the grandmother.

We sat together at a table. With its glossy wood-paneled walls,
brass-fitted sconces, and white lace curtains and tablecloths, the train
car had the look of a country manor from the foreign movies.

It was early January, about two months after we'd left Beijing. I
hadn't known we would be gone this long and with each passing day,
I feared I might never go back. Although I tried to read a book of
political theory I'd found in the library of the last villa, the train diz-
zied me. I wished I could have asked Secretary Sun how to keep
preparing, but he'd remained behind to keep track of the President
and his allies. It was hard to accept he'd finished his duties to me,
that he'd no longer prod me, challenge me. Protect me. Both he and
Teacher Fan were too busy, it seemed, to get word to me about my
family.

"She'll picture you as a husband, a father," the Chairman told
the bodyguard. "Women measure a man by how they treat their
family."

Bodyguard Wei grimaced. "I hope she doesn't consider me *her*
father. She's nothing like my mother."

"Everyone seeks out what they first know!" the Chairman said.
"If you want to make a life with her, take a long look at her mother.
You'll see how that girl might turn out. If she henpecks her husband.
If she's much of a cook."

"She's kept her looks," Bodyguard Wei said.

"So you've already checked!"

Bodyguard Wei looked down in embarrassment.

"Men your age are like dogs, gazing at every tree, at every possibility," the Chairman said.

Bodyguard Wei was a favorite of the Chairman—earnest and
shy, despite his towering size. But if I had to listen to him talk about

his romances a minute longer, I'd jump off the train. When I asked how much longer until we arrived in Shanghai, the Chairman unfurled a map of our country across the table. My village was a pinky's length from the capital, and in our months away, we would travel a hand's length, two, and then three. I was very far from my family, far from anyone I knew.

I looked at the map again. More American troops had landed in Vietnam, which curled off our southern border. It was only a matter of time until they invaded us, too.

The Chairman stretched his arms above his head. "I've been sitting so long, I can hardly move."

My body felt just as gnarled and knotted. I looked outside at the barren fields and overcast skies. In the distance, curls of smoke drifted up from a cluster of gray-brick homes. Usually, our train would speed through empty stations, soldiers from the closest base spaced out along the platform as we passed. Yet hadn't he always complained that no one told him anything? He'd long been suspicious that the President left out details in his reports. He'd want to see if capitalism—if greed and selfishness—had taken root in the countryside.

I tapped on the map. "There's a station coming up. Do you want to stop and walk around a bit?" I asked the Chairman. "Stretch our legs?"

He smiled.

"We can look around," I added.

Bodyguard Wei couldn't hide his shock. "It's not scheduled. There isn't any security in place. Local officials will insist on precautions."

"Precautions!" the Chairman snorted. "You mean the way cadre sweep away what they don't want me to see in every city we've visited? They might as well prop up dolls when I'm there! I'm tired of talking to people who've memorized their lines, who have no thought other than what they're told."

Bowing his head, Bodyguard Wei left the car to make arrangements. Although the Chairman should have been able to leave at any time, go anywhere in the country in the fastest, sleekest form of transport, it was impossible for him to observe without being observed, without a convoy of armed guards who cleared traffic and held back crowds. Making an unplanned stop was the only way he could see how the people lived.

"They'll radio ahead, but there's not much they can do to prepare," the Chairman told me. He didn't bother to change out of his wrinkled tunic and slacks. I wished I could get into my outfit from National Day, but it was packed away. The Chairman drummed his fingers on the table, impatient, and soon enough, we arrived at the station.

Even though it was winter, he exited the train without putting on a jacket, and without stopping to wait for me or Bodyguard Wei. I grabbed my padded coat, shouldering it over my plaid skirt and fitted gray sweater.

"Is he coming?" I heard someone ask on the platform.

"Not yet. Just the porter."

They must not recognize the Chairman in his shabby clothes. None of them broke formation as he moved down the platform.

"You from here?" the Chairman asked the gangly soldier, who seemed confused until understanding dawned on him.

"Yes, Chairman."

The Chairman offered him a cigarette, lighting it for him. "How's life?" he asked.

The soldier stared at the cigarette as if it might explode in his hand. He looked between the Chairman and the cigarette before puffing on it.

The Chairmen repeated his question. "How's life?"

"It's okay," the soldier answered.

The Chairman frowned.

The soldier straightened. "It's very good."

"Better than when you were a child?" the Chairman asked.

The soldier froze, the cigarette smoldering in his fingers, until I nodded at him, which reminded him to bob his head. He had a fox's face and sooty eyelashes. I didn't know his name and would never know it, but I felt a tenderness toward him and everyone I might meet as a model revolutionary when I'd make stops like this one— not only to share my story but to hear theirs.

"How long have you been in the Army?" I asked. He didn't appear much older than me; he had to grow into his oversized feet.

His relief was undisguised. It was easier talking to a teenage girl than with the Chairman.

"About a year." He took another drag.

When we were children, I wondered, did we worship the same heroes? Did we now? Lei Feng the soldier called himself "the tiny screw in the machine of revolution." Sister Yu and Iron Girl, the model revolutionaries from my childhood.

"I bet you didn't expect to meet the Chairman today," I said.

He cracked a smile. "It's an honor."

If he'd encountered me in the village, if I'd worn ragged pants, he might have ignored me for a prettier girl. Here, next to the Chairman, he had to pay attention, pay respect to me.

The Chairman continued down the platform, the stilted conversation much the same with each soldier. The men, studying me curiously, must have thought I was an attendant or an aide.

Whatever the Chairman imagined he'd hear and see, he hadn't found it yet. His face got in the way. Above a cracked clock his portrait hung, rosy-cheeked, with a closemouthed, mirthful smile. His eyes were kind. None of his quarters held such pictures, and seeing it here reminded me that what I thought was a private smile was for the country.

The portrait must have been painted at least a decade or two ago. His face was plumper now, his hairline pushed farther back, and his sideburns edged with gray.

Bodyguard Wei hung back with me. I had to stop him from hustling us back onto the train. "You see? No one would dare hurt the Chairman," I said. "They'd be torn to pieces!"

"Last year, a woman hanging laundry spotted him in his sedan when he rolled down the window to wave," he said. "She screamed, and crowds clogged the roads for six hours."

"Six hours?" I said. "People would wait six hours, six days to see the Chairman. You've gotten too used to being around him. No one here will ever forget this day."

"A little girl died," Bodyguard Wei said softly. "Crushed to death in the crowd."

Stunned, I didn't know what to say. Swallowing hard, I hurried to catch up with the Chairman as he left the station, heading toward the village a hundred meters down a dirt road. It must have been built long before the tracks came through. As my heels sank into the dust, I stumbled and touched his arm to steady myself.

"I can't ever find out the truth," he grumbled.

"They must have been nervous," I said.

"You got over it." The steam from our breath twisted in the air.

"Not at first," I said. We passed a stand of barren trees. "The guards probably aren't so talkative. You know how hard it is to get anything out of Bodyguard Wei! Three words is a speech from him. Here, you'll find someone. There's always a gossip who won't stop talking."

The Chairman grinned. "Everywhere."

As we reached the outskirts, people raced to prepare. In a doorway, a granny swept, dust whirling around her. Next door, a man stepped out, smoothing his hair, which stood on end. He rubbed his eyes, as if he'd woken up from a nap. If the Chairman had descended upon my village, we would have been as frantic. The familiar stink of straw-burning stoves and manure drifted on the breeze. My breath caught; it felt as if at any moment, Ma might step around the corner, and Ba might emerge from one of these homes.

Through the open doorway, we could see a mother swipe her daughter's face with a rag. "Hurry, hurry," she said. At the door, they slipped on straw sandals over their socks. The girl wore two thick sweaters, the wrists fraying. She might have been seven. When she stared at me, I tightened my coat around myself. Even without a jacket, the Chairman didn't seem to mind the cold.

"Looks like it's time for a haircut," the Chairman joked. The man smiled tentatively.

Bodyguard Wei joined us, scanning the gathering crowd.

The Chairman asked the man his name, his age. "How many children do you have, Brother Huang?"

"Two," he said.

The Chairman peered behind the man. "Where are they?"

"We have one child," Brother Huang blurted.

The Chairman chuckled. "Well, what is it?"

The man hunched his shoulders. "One."

I peeked inside: a bed, a stove, and a table with four stools. Yet there were only three people standing before us now. A family of four, until recently or not so recently. I might have been assuming too much; maybe they'd always been a family of three, and the stool was for guests. I doubted it. Something in the hollowness of the man's cheeks, in the listlessness in his wife and the fussiness of their daughter made me wonder if they'd lost someone not so long ago.

Did my family keep my sister's bowl? Did they keep mine?

When the girl peeked out from behind her mother's legs, the Chairman tickled her under her chin. He was easy with her, and it made me wonder if he'd been a playful father. Though she giggled, her parents remained on edge.

"How old are you?" he asked her. "Do you know who I am?"

Tugging on his hand, she pointed at the ceiling, where newspapers had been pasted. The Chairman beamed down from above their heads.

"How was your harvest this year?" the Chairman asked Brother Huang.

He cleared his throat. "Never better."

The Chairman clapped his hands together and the girl imitated him. He smiled at her. I hadn't been around children in months and realized how much I missed their high sweet voices, the way they flung themselves around without embarrassment. If I hadn't been wearing a skirt and heels, if I'd worn straw sandals like hers, I would have squatted or kneeled beside her.

"Do you like stories?" I asked her.

She nodded.

"Do you want to hear about the peasant girl who tricked . . ." I paused. How could I describe the President? "Who tricked a man who was mean to people like her? Do you know anyone like that?"

She nodded again. Her father put his hand on her shoulder. The Chairman was watching me—the parents and a few neighbors, too. It was starting to feel like an audition. I'd been hazy, but here I could gleam like I had on National Day.

"Just because of how this girl talked, because of what she looked like, the man thought she and people like her were meant to serve him," I said. The President scorned people like her, like me. If only I had the chance, I could inspire girls to defend the revolution. "Is that fair?"

She shook her head, her two braids whipping around her shoulders.

"What would be fair?" I asked. "Shouldn't he serve her sometime?"

"Who was it?" the girl asked. "A landlord?"

"Even more powerful," I said.

"The emperor?" she asked.

Her father shot a glance at his wife.

"The emperor's assistant," I said. "Who wanted to be emperor himself."

"You have many people who want to meet you," the mother said anxiously, her voice high and thin.

Much later, I'd understand they might have feared I was making a veiled comparison to the Chairman, trying to draw them into saying something disloyal.

Before I could say more, the headman interrupted us. "Welcome!"

The Chairman gazed over the village, asking how many people lived here.

"Forty families," the headman said. His ruddy cheeks and nose gave him the look of a drunk. He pointed toward the village plaza. "This way! Come sit!"

"We've been sitting all day," the Chairman said. "Let's have a tour."

"After you take a rest," the headman said. "We're preparing a feast."

"Local specialties?" the Chairman asked.

The headman hesitated. "With the supplies you so generously provided."

Villagers were coming up the path, carrying crates of food from the train, fresh greens and radishes, and a red slab of pork. Food that we wouldn't miss, food that would get replenished with ease to make meals that we would forget the next day.

I must admit, I didn't feel guilty for having so much more than them. Back then, I believed I was helping the Chairman make sure they would have the same as us someday. I took the girl's grimy hand, moist and hot despite the chilly weather, and promised I'd come back to finish my story.

She ducked behind her mother's legs, and we followed the headman, now accompanied by what seemed like most of the village. The bodyguards had formed a loose circle around us. After I noticed what might have been the storehouse, I nudged the Chairman, certain he'd want to see inside.

As we veered toward it, the headman hurried beside us. "It's a mess. Not worth your time to see."

The Chairman kept going until the headman had to let us into the storehouse, which was half-empty, its upper shelves cobwebbed, a pot tipped onto its side, and a cover sitting askew on a yawning bin. The storehouse should have still been crowded with grain, gourds, and dried vegetables. You were fat this month, thin in February, half-dead by March, the saying went, having eaten through your stores.

I wondered what had gone wrong, if the harvest had been poor this year. We followed the headman back outside, where he made excuses, telling us they'd had a bumper crop. Winter had come early, though, and they'd dipped into their stores faster than they'd intended. But families also had what they'd reaped from their individual plots.

The Chairman studied the shorn fields, his mouth grim. Whether or not the communal harvest had been enough, we'd never know. But the people had taken it upon themselves to go it alone, working hardest for themselves.

"Early winter means an early spring," the headman was saying. "We'll double the harvest from one year to the next and have you back then."

"Only fools depend on the weather," the Chairman snapped.

We left soon after.

CHAPTER 21

*A*S WE SPED TOWARD SHANGHAI, I STAYED OUT OF THE Chairman's way. He looked out the window, ignoring the book in his lap. But I didn't regret suggesting the stop, not when I remembered how the little girl had listened to me, looked at me.

Someday, as a model revolutionary, I wouldn't only give speeches in village plazas. I'd go from home to home and find someone who might feel lonely or alone, someone who might tell me what they and their family needed. And I'd get them the help that no one else could.

Looking back, I know what I'm saying sounds grandiose, self-serving. I can imagine your questions: *Didn't you know how childish your dreams seemed?* Listen, though: I was a child, taught to believe I had no higher cause than to serve the people.

Visiting the village also made me think of my family. The rawness of my sorrow had scabbed over, but sometimes ripped open. The wailing and keening that accompanies funeral processions, the beating of the chest, the firecrackers, were to impress the living—so much wasted pain, flaming up like kindling, not the long-burning coal that the dead deserve.

I longed for my mother's recovery. The sister who died didn't care if I knew or not, and I must seem dead to the one who'd lived.

I looked down at the Yangtze, swirling below. Our country's mother river, it began in the mountains in the far west, a clear stream that turned turbulent in high narrow gorges, becoming wide and slow, before ending in the eastern seas. It was every superlative: the swiftest and the most treacherous, with a current that the mightiest ship struggled against and whirlpools that spun everything around.

"Everyone told me not to swim in there," the Chairman said.

I stared at the froth. "Why would you go in? Did someone tell you where it might be safe?"

"No one ever went in to swim. By the time you wade up to your knees, the current knocks you down. Now a crowd goes in every summer!"

I palmed the window. High above, hawks wheeled, floating on the wind. If I drew out his memory, it could lighten his dour mood. "You just had to show them how."

He nodded. "They told me I'd drown, but I didn't listen."

"They?" I asked.

"Everyone who's supposed to look after me," he said. "What did they know? Some of them didn't even know how to swim!" He frowned. "I swam the Yangtze three times in all."

The muddy waters didn't look inviting. "You wanted to show them the first time wasn't just luck," I said.

He nodded. "That's why I swam a second time. And the third?"

Studying the river again, I pictured him stroking through the current. Each time he plunged back in, it must have put pressure on the men onshore to join him. "To show others they should follow."

"Exactly! You would have thought they were going to their deaths! Once they got in, they kept going. They had to, or they'd drown. If you talk and talk, you'll never get anything done. So many cadre were like that—are like that now—afraid to take risks necessary for our country to become strong. They fall back into what they know."

"When was this?" I asked.

"Back in fifty-six," he said. "Were you even walking then?"

"I was running."

He laughed and returned to his book. Staring at the river, I thought about the timing of that swim: back when the Chairman had been pushing for collectives, in the countryside and in the factories.

The Party had been divided in those days, Secretary Sun had said. The President and his allies had wanted to turn socialist slowly—so slowly, the Chairman suspected they might have been secret capitalists.

The swim had emboldened the Chairman, I suspected. Afterward, hadn't he insisted on the Great Leap Forward? A plan no one but the Chairman could have imagined; in school, we'd learned that it was supposed to make China a leader of socialists around the world. He had led the country the way he swam—with daring.

As the track curved away from the river and entered a grove of pine trees, he reached over and stroked my hand with an absentminded affection. These moments helped me endure the mechanics of what happened every few nights: his mottled hands tugging at me, rolling me over, his tea-steeped breath at my neck, and the weight of him, pinning me to the bed. My body responding automatically to what he did, what we did.

I put my other hand on top of his. The annual swim in the Yangtze River made me think the plunge must have been important not only to the Chairman but also to the officials who had doubted him, and then changed their minds. It mattered to those who still followed him into the river, inspired by his strength and his fearlessness.

"Some people will hold you back because of their own fears," he said. "Don't let them."

AT THE MEETING THE next day, I sat on the far side of the cavernous room, listening to the Premier, the Defense Minister, and the President, who'd all traveled to Shanghai. The Defense Minister was wintering in a villa about an hour away and the other two had flown in. They, along with a few officials I didn't know, were discussing whether to replace someone at the Ministry of Public Security, but I didn't recognize any of the names.

The men, clustered on couches and seats around the Chairman, glanced at me every once in a while, except for the President, who never looked in my direction, as if his head was clamped in place. It was the first time I'd seen him since National Day. Though I'd searched the newspapers for reports about him, I never turned up hints of his impending ruin. We'd heard his cadre planned to visit the universities starting in the spring, and right now, he didn't seem worried in the least. The men laughed, the Chairman loudest of all; I looked up and realized the President had said something amusing and well received. He leaned back in his chair, legs crossed, his foot propped up on his knee, comfortable. He reached for his cup of tea, one of many cluttering the low wooden tables.

I twined the fringe on a pillow around my finger until my skin became pale and bloodless. The throb mirrored my confusion. How could the officials go back to joking around with one another? I'd never felt so young. Young and naïve, as if I hadn't convinced the President to nose around schools, as if my training didn't matter and I remained an ignorant peasant girl.

After the trouble in the village, I felt I had to convince the Chairman that what I'd accomplished on National Day hadn't been an accident, hadn't been luck. Maybe I could give him advice after hearing their discussion. But I couldn't follow the conversation, because there were too many terms, too many names, too many histories, I didn't understand. Why did I ever think I could keep up? I hated my stupidity, and I hated the President even more. It had to be his fault somehow. I tell you, if locusts had descended, if the moon had fallen from the sky, he also would have been to blame.

As the talk droned, I struggled to stay awake. When my head dipped, I jerked up, hoping no one had noticed, but that afternoon, the Chairman sent me to the library of the redbrick estate, which had been built by a wealthy Frenchman. I tried to read verses by Du Fu, a favorite of the Chairman's, a poet, historian, and sage who lived centuries ago and wandered for eight years while rebellion and famine devastated the country.

On our old home, the moon is bright. The moon renewed itself each month and so could I. But in the next few lines, the poet lost hope.

My brothers are scattered far
Nowhere I might learn if they are dead or alive
I send letters, but none reply
The land rings with the clash of arms

The poem seemed like a bad omen.

At the window, I studied the villa's peaked turrets and spiked, delicate iron gates, a design that had come to the Frenchman's eleven-year-old daughter in a dream. All I could think of then was that a child had more control over her surroundings than I did.

At dinner, I asked about the meeting, apologizing for losing track of the names.

"Soon you won't have to remember them," the Chairman said.

"They're getting forced out?" I asked.

He pulled out a fish ball from the bubbling pot and popped it into his mouth. "These are ready." He plopped one into my bowl.

Cagey as always. I dumped in cabbage and black mushrooms, the broth spattering, until the boiling water went quiet.

"You've overloaded the pot," the Chairman scolded. "We'll have to wait for it to boil again."

"I'm tired of dipping a piece here, a piece there. I've been nibbling all night and I'm no closer to being full," I said. The smell of gas wafting from the portable stove on the dining table made me nauseous.

"Always trying to get more with less work," he joked. Probably sensing my frustration, he hinted at what was happening. "Those who try to keep their own kingdom won't for much longer."

"Are you talking about the President?" I asked.

Pushing his chair back from the table, he walked over to the mahjong set. He grabbed fistfuls of the ivory tiles—big and yellow as horse teeth but polished like piano keys—and stacked them vertically, two in each row, each level crosswise from the one below.

He motioned for me to join him and pointed at the tile perched on top. "How would you get rid of that one?"

When I reached for it, he pushed my hand away. "Those at the top can see you coming," he said. From the middle, he slid out a tile and dropped it with a clatter onto the table. I tried to ease one out, but the stack tottered.

"Careful," he said.

I nudged aside another tile to steady the stack, and then pulled mine out. We traded turns, until the top tiles teetered on the few left beneath them.

One flick of a finger, and the rest would topple.

"We start in the middle," he said. "With the President's cronies. The others will follow."

IN THOSE MONTHS, THE Madame was on the advance, that much I'd gathered after reading her correspondence with the Chairman. In one letter, she described calling upon an army base, where she'd screened ideologically flawed movies to senior officers, teaching them how to spot what secretly undermined the revolution. In another, she wrote about a meeting with the Defense Minister. In late February, seeking the Chairman's advice, the Madame visited us in Hangzhou, at Liuzhuang, the estate of a former tea merchant. It overlooked the tranquil West Lake, its shores thick with bamboo groves and pavilions.

I wasn't invited; he told me to go to the library, located on the other side of the villa. She would stay for about half a day before returning to Shanghai. I looked up at the lotus flowers carved in the library's ceiling, their petals tipped in gold. Cabinets, inlaid with mother-of-pearl phoenix and dragon designs, were crammed with books. Another cabinet held magazines with glossy photos of foreigners, treasures that were mine alone today, that should have awed me, but only made me feel more apprehensive. How many of these books hadn't been touched in years, shelved and never read? I felt just as musty.

Although I should've looked for something to study on the shelves, the library was drafty, and I tucked my hands into the sleeves of my sweater to warm up. If I was quiet, I could make my way to their room and press my ear to the door. I pictured him with his wife, their heads bent over a page. The thought of them together made me itch, pale bumps breaking out on my forearms. I'd scratch myself raw if I had to stay in here.

In the garden, most of the trees were barren, their branches stark. Not a creature stirred. I turned back toward the villa. Even though the room where they were probably meeting didn't face the garden, I ducked onto a bench behind a bush to stay out of view.

The damp chill seeped into my skirt. Rubbing my arms, I wished I'd grabbed a jacket to wear over my thin sweater. I looked down, letting hair curtain my face, and blowing at the strands that got caught in my mouth. I'd make him forget her as soon as she left. I wouldn't let her keep me from becoming a model revolutionary, from helping people like the ones we'd met in the village.

The Chairman never mentioned that visit, and for all I knew, he'd forgotten it already. But I'd never stopped thinking about it. The little girl had squeezed my hand in what felt like a wordless plea: *Don't forget me.*

Before long, I went back inside.

In the hallway, I came face-to-face with the Madame. She stood tall, her eyes brighter than I remembered, no trace of the crone she'd seemed in danger of becoming. Though she had a hint of a double chin, she gave off the impression of a piece of jade rubbed until gleaming, lavishly cared for in every way.

I touched my tangled hair and glanced at my mud-spattered shoes. Although I thought she might turn without acknowledging me, she surprised me. "How's he been sleeping?" she asked.

"When he wants," I said. "When he can."

I didn't tell her that the night before some meetings, he'd down handfuls of pills—surely more than what the doctor would have ever allowed.

I was taller than her, but she had a presence that took up so much space, her head could have brushed the ceiling.

She wagged her finger at me. "You have to make sure he eats well, sleeps well. I've told the doctor what he needs, but he won't listen!" she said. "Dr. Li never listens. You can't trust him." She shook her head. "If his condition changes, you get word to me. You can come to me."

How many times had she seen him sink into his melancholy? "The Chairman wants me to?" I asked.

She pressed her lips into a thin line.

"He gave his permission?" I asked.

"He knows that I value his health above mine," she said. Fine lines crinkled around her eyes. When she folded her arms across her chest, I noticed her veined and spotted hands. For all the power she had, she'd never be sixteen again.

"No one's looked after him like I have," she said.

I should have agreed and walked away, but I remembered then how she'd called me a silly whore. How she'd blamed me for the Chairman's illness, telling Teacher Fan, probably Midnight Chang and anyone she came across at the Lake Palaces.

And now she expected me to report to her? We both knew that he traveled with me.

Maybe she could tell what I thought as the silence stretched on. "You're no different than the other girls who've passed through his bed," she said. She looked at me with a disdain meant to show me my time would soon run out.

If anything happened to the Chairman, I'd be nothing. But I could say the same about her.

I had wondered if Midnight Chang had become the Madame's aide; she had never mentioned it in her letters to the Chairman. "You don't think Midnight Chang will turn on you the first chance she gets?" I asked.

She inhaled sharply. She'd chosen the wrong protégé. She might have thought Midnight Chang could entice the Chairman away from me, but they'd failed.

"If she ever gets out of line, you could tell her to rub mud in her hair," I said. Just like the prank the Chairman played on her in Yan'an.

The Madame went taut, her strike withheld.

———

THE NEXT TWO MONTHS blurred like the view from the train. We stayed away from Beijing. As we entered spring, we traveled along the Yangtze, where the rows of wheat and corn of the north gave way to patchworks of terraced rice paddies. Though many days dripped as slowly as a leaking tap, I could tell something simmered, threatening to boil over, that the Chairman wanted to watch from afar.

The President kept postponing when he'd send his cadre into the universities. He traveled out of the country for much of April, on state visits with his wife to Pakistan, Afghanistan, and Burma. As soon as he returned and settled on a date, the pace of the Chairman's calls and letters to the Madame, the Defense Minister, and his other allies sped up to daily and sometimes twice a day.

Late one night, when I asked the Chairman what he planned, he gave a little smile, as if to say this matter was too great for my understanding. "There's nothing left to do but wait," he said. Action through inaction: a tactic employed by emperors and rebels alike.

"For what?" I asked.

"Wait and see," he said. He got out of bed to put on a record, meandering horns that made me think of sunlight glinting off dark water.

My hands knotted the sheets. Hadn't *I* tricked the President? If I pressed the Chairman, though, he'd lash out at me.

In May, after the Chairman got off the phone with the Madame, he couldn't hide his pleasure at what she'd told him. At a meeting of Party leaders in the capital, officials agreed: Bad elements had infiltrated the country, all bent on restoring capitalism.

I sucked on my forefinger, bleeding after I'd torn off my hangnails during the call. I hated that she'd delivered the good news. "What does that mean?" I asked.

"There's corruption in the Party, the Army, the government, the courts, the police, everywhere you look!" he said.

His absence from the meeting puzzled me. "Why didn't you go?"

Even as I asked, I remembered the stack of mahjong tiles. He'd shown me how to knock flat the top tile by wiggling loose the ones underneath. It was best not to act publicly, directly. If he hung back, he could deny responsibility if and when trouble arose. "Because you didn't have to," I said.

He nodded. "Why run off your mouth when you can leave them guessing?"

A courier brought us the full report, and details soon hit the newspaper headlines: Only a campaign of violent class struggle would rid us of the monsters that my generation had been taught to fear, taught to hate before we took our first steps—the capitalist wolf at the front door who would snap you in its jaws. Students in Beijing were among the first to join the new Great Proletarian Revolution, and the President's cadre had to contend with their defiance.

In villas serene as the inside of an egg, the distant turmoil didn't seem quite real. Over lunch, I stared at a newspaper photo of giant protest posters, accusing top school officials of scheming against the Chairman. Each poster seemed big and tall as a man with his arms and legs spread. The characters looked frenzied, almost vibrating, as though they might fly off the page.

"Where are these?" I asked, trying to figure out how I might join the campaign.

"Everywhere," the Chairman crowed. "All over campus. Even glued onto the backs of professors!"

I pushed my bowl away. What remained of our dishes congealed in pools of grease.

"Those are the lucky ones. Some professors had ink thrown into their faces," he said. "It's catching on. It's not just students at the universities; their little brothers and sisters won't be outdone."

With a smile, he tapped another photo in the newspaper. At a middle school, the students declared themselves Red Guard, vowing to defend the Chairman. They wanted to live up to the ideal of Yan'an, where you were worker, soldier, and student all in one. They'd put on old military uniforms and red armbands.

"Child's play," he said. "But they're also foot soldiers of this new revolution. They took it upon themselves to uncover these traitors. You have to be young, to make change like this."

It didn't seem fair; children younger than me had joined the revolution. All their lives, like me, they might have dreamed of becoming fighters. All they'd needed was an enemy, and they found one in the capitalists in disguise.

I had a sudden yearning for other teenagers, for our buzz and clamor. In the troupe, we fed off one another, egging one another on. Around the Chairman, sometimes I felt like a sound that had lost its echo.

"When will we go see?" I asked. I didn't want to miss out on what everyone else my age seemed to have a part in.

"I know you're impatient," he said, his tone genial. He rubbed the back of my hand.

They were so far ahead of me, I'd never catch up. "I've tried to read the books you and Secretary Sun recommended."

He nodded. "Some of the same books I read when I worked as a library clerk."

"But I can't learn on my own, not like you!" I said. "Can you— can we study together?"

"Let others stay busy with their politics," he said. "We're taking a rest."

"Others?" I asked.

He slid a piece of paper at me, with a list of names and titles. "The group helping guide the campaign."

The page picked up spots of grease. I didn't recognize any of the names except for one that jumped out: the Madame, the deputy director. A hot flush rose through me. All this time, I'd been dreading her revenge, but she didn't need to trifle with me. She had a role at the center of the Cultural Revolution, and it seemed her decades of loyalty had paid off.

"I should go. Go in disguise. Seek out corrupt intellectuals," I said. Now that the campaign had a name, had a form to the smoke and shadow, I wanted a place for myself in it.

Interrupting me, he asked Bodyguard Wei to bring in the movie projector.

"I could go around the country," I went on.

"Let the President keep sending in his cadre. You're ready, but the time's not," he said.

I looked at the list again. The Madame's prominence made me suspect that the group's members were just as loyal to the Chairman. Barking—and biting—where the Chairman couldn't: at the President. No one yet knew that the Madame and her cronies would rule the country in the decade to come.

Back then, I only wanted our wandering to come to an end.

NOT LONG AFTER, I woke up to a frenzied scream as the Chairman thrashed beside me.

"I'm here, I'm here." I turned on the light and touched his shoulder.

He opened his eyes. "I thought I saw someone standing in the corner."

The President? "There's no one but me," I said.

He grabbed my wrist, his fingers damp and slippery. "Do you hear that?"

Branches tapped against the tall window.

"It's the wind," I said. Trying to keep my voice even, I drew the sheets around him. He shrugged them off, for he was always too warm. Though the attendants aired out the rooms, mustiness remained, the green-black scent of dampness and darkness sealed up in the long months between his visits.

"Someone's in the attic." He bunched the sheets in his fist. We heard skittering, light footsteps, and rocks scattering.

"It's nothing," I said.

"Nothing? Nothing?" The Chairman sat up.

"I'll tell the guards." The bed creaked under us.

"It's too late," he said, his voice hoarse. "They'll never find her."

Her? Not the President, then. Who haunted him? His wife, Martyr Yang? His mother? I gripped the edge of the bed, as if we were adrift on a boat at sea. His recovery from his sadness and exhaustion had been fitful and incomplete, with nightmares like this one, or days he almost didn't get out of bed. It could have been another reason he put off returning to the capital. It was why I didn't press him about what he planned for me.

An American newspaper had just claimed that he'd needed help on the stairs on National Day, his face had become an expressionless mask, and that he sounded hoarse and might have throat cancer. "Imperialist lies," he'd said, then argued America was crumbling: demonstrations against the war in Vietnam and riots where whole city blocks burned to the ground. "Their people are rising up. Taking down capitalism from the inside."

Even so, the rumors about his health must have tormented him. Long after I turned off the light, his body remained tense as a sapling tied into a snare. His suspicions about everything and everyone seemed to be running high, as if his own shadow might be out to get him. He hadn't touched me in days, and I knew he hadn't bedded anyone else since our travels began. Although I wanted to believe his faithfulness meant something, he might just have been wary of letting in someone new.

We were protected here, behind walls, behind soldiers with guns. How could he lead the new revolution, if shadows terrified him? People twice, three times or more my age didn't know how to calm him. Many days, I threatened to spill out everywhere, on the verge of tears, on the verge of screaming. If I couldn't help my family or Busy Shan, how could I possibly help him?

The next morning, I told Bodyguard Wei about the noise, and he set a trap on the roof that caught two huge rats. He brought them to us, their fur matted and their necks broken, but such proof didn't convince the Chairman.

"Something isn't right here," he said after he'd dismissed the bodyguard. He smelled like dried sweat. Books were spread face-down around him in bed; he'd been unable to concentrate on anything for long. "There's something poisonous about this place."

In the grass, in the trees, everything seems a soldier, so the proverb went. A guerilla who'd been looking for threats for so long, the Chairman didn't know how to live any other way—not now, while waiting for his foes to fall. Or maybe a hungry ghost haunted him, a forgotten ancestor who wouldn't leave him in peace unless he returned to pay tribute to the place where he began. A fly buzzed somewhere, a circling taunt.

"Let's go home," I said. "To your hometown."

CHAPTER 22

THE FIRST PLACE WE VISITED IN SHAOSHAN WASN'T THE grave of his parents, or his childhood home, but a huge rock in a clearing on a hill forested with groves of pine and bamboo, where he used to gather firewood, taking as long as possible for a few moments to himself, away from the endless demands of his father.

"Hello, Grandmother Rock," he said. Dried pine needles crunched underfoot, the air heavy with their scent.

He told me how as a boy, he had spent many afternoons here napping, hiding from field work and lessons. He bowed three times to the rock to show respect to his elder—the only deference I would ever see him make, to anyone or to anything. His mother had nicknamed him Shisanyazi, he said. A child of stone, the third son she'd borne but the first to survive. If he'd followed his mother's wishes, he could have become a monk, but the call of the revolution had been louder than the call of enlightenment.

In the wet heat, sweat trickled down my back, pooling at my waistband, which chafed against my skin. I rubbed my hands over the smooth curves of the dark gray stone, speckled white, pink, and black, here long before and long after me. As I pressed my face against the sun-warmed bulk, calm settled over me, in this place whose memory might have sustained the Chairman in his lowest moments. Here I felt closest to touching the boy he'd been, solitary and dreamy, first sensing the possibilities of a larger world. Here I might persuade him to consider the future again.

We didn't stay long at his home, which had been turned into a museum. It was grander than I had imagined, not a single-room home with a single bed like my family's, but a house with several rooms, with packed earth floors, two wings around a courtyard—signs his family had been far more prosperous than mine. As a baby, the Chairman stumbled through the courtyard, and later on, read in the shade of the mulberry bush. Everything seemed off-kilter, missing the smells and sounds of a family, without the sweetness of steamed rice in the kitchen, or the stink of chickens in the yard. It must sound strange to you, but I wanted to climb into the way it used to be, and into his childhood bed, hung with nets and a battered oil lamp, and inhale his memories.

The museum director lingered a few meters away. When I tried to sit on a low, sturdy stool in the kitchen, the Chairman elbowed me aside and ran his hand along the wood. "I was the only one allowed here beside Ma."

"Where she could keep an eye on you," I teased. "Who knew what trouble you must have been getting into?"

"I was no trouble at all." He grinned. "A model child. To her, at least."

His mother must have indulged him from early on. I pictured her presenting him with a surprise after every chore: a long bean set aside for him to chew or a scrap of red thread to tie around his plump wrist.

"She'd given up on my younger brothers. They were no good at sums, at books. She always told me the family depended on me," he said.

She must have believed him destined for greatness, never imagining how far he'd go.

I had a family, too, but he never asked. By now, they would be long past the forty-nine days of mourning for my sister, with offerings left at her burial mound. Grains of corn, a splash of liquor. Her spirit, forever seeking a place in our home, because she had never married, never had children to honor and remember her.

I couldn't ask the Chairman to help me find out which sister had died. He had endured years, decades even, of not knowing the fate of his family. He'd swallowed whatever he felt about those losses, just like I had to if I wanted to become a model revolutionary.

AT THE LOCAL RESERVOIR, a turtle sunned itself under skies that looked draped in gauze. The air twitched with a green scent that teemed with vitality, as if every flower, bush, and tree might grow twice in size overnight. My father would have loved this landscape, the patchwork of rice paddies climbing the hills and the misty peaks.

The Chairman used to fish from its banks and swim in the warm shallows with his brothers. Bodyguard Wei paced the banks, keeping an eye out for onlookers. The museum director had been sworn to secrecy about the Chairman's visit, but someone might accidentally come by.

We'd changed into our suits at the museum. Now, as we floated on our backs, I gazed through the willow trees fringing the shore, their branches billowing like imperial robes. I remembered when the Chairman first taught me to swim: I'd paddled around, straining to keep my head above water in the pool at the Lake Palaces. When I'd discovered that the pool sloped down and I was no longer touching the bottom, I'd panicked, thrashing back toward the Chairman.

"Put your face in the water," he'd called to me. "Hold your breath."

I'd leaned over, my face about to break the surface, when I pulled back, certain I'd drown. "I can't."

"I'm here," he'd said. At the count of 3-2-1, he held me and we plunged in, but the moment my nose touched the water, I'd jerked back up, coughing, my lungs shredded.

After I could breathe again, he'd taken my hands. "Blow out," he'd said, stroking my hands with his thumbs. "It will keep the water from coming in."

I'd held myself together in the grip of his fingers. He had counted down again, and when we went underwater, we had stared at each other, bubbles cascading from our noses. The sight so beautiful, the gurgling so funny, I'd forgotten my fear.

Did the Chairman remember that day? He backstroked across the pond, the splashes causing a pair of ducks to flap out of the water. Drifting here as a child, he could have imagined himself in the clouds, slipped free. Maybe I would find the boy he'd been by swimming here: my arms curling as his curled, my legs kicking as his kicked, listening to frogs a thousand generations removed from those that sang to him.

I glided toward him, relishing the pull of my muscles, the push of the water against me.

You never saw me swim, never saw how I became more of myself. I felt reborn. Free.

Years later, I've thought about what might have happened if I hadn't persuaded the Chairman to go to Shaoshan. If his whims had taken him to somewhere with cooler temperatures, to his villas in Moganshan or Beihei. If we had detoured north, to the model village tucked in a steep mountain valley in Shanxi province, he might have sunk back into his strange illness. If the Chairman had been completely unavailable, the President could have quashed the student protests before they spiraled out of control. So many during the Cultural Revolution might not have perished, might never have been forced from their homes. I might never have met you. It's impossible to know.

And yet I have no doubt the visit to Shaoshan became a turning point for the Chairman and so, too, his campaign. Over the next few days, seeing where he came from seemed to bolster his resolve to destroy those who would lay waste to his legacy.

THE VILLA WHERE WE stayed nestled on the slopes of Mount Dishui. The gardens hung heavy with the scent of magnolia, the snowy blossoms bursting in an exhausted abundance.

Next to the pavilion where we napped every afternoon, a waterfall tumbled from a miniature mountain and into a deep pond that brimmed with lotus flowers, croaking frogs, and fat orange-and-white carp flicking their fins.

Every three days or so, couriers arrived. The reports were short and oblique: The Cultural Revolution was proceeding. After administrators had canceled classes in June, more and more students at middle schools and universities were calling themselves Red Guards, with ferocious names to match: Red Descendants, Soldiers for the Annihilation of the Bourgeoisie, Little Red Devils, and the Red Flag Combat Team.

The Chairman—and the group led by the Madame—wanted even more turmoil. "Great chaos will lead to great order. The demons will out themselves. Their class character dictates it," the Chairman wrote his wife.

It was now early July, more than a year after I'd left home. I felt no closer to convincing the Chairman to return to the capital. Only there could I become a revolutionary myself. Only there could I make plans to see my family, help them and people like them, and report to the Chairman what I'd seen. My dreams may seem muddled now, but I tell you, back then, they made sense when little else did.

He dropped the latest stack of reports on the table in the pavilion shaded by towering sycamores. Amid the protests, the President's cadre struggled to regain control. It was just what we'd hoped might happen when we'd suggested he send Party officials to campus. Across the country, tens of thousands of cadre followed his lead and rushed into schools to put the students in check.

The President had also banned street demonstrations and attacks by students against those they accused. I flipped open a report that detailed how they were chafing against the restrictions, turning against the cadre.

"Will the students start blaming the President?" I asked.

"Of course! The cadre arrived in his name, on his behalf, on his authority," the Chairman said.

"But what if they think he's carrying out your orders?" I asked. Until then, it hadn't occurred to me they might hold the Chairman accountable.

He smirked. "Back home, what did you think the President did?"

Heat rose in my cheeks. "I didn't think about him much at all."

"Do you know what he does now?" he asked.

I stared at the weathered planks of the table. He'd never bothered to explain.

"Most people in this country couldn't quite say, either. Just know it's no secret to these students that I've stepped back from daily matters and that I have for years. I take the long view. Five years, a decade. Anything that might happen tomorrow, next week, or next month is an act of the President."

"Maybe they'll think the President is downplaying the crackdown to you?" I asked.

"They might." He pawed through the mail, tossing aside something—an invitation for an annual swim in the Yangtze that commemorated his historic plunge. How proud, how pleased he'd been, telling me about that day. The letter promised thousands of swimmers would be there, and a dance party that evening.

A courier arrived with a sheaf of papers. "Tell me what you've seen," the Chairman said to him.

"There have been—" The courier paused, his scarecrow's rigid shoulders and downcast eyes betraying more. His mouth hung open with the expression of a guard discovering treasures gone missing.

The Chairman clapped his hands by the courier's ears. "I can see you're not a deaf-mute." Ever since we'd returned to his hometown, his questions for his couriers had become pointed, probing. He tented his fingers, his eyes fixed on the courier. If the Chairman had been a smell, he would have been hot metal, the clean metallic scent before a lightning storm.

The courier squirmed. "The students aren't listening to the cadre," he answered. "The demonstrations and the struggle sessions haven't stopped."

I imagined the students in old army uniforms, striking fierce poses. Foot soldiers of the revolution. From the little I knew then, the students sounded devoted to the Chairman. If they had taken to the streets in the same numbers as they had on National Day, the capital must be overrun. I'd taken part in struggle sessions in the troupe and in my village, and heard the stories from my parents, but I didn't understand the scale or the intensity of the latest ones. No one told me that some victims had been forced to kneel on broken glass, and how the worst beatings left them crippled. The most despondent and desperate stepped in front of trains or swallowed rat poison.

"Even more students are joining up," the Chairman said. He loosened a clump of gristle with his toothpick and spat onto the ground. "This is what happens when you pour gasoline onto a fire."

He showed me a letter from the President, asking if he should send in reinforcements for his cadre. The new courier couldn't hide his surprise that the Chairman let me read his correspondence.

I fingered the page. "That will fail, too. The students will fight back even more."

The Chairman nodded. "The President is suppressing the students."

Suppress. It was the first time I'd heard him use that word to describe what was happening.

Even though the courier didn't register its weight, I understood: To put down the students was to put down the masses. The people had once revolted against greedy landlords and imperial officials, and now the danger came from within the Party—from the very top, from the President and the cadre who followed his orders without question.

"Do you have anything for the President?" the courier asked. "Anything at all?"

The President must have hoped for advice, but the Chairman refused him any. "You could go by the university, investigate on your own," I told the courier. The Chairman would never believe I could inspire people, unless I showed him. "You don't have to let your bosses know. Then come report to the Chairman."

He didn't acknowledge me. The Chairman smiled, but said nothing. I fidgeted with my cup, wondering if he thought I'd been presumptuous.

"The courier won't thank you," the Chairman said after the courier left. "He'll hate you."

"For helping him?" I asked.

"For telling him what to do," he said. "Let him fail. Let him fail, and then he'll learn."

The Chairman was waiting. For what, he wouldn't tell me. Maybe he wanted a certain number of schools to join the movement or certain intellectuals and their political patrons had to fall before he knew if his revolution had taken hold. It was clear, though, that the Chairman wanted the students set free to keep the revolution alive, not guided by him or anyone else.

Years later, I would realize that for all the time he spent with the teenage girls in the troupe, he didn't understand how dangerous liberating us could be.

My neck stiff, I stretched my arms above my head. "If I'm to be a model revolutionary, why shouldn't I teach them?"

"You'll inspire the youth. But they'll learn on their own." He peeled an orange, the scent sweet, innocent, and purifying.

"You ask for details that aren't included in the report, but the couriers don't know," I said. "They'll never know what the students will do next."

"The grass will be milk soon enough," he said.

The breeze picked up, and I snatched the swim invitation fluttering off the table. "If we—if you could just see for yourself." The sound of hammers tinkled and echoed on the villa's grounds. Maybe it wasn't only the President he was after. Maybe he wanted other officials to guess if they would fall, fearful that he targeted them. In the troupe, weren't the struggle sessions more ominous because we never knew who might strike or who among us might get attacked next?

By the river, someone was playing the flute and the song flickered in and out of the breeze. My neighbor Fatty Song used to play in the evenings, in clear, bright tones like water falling.

I placed my hand on his thigh. When he reached for me, my fingers darted to his sides, where he was most ticklish. "Not now." He batted my hand away.

When I persisted, he started coughing. His face turned a deep, alarming red, and then he stormed off.

A spider hung from the rafters of the pavilion, swaying on an invisible thread that I wanted to glide up and away on. I lit one of his cigarettes, seeking the comfort it gave him. The first drag burned my lungs and made me jittery. I'd already been feeling run-down, on the early days of my flow. Though my worries about getting pregnant remained, they'd also receded, now that month after month my flow arrived, regular as the moon.

Ma's own struggle to conceive might protect me now.

I yearned for my family, for my village and our routine. There, I had no doubt of my purpose, of the weeds to be plucked, the porridge to be cooked, the kindling to be gathered. There, I was just another teenager, easily ignored, who didn't have to soothe the Chairman's moods.

As I strolled to a nearby pond, I told myself his quarrel wasn't with me. The biggest carp I'd ever seen lived among its winding banks—its scales orange as the hottest part of a fire and golden eyes so intelligent it seemed like one of those guardian spirits in disguise. It always came up to the water's edge when I peered in, as if it were from the fairy tale that granted wishes to an unwanted daughter. But he was nowhere to be found now.

Wait, Secretary Sun would have told me. I missed him keenly, an ache in my chest, missed him more than I'd admitted to myself until then. *Wait*. But I'd been waiting long enough. If the Chairman wanted to know more about the universities than what could be found in a report, I could go on his behalf, disguised as a student. It would become part of my legend: the revolutionaries and scheming counter-revolutionaries, all schooled by a peasant girl.

I CAME UP WITH a plan. No matter how far the Chairman traveled, he must feel suffocated—never more so than in this villa, which had no air-conditioning. The electric fans that surrounded our bed only pushed around the hot air. Our trip to the village hadn't turned up much, and his frustration could have been mounting all this time.

When I came back inside, he didn't turn to greet me.

"You need new eyes in the capital," I told him.

He was looking out the bedroom window, the glass rippled and warped, its wooden sill dusty and littered with flies. "I have enough eyes."

"You need new hands," I said. "I won't hang around at the edges. Not like the couriers, who perch on a cliff to study an anthill below. I'll bring the revolution back to you."

CHAPTER 23

SECRETARY SUN MET ME AT THE TRAIN STATION, WHICH smelled like cigarettes and fried dough. Vendors manned bubbling cauldrons of oil, claiming their treats the plumpest, the crispest you'd ever have. The Chairman had phoned him, ordering the two of us to return to Peking University, where the student battles against the school's leaders had raged first and fiercest in the name of the Cultural Revolution.

I'd traveled to the capital with a confidential courier who'd been eager to hand me off to Secretary Sun. In the backseat of the sedan, we were quiet, the air heavy with everything unsaid since we'd parted. I centered my red-star cap over two tight braids, now grown out from my bob, and smoothed down my tortoise-green army uniform, belted at the waist. All students were now wearing similar outfits, and so, too, Secretary Sun, no longer in his usual button-down shirt and slacks. He'd lost weight, his cheeks gaunt and his face drawn, lines etched around his mouth. He was just as handsome— refined somehow—as if his true self were emerging, a carving from stone. I studied him in the rearview mirror, wondering what he thought of me, or if he'd thought of me at all.

"What—" "How—" we said at the same time. Eight months had passed since we'd last seen each other, when the Chairman and I left the Lake Palaces.

He looked at the driver and back at me, a silent reminder that anything we said could get reported to the Chairman. We started over. Secretary Sun said he'd just returned from an inspection of

Fudan University in Shanghai. His voice sounded hoarse, from a cold, he said, that wouldn't go away. He asked about Shaoshan.

Hot, I said. "The only thing hotter is the food that the chef prepares."

"Is it spicy enough for the Chairman?"

"Probably not!" I said. "The other day, the attendant warned me when she set down the dish. There were so many fried and fresh chilies you couldn't see underneath them. 'Not for you. For the Chairman,' she said. To show her that I could take it, I swallowed a huge bite. 'Delicious,' I said, but then I downed a pot of tea. The Chairman finished off the rest, never blinking."

"When *I* tried to match the Chairman, I tasted fire for days," Secretary Sun said.

We both laughed. It was like hearing a chime, to have him beside me.

Puddles steamed in the street, what remained of the storm that had just blown through. We swerved around a pedicab piled high with wooden crates, its rubber tires nearly bald, and startled the man who steered and held up the wobbly load. He jerked back to avoid getting hit. Traffic soon came to a standstill. The driver leaned on his horn, but the cars didn't move, and after a minute, he got out to investigate.

Secretary Sun appraised me. "I never would have believed what you have become."

My face went hot. "And you, what's become of you?" I asked. "The sun's in your skin."

He'd turned lacquered brown as a roast duck. Dark as a peasant, dark as me. The color sharpened his high cheekbones and gave off the heat of those hours outside.

"In yours, too," he said.

In my Red Guard uniform, I might have seemed older to him, not sixteen, but old enough to be in college. In his, he seemed younger than he'd been at the Lake Palaces, where he'd been so solemn in his dress and his manner, but now could have been a university student joining the cause.

The driver yanked open the door, breathing hard, his expression grim. He honked again and again, until the cars ahead of us inched forward and he nosed into an opening. He gripped the steering wheel, his knuckles white.

"What is it?" Secretary Sun asked.

"It's a student demonstration," he said. "They're blocking the gates of a factory. No trucks can go in or out."

"Let's go," I said, eager for my first chance to see Red Guard up close.

The driver snorted. "You don't want to be anywhere near there. A cadre tried to clear them away, so they tied him up! They're shoving him around now."

Prickles shot up my back. I would have expected them to shout down the cadre, but grabbing him like that showed how little the students now thought of these Party officials.

"Come on, come on," the driver muttered under his breath. He rolled down the window. "You donkeys. Move!"

"There's nowhere to go," I said.

"The demonstration is moving toward us," he said. "Who knows what else the Red Guard might want to smash up?"

I locked the door. Surely they wouldn't attack an official sedan, or maybe we were the kind of target they wanted. I sank down, humiliated; at the first sign of danger, I wanted to hide.

"Have you seen anything like this?" I asked the driver.

"It's been a mess. Impossible to go anywhere without detours." He raised his hand to honk, but held back as Red Guard came into sight, maybe fifty in all.

They prodded the cadre whose arms were tied down under loops of coarse rope. When he stumbled, a Red Guard kicked him in the back of his knees. They couldn't see us through the tinted glass, but we could see them, the excitement in their faces, the fear in the cadre's, that of an animal who would gnaw off its leg to escape. He wobbled for a few steps, then tripped and fell against our car. A Red Guard pulled him back, then slammed him against the hood.

The jolt flattened me. After they finished going by, cars haltingly inched forward, and space opened up, enough for our sedan to veer toward an alley and speed through. I clutched the door handle, my heart pounding, until we emerged on the other side, and I let out a shuddering breath.

"Do you need to take a rest?" Secretary Sun asked after a long moment.

"We're already late," I said, trying to sound braver than I felt.

"It's probably not the welcome you expected. But it's not the first time something like this has happened," he said.

"The Chairman knows this?"

"The Chairman would probably think the cadre should all be tied up!" He sighed. "He thinks the cadre are suppressing the students. But no one is controlling them. No one could."

"No one but the Chairman," I said.

He hesitated, and then nodded. By the side of the road, a granny shuffled along, toting two baskets on a carrying pole piled high with melons, and a mother pushed her baby in a bamboo stroller, each oblivious to the turmoil a few blocks away.

"How's Teacher Fan?" I asked.

He looked out the window. "The troupe has disbanded."

Something lurched in my chest. "Because the Chairman's been gone?"

He nodded, still not looking at me.

"What about Midnight Chang?"

"She's gone, too," he said.

Midnight Chang had jabbed at me at every turn, but all her scheming had amounted to nothing. "Is she back home?"

He nodded.

After we arrived at the university and passed between a pair of stone guardian lions that flanked the red-lacquered gate, I noticed the biggest change since my last visit to the main plaza: There were posters everywhere, posters pasted on posters, the paper gone limp in the humid air.

As we got out of the car, my legs were shaky. The Red Guard on a rampage at the factory had rattled me more than I wanted to admit.

I wheeled around the plaza, trying to take it all in. The characters on the posters were painted on newsprint in a furious scrawl that all but poked you in the eye if you got too close. PROFESSOR TANG IS A BLACK-HEARTED WOLF!, THE CHANCELLOR TAKES THE CAPITALIST ROAD!, and SAFEGUARD THE CHAIRMAN!

Where students had once rushed through, they now clotted around posters, pointing and murmuring. The campus seemed chaotic as a market that has run out of its goods, the buyers still clamoring for the wares they can't have. Bicycles were parked everywhere. A pair of young men applied a new poster with a broom and bucket of paste that faintly wafted the scent of roasted sweet potatoes.

"There are more posters than people," I said.

"If you don't put one up, people think you're against the revolution," Secretary Sun said.

Reports had indicated that students believed the campus was overrun with capitalists, and I'd seen for myself how they'd attack anyone they thought undermined the Chairman. Students had been searching for threats everywhere, the couriers had said, in novels, newspapers, and movies, finding threatening signs and symbols wherever they looked.

The Chairman hadn't expected, hadn't counted on the extent of the student involvement. I'd tell him how the crowds offered safety in numbers. The collective offered courage, strength—and anonymity. None of the students strutting around me wanted to be the first to back down, no different in a school walkway than on a battlefield.

When the President pushed back against the students, they grew more frenzied, just as we'd wanted, just as we'd planned. After what I had seen so far, I felt like I'd gulped down ten shots of maotai—giddy but also queasy about what I'd set into motion.

After we agreed to meet back at the sedan in an hour, I slipped into a nearby group, a few students clustered around a poster. If they asked, I'd go by Dong Feng, the East Wind, a name they'd believe fit for a model revolutionary.

I wondered if I could pass muster as a student. I'd fooled the

President, but what would they see? If they realized I wasn't a student, would they turn against me as quickly as those Red Guard at the factory?

A teenage boy tapped on a wrinkled poster about the President's cadre. "They call the students counter-revolutionary?" he spat. His inflamed, pimply skin reminded me of lumps of tofu swimming in chili sauce. "Nonsense!"

The others gathered nodded.

"They don't intimidate us," said a girl whose thick glasses magnified her eyes, giving her the look of a frog. "We'd rather die than submit to their lies."

"I heard that some of the work teams aren't cadre at all," the boy said. The President's cadre collaborated in what were known as work teams. "They're thugs who got released from jail, to shut us up once and for all."

"Don't let rumors distract you from the real enemy!" the girl answered.

He gave her a wary look. The other students eyed her, too. I wondered if they knew one another, or if students were always trying to get the better of one another. If you didn't seem revolutionary enough, maybe you risked getting blamed.

She pointed at a poster about a student who had killed herself by jumping in front of the train. Cadre had accused her of trying to overturn the revolution. "Her blood is on the President's hands."

He bobbed his head. "He all but pushed her!"

Neither of them seemed nervous saying what amounted to treason. Blaming the President wasn't new to them. How quickly would a rumor spread? If they hated the President so much, I could come up with gossip of my own. But what? The Chairman had implied the President had certain appetites, and he might be capable of what I claimed—maybe only once, but one too many times.

"I heard he went after a fifteen-year-old girl," I blurted. "A friend of his daughter's. After a party at their house."

"Who told you that?" the girl said, sizing me up. My uniform was in better shape than hers, which was moth-eaten at the shoulders, baggy on her wiry frame.

"Garbage talk," the boy proclaimed, with the authority and flash of a cleaver.

He couldn't dismiss me like that! "Call it what you want, but it's true," I said.

"What happened to her?" the girl asked.

"She killed herself," I said.

Her face crumpled, and she blinked away tears. She seemed so devastated, I should take it back. And yet, I could see something else in her, in all the students crowded around the poster—a shiftiness born from an itch to spread a rumor.

"I heard she was thirteen," the boy said, as if a moment ago he hadn't called me a liar. He wanted to claim authority, and I sensed then how my lies, everyone's lies, could spin out of control, joining other people's exaggerations, unpredictable as marbles tumbling across the floor.

"I . . ." I trailed off. I didn't want to admit I'd been lying. I peeked at Secretary Sun, who was reading a poster on the side of a brick building a dozen meters away.

The group noticed him. "He looks like a spy!" the girl said. "He could be a cadre in disguise, pretending to be a Red Guard."

"He could be a convict!" the boy added.

For a few seconds, the girl let slip her fear. Then she squinted with such a fury I thought if I didn't stop her, she might push Secretary Sun onto the ground. She marched toward him. She would have been a toddler at the time of Liberation; I'd been a baby a couple weeks old. We'd missed the glory of the revolution, but our time was coming.

I grabbed her arm. "Shouldn't we watch him first? Spy on the spy?"

"Spies!" the boy said. "You think I wouldn't know about this? Nothing happens here without my knowledge. The No. 1 Red Brigade leads the way."

The girl frowned. "The No. 1 Red *Light* Brigade will defeat every enemy."

The No. 1 Red Light Brigade and the No. 1 Red Brigade. Their names were so close. Was she talking about the same brigade, or had they run out of revolutionary names?

The way they glared at each other made me suspect they had to be rivals. In a country of hundreds of millions, we couldn't all be No. 1. Yet no one ever dreamed of being in the middle.

When the girl stalked off, the boy yanked her braid.

"Wah!" the girl shouted.

Shaking free of him, she shoved him in the chest with both hands. I backed away from the wall, along with the others trying to get out of the way. He seized me by my shoulders. "You, I've never seen you." I knew his kind: Too young for a wife, he still needed the care of his mother. When he fell short in his struggle to become a man, his rage would follow.

"Maybe *she's* the spy," the girl said.

"I—" When I hesitated, he squeezed my shoulders until it felt like my bones ground together. The rest of the group had retreated a few meters away. I looked around the plaza, hoping that someone might stop him, but everyone seemed caught up in their own quarrels.

Secretary Sun hurried over. In a moment, he'd pull us apart. In a moment, he'd send me back to the Chairman. I had to make up a story: I was in high school, I said to him. "I had to come; I've heard so much about what you're doing here."

Flattered, the boy let go of me.

"Little Sister, be careful," the girl said. She cut her eyes at him. "Don't trust paper tigers."

He frowned as she invited me to her brigade's meeting at the library, later that afternoon. "All talk," he said. In an hour, he bragged, he could bring me to a struggle session, attacking an economics professor with capitalist leanings.

"I'll take you to a cowshed," she countered. The nickname for the makeshift prisons in classrooms and dormitories. "I know the guard on duty. He'll let you look through the window. The way they beg to get out—it's pathetic."

Sweat dripped down my back, the sun making me feel woozy. I tried to move away, but I was caught between them—like a rag that a pair of dogs would sooner shred than let the other have. Secretary Sun lingered nearby in front of another poster, other students milling around him. In the time since we'd arrived, the crowd in the plaza had thickened, the lines around the posters five deep.

I told them that I was meeting a friend. As I walked away from the plaza, past classrooms and deeper into the campus, Secretary Sun fell into step with me.

"All right?" he asked.

"Melon-headed idiots. *They're* supposed to lead us?"

"They're more destructive than they seem," he said. A pair of ducks glided along the shore.

"To his enemies? To themselves!" I kicked aside a fallen pine cone. "Who needs the cadre to suppress the students? Set them against each other!"

"The infighting isn't new. It's part of every revolution," he said.

He had a point: The students still had many of the Chairman's enemies on guard—on the run. And yet, if the Chairman wanted the Cultural Revolution to go on, he would have to find another way to dazzle those who doubted him. He'd been in seclusion for so long, fading from their present, but he had to appear to be as vital, as invincible as ever. Yet another appearance from high above Tiananmen, another speech crackling over the radio, or a gleaming portrait in every village wouldn't do.

IN MY WEEK AWAY, I talked to scores of Red Guard on dozens of campuses in the capital and witnessed struggle sessions, sometimes two or three times a day, in abandoned classrooms or in the plaza. Sometimes, if the victims groveled enough, they left the struggle sessions humiliated but unharmed; it depended on the whims of the students. The punishments became increasingly violent and warped, like a weird echo that grows louder, not softer, with each repetition.

The most terrifying afternoon I witnessed began when a Red Guard shaved a portly university official's head at the front of a large lecture hall. He was the highest-ranking administrator the students had gone after so far on my visit, and I wanted to include him in my report to the Chairman. I scanned the crowd—three dozen students or so along the walls and the aisles—and was relieved that the Red Guards who'd quarreled with me weren't among them.

"Tell the President he's next!" a girl shouted at the man, now bald and weeping.

Articles denouncing his allies had begun appearing in newspapers and magazines. Radio broadcasters read the accusations aloud, people shared them at meetings and posted them at crowded intersections. What you might settle with your fists in the village, here you could lay out in words, with the power to humiliate your opponent across the entire country.

I pressed myself against the wall as the students paraded the university official toward the door. Blood trickled from cuts on his freshly shorn scalp, one rivulet dripping into his eye that the man couldn't wipe away because his arms were pinned behind his back. He wheezed, wild-eyed as someone drowning. A dark stain spread across his crotch.

I was surprised at how personal their hatred seemed, as if the President and his proxies had slapped them, spit on them. As if he himself might come at them with a knife around the next corner.

The Red Guard was shorter than the official, the top of her head at his chin. With a shriek, she splashed ink into his eyes. He didn't blink. He must have sunk deep inside himself; otherwise, he wouldn't last the day.

Secretary Sun remained behind with me as everyone else left. We would have to follow them, but I had to gather myself first. The more I witnessed, the less certain I felt about what to tell the Chairman. I didn't know how to convince him to return to the capital.

"They act like the President is out to get them. As if any of them matter that much," I said, keeping my voice low.

"It's not about what the President did to them, or might do to them," he said. "The man they marched out of here? He shut down a cheating ring a few months ago."

"They're getting revenge?" I asked. Outside, the students jeered. "But is he guilty of what they said? Is he a secret capitalist?"

"Guilty enough," Secretary Sun said. "We're all guilty of not doing enough for the revolution. But yes, people are settling grudges now. Years and years of them."

"Then there's no end to it," I murmured. "What happens when the Chairman wants it to stop?"

Secretary Sun didn't answer.

"We have to tell him," I said. The students had written slogans on the chalkboard, on top of faint math equations that they couldn't completely erase, from classes canceled weeks ago.

"He's been told," he said.

I leaned against the wall, wanting to slide down to the floor. The smell of burning wafted through the shattered window, and glass littered the floor beside an overturned desk.

"If they're this angry, what if they turn on the Chairman?" I asked.

"Have you heard anything like that?" he asked.

I shook my head.

"You won't," he said.

"You don't know that!" I said. Chanting began.

"In all your life, did you or your family ever blame the Chairman for anything?" It was as if he'd asked if we would ever consider carving off our faces.

"A girl was saying that the President must have done something to the Chairman," I said. "How the Chairman hadn't been seen in months. Her friend disagreed, but the girl insisted, asking, 'Why haven't we seen his photo in the newspaper? Why hasn't he been on the radio?' "

"I've heard that rumor, too," he said.

"Shouldn't the Chairman do something?" I asked. "Make a public appearance?"

"He knows," Secretary Sun said.

"The reports don't really explain what it's like here," I said. "But I will."

The suffering official bellowed incoherently. We ran to find him getting marched off toward the main plaza, which was already crowded with a competing commotion: a pair of students lugging a woman in a basket onto a stage. "Whore! Whore! Bourgeoisie whore!" they shouted.

Her long hair hung in her face, matted with blood. The stage was on the other end of the plaza but when I moved in for a closer look, Secretary Sun tugged on my arm. "They're going that way."

The Red Guard we'd been following had led the official in another direction. The sound of pelting started up, and I turned to see the crowd now hurling stones at the woman onstage. Most missed her, hitting the floorboards, but when one glanced off her shoulder, she didn't flinch.

I faltered and would have tumbled to my knees if Secretary Sun hadn't caught my arm. When I staggered toward her, he jerked me back and clapped a hand over my mouth.

I realized then I was screaming. "Stop! Stop!"

He released me after I went quiet.

"Don't you want to see what happens to him? For your report to the Chairman?" he said, with a bitterness I didn't yet understand.

My throat felt scraped, swollen. I'd been lucky; no one else had noticed. Why did I want to keep screaming then—*for* her, *at* her?

"There's nothing here the Chairman hasn't heard about already," he said. "And nothing you can do for her."

I followed him in a daze, blind to everything around me. We ended up by a squat structure, a temporary classroom that had fallen into disrepair, now turned into a makeshift prison. Later I would learn how the accused slept on the floor, shoulder to shoulder, and started each day memorizing the Chairman's words, beaten or slapped if they missed a single line. Then they'd get carted off to scrub toilets, pull nails from boards and stack bricks, and perform other acts of reform through labor.

Two student guards stood by the door, one with a metal pipe tucked under his arm, and the other with a wooden cudgel. Screams were coming out of a smashed window, along with the sound of fists and feet against flesh, the thump of something more, followed by high hooting laughter. The university official shook his head, no-no-no, dragging his feet, until the Red Guard forced him inside.

I dug a fist into my mouth, regretting my part in this turmoil. Then, I could barely describe the feeling, let alone admit it to myself or to Secretary Sun, that the violence was anything but necessary.

Now, though, I struggle with it. I wonder if I'm giving myself too much foresight, as if recognizing their brutality somehow washed my hands clean.

CHAPTER 24

SWAYING AS THE TRAIN FOLLOWED THE CURVED TRACK, I pictured myself in the muddy waters of the Yangtze below, tossed around in the foam. Spotting a stick, I tried to track its movement but it soon disappeared out of sight.

We were returning to Wuhan, to the villa tucked into an inlet of East Lake. Across from me, Secretary Sun dozed. We'd taken the overnight train from Beijing, in a car that smelled like coal dust and old sweat, and I'd fallen asleep before him. I'd woken up a few times, confused where I was, before drowsing again.

Dawn was breaking now. His mouth parted, his arms loose at his sides, he seemed younger. Vulnerable. It was the first time I'd ever seen him asleep, which made me feel close to him.

In the end, I hadn't found any monsters or freaks, any blood-thirsty bourgeoisie of the sort the Chairman railed against. I'd only witnessed students waving wooden swords, terrifying professors and school administrators who confessed to every accusation to stop the beatings. I wrapped my arms around myself. I'd never forget the helpless woman in the basket. After the Red Guard finished with her that day, what did they do to her?

Secretary Sun twitched, his head dipping into his chest. He woke up embarrassed and shuffled the papers on the seat beside him.

"How long have you been up?" he asked.

"I couldn't sleep much," I said. "I've been thinking about what I'll tell the Chairman. No matter what I say, he'll think it was a waste of time."

"No one could have tried harder," he said.

"So you agree," I said dully. "Anything I tell him is pointless."

"I didn't say that." He'd been preoccupied last night, as we left the government guesthouse and as the train pulled out of the station, perhaps because he, too, was preparing to see the Chairman. But it turned out he'd been wondering when to tell me about my family. "Your mother recovered," he said. "And much of the village, too."

"What are you talking about?" Most days, most of the time, I pushed my family from my mind. I'd all but given up on getting any report about what happened after the fever struck them last autumn; I'd have to go there and find out for myself someday.

"I got word last night." As we'd finished dinner at the government canteen, he'd been given a folder. Reports for the Chairman, I'd assumed.

I pictured my mother, gaunt and bent. But—my sister. My sister, my sister. "You should have told me!"

"The canteen was crowded," he said. "I thought I should wait until I was alone with you."

"We were alone after we boarded the train last night," I snapped.

"I wanted to wait until after you spoke with the Chairman."

More excuses.

"You just told me you couldn't sleep," he said. "I didn't want to add to that."

I glared at him. "You always think you know better. If it was your family, wouldn't you want to know immediately?"

He didn't answer.

"Did it say which sister died?" I asked.

"Song Mei Tian," he said.

"First Daughter." I gripped the armrests, a howl climbing up my throat. All my life, I'd trailed her shadow. My big sister, who'd rained down clever insults that silenced a neighbor boy, an uncle, a classmate, anyone who dared to laugh at our family. Quick to shove, quick to slap anyone who filched from our garden plot. She taught me to defend what was ours, what was mine, and made me fierce.

"The report said it was the middle sister." He opened a letter that I grabbed from him.

"That's Mei Ling!" Second Daughter, in the middle, her hands always clasping us together. I tried to read the page, but my tears turned the words hazy. Mei Tian, Mei Ling, Mei Xiang. First, Second, and Third Daughters. Three plum flowers, now two. Both my sisters were with me always, if not in my thoughts, but in how I had survived the Lake Palaces.

"It says Mei Tian," he said quietly. Though we were in a private passenger car, I wanted to scream loud enough to wake everyone up on the length of the train.

"That's not my middle sister. Admit it: You don't know!" The words lacerated like shards of glass. "You think we're all the same. This sister, that sister, this girl, that girl—you can't tell the difference. You think people like us aren't worthy of your full attention."

"Your family's proud of you," he said, with the slightest catch in his voice.

"What do you know?" I said. He couldn't speak for my family, any more than he could speak for me.

Secretary Sun cleared his throat. "Your father told the courier. He called you a hero."

I looked out the window, the trees blurring green, as I roiled with regret and confusion, raw and burnt at the same time.

WHEN WE RETURNED TO the villa, they were waiting for us.

At the mahjong table, Midnight Chang seemed more beautiful than in my memory, her hair braided into an elegant coil. Though she too wore a Red Guard uniform, she seemed ethereal as a princess in a watercolor scroll. I was grimy and smudged all over from my travels.

"You're just in time!" the Chairman said, beckoning us. They sat across from each other at the mahjong table. Usually off to the side, by a bookcase, it had been moved closer to his desk, at the center of his quarters.

"Maybe they'd like to take a rest? To wash up first?" Midnight Chang asked, her tone solicitous. "You must be tired." She rubbed her thumb on a tile.

The Chairman waved off her suggestion. "They slept the whole way." He studied Secretary Sun. "Though it looks like you could sleep another week! Your years have caught up with you at last."

Secretary Sun forced a smile. We lingered in the doorway, the surprise plain on his face. It seemed he hadn't known she'd come for a visit. In grief, in anger, I'd stopped talking to him on the train, but now I was glad that I wouldn't have to face Midnight Chang alone. As long as I'd been traveling with the Chairman, I hadn't had to think much about her. Secretary Sun had mentioned that the troupe had scattered, but said nothing about Midnight Chang remaining under the Madame's orders from afar.

I wondered if she'd been part of a Red Guard detachment that visited a campus somewhere nearby. If she'd spent a night—or two?—with the Chairman while I'd been away.

On the other side of the desk, the bed was rumpled. I couldn't tell if she'd been there, if she'd lain in sheets where I'd lain under the Chairman. At least the drapes had been pulled back from the windows. If his quarters had been shadowy as usual, I might have fled. I reluctantly took a seat—the Chairman to my right, Midnight Chang to my left, Secretary Sun across from me—everyone elbow-to-elbow around the tight square of the table.

We began. Judging from the discards piling up, I guessed she was searching for the North Wind tile to complete one of her sets of three. I had to watch not only my own tiles, but those in play. Mahjong is a game of probability, a battle, a world laid out in the tiles—all reasons the Chairman loved to play.

Though he probably could have beaten me each time, I'd also figured out how to ease his victories, discarding tiles that he needed or breaking apart my pairs and triples. Midnight Chang grabbed my discarded tile and shouted, *"Peng!"*

Her arm bumped mine as she reached for the last of the roasted peanuts, which had been laid out on the edge of his desk. She summoned the attendant, never shy about asking for what she believed was her due. I hid my smile. If she won the hand, the Chairman would become annoyed and cut the game short. He examined her as if she were a tile that he'd planned to relinquish before discovering it was the one he'd needed all along.

The bones were sharp in her face. How often did she starve herself, slap herself to achieve perfection?

Later on, Secretary Sun set down a tile, one that I was almost certain that Midnight Chang needed.

"*Hu le!*" she shouted in victory.

The Chairman pointed at me. "This one, I taught her the game, but she's not as quick as you."

"And you!" He turned to Secretary Sun. "You wasted no time on games while away, did you?"

"I'm out of practice," Secretary Sun admitted.

"My luck is good today," Midnight Chang said.

My strategy had backfired. Midnight Chang winning kept him interested, not irritated.

Shadows hollowed the Chairman's eyes, and he had a punchiness about him that emerged after too many days of too little sleep. His tremors might return. In these moments, he was at his most impulsive. If he'd been a dog, he would have chased after anything that hurtled by.

We shuffled the ivory tiles, swirling them in hissing circles on the green felt table, their clacking like a bamboo grove in a high wind. The tiles held the colors of the universe: the red of blood, of the people; the blue of the sky, of the heavens and the seas; and the green of the earth, of the fields my family worked, of the hills behind our village.

Midnight Chang stacked tiles horizontally, lifting a long row on top of another. Within moments, she could build a wall around me. A prison cell. She leaned forward, and when I heard the sound of shuffling on the wooden floor, I realized that the Chairman had nudged his foot against hers. I heard what sounded like her nudging back, the two of them playing around. Her eyes, bright as stars. I stacked my tiles, trying to keep my hands from trembling. The tiles were cool and slick, perfect as stones washed in a river, everything that I wasn't.

After she won a few more hands, the Chairman turned to her. "My wife said that you are an excellent player." He drew off his cigarette, smoke curling around his head. I dropped my tile, which bounced with a muffled thump on the table.

He ashed into a teacup. "It turns out mahjong players make excellent revolutionaries. The Fudan club has been quite active, she tells me: The strategy at the table serves them well when they fight back against the cadre."

"It's a reminder to keep looking in unexpected places," Secretary Sun said.

My campus report shriveled in my mouth. I had nothing so clever to tell—except for the rumor I'd spun about the President, that I was too ashamed to say out loud.

The Chairman must have mentioned my university visits to his wife, and I couldn't shake the sense of betrayal. Was the Madame copying me, or had the Chairman pushed for Midnight Chang also to go in disguise?

His wife could have urged him on. "Why settle on one?" she might have asked. "See what they both might turn up."

I wanted to flip the table, sending the tiles flying like teeth knocked out; I wanted Midnight Chang to tumble into the Yangtze and get carried out to sea.

She placed her tiles in a perfect line, her refinement a reminder of my fumbling. "Did you see your family yet?" she asked me.

"My duties have kept me," I said.

The Chairman leaned forward, eager to see us fight. The wooden chair squeaked under him. I was a tile to him, but I wouldn't be easily tossed, easily replaced.

"Duties," she said. As if she hadn't been selected for the same duties in the troupe, as if she hadn't yearned to be in my place. She wouldn't be so smug if she knew about the report that spilled the troupe's secrets, if she realized I'd discovered that her father was a drunk. "Have you seen Teacher Fan?" I asked.

"You haven't heard?" She paused, relishing that she knew something that I didn't. "After she'd been relieved of her duties, she tried to kill herself."

"Is she . . . what happened?" I asked.

"She jumped out the window," Midnight Chang said. "But she lived. She didn't have the right technique. If you're going to kill yourself, you have to go headfirst. Make sure you're top-heavy. But she jumped feet first."

Their voices suddenly sounded distant, and the room turned sweltering. I leaned forward, my head hanging down, trying not to faint.

"She looked like an ice pop," the Chairman said, his tone mocking. Her feet first, arms at her sides. He and Secretary Sun had known—for weeks or for months?—but neither had told me. From what Secretary Sun had said, I had assumed she'd taken up other responsibilities. He'd evaded my questions about her, I now realized.

It took everything in me to look up at Secretary Sun, who gripped a tile in his fist. They must have respected each other, in that way capable people recognize that quality in one another. Did he mourn her? He might have said nothing about what happened because he wanted to protect me. As for the Chairman, I guessed why he hadn't bothered to tell me: After he'd received the news, she hadn't crossed his mind again.

"Why did she jump?" I asked. I couldn't imagine what Teacher Fan had done wrong. Maybe someone in the troupe had reported her to the Red Guard for teaching dances that were backward and bourgeoisie. Midnight Chang could have done it, any and all of the girls eager to turn on her for the crime of not recommending them to the Chairman.

The Madame hadn't saved her, or maybe she'd made the decision that Teacher Fan harbored too many secrets. I never should have hinted that I knew she'd rubbed mud in her hair at Yan'an. The Madame would have suspected either the Chairman or Teacher Fan had told me; maybe she'd found it easier to blame her friend.

"She could no longer tell gold from straw." Midnight Chang stared pointedly at me. "She'd lost sight of good character, of who best served the Chairman. You didn't see her at the university? She gets carried around in a cabbage basket and onto the stage for struggle sessions."

She must have been crippled after she jumped. I realized then that we'd spotted her at Peking University, the woman with the bloody, matted hair, but Secretary Sun had led me away before I could discover it was her. I hated that he'd kept it from me, just like he'd withheld my sister's fate. If I'd known it was her, I might have— I would have—what? Shouted her name, told the Red Guard to stop throwing stones? They would have shoved me down next to her.

Midnight Chang smirked. Her glee. The Chairman's indifference— his cruelty that had been apparent all along, that I could no longer deny.

"People are saying she's the one who brought the President that twelve-year-old," she said.

Twelve? Tiles jumbled in the center of the mahjong table, a few on their sides, ready to be knocked over.

Midnight Chang ran her hand across her row of tiles, a paved path out of this muddy fight. "All those special hands, I can't remember," she said. "The Thirteen Orphans. The Great Winds. The Pearl Dragon. The Ruby Dragon. Can you teach me?"

"You've already beaten me," the Chairman said.

"You can't depend on luck," she said.

Secretary Sun clapped two tiles together: The sound of a gunshot. A call to action, to fight back. The Chairman darted a glance at him.

I felt as though I were wading waist-deep through a swamp. "You want a lesson tomorrow morning?" I asked with as much brightness as I could force out. Midnight Chang might not know that the Chairman resisted appointments, any schedule other than the one set by his whims. If she pushed for a time, he'd skip the lesson altogether.

"Or in the afternoon?" Midnight Chang asked him. "Tomorrow night?"

The Chairman swept tiles into the case. She pushed hers toward him. If she'd known better, she wouldn't have asked for lessons; she would have asked him to tell her the stories behind each special hand. With a nod from the Chairman signaling that he was finished with the game—and with Midnight Chang—Secretary Sun ushered her away.

She turned for a final look, not at the Chairman but at me. An acknowledgment or an appraisal, I would have expected, not the briefest sorrow I found in her expression. As she turned away, she flicked her braid over her shoulder. For the first time, I noticed she'd adorned it with a wooden bead carved into a plum flower. Stained a reddish chestnut, a shade I'd seen nowhere except my village.

I couldn't breathe.

To her, the plum flower bead must have seemed crude, a knot of wood, but the pair I owned were my only keepsake. Who had taken it from Ma? Been where I'd yearned to return, if only for an hour, to see my sister, my parents. Pinned to my seat, I wished I'd never taunted the Madame. She would—or had already—ordered punishments for them. What she couldn't do to me, she would do to my family. My father, paraded as a counter-revolutionary, taunted with hurled eggs and spit. Ma, whipped, her back slashed and bloody.

I bit back my question: *Which sister died?* I couldn't ask about my family, not in front of the Chairman.

Midnight Chang flicked her braid again. A taunt, *Know your place;* a curse, as if she'd stomped upon the graves of my ancestors. She wouldn't grant me any mercy, any more than I would grant it to her, and in truth, neither of us could stop what the Chairman and his wife had begun. Bees swarmed inside me. The buzz warped into keening, a high long note for Teacher Fan, who might have no one else to mourn her. For my sisters, whose fates I didn't yet know.

As Secretary Sun motioned for her to keep walking, the Chairman rose, flung off his shirt, and reached for his swimming suit, drying on top of a rosewood screen on the other side of the bed. The wood was swollen, the finish faded from the constant dampness.

After they left, I turned to him. "The reports you've been getting . . . did you know the students are attacking each other?" I asked. "Red Guard against Red Guard."

"So I've heard," he said. "Any other news?"

"It's not just with words. They'll rip each other apart, until there's nothing left!" I said. Bitterness rose up my throat, flooding my mouth, as I remembered Teacher Fan, tormented and crammed into a basket. My hands, palms up, splayed open in my lap, useless as I felt.

"Midnight Chang said much the same. But neither of you knows much about revolution," he said.

Did he know if she'd visited my village? If I asked, he'd take it as proof my loyalties lay with my family, and not the revolution.

"The students are blaming the President," I said.

He nodded.

"They're getting revenge on their classmates, their professors, their neighbors, for things that have nothing to do with revolution," I said. "Even though they're calling themselves your soldiers."

He shrugged.

"I started the rumor that the President went after one of his daughter's friends," I blurted, desperate to impress the Chairman.

He laughed, shouldering on his robe. "So you're behind that dirty talk! Clever. There's a lot of that going around—it makes for the most amusing reports. He's so unpopular right now you could have announced he'd killed and eaten a girl, and everyone would believe it."

It didn't seem to trouble him that the girls in the troupe weren't much older than the one from the rumor. I got up from the table.

He rubbed his temples. He hadn't been sleeping well, I could tell, and soon he'd want to move on from Wuhan. With or without me? He tossed me my suit, but I didn't catch it. Crumpled at my feet, it looked like the skin of a snake, like something outgrown. "Get dressed."

"For the pool?" I asked.

"No, for a Politburo meeting!" he said. "Yes—the pool."

He searched for his plastic slippers, kicking aside piles of clothes before he found them.

"I'll get back into the routine," I said.

"Routine," he muttered, as if I'd hurled a curse at him. In a way, I had.

As I got dressed, I thought about how the villa's pool was placid and predictable, where I'd watched the Chairman take endless laps in the past and where he would again today. It must remind him of tedium without end, a rut that he'd been unable to escape, no matter how often he moved from villa to villa.

I scooped up a tile that had fallen to the floor of his bedchamber and rubbed my thumb across the blue circles: the blue of the sky at the height of summer, the blue of the deepest waters. He'd had no cares, paddling around in the pond by his childhood home. Maybe we could swim somewhere else outside, or would that seem like more of the same, the banks of a pond closing in on him?

I'd been thinking about how he might fire up the Red Guard, and it came to me then. "If you want to swim, swim in the Yangzte."

Almost a decade ago, to prove he could achieve the impossible, he'd swum in three rivers that defined our country. It was how our legends unfolded: in threes. No other number as perfect, as whole.

In the south, he'd dipped into the Pearl River, though his advisors had warned its foul waters brimmed with trash and shit. In the heartland, near his hometown, the Xiang River had been flood-high and infested with snakes. And in the Yangtze, the mightiest of them all.

He draped a towel around his neck. "The pool's gotten too small, hasn't it? It's time you swam in the river, time you met the current."

CHAPTER 25

*T*RIMMED IN SILVER, THE CHAIRMAN'S ARMORED SEDAN SEEMED impenetrable, its engine rumbling through my body like thunder. When I asked Secretary Sun to pull aside the stiff brown curtains, I glimpsed the steamboats, their brass fittings bright and blinding. They chugged in place, billowing acrid, greasy coal smoke. Downstream, photographers jostled on a floating platform, their cameras glittering in the sunshine like a many-eyed monster.

Thousands of swimmers massed on the bank, scores of them carrying huge crimson flags and banners. Giant slogans, praising the Chairman and the revolution, had been carved into the hills: STRUGGLE AGAINST HEAVEN AND EARTH! With three sharp blasts of a whistle, the flag-bearers plunged into the water. Firecrackers exploded. As smoke twisted into the air, a man stumbled, his flag almost dipping into the river before another swimmer swooped in to rescue it.

"You can't cling to the edge. There's no stopping," Secretary Sun warned me. He'd been trying to persuade me not to go in ever since the Chairman had informed him that we'd be joining the swim. Each year at this event commemorating the Chairman's original swim, a few people drowned, dragged by the fast, swirling current, or snagged underwater by branches.

"What do you know?" the Chairman scolded Secretary Sun. "You don't even know how to swim."

"I can float when I get tired," I said.

The Chairman snorted. "You should float the whole way. When you swim, you thrash about, like you're covered in fire ants."

Though he'd taken my suggestion to swim in the Yangtze, he'd been short with me ever since. When I touched his shoulder, he didn't reach for me. I dropped my hand into my lap.

"Exactly why she shouldn't go in," Secretary Sun said.

The crowd surged on land, sure to surge in the water. "Maybe we should both wait, and go in when it's safe . . ." I said. If his tremors overtook him during his swim, he could drown.

"Enough!" the Chairman said. "I've waited long enough. Do what you like," he told me.

Eyes stinging, I turned away. I didn't want him doubting my commitment to him, to the revolution. The Chairman ordered the driver to bring us around to the grandstand where dignitaries awaited. After the guard waved our three-car caravan into the fenced-off staging area, the Chairman climbed out, grunting as he pushed off the seat.

In his white swim trunks, white bathrobe, and white sandals, he glowed. Though his sleep had been fitful lately, his months outside of the capital, spent in the sunshine, our many tranquil swims and hearty meals, had invigorated him.

Without stopping to talk to any of the officials, he headed straight for the river. Bodyguards flanked him, shouting at people to give way, but a crowd that big could never be contained. That was what attracted the Chairman, a chance to lose himself among the masses, as others lost themselves in him.

On the grandstand, I noticed the Madame and Midnight Chang peering over the water, each shaded by a tan parasol. They wore matching green pantsuits and sunglasses, with binoculars hanging around their necks. The fact that they weren't dressed for a swim made me more determined to follow the Chairman into the water. I had to show him Midnight Chang couldn't match me.

I didn't see the President, the Premier, the Defense Minister, or other top cadre from National Day. The Chairman's decision to join the swim had been so last-minute, they might not have been able to pull away from their duties in the capital. None of them yet realized how this day would mark a turn in the Cultural Revolution.

My thoughts returned to Teacher Fan. Dancing with her had been like flying; she belonged in spins and soars. All her connections, all her matchmaking hadn't saved her. She'd sacrificed everything for the Party and had ended up worse than dead.

The Chairman could want the same for the President. With each push, did I send him tumbling toward the same end? The President had a daughter, he'd said. A daughter close to my age.

Had the President heard the rumor about the girl? Had *she*?

The Chairman's bald spot glinted in the sunshine as he paused to shake hands and pat shoulders. He wanted to be carried along the stream of people, to forget the sound of his own labored breathing as he became something greater, once more a spark turned into a prairie fire.

Waving all the while, the Chairman climbed aboard a motor launch, which cruised toward the center of the river, so broad that the spectators on the other side were dots. He flung off his robe and jumped in, throwing up a huge splash. Only the wide Yangtze surged and seethed as chaotic as the revolution he wanted to take hold. Only the Yangtze could show the people what he had mastered, and into the Yangtze he went.

A chant started up. "Long live the Chairman! A long life to the Chairman!" Bodyguard Wei and five others followed him into the river, along with swimmers whose black rubber caps turned them identical, like ants swarming toward honey. Floating posters of the Chairman bobbed alongside them. The call to defend the Chairman had sounded out beyond the schools and universities. People across the country were preparing for attacks by enemies of the socialist revolution, both from within and beyond our borders.

"Are you getting out here?" the driver asked me.

I didn't want the Madame and Midnight Chang watching me flail in the current. I'd get out elsewhere and make my way to the river, I told him. The Chairman's sedan was always parked separately, to ensure no assassin took note of his license plate number.

The driver started up the engine, pulled away from the caravan, and drove to a grassy bank overlooking the river. Weighed down by the armor, the sedan never jounced, not even on dirt. The driver nodded at us in the rearview mirror. After exiting the sedan, he lit a cigarette before ambling closer toward the shore to watch the swimmers.

With the air-conditioning turned off, the temperature rose inside the sedan. Cracking the door open, I leaned back in my seat until my head stopped spinning, and adjusted the strap of my bathing suit, grown loose after much use. The sleeves of my robe—a castoff of the Chairman's—dangled past my hand and slid off my shoulders. I pushed back the strap of my worn bathing suit, but not before Secretary Sun glimpsed my right nipple. He twisted away as though I'd struck him.

Sweat trickled between my breasts, a slickness that I realized I wanted Secretary Sun to trace down the length of my body. The Chairman had awoken something in me, something I couldn't admit until now that had nothing to do with him and entirely with me. To fall into that ache now seemed irresistible, inevitable.

"You don't have to swim," Secretary Sun said. "It's dangerous."

"It's just as dangerous not to," I said. "The Chairman's waiting. If I don't go, Midnight Chang or someone else will." I pictured the dowry bead, hanging on the end of her braid. Soldiers tearing up our home, ripping the pouch from my mother's hand. Ma, begging for them to stop.

"Is the Madame trying to hurt my family?" I asked.

"She can't do anything if you keep the Chairman pleased," he said. "You're not like the others. You notice what others don't. When you're used to being the most . . ." He paused. He didn't say beautiful, but that was what he meant. "If the troupe is full of girls like that, they end up fighting. Weren't the girls always fighting?"

Teacher Fan never stopped it. She might have encouraged it. "Why didn't you tell me about Teacher Fan?"

He winced. "There's nothing you could do for her."

"Was it because of me?" I asked. "Because she defended me?"

He didn't reply.

"If it wasn't for me, the Madame never would have gone after her." I dug my fingernails into my palms.

"The Madame can go after anyone she likes now. This goes all the way back to Yan'an."

I stared at him. "But they were friends."

"Until they weren't. Until the Madame no longer needed her," he said.

Teacher Fan knew too much, but I still deserved the blame.

"Teacher Fan—we both agreed that you see things as they are," he said.

"So do you."

"You say it, though. The way you see, you make me see." He took my hand, the gesture easy as if he had done so thousands of times. Palm to palm, the heat passed through us, and those gentle fingers undid me.

We kissed, my mouth opening up to his, tentative, then devouring. My hands clutched his head, and moved across all his surfaces, his stubble, his jaw, the notch at his waist, and his sweat-slicked back.

He jerked away. With a shudder, I gripped something on the seat beside me, a wide lace drape that I must have yanked down. Nudging aside the curtain, I didn't see the driver through the dark glass. It was reckless, madness, even if the sedan's passenger compartment appeared sealed up tight as a tomb. I dropped the edge of the curtain and the interior of the car went dim again.

I locked the doors and then we fell into each other at the same time, our kisses even more urgent than before. Sinking onto the floor of the sedan, I undid the buttons of his pants, touching him. His fingers slid beneath the leg band of my swimsuit and then inside me, touching, touching, and touching, delicate and insistent. His lips crushed against my neck, and our bodies slid together.

Soap bubbles floating, bursting.

Still pressed against him, I slowly became aware again of our surroundings. The cheering swelled, the sound muffled by the pounding in my ears. The air inside the sedan had turned scorching, pungent with the salt and tang of our bodies. With each breath, I regained myself.

When I left this time, he didn't try to stop me. It took a minute to reach the edge of the crowd, and a few more before I arrived at the riverbank. My lips felt swollen, bee-stung. Without a backward glance, I shrugged off my robe, kicked off my sandals, and pushed into the breeze carrying the muddy, wet scent of the water.

After I leapt in, splashes pounded around me. Arms, elbows, knees, legs pummeled my face, my sides, my back, and I lost sense of where I was, swimming to shore or into the river, sinking or sur-facing. I'd forgotten my goggles and cap, and I swam blindly in the cloudy water, my hair slipping loose from its ponytail and tangling in my face like choking weeds.

Ahead of me, a swimmer called for help, all wild arms and choked screams. "Float on your back!" a woman shouted. "I'm coming!" a man cried. Amid the commotion, I couldn't tell what happened to the drowning swimmer. Someone kicked me in the face and coppery blood flooded my mouth. Another kick, to my side, and I inhaled water, foul and turbulent as my desires. The Chairman didn't know what I'd done with Secretary Sun, but he still could punish me for my every selfish wish. He would have known what would happen in the river, and that the swimmers would engulf me. Blows battered me, from my sisters, dead and alive. From Midnight Chang. From Busy Shan, Teacher Fan, and the President. Another from the Ma-dame. From the Chairman himself.

I gave in to the kicks and slaps and slipped beneath the surface, beneath the churn and into the darkness. It would be easy to sink, to let the water fill my lungs, to sink to the bottom where I belonged for my every betrayal.

I broke free, clawing each stroke until I pushed back up through the surface, gasping. I swam and swam, toward the center of the river and away from the crowds. When the current pulled me, I flipped onto my back, inhaling the scent of osmanthus on the breeze. Floating, I drifted faster than the clouds.

AS I WALKED BACK toward the start, pebbles bit into my bare feet. The Chairman's sedan pulled up beside me. There weren't many cars on the road, and I'd been turning to look as each one passed by. Although I dreaded facing the Chairman, when I opened the door, I discovered the backseat empty.

Secretary Sun, in front beside the driver, turned to look at me. When our eyes met, embers kicked up inside me. He told me the Chairman had already returned to the villa. I nodded and got in, draping a towel around myself from a stack in the backseat.

Neither of us said another word on the drive. I stared at the back of his head, hairline to neck to shoulder to those arms that had wrapped around me. He might have been without a woman for months, years, when I'd climbed into his lap. Though my attraction to him was just as muddled as his might be to me, I couldn't deny that I wanted him to touch me again.

We had to act as if nothing had happened. He had to protect his position—his life.

I glanced at the floor of the car where we'd twisted around and tightened the towel around my shoulders. If we'd been alone, I wouldn't have known what to call him. His given name—which he'd mentioned only once to me—seemed too strange, too intimate, too brazen.

Anywhere but the Lake Palaces, new lovers might have traded honorifics that doubled as endearments.

"Old Sun," I might have called him.

"Little Song," he might have replied.

Here, though, I'd have to refer to him as Secretary Sun. If I called him a nickname—even if I kept it to myself, even if I kept it from him—it might slip out by accident. In truth, the formality of his title suited him, reflecting the patriotism, the passion and purpose that drew me to him.

After everything, I thought of him as Secretary Sun, and still do.

———

EVEN THOUGH HIS PORTRAITS were everywhere, the Chairman still delighted in newspaper photos, in this near-instant historical record, reproduced millions of times and raising him from the dead. A little over a week after his swim in the Yangtze, his photos took up the entire top half of the front page. Here, he bobbed in the river; in another, clad in his gleaming white bathrobe, he might as well have descended from the heavens. "Follow the Chairman through the wind and the waves," the story proclaimed.

The cameras missed me. Although I shouldn't have craved this attention, although the public wasn't supposed to know I shared the Chairman's bed, it gnawed at me. I stared at the photographs, as if I might appear at the edges. At least the Madame and Midnight Chang were missing from the photos, too. It lulled me into thinking they mattered as little as me.

"A World Record!" the headline proclaimed. In recent years, there had been few widely circulated photos of him, and across the country, people seized upon this new image as proof of his strength and his courage. For years, the Chairman had been fading into history, more legend than real. Showing off this feat, at his age, was no less astonishing, no less inspiring, than if he'd shown he could fly.

Just when students might have tired of the Cultural Revolution, the Chairman's superhuman accomplishment inspired millions more to join in. In the coming weeks, thousands around the country would copy him: In Beijing, swimmers would plunge into the lake at the Summer Palace, and in Shanghai, dockworkers jumped into a floating pool at the port. The President never could have inspired them to follow; he never would have taken the plunge—that much was clear to the country now. We had to leave him behind.

I still hoped the Chairman might praise me for urging him to swim. Hadn't I proved I could be as tactical as any guerilla at Yan'an? Maybe now he would announce that I was ready to serve as a model revolutionary.

"Will you go back every year from now on?" I asked.

The Chairman didn't answer. Instead, he fanned the newspapers on top of his desk to admire himself. Different headlines, the same pictures, repeated in newspapers in cities large and small. The article claimed that the Chairman swam fourteen kilometers in sixty-five minutes, an achievement that few could have matched. He'd swum little of that, floating for no more than a quarter of the distance before the security detail closed in behind him, cutting off the other swimmers.

The Chairman turned the page, searching for more pictures of himself. The ink stained his fingertips, which looked smudged with coal dust. I will always remember the oily smell of the newspapers that day, combustible as my heart.

I tapped at a headline. "An Olympian!"

He repeated it after me, crowing at the description. A question rose up in me, a familiar one that I buried immediately: If he could no longer see the truth about himself, how could he see the truth about the country?

CHAPTER 26

THE RUMBLE OF RED GUARD IN TIANANMEN SQUARE SEEMED like a single heart beating, even louder than on National Day. Down below, they waved red flags, beat drums, and brandished signs that proclaimed REVOLUTION IS NOT A CRIME and REBELLION IS JUST! Their red armbands flickered across the olive green of their uniforms. They were dressed just like me, the centerpiece of this rally to kick off the next phase of the youth campaign, and the first of several that unfolded beneath the Chairman's feet that summer and fall.

I waited in the staging area of the balcony, next to Secretary Sun. We hadn't been alone again since the day of the swim; we could hardly stand to look at each other and might never again. The Premier and the Defense Minister sat in front of us, as well as the Madame. To my dismay, Midnight Chang sat beside her. Her Red Guard uniform was identical to mine, her hair in two braids styled like mine, probably one more attempt to unnerve me.

The Chairman sat on the other side of Midnight Chang, whose head dipped toward his. Grinning, he stroked his arms through the air, as if to replicate his feat on the Yangtze, as if to teach her how to swim. She followed along enthusiastically.

I'd woken up feeling swollen, on edge yet also vigilant, as if I'd drained three pots of tea. I was glad there were no mirrors in the Chairman's quarters. If I looked at myself, I might have curled into a ball. My new uniform felt rough against my skin. I'd stuffed a precautionary rag between my legs because my flow was more than a week late, and I was terrified I might bleed through if it arrived on-stage. My back felt so sore, it was bound to be heavy.

At the podium, the President mumbled from notes, announcing he would disband the work teams. "I honestly don't know how to carry out the Cultural Revolution," he said. A page fluttered to the ground, and he retrieved it, flustered, trying to find his place. He blinked, his eyes dark pits.

How old, how lost he seemed, the skin sagging around his neck like melted candle wax. Last autumn, I had plotted for his downfall, and for months after, I had tracked his every misstep. Now that it had come, I'd gone numb. I could have been watching a fly circling weakly, about to expire. If I let myself feel anything at all, I might shatter.

"I'm an old revolutionary, still learning," he said.

"An old revolutionary who likes little girls," Midnight Chang joked, clear over the din.

The Chairman laughed. "Old revolutionary? More like a counter-revolutionary!"

As the President shuffled away from the podium, Red Guard booed him. He walked past me, his head down and body gnarled with shame. For months, I'd waited and watched for his downfall. I could have apologized for the hand I'd had in his misery, promised to make amends, to find his daughters and tell them the truth, but I said nothing as he lurched into the reception hall. He must know he would soon be stripped of his duties, called a renegade, a traitor, a scab, be arrested and expelled from the Party.

Something nagged at me. I wanted to ask Secretary Sun, but when I looked at him, I felt awkward. Would he still tell me what no one else did? Until then, I hadn't admitted to myself that I was afraid such conversations had come to an end.

"Why did he do it?" I asked him.

He didn't answer, but from the way his shoulders tensed, I could tell he'd heard me. I leaned closer and asked again. "After all these years, why did the President turn on the Chairman?"

In his silence, I wanted to shrink into nothing.

At last, he looked at me. "It wasn't sudden," he said.

My face flushed from the heat of his stare. "Nothing is," I said. "What started it?"

He hesitated, glancing at the Chairman, who remained preoccupied with Midnight Chang.

"Tell me," I insisted.

"It started with lies," he said, his voice hushed.

"The President lied?"

He shook his head. "Not the President. Some officials in the countryside didn't report problems during the Great Leap Forward."

"What kind of problems?" I asked.

"Lies about the harvest," he said. "When they couldn't keep up with production goals, they claimed bumper crops where there had been none."

After officials reported higher and higher yields, the cities took more food, he said. In some villages, people were so busy tending to their homemade steel furnaces that the crops rotted in the fields. "The weather got blamed."

"People starved," I said.

He didn't deny it. We both knew where I was from, and the hunger I'd survived in my childhood: every bone stark as our bodies receded. Shallow graves. Buzzards, circling, circling.

So it wasn't just in my village. "People all over?" I asked. I shrank into the memory of those years, picking through the dirt for hours, in the hopes of finding a single fallen grain.

I glanced at the Chairman. "Did he know?"

Secretary Sun followed my eyes. "The President stepped in," he said. "And that was the end of him."

I didn't think about what he'd left unsaid. Instead, I told myself the Chairman couldn't have known, because if he had, he would have stopped the campaign. The President must have kept it from him, so that he might act first, act the hero. And that strategy now brought the President to his knees.

As officials gave speech after speech, calling upon the Red Guard to destroy old ideas, old culture, old customs, and old habits, I silently practiced my opening lines. After the Defense Minister finished, the Premier took to the podium. Soon, very soon, I'd appear on the cover of newspapers and on the radio, too, he had said. He would arrange for my meetings with provincial leaders and set up tours of villages.

Sweat dotted the Premier's forehead and circles of wetness ringed his armpits and soaked his back. The Chairman still favored him. Did the President's humiliation hang over him, too, or was he simply relieved that the Chairman had found a different target?

The Premier began to praise a young revolutionary. "At the age of five, she memorized the Chairman's poetry and recited it each night in her village. By the time she was eight, she could hoe an entire wheat field by herself." He must be referring to an earlier hero, someone like Sister Yu or Iron Girl, or someone from the model village. "At the age of ten, she terraced a hillside that doubled the village crop yield."

He held his hand out to me, and the crowd clapped and roared. No—the Premier was talking about me.

To most of the Red Guard I was a smear of green on the balcony of Tiananmen. My face must look blank, a sun-darkened spot to help the audience imagine themselves in my place. The Chairman could have taken any girl from the troupe, dressed her in the same uniform, and given her the same story to share with the masses. It didn't matter what I had sacrificed at the Lake Palaces, so long as I fit the part from afar. He had rewritten my history. To be everything to everyone, I'd become no one.

I might lead, but only from a distance.

Yet I wasn't someone else's words on a page; I was me, I was me, I was me. The Premier turned back to face the square. After I stood up and raised my left hand, a few Red Guard in front copied me. Up, up, up went their arms, the people behind following, no words necessary, no words interfering with our communion. Secretary Sun didn't stop me. I raised my right hand, waving the Little Red Book, and when the Red Guard followed, we were like wind over wheat.

I would always remember the first and only time I felt as the Chairman must have when he faced his people: I was without end.

After I dropped my arm, the crowd settled down and resumed chanting. I took my seat again. The Premier beamed, pleased at the seemingly enthusiastic response to his speech; he didn't seem to realize I'd been controlling the Red Guard from behind his back. As the youth drowned out his words, he must have understood that they weren't listening to him. His expression turned heavy, and he shouted for silence. Quiet swept over the crowd, back and back and back, sound fading like the last drops of a rainstorm. Soon, coughing, murmuring, and shuffling spread from the rear—a many-legged insect that couldn't stop moving.

When I glanced at the Chairman, I noticed his hand on Midnight Chang's knee. I knew then that he would soon issue an invitation to join him in his bed. Or had he already? On the other side of Midnight Chang, his wife sat so rigidly I could tell she forced herself not to look at them.

Studying Midnight Chang, I realized her Red Guard uniform matched mine in every way but one: Her red-star cap sat loose on her head, sized for someone bigger, and in a lighter shade than mine, as if faded from the sun. Was it the Chairman's? His cap was brand-new, its brim stiff as a salute. When I'd been practicing my speech with Secretary Sun, the Chairman could have bedded her, in the same bed I returned to that night. Maybe she'd put on the cap, posed and pranced naked, and he'd let her borrow it, a promise of the games they might soon play again. Had her scent slipped by me, the trace of her body in the sheets?

I slumped down. "I can't do this."

"You must," Secretary Sun said. I couldn't look at him. "You will. You always do."

The Chairman would soon finish with me, on to the next girl, then another, and another, until the end of his days. Perhaps he already had. I'd outlived my usefulness to him, just as Teacher Fan had outlived hers. Both of us had been a means to an end, sacrificed not for our country, as we'd believed, but for the Chairman.

In the months we'd been together, the static of my doubt had grown noisier. Even still, I might have ignored the signs that I couldn't trust him, that he wasn't fit to lead us any longer, but for what Secretary Sun had told me moments ago: that the President had ended the famine.

The Chairman also must have known about the lies that caused us to starve—as soon as the President did, I realized. Maybe sooner than his rival, and yet the Chairman kept up the deadly campaign to hold on to his power. Now he'd let the Cultural Revolution destroy us once again.

My head reeled. I felt so jangled, the rag rubbing between my legs, preparations for the blood that still hadn't come.

What if—what if I was pregnant?

And was it the Chairman's?

At the start of his melancholy, he'd called himself a eunuch. What did he mean? Not by definition, but maybe that he couldn't father children, or at least, no longer? In the village, a few couples struggled to conceive, the women begging Ma for a cure. Sometimes the fault lay with the men, my mother said, even if no husband wanted to hear it.

How often had I agonized, thinking that I might be carrying the Chairman's child? No baby ever took hold from our many nights together. Maybe I'd never needed the *dong quai*. Maybe that explained why Teacher Fan didn't provide any to the troupe. Why Secretary Sun told me we didn't need to stop at the herbalist. I understood then why girls got expelled from the troupe if we carried a child: A baby served as proof they'd betrayed the Chairman with another man.

Even if the Chairman could no longer father a child, Secretary Sun could. He'd immediately suspect his aide. If the Chairman discovered that I was pregnant, he would destroy us both. Could I end it with herbs I'd somehow have to find—would the blood come in time—and did I want to?

Secretary Sun looked at me. Could he see the panic in my face? Because of the Madame's gossip, the Chairman may have already had us watched.

"At the age of thirteen, she composed a revolutionary song to help villagers work for twenty hours a day," the Premier continued. "At the age of sixteen she led a team at a dam that brought electricity to half the province, collecting rocks that she carried in a basket on her back. She is a true daughter of the revolution. A little cog in the revolutionary machine, who serves the people wholeheartedly. Spread her spirit and walk in her path. I present to you—Dong Feng."

Dong Feng? The name the Chairman had given me when I deceived the President now felt like a slap, the final and worst insult. Today I was supposed to reclaim my name, my story: Mei Xiang, the name my parents had given me. My village would never know that Dong Feng was the girl they once sang with, ate with, worked with.

The Premier turned to me. "Dong Feng, don't you want to greet your young comrades?" he asked.

"Dong Feng! Dong Feng! Dong Feng!" they shouted, arms waving, feet stomping. If I were standing beside them, I might have been swayed to join them and their revolution. From above, I saw how easily they were led.

At the podium, I peered over the edge. It would be easy to tip over, falling down to the ground where I belonged. The Premier steadied me, and I adjusted the microphone until my lips were almost touching the metal mesh. Finding the words I was supposed to say was like drawing water from a dried-up spring, but the remarks the Chairman prepared welled up in me—almost against my will. "My fellow youth, we must seize the torch of revolution that our parents carried."

From the corner of my eye, I noticed the Chairman leaning forward, mouthing the speech along with me. In spite of everything, it was as if his hand was on my back, like the night I read aloud from the Little Red Book to my family. The Chairman protects, the Chairman provides. I fell into the rhythm of his words, keeping an even pace, aware that if I spoke rapidly, my time at the podium would end sooner.

Photographers snapped away, their flashbulbs exploding with the violence of battle. The sunlight glinting off the cameras blinded me, and I blinked, dizzy, feeling as if I might float away. I forced myself back inside my skin, but I'd paused so long that the Premier prompted me with the next line of my speech.

"May you learn from my example, as I have learned from the Chairman's."

The Chairman's example? If I followed my orders, if I wasn't pregnant, the Chairman might grant me a position in the Lake Palaces, plenty of food, a warm bed, and a chance to visit my family. I wanted none of it. The Chairman claimed not to be a god, though he lived as one. A god descends from the heavens to become a man, a monster. If the Chairman had created me in his image, I was a monster, too.

"May you learn . . ." the Premier prompted again.

The truth was all I had left. The truth was all I had to give.

"The revolution must never die," I shouted. "The battle will be long and difficult, the greatest challenge we have yet to face, and it is up to our youth. Old fools are lost in the past. But you, the youth, are the future of this country."

A single tile could change the course of a mahjong game, a single cry could turn a crowd. I gripped the microphone stand. "I warn you. The Chairman isn't what he seems. He's a hero but his time has passed. We must stop the lies. It's—"

Someone silenced my microphone, and my words were drowned out by the cheers that the Premier summoned with a wave of his hand. My tongue felt grotesque, swollen as a slug. What else would I say, if I had a chance? It didn't matter. They weren't ready to listen.

The Premier yanked me from the podium, and I stumbled, falling into his arms before he dumped me onto my chair. It was so loud below that I didn't hear the students behind me, not until dozens of them had squeezed onto the balcony, invited here to meet top officials. The speakers crackled, the Chairman's anthem played, and the screams around us rose in loudness and pitch, like wind at the height of a storm.

My legs had gone stiff and heavy, and I heard nothing else. Guards would beat me, break my legs. Tear hair from my scalp, plunge my head into a bucket of night soil. Drown me in a well, slit my throat, or put a bullet in my head. Force me into a dark, silent cell, alive but in a life withheld.

Secretary Sun took me by the elbow and in a daze, I tottered to my feet and dimly heard him saying we had to go. Students in uniforms almost identical to mine flocked around the Chairman, clutching red armbands, each jostling for a chance to tie theirs on him. I was them, they were me, doubles upon doubles. One pushed toward me with a thin, pitiful mustache that gave him the look of a catfish. "Dong Feng!" he shouted, pleading, reaching for me. It was as if he hadn't heard my warning to the crowd, as if my words had been swallowed up by their roar.

More Red Guard and photographers surged onto the balcony. Though security officers pushed them back into the jammed reception area, telling them they had to wait their turn, to remain in place, they couldn't be contained much longer. For every student they pushed back, another two slipped through.

Secretary Sun had lost his grip on me. I swiveled my head, unable to pick him out from the crowd, unable to call out for him, and then the Chairman was upon me. His legs spread wide, his shoulders back—a mountain. "You dare to make a fool out of me?" he shouted.

My knees buckled, but then I straightened, revived by the same rage that had gripped me at the microphone. I had spoken against the Chairman, and the earth hadn't split open, and I hadn't disappeared. I wanted to cough up the air we shared and to spit his words from my mouth.

"You're nothing! Less than nothing!"

I had no reply for him but in my feet. There was nothing left to believe in, no heroes who weren't selfish and grasping. Nothing to believe in except you. In his face I could see regret. I will never know what he chose to see in mine.

Someone shrieked, "Help me! Get off! I can't breathe."

"Back up, back up!"

The crowd surged left and then right, and in the commotion, I bolted toward the soldiers, whose backs were to me.

"Somebody get a doctor!"

I zigzagged on the balcony before slipping into a gap. A Red Guard elbowed past me, shoving me deeper into the reception area, where more students crowded in.

Shouts rose behind me, and hands flailed for my wrist. When arms tightened around me, I squirmed away. As students surrounded us, tight as mortar to brick, a high thin scream rose up behind me, and a woman shouted, "Let me go! I've done nothing wrong."

"Shut up!" a man yelled. "Got her."

They'd mixed me up with someone else. More shouts followed and what sounded like a scuffle, someone getting thrown into the heavy wooden furniture, and the crash of glass. Without a backward glance, I flew down the wide stone stairs, one step, then the next and the next.

The crowd swept around me. My legs, my arms, my breath were no longer mine, a relief to give in to the surge after holding on tightly for so long. Not fighting, not gliding, not riding the current but becoming the current itself, one more young revolutionary among a million in the capital.

FANNING OUT FROM TIANANMEN SQUARE, the students waved banners and shouted slogans, brandished tasseled wooden spears and rifles, and beat bamboo clappers, shouting out slogans: "Five lakes! Four seas! One revolution!" According to the Chairman himself, they owned the future, and now they had their strongest claim yet over the capital. "Bombard the headquarters!" he'd told them. The sight of so many young revolutionaries made me shine with the light of ten thousand suns.

I tasted blood from a cut on the inside of my cheek, and felt it pumping through my chest, coursing through every part of me. Having lost my center, my world, I gave in to the crowd.

The sound of many marching feet rumbled down the street—the

Red Guard chanting, their energy unflagging. Detachments from across the country had poured into the capital, girls in colorful head-wraps and ruddy boys from the grasslands in leather boots.

A group splintered off and I followed them, zigzagging through alleys until we joined a struggle session in front of a courtyard home. I wish I could tell you I couldn't bear to take part in the violence, and that I only did so to blend in. That having spoken the truth from Tiananmen, I wanted to escape the capital as soon as possible. For once, though, the turmoil around me matched the turmoil inside.

"Landlord! Traitor!" I found myself spitting at a scrawny professor, whose crime was either that he could speak English or that he put on airs. Shouting that the professor was a spy, a Red Guard twisted the man's arms back, and forced him to kneel on shards of charcoal and bricks, and then kowtow, pressing his forehead to the steaming, filthy pavement.

Blood dripped from the professor's temple, the scent of a hot iron wok. Piled before him were books, a jade Buddha, and a pair of glasses.

Freed from everything that ever dared to hold us back, a Red Guard flung records on the bonfire, which oozed and melted, releasing an evil black scent. I might have kicked the professor in the buttocks, kicked him as I wanted to kick the Chairman, but then I caught myself. If I tortured him, I'd become the monster I'd fled.

When someone else knocked him onto his hands and knees, a girl—probably the professor's daughter—rushed toward us. Dozens of teenagers pushed her back.

"Burn the bourgeois professor!" a pockmarked Red Guard shouted. Not long ago, he'd been a schoolboy, and it appeared he'd never known such power until today, fighting enemies of the people.

"I'm loyal," the professor insisted. "I've always served the Party."

The Red Guard stomped on the professor's ribs, which broke with a sickening crunch.

"Beat the drowning dog!"

"Deep-fry the reactionary!"

The pockmarked Red Guard pried open the professor's mouth

with a stick and poured from a bucket of shit and piss. Thrashing his head, he swallowed with the wet sputters of a man drowning. When he vomited, several Red Guard forced him to gulp it back down.

A beam inside the house collapsed with a crash and a shower of sparks, taking down the red door. It looked familiar, and I realized then that I'd been here before, in Secretary Sun's neighborhood. Was the professor Grandfather Pang's son?

When the girl bit the hand of her captor, the Red Guard slapped her glasses off her face. She was no more than eight years old. She struggled against him, her braids thrashing back and forth, butting her head into his chest. The Red Guard tore off his belt, forced it into the daughter's hand, and raising her arm with his, whipped the professor's head. The clasp glinted, like a sliver of ice, a shard of a mirror, the barrel of a rifle.

Grandfather Pang hobbled out. Trying to get to the girl, he tottered and fell. The crowd swarmed around him. The professor groaned, deep and low, and the look he gave me, begging me to see him, sent me fleeing.

I ran until my lungs were bursting, into an alley where I doubled over. My body tingled, threatening to dissolve into the muggy air.

Somehow, I'd escaped. But what had I done? I had cursed the Chairman—and in doing so, cursed myself. And you. To escape imprisonment or death, I would have to leave the capital, maybe the country, destined for years on the run. I had cursed Secretary Sun, Teacher Fan, anyone associated with my rise at the Lake Palaces. If the Chairman couldn't punish me, Secretary Sun would serve in my place.

I had cursed my family, not only my parents and my sister, but all our descendants. A mob would converge, tearing down our house. My parents would have to denounce me, scratch me from their memories, and still might not escape retribution. What had I done to them? To you?

If I kept you. I could seek out an herbalist, beg for something that might bring my flow on. It might not work, though; such cures often didn't, and in truth, I didn't know if I wanted you to end.

I was already thinking of you.

———

I RETURNED TO A world set afire. Smoke smudged the stars, from conflagrations of books and record albums, from blazing courtyard homes and from burning debris piled in the middle of the street, from tailors and barbers and booksellers who provided services to the stinking bourgeoisie. Not even the Chairman's soldiers could halt these young revolutionaries. The Red Guard could march on the Great Hall of the People, the Forbidden City, and the Lake Palaces if they wanted. Only their adoration of the Chairman kept him safe. But if Red Guards were turning on their parents, and their neighbors, someday they could turn on him.

The mob surged around me in every direction, the budding revolutionaries uncertain where to charge next. An elbow dug into my back and I almost tumbled to the ground. I had to keep moving or get swept under their feet.

After midnight, the streets emptied, taking away my cover. Noises rattled me: a mangy dog nosing through garbage, a welter of rats fighting over scraps, and distant footsteps. Cuts covered my hands. When I heard the whine of a jeep, I leapt in an alley and crouched in a fetid puddle behind a cracked clay urn. I spied the bright beams cutting through the darkness and four silhouetted men riding along—soldiers in search of me? I covered my mouth with my hands, trying not to shudder.

A few minutes later, the jeep circled back and passed out of the neighborhood. Waiting to see if the soldiers would return, I huddled in the alley, surrounded by the stink of rot and urine. After I started walking again, carrying a crumbling brick for protection, this part of the capital had fallen asleep, the night hushed as though after a snowfall.

I imagined the Chairman chain-smoking, refusing his dinner, his doctor, and his advisors. His face would be sallow and drawn, his breath short and sour, and his hand trembling, spilling his tea and cigarettes. Waiting for reports every hour about me. When none came, the Chairman would curse Midnight Chang. She'd been left alone with him on such a day, in such a mood.

Or else, he'd couple with her in the bed I no longer shared with him. Their arms and legs twined, her body bent over to receive him, or on top of him, every position he'd put me in, as though by casting her in my place, he'd rid himself of my memory. His quickening breath, her mouth open in pleasure.

She would throw out my few possessions but, in the days to come, find reminders of me everywhere, my scent, the strands of my hair, and notes folded into pages in the books I had studied.

Tonight, Secretary Sun would have faced the Chairman's bloodshot gaze. If he so much as blinked, he risked revealing what happened in the sedan. He had survived at the Lake Palaces for this long, I told myself, and might longer still. Clouds scudded across the moon. Did Secretary Sun look at the moon and think of me, hoping it might light my way? I grazed my hand across my belly. If only I could have told him about you. If only I could have said what I had sensed for months but could now say: The difference between a peasant and an intellectual isn't how they talk or how they dress. Anyone could learn that. Anyone—my mother, my father, my sisters—could pretend if they had the right teachers. The difference was in how they were treated. Secretary Sun treated me like I was something more, but I would always be a peasant to the Chairman.

Secretary Sun would have listened to me speak. He would have agreed. But he hadn't followed me.

A BAT WHIZZED BY, hunting for insects. Crouching, I covered my head, but not long after, a silver cloud descended upon me. Yelping, I struck at the humid air, hitting nothing. I'd stumbled into moths that scattered like torn scraps of paper in a gust. No one poked their head out a window to check on me, perhaps unwilling to intervene on behalf of yet another person screaming for help, a sound they'd grown accustomed to in Beijing that summer.

I walked all night. Just before dawn, I reached the outskirts of the capital. Fields of corn and sorghum began at the foot of a factory's high cracked walls, spreading toward a village. Inhaling the loamy scent of ripening, I couldn't quite believe that I had eluded the Chairman. The road loomed before me, no one ahead of me, and no one behind me. At the next crossroads, I could go anywhere, everywhere that the Chairman couldn't. For the rest of his life, he'd remain trapped, whether behind the high walls of the Lake Palaces or at his villas under twenty-four-hour guard. I hadn't been alone for this long in more than a year, maybe not my entire life. Who was I, outside of the schedule and the lessons of the Lake Palaces, away from the Chairman and my family? Who would I be to you, you who were still only a hunch? I didn't yet know.

Mosquitoes attacked as the sun rose, nipping wherever I was exposed, at the cuffs of my shirt, the hem of my pants, and the brim of my cap. Lumps swelled on my forehead and ankles, and gnats followed me, drinking at my eyes. Threads of smoke from cooking fires drifted over the rise of a hill. Perhaps no one here knew what happened in the capital yesterday, about my speech or the young revolutionaries on a rampage. Though the village was less than a day's walk away from the Lake Palaces, their daily chores would have been more urgent.

The corn was at shoulder height, with its scent of late summer, of long sunshine. I found shelter between the rows thick with weeds, on the far edge that the villagers neglected, if they were anything like my neighbors. My uniform was stiff with sweat, pants splashed with filth, and a stray ember had burned a hole in my sleeve. Aching with hunger, I pulled down an unripe ear and bit into the starchy kernels. I gagged, wondering if I could survive the journey ahead, the sporadic meals and dangerous roads, trying to sustain you in my body and later, outside of it, wherever I ended up. In the countryside or in a city? On the classroom map at the Lake Palaces, dots had been cities of millions, and ridges the length of my thumb had been mountains. I was nothing, not even a speck.

The Little Red Book spilled out of my pocket, fallen open to the passage I first used to impress the Chairman, and had turned to many times since then to bolster my confidence: "We are not only good at destroying the Old World, we are also good at building the new." Whenever I held a copy, I'd reverently handled the pages with my fingertips. The book held his wisdom, unsullied and unchanging, serving as a constant when so much at the Lake Palaces wasn't. It stood apart from the Chairman's foul moods and petty actions.

I ripped out the page and the one that followed, and then tore up the binding, surprised and gratified at how easily the book came apart. Kneeling, I clawed at the cracked earth, a grave for the Little Red Book, a grave for Dong Feng, the revolutionary hero. Hearing a caw, I glanced up at a raven wheeling above, its feathers glossy as calligraphy ink against the sky lightening into a pale blue.

As I finished patting down the dirt over the book, voices approached. Before I could hide, a mother and her young son arrived. She'd tied a faded rag onto her head, to keep off the sun, and carried a hoe, its sharp tip glinting in the sun. If I ran, she'd raise the alarm and everyone would chase me. I would have to convince her to help me. If I could do this, then I might survive this day, and the next.

"What are you doing?" asked the woman, who had a squirrel's darting quickness.

Her round-faced son clung to her pant leg, staring at me. A water gourd slung on his arm. She could have shaken him off, but she stroked his cheek. He buried his face into her leg and she swung him onto her hip, kissing him on the top of his head. His perfection, her pride.

"My father's sick," I blurted. "I'm on my way to him." A child's love might persuade her not to turn me in.

"Get the headman," she told her son.

"Wait!" I said, taking a step toward them. She set down her son, shielding him with her body. I raised my hands, palms up, pleading. From my left breast pocket, I pulled off a pin, a yellow star against a shiny red background, the enamel smooth and cool, that I pressed into the boy's hand. To win over his mother, I had to win him. He looked over my shoulder and without warning, his mother shoved me into the corn. My face plowed into the dust and I rolled hidden behind the row, shielded by the stalks. I sputtered, my mouth full of grit. When I propped myself onto my side, I saw that two men had arrived. If they'd peered into the cornfields, they might have noticed the rustling, but one was busy picking at his nails with a small knife, while the other fiddled with his dull and rusty hoe.

The men told her that strangers had arrived, and that the headman had summoned everyone to the plaza for a meeting. They called her Sister Chen. From the rigid set of her shoulders and the tone of her voice, it seemed she didn't like these men. Maybe she'd heard their excuses too many times, and they were unreliable, creating messes that people like her had to clean up. That they—and not someone she trusted—delivered the message might be what kept her from turning me in.

The revolutionary pin in her son's fist glittered in his fingers. When he started to open his hand, Sister Chen gripped his shoulder to stop him.

"Something to do with the capital," said the man picking at his nails. "Old Shorty tried to deliver eggs this morning but was stopped at a blockade. Soldiers turned him around."

"There's been trouble all summer," Sister Chen said. "Nothing that has much to do with us."

"Maybe they're looking for someone," he said.

"Maybe they're announcing a reward," the other said, leaning on his hoe.

"A reward," Sister Chen scoffed. Her son looked straight at me, as if we were engaged in a private game.

"The headman will keep it for himself." He put away his knife.

Sister Chen shrugged. With her hoe, she chopped at weeds less than a meter from my face. I recoiled, the sheaves rustling.

"What was that?" Now nibbling his thumbnail, he peered above the row.

"A crow!" She shuffled her feet until she blocked the gap into which I had disappeared. The men attempted to persuade her to join the meeting, but soon gave up. After they left, Sister Chen pulled me out and handed me the water gourd. I gulped down water as her son tried to put on the pin. She whispered he should slip it in his pocket.

"Why don't we follow Uncle?" he asked.

"Have you ever known them to lead you to anywhere but trouble?" she asked. "I wouldn't follow them to heaven."

Sister Chen gave me a bundle of corn cakes, fragrant with grease, and haltingly mentioned that her mother passed away last year. "I didn't get to see her before she died."

I thanked her and fled.

THE COUNTRY WAS ON the move, and it wasn't as unusual as it once might have been for someone my age to be traveling by herself. Beating drums and waving banners, youth marched into the cities and the countryside, calling themselves "Descendants of the Revolutionary Army" and a "Propaganda Force of the Chairman's Thought." They made pilgrimages to Shaoshan, Shanghai, Jinggang Mountain, Zunyi, Yan'an, and other places from revolutionary history. Transportation, meals, and lodging were free, provided by the government. Teenagers packed into trains and army trucks, slept in government offices and dormitories, and ate in canteens serving pickled vegetables and stale buns in the cities, or found shelter in barns and ate watery porridge in the villages.

On the run, I stole from the Red Guard, pilfering identification cards, a bedroll, and extra clothes from their unattended knapsacks. Most teenagers, leaving home for the first time, were ideal victims: well-fed travelers who likely had been misplacing their belongings, who'd notice their identification cards, cash, and ration coupons gone only days later. Careless and trusting, they called me their sister, their comrade, treating me as they expected to be treated.

When Red Guard tried to work for the peasants, the enthusiastic but incompetent students mistook shoots for weeds and built wobbly terraces that tumbled overnight. I came upon their destruction. If I hadn't left home for the Lake Palaces, these spoiled teenagers could have been lecturing me. "I'm a straggler," I told villagers who fed and housed me. In return, I planted, weeded, bound sheaves, collected and spread dung. I hung tiny red chilies and bundles of cabbages to dry from the eaves, fetched kindling, and left at dawn.

The autumn stayed warm and fine, as I followed the sun and charted a westerly course into the interior of the country. I walked for as many hours as I could each day, on paths that climbed over ridges, skirted fields and marshes, and crossed rivers. Reason suggested I pray for blood, that I seek out an end to the pregnancy, but when my flow still didn't come, I suspected—I hoped—that I held you within me. You alone of my family hadn't been taken from me.

I'd never been so weary, and yet, my senses had never been so heightened, either: The orange-red of the turning leaves pulsed in my blood, and every earthly scent seemed to reach deep into my nose and my throat. It was then I started talking to you—a one-sided conversation. Or maybe it wasn't quite a conversation but an acknowledgment of you, of us, of an "us." Keeping me company, then and now.

Although my feet had been toughened by a lifetime of going bare, they blistered from so much walking, the tender flesh weeping and the tread on my leather boots wearing thin. Each step took me away from the Chairman and the world he envisioned, and into the one that existed.

My birthday came and went; I might have forgotten I turned seventeen if another Red Guard hadn't remarked she had a craving for moon cakes. I couldn't go home, as much as I wanted Ma and her remedies to ease my pregnancy and help me bring you safely into this world. Our village would have spies, and on the road, I could hide. By springtime, though, I'd have to find shelter, somewhere to give birth—all of which seemed impossibly far off and yet impossibly soon, too. I knew only that I'd cover as much ground while I still could, more nimble with a baby hidden under my clothes than tucked onto my back in a sling.

Every night, I prayed for you and for my family. They were blameless, save for the fact they had raised a traitor. Maybe they had disowned me, but it still might not have mattered. In ancient times, emperors had killed entire clans for a son's crimes. I pictured Ma forced to her knees, her forehead to the ground, and her arms twisted behind her. Ba, his other pinky sliced off, with the hiss of the knife and crack of the bone. My sister—Which one? Which one lived?—forced into a cowshed, and shit dumped onto her bowed head.

Until now, I didn't understand the horror of exile, the loss of my bearings and the loss of myself. No one to remind me of who I had been before Dong Feng, no one who could summon the same memories of my childhood as Mei Xiang. My village and my family seemed as much of an invention as the lies I told to strangers. Having left no mark on the past, I left none in the present, either. My footsteps and my life, flung to the wind—except for you.

CHAPTER 27

*I*N LATE FALL, I FLAGGED DOWN A CART, SEEKING A RIDE TO Taiyuan, the capital of Shanxi province, the skies in the distance low and gray from the iron foundries and factories sending up gritty smoke. The first frosts had arrived, glimmering on rocks in silvery patterns like the etchings on oracle bones. The Chairman had told me the ancients read the bones to divine the future. What would mine hold?

The driver's left eye drooped in a permanent wink, a sidelong glance that appraised the world and seemed to find it wanting. I could tell he wouldn't ask many questions, not like the grandfathers who wanted to trace back generations of my ancestors or the mothers who questioned my solitary travels.

"Thank you, Uncle," I said.

"Uncle Lin," he said.

By then, I was more than three months pregnant, and hungry all the time, feeling as if I might cave in. I had the appetite of ten men. A hundred. As soon as I finished a meal, I wanted another. You hadn't kicked yet, and I hoped that you might soon. I felt you, though, in the creak of my joints, and the spread of my hips, creating a looseness like a rubber band pulled nearly to breaking and then released.

Ma had struggled to keep children in her, and almost died giving birth to me. But I couldn't dwell on such possibilities, intent on keeping us fed and ahead of the Chairman.

In the city, I needed to find small goods scarce in the villages that

I could trade for food: needles, salt, star anise, and peppercorns. I'd also begun to forage for cures that I could offer, tying them off in clean rags that I stored at the bottom of my rucksack.

Though Ma never praised me, I knew she always brought me foraging—and not my sisters—because I was patient and sharp-eyed. Once, she had clasped my hands around a root that I'd missed. She'd gripped until I thought my hands would break, and I shook free and threw down the root. She caught me by the shoulders, wordlessly telling me that I had to learn, and that this skill would someday serve me. Even as a child I'd known that I didn't have beauty or blessings. I longed for her now.

When the wind gusted, I tucked my hands into my sleeves to keep warm. Irrigation ditches flowed beside neat fields that could have been another commune but for the high fences and the barracks. A labor camp? I wondered if Busy Shan lived in a place like this one, or if they'd let her go home yet.

We passed men weeding a row. "Their punishment is forcing them into our lives," Uncle Lin muttered.

"Peasants have dirty hands and cow-shit-soaked feet, but they are cleaner than intellectuals," I said. A popular saying among the Red Guard.

He snorted. "Cleaner? Only if you've dipped the intellectual into a pit of pig shit."

I laughed, a real one, an unexpected one, that made me realize how long it had been since I'd found anything funny. He began to hum tunelessly. As we entered the city, we passed new street signs— RED FOREVER ROAD and STRUGGLE FOREVER LANE and RED KERCHIEF PARK, names changed by Red Guards. As adrift as I felt on the run, people must feel the same where parks, markets, and landmarks of daily life had lost their familiar names overnight.

The Chairman couldn't track me here, or could he? The mountains were high, and the emperor far away. I pulled down the brim of my cap. My escape must have frustrated him; every day I remained unfound reminded him of the limits of his power. Or perhaps I remained free at the Chairman's whim. I had also considered and rejected another possibility: that the Chairman had stopped looking for me or had never gone after me at all.

I would have been fortunate, but I couldn't bear his indifference.

The cart wheels squeaked and rattled on the cobblestones. Uncle Lin parked in front of a gleaming bronze statue, freshly polished, of a local hero, a peasant with a blunt, obstinate chin who gazed to the east, where the sun rose and revolution began. He helped me down from the cart. When his hand lingered at my waist, I pulled away. My belly had begun to swell, but only barely. To him, I might have seemed like another soft city dweller turned Red Guard, a teenage girl not long out of childhood.

I hobbled off, my legs and back aching from the jolting ride. As I swept dust from my clothes, I spotted an officer standing by a jeep in a uniform that bore what looked like the yellow braid of the Lake Palaces. His haircut seemed too short and neat, and the crease in his pants too crisp, straight lines in this remote city of blurs and smudges, of mist and coal smoke.

Searching for an alley I could slip into, I realized I'd have to cross the square. The officer looked past me, another negligible detail in a negligible city. I exhaled in relief, wondering what brought him to this outpost. Maybe he was escorting someone from the Lake Palaces to the labor camp. I tried to remember if he'd been a guard at a dance party. Had he heard rumors of a disobedient lover, of a dismissed advisor? In the tales that followed my flight, the Lake Palaces might have gossiped about Secretary Sun and I being lovers, that the Chairman had been a fool to leave his mistress in the care of his younger aide.

To my horror, I recognized the prisoner: Secretary Sun, his back hunched, as though under a load of rocks, and his right arm hung crippled, his fingers curled into claws. He'd grown thin, the tendons tight in his neck and his prisoner's uniform baggy on his body. The Chairman's revenge must have been swift.

If he, too, had escaped, if I could tell him about you, I might be redeemed. I had to soothe his pain at least, offer him a drink of water, press my hand to his broken body, and beg for his forgiveness.

He turned his head, and became someone else, too tall and years older. His features were crooked, one eye lower than the other, and his mouth knocked to the side. The prisoner was a stranger. For a moment, I'd let myself believe that we could flee together and that my travels alone would come to an end. Never a meal, never a bed, never a day again without him, a wish I hadn't admitted to myself until now, and having him transform and disappear before me felt as if I'd lost him once more.

For a long time, I had known what I wanted, even if I couldn't say it out loud. I'd suppressed our attraction as forbidden, impossible, strange—how could I want a man without worship and fear?—and it rocked me, this reminder that I might never find that again.

After ordering the prisoner to stand still, the officer walked toward me. Without thinking, I ran. He chased me, shouting for me to stop. I hurried through the tight lanes of an outdoor market, turning right and left and left, where vendors were unloading heaps of cabbages, ruddy apples, and pungent piles of scallions, more food than I'd seen in a long while, which made me stumble from hunger.

The vendors gaped, but no one stopped me. I burst into a wet market, noisy and rank with fish guts, chicken feathers, and rotting produce. Shoppers fought over scraps of meat, their haggles echoing off the tiled wall streaked with mold. Running toward an exit, I passed two wrinkled women arguing over the last rabbit haunch. "I was in front of you!" "You reached for the liver first!" "Rules never apply to you!"

I slowed, panting, and could no longer hear the officer running after me. Maybe he'd halted without going too far into the warren of stalls, but he still could alert local police. As I squeezed past a stall, my rucksack brushed against a slab of pork, knocking it into a stinking pool of water. I cringed. The butcher and his shoppers shouted at me and someone grabbed at my arm. Wrestling free, I dashed outside, where I discovered I'd traveled in a circle, to a side entrance overlooking the plaza. The officer stood with his back to me, scanning the market. His prisoner was back in the jeep, watched over by the driver.

I knew no one in this city, no one who could hide me. Except for Uncle Lin. He was parked where I'd left him, blocked from the officer's view by the statue. Tearing off my red-star cap, I unknotted by braids, my hair falling in wavy tangles to my shoulders. I stopped running like a thief and walked briskly toward him. With a pleading look, I gestured toward the officer, and then to the back of the cart.

Uncle Lin beckoned me, and as soon as I climbed in, he dumped a basket of dusty yams on top of me, battering against me like dozens of fists. One hit the back of my head while I tried to protect my belly, yams wedged between my arms and my body. I wiggled my arms, trying to shield you. After he strapped down a cloth, he whipped his donkey and the cart creaked away. I held still, convinced the cover would come loose, and the officer would yank me out by my hair.

The cart stopped and a man questioned Uncle Lin, asking why he was returning home instead of selling his yams. Uncle Lin coughed, spitting and snorting, and explained that he was ill, he'd had a late start, and the trip here had worsened his symptoms. The yams would keep until the next market day, later that week. He added another cough and the footsteps backed off.

We rolled out of the city, creaking over what sounded like the bridge where he had picked me up. I wondered where he was taking me. I had encountered the desire of other men on this journey, until a jealous wife, a nosy sister, or a meddling neighbor had stopped their advances and midnight gropes. Would my luck end now?

Although I thrashed, attempting to gain leverage, my rucksack remained stuck, no matter how hard I tugged. We hit a pothole and yams rolled over me, wedging my body tighter into the cart. My jaw throbbed, jammed together by the weight of the yams, and I fought against sneezes, circling deep in my head. Rain pattered, followed by a downpour, and muddy rivulets washed off the yams and into my face, soaking my clothes. We turned off the main road, onto a rutted track at an incline.

When we stopped, my body had gone numb and my wet hair clung to my scalp. As I heard a door open, I wriggled, and the yams shifted but not enough to free me. After he pulled off the tarp and cleared away yams, Uncle Lin threw a blanket around me. Though he was also soaked, he didn't bother to cover himself. His home stood alone, at the edge of shorn fields.

Inside he stoked the fire, poured water into a chipped enamel basin, and handed me a clean rag and a bundle of clothes. He busied himself at the stove. Aware of my stink, I rinsed my gummy mouth, wiped grime from my neck and my face, and worked out the dirt from beneath my fingernails, until the water in the basin turned dark. The air was tinged with chimney smoke, mildewed straw, and what encroaches in dark, closed places. I hadn't bathed since leaving the Lake Palaces, and as I cleaned myself up, the heaviness within me eased. My back twinged, and I rubbed my bloated belly.

I slipped on the homespun clothes: a clean, threadbare top, tight around the shoulders, and pants that hovered above my ankles. Not his, but some woman's. I thanked him. His walls were bare, the first I'd seen without a portrait of the Chairman that everyone hung up in those days. Maybe he only put it up if he thought his visitor would care; maybe he didn't have many visitors.

He could see I'd noticed the blank walls.

"He's not watching here," Uncle Lin said. He had also changed into dry clothes. He sat on a rattan chair, the cane worn smooth and dark, with a hole punched in the seat between his legs.

"Nothing to see," I said.

"There usually isn't." He gave me a cup of hot water. As I sipped, warming my hands on the cup, he split open a pomegranate. I savored each crunchy jeweled seed, until my hands were stained red, while he boiled cornmeal noodles. He seasoned the dish with vinegar and hot peppers, then placed the bowl before me. We'd dine, one after the other, because he had one bowl, one cup, and one set of wooden chopsticks. I pushed the bowl toward him, but he insisted, and I slurped down the noodles, coarse yet delicious, topped with red-stemmed wild greens, tart with the faint taste of lemon, the kind that my mother pickled to see us through the winter.

The fire had grown low, and darkness had fallen in the room.

"You didn't hand me a leaflet as soon as you climbed aboard," Uncle Lin said. "Didn't attempt to educate me."

"I'm not much of a teacher," I said.

"I'm not much of a student," he said. I wondered if he'd hungered for company, for someone who didn't exclaim and demand revolutionary proclamations.

When he stroked my cheek with his thumb, I flinched, and he dropped his hand, his mouth twisted in embarrassment. Inside I felt stirred up, like the soft, muddy bottom of a pond, rousing what I'd buried for months. To rid myself of the Chairman's touch, I had to find another. I reached for him.

As he hovered above me, I couldn't escape the vision of the Chairman, sneering at us. Probably, he no longer cared. I rocked wildly. Just as I felt I might escape into sensation, into myself, Uncle Lin gasped.

We spooned together, my head tucked into the crook of his arm, both of us facing the wall where the fire's shadow flickered.

On my journey, I would sleep with a handful of men. Sometimes for survival and for their silence, sometimes against my will, and sometimes because of what the Chairman had awoken in me.

UNCLE LIN'S CHEST AT my back was pleasingly solid, until our feet touched, and I pulled away, the moment too intimate. I rolled over to face him, glad of the darkness. He told me about his pregnant wife, forced by the commune to fetch buckets of water all day. Their family had been marked as landlords because his grandfather bought a small plot of land before Liberation.

She went into labor too early. "She bled," he said. She and the baby had died within hours—lost to him, but saved from the revolution.

The next morning, we ate spicy pickled cabbage and roasted yams, and split a single dried date. I chewed slowly, holding the sweetness in my mouth as long as I could. I considered stepping into this home, making a place for myself here, and though I might soothe Uncle Lin's pain—and mine, too—I had nothing left to give. If I had stayed, it might have changed what happened next. If I'd known, I would have stepped back over the threshold, trying to stop what rushed toward us.

*A*S WINTER SET IN, I STUFFED MY WORN BOOTS WITH RAGS, slipped on wool long underwear that poked out from the hem of my pants. I stole sweaters from clotheslines and layered them underneath my padded jacket. I could hardly bend my arms, but the clothes hid my thick waist and the new heaviness in my breasts. Even as I headed south in search of milder weather, cold bit into me. And so, I lingered where I could.

For a time, I emptied the chamber pot and cooked for a crippled woman in her damp hovel. For a time, I gathered dung to fuel the stove of a granny who lived at the edge of a pine forest. For a time, I patched and mended the clothes of a family whose mother had passed away a year ago, people for whom the revolution hadn't fulfilled its promise and never would. I told them I was on my way to help a sick father, to marry, to join my cousin's Red Guard detachment, whatever excuse seemed to fit their expectations.

I never sought help from people with plenty, with the most to lose, who might question a stranger. Like the Chairman before me had, I discovered that those with the least were the most generous with a bowl of rice or a warm spot on a brick bed. Calling upon the neediest, I slid into what they were missing. Like the demons who drape themselves in pelts of human skin, I assumed different forms, inventing siblings, maladies, and dilemmas to explain why I traveled alone. My acting lessons from Teacher Fan served me well. I was never the youngest of three daughters—I kept that story for myself.

When worried that local authorities were about to detain me, I left to avoid bringing harm to those who had helped me.

In early January, I traveled through an unwelcoming county in Anhui province, where the distances between villages were far and the mountains so steep that the highest terraced fields were nearly vertical. One day near twilight, a cramp stopped me in my tracks. I undid the third button on my pants. The waistband had been digging into my middle and soon I'd have to get bigger clothes. The cramp eased, but a dull ache remained. My breasts were always tender, veined as a bloodshot eye. Wincing, I gathered kindling, tucking a few branches under my arm until the throb started up again. I never arrived at a stranger's doorstep empty-handed.

The gnarled arms of a pine tree held the little house whose chimney smoldered, probably from wet wood in the fire. I knocked on the front door, painted with worn characters for good luck. A girl answered, her face closed until I offered her the heap of branches. She might have been ten. Inside, the house was barely warmer than outside. A bundle shivered on the bed, the blanket slipping down to reveal the most ancient face I'd ever seen, spider-web wrinkles on skin translucent as rice paper, fine white hair, and a puckered toothless mouth. She seemed like a character from one of Ma's tales, cursed by the gods with eternal life but not youth. Granny Deng, the girl said when I asked.

I took off my cap. At the stove, the girl poured water and cornmeal together for porridge. To stoke the fire, I rearranged the kindling, and then blew on my hands for warmth, rubbing my palms together. It had been weeks since I'd tasted grease, and my skin had become tight and flaky. After I poured out the extra water and stirred, I set another pot to boil, and dropped in a handful of *dangshen,* a cure for Granny's cough, I explained.

Granny Deng yawned as steam rose off the porridge. I hadn't eaten anything in two days. Swallowing saliva to quell my own hunger, I ladled porridge into a wooden bowl and diluted it with water.

"Bao Bao," Granny Deng whispered to her granddaughter. Little Bao, little precious one.

Granny Deng finished eating, and Little Bao slurped a few spoonfuls before offering the last to me. I sucked the porridge through my teeth, savoring the comforting blandness, and the girl licked the bowl clean, thoroughly and efficiently as a cat. She handed me the bowl, into which I poured the medicinal brew, and offered it to Granny Deng, who took it without complaint.

Little Bao climbed onto the bed, tucking a quilt around the feet of her grandmother, and motioned for me to join her under another quilt. We faced each other, our knees drawn up, enveloped by the scent of our damp wool clothes. Granny Deng snored. The crackling fire turned their home cozy, and I wiggled my toes and my fingers, drowsing despite the tightness that had spread to my back.

"Why aren't you with the others?" She fingered my cap. Red Guard might have passed through the village. There was a revolutionary martyrs' site a half-day's walk from here, where a major battle had taken place, putting the village in the unfortunate path of the Red Guard.

"I had to go home," I said. I was returning to my detachment after taking care of my ill mother, I added, for Little Bao would understand such responsibilities.

From a shelf sunk into the wall, Little Bao pulled down a wooden sheep with curls of fur, rearing up on sturdy hooves, and a polished turtle, its neck outstretched as though sunning itself. Her father's carvings were her family's only treasure. Little Bao told me she'd been orphaned after her parents' cart plunged down a ravine. She showed off her own crude attempts: an ox, its legs blocky and eyes gouged in, and a one-eared rabbit with square paws. "It never looks like what's in my head," she said.

"Nothing ever does," I said.

Granny Deng's mouth fell open and her snores grew louder.

"Will the revolution last into spring?" She mumbled that she'd tried reading aloud from the Chairman's writings to cure her grandmother. Her face hopeful, she held out her copy of the Little Red Book; it could have been a gift from Red Guards, and I wanted to slap it from her hands.

A leaflet fell out, featuring a photo of a young woman in revolutionary uniform, her fist raised. She could have been Iron Girl or Sister Yu. She could have been me. Holding the leaflet up in the dim light, I squinted at the words but recognized who it was even before reading about her advertised appearance in Luoyang. There, Red Guard had hacked off the heads of tens of thousands of Buddhas carved into the limestone cliffs. Busy as the town was in the aftermath, an uneasiness had hovered when I'd passed through in late autumn. I'd missed Midnight Chang by a matter of weeks.

"Flower of the revolution." Little Bao touched her fingertips to Midnight Chang's face. The Lake Palaces had let her keep her name; she had prevailed over me in every way.

It should have been me.

I no longer believed in the revolution, but a large part of me still craved that fame, that certainty and purpose. I hated her, hated the Chairman all the more for it, for uncovering it, for stoking it in me.

If, years ago, my family had told me that heroes no longer existed and never did, that the revolution was long past, I wouldn't have believed them. Now I understood Ba had tried to warn me, each time he told me an ancient story, where truth existed outside of the official record. Ma had also prepared me when we foraged roots and tubers that we didn't share with our neighbors. We provided for ourselves.

I brushed my fingers across my pocket but didn't feel Ma's beads. Gone. Panicking, I dug into the pocket until my fingers tore through the threadbare cloth. If only—I could have—should have—

The beads dropped onto the covers and I clenched my fist around them. I would teach my parents' lessons to Little Bao—secretly, cautiously. When she discovered the revolution had withered, that her idols were a sham, she wouldn't feel as though the world had conspired against her.

———

THE NEXT DAY, I took Little Bao out to forage. Maybe we could find crisp winter bamboo shoots. Most trees had shed their leaves, but by the river, I found a stand of burdock whose roots we could stew. The odd jabbing in my side continued. I thought you had quickened inside me. Maybe that was what women meant, when they said their babies kicked. I had another season to go before you arrived, time enough to rest, all the time and no time in the world.

That night, snow fell, and we stayed in bed most of the next day. The village hid under an endless white shroud. Silent, the birdsong hushed, with a cold so dry and piercing my lungs ached when I fetched a bucket of snow to melt on the stove. In bed, Granny Deng curled between us, three spoons nested together, my chest to her back, my arm across her and resting on Little Bao's waist. The sleep of families who warmed one another, swatting, snoring, and tugging for a share of the blankets.

I braided Little Bao's hair, wiped her face clean, and acted out scenes with her carvings. Granny Deng crooned songs in her creaky voice, and though I tried to nap again, my stomach knotted like a rat's nest. The other day, still on the road and desperately thirsty, I'd cracked ice over a puddle with my boot heel and scooped a few muddy drops into my mouth, and now my body could be rebelling.

Sometime later, I squatted over the wooden bucket that served as their chamber pot. When my legs gave out, I ended up on my hands and knees, folding and unfolding into a caterpillar, chrysalis, and moth. What I remember next was the screaming. Not my own, but Little Bao's. She huddled in the bed, covers drawn over her head. A pool of blood widened around me, sinking into the packed dirt floor, the scent of mown hay, dampness, and rust everywhere. My body felt as if I'd been encased in sand, to put out a fire that burned yet left me shivering, my teeth chattering so hard that my jaw ached.

And then I met you.

Your skin damp and translucent as a salamander's, crisscrossed with veins no thicker than a thread, your arms no bigger than my middle finger, your own fingers in miniature but perfect all the same. The miracle of your mouth opened and closed. I picked you up, palming the tiny crown of your head, your body laid out against the length of my arm as if you belonged nowhere else.

My son.

When I kissed your forehead, light as a feather, I felt as if we might pass into each other, into one flesh one last time. Every wordless promise I made to you then, I meant. Did you understand any of it? I gazed down at you, not daring to blink. If I never blinked, I might keep you alive, might give you infancy, childhood, children and grandchildren of your own.

In that eternity, Granny Deng tottered out of bed and despite her seeming frailty, her hands were sure as she cut the cord between us. She could have been mustering her strength for a while. She'd been a midwife, I would learn, who'd ushered hundreds of babies into the world, who remembered the motions of labor long after becoming forgetful about much else. When she reached for you, I jerked away but I couldn't protect you, couldn't outrun what was happening. The rosiness in your skin disappeared, your sunrise fading into sunset, into night.

IN THE DAYS THAT followed, I tossed with fever. Granny Deng and other women swarmed in and out of my vision, pressing bitter brews to my lips and smearing on stinking salves. A scowling man studied me—the headman? In my dreams, you and my family and Secretary Sun vanished, slipping out of my reach, into mist, over a cliff, into turbulent waters, into a deep pit.

Whenever I started awake, certain I'd heard you wailing, my breasts throbbed, leaking the milk that had come in. But you were never there.

I shouldn't have walked for so long, for so far. I should have found food and shelter, begged for mercy from whoever took me in, done whatever they'd asked to keep you safe.

They buried you without me. To join you, to die anonymously, far from home, seemed just punishment for failing you. Animals would pick at my flesh, birds line their nests with my hair, and the wind scatter the dust of my bones.

But I didn't die. One afternoon, I crawled to the door, drawn by a green scent in the air. The house was empty, and I dimly remembered a knock earlier, hushed conversation, and the sound of footsteps. Now I nudged open the door and pushed myself up to sitting. My jagged bones might poke through my skin if I moved too quickly.

Snow lay in patches on the ground. A dozen meters away, plum blossoms had arrived, bright white blooms against the stark black branches. Resilience, perseverance. My father's name for me, Mei Xiang. His fragrant plum blossom.

What called me back to life was the understanding that my death would be another victory for the Chairman. That realization had driven my flight, from the beginning.

Until now, the snow might have kept the headman trapped in the village and unable to report me—an apparently luckless Red Guard—to higher authorities, but the weather was turning and I couldn't bring further trouble to Granny Deng and Little Bao, whose only crime had been of kindness.

CHAPTER 29

ROAMING, I EMPTIED MYSELF INTO THE FURROWS IN THE field, into the geese flying overhead, into the roads shimmering with a fine white dust that bleached travelers into skeletons, and into other preoccupations of day-to-day survival. Impossible to settle down or plan beyond next week. I never stayed in any home longer than a night or two, resisting the sway of routine and fidelity.

I tried to forget about you, about your rosebud mouth. Your burial mound heaped with white stones, one of my mother's dowry beads tucked among them. The other I kept. No one I met on the road knew that I'd been pregnant—that I'd been your mother. Mother to you, to Fei Hong, a soaring bird, never to land.

My hidden past was a blessing, though sometimes I wanted to scream that I wasn't who they assumed: a teenager with no care in the world except for her next adventure, with a comfortable home and a family who would welcome her any time she returned.

I couldn't avoid the Chairman, who appeared everywhere: on posters as a revolutionary soldier in an olive uniform at thirty, and as a vigorous statesman at fifty; on the cover of the Little Red Book and on collections of his poetry; in a mural in which he strode through a bright field of poppies; and as white plaster busts people kept in their homes and bowed before in the morning, to ask for instructions, and in the evening, to report on their day. Because I saw nothing from the present, not his shaking hand nor his wasting despair, I began to doubt my memories of his ailing. I wanted the twitches to travel up the length of his body, until he choked. With his death, order might get restored and the violence around me might end.

He endured, though, and so did his revolution. The frenzy had intensified, a flood that gained force from the debris swept up in its path. Class enemies, bad elements, ox devils, and snake demons kneeled and repented. I tried to keep clear of the Red Guard, who smashed teeth, broke arms, and cobbled together prisons. In the temples, they kicked over altars, toppled urns, and set worship halls on fire.

Sometimes I couldn't avoid the chaos, though. When loudspeakers in the parks recited the Chairman's words and revolutionary music, we had to dance along, skipping in place, raising our arms above our heads, our knees rising to waist height. Each dancer solitary, no hands touching, to show how we put the revolution first. No one around me could have imagined the Chairman swing dancing, twirling me under his arm in the pavilion or alone in his bedchambers.

I turned away from factories where workers battled one another, convinced they each upheld the revolution. Production halted, everyone too busy to run the assembly lines. In Shanghai, in Wuhan, and around the country, Red Guard split into factions, proclaiming themselves as the true inheritors of the Chairman. They had turned on one another in what amounted to an all-out civil war, with insults and now violence, with stolen grenades and machine guns. I stayed far from the cities rumored to have the bloodiest battles, places with access to weapons from the munitions factories, places where rivals sprayed pesticides at one another through fire hoses. In Chongqing, Xiamen, and Changchun, to the west, the south, and the north, tanks rolled and warships fired cannons, helmed by these would-be revolutionaries. Those fleeing warned me about teenagers barely big enough to hold machine guns, who fired off their ammunition for fun, who would take down anyone whose fate put them in their crosshairs.

Finally, the Army cracked down. From the news, it seemed the Defense Minister argued that only the armed forces could restore order, only they could defeat capitalist infiltrators. Soldiers crushed the rioters, with turmoil continuing for months.

I was neither the first, nor the last, of the heroes that the Party exalted during the Cultural Revolution. In my travels, I'd asked Red Guard if they had seen Midnight Chang speak, or if they knew of upcoming appearances. No one did. In grimy Hengyang, along the muddy Xiang River, where the Chairman's Hunanese accent echoed around me, I discovered her giant portrait on a factory wall. She brandished a shiny wrench, as though poised to swing it on a battlefield. The portrait appeared new, with the glistening perfection of a flower petal captured in a drop of dew. On this broiling day, everything else blurred behind soot raining down from the crooked chimneys.

A Red Guard coming out of the gates saw me staring and told me what she knew of this woman: a hero with a talent for fixing broken machines. While reciting the Chairman's words, she'd clutched shut an exploding boiler in a munitions factory, allowing her fellow workers to escape. "The blast left a pit the size of a lake!" the girl exclaimed. "They found her left hand in a schoolyard. Three blocks away! It's on display at the factory they rebuilt. Still wet with her blood."

Blood that had flushed Midnight Chang's cheeks and powered her breath, her step. Perhaps she'd volunteered for a propaganda film, something maybe that could guide the wayward Red Guard. The boiler could have scorched her back, singeing her braid, the metal buttons on her coveralls branding her flesh. She didn't dare move. She couldn't back out, not after hours of makeup and costume, not after days assembling a film crew and preparing the factory. The boiler could have been stoked to the highest levels, for the sake of a compelling scene—straining, rattling, and exploding. Only in her death would she succeed in pleasing her masters.

"She served the people," the Red Guard said. "With all she had."

Like Midnight Chang, she would have gladly died for the revolution. Even in the wet heat, this girl's uniform remained spotless and her braids tidy. Pins with the Chairman's profile, plastic and ceramic, glittered on her shirt like dragonfly eyes. She scrutinized my callused fingers, my matted hair, and my tattered uniform, then slid her hands into her pants pockets, hiding her soft palms and neat fingernails. I wanted to slap her until she understood she shouldn't give herself up to a revolution that offered nothing in return. What a stupid girl, to worship Midnight Chang. What stupid girls we were.

AFTER THAT, I STOPPED traveling as a Red Guard. I wanted nothing more to do with the Chairman's revolution, not even as a disguise. I had been one of millions of young revolutionaries, and now I would be among tens of millions of peasants and proletariats. I worked and bartered, slept under bridges, peddled herbal remedies, told fortunes. I lied and stole muddy shoes drying on a doorstep, a patched shirt from a clothesline, a sweater from an outdoor theatrical troupe.

All the while, I harbored the faint hope that my family was safe, a hope like a single candle shining, flickering but persistent in the wind. As the Chairman withdrew from the public eye, I hoped he might be in decline.

Every time I thought of you in your shallow grave, I almost collapsed, wanting to hear my father's stories, feel my mother's hand, and curl beside my sister. But I told myself to stay away from our village, and I traveled as far as I could to protect them.

My third winter on the road, hundreds of thousands of people left for the countryside to be reeducated, a government purge to end the unrest. Eventually, millions would get forced out of the cities, many of them former Red Guard sentenced to an uncertain future.

Around then, I found my neighbor Fatty Song. Impossible, but so it happened. In Ganzhou, a damp backwater, I thought I might find work as a laborer, bricklayer, maid, or washerwoman, any job that existed between the cracks that kept me from becoming a beggar, pickpocket, or prostitute—though I'd considered those, too.

He was slumped outside a train station, his eyes closed, holding out his smudged palms. It couldn't be him, so far from our village, but he had the same scar above his eye where his father's hoe had hit him by accident back when he was a child.

Squatting beside Fatty Song, I slipped a steamed bun into his hand, which he stuffed into his mouth. I uttered his name, my breath twisting in the cold. "Fatty Song." The nickname made him recognize me.

"Little Mei," he said.

I asked how he came to be here. He'd worked at a steel mill. "The heat was worse than any hell," he said, his voice raspy. He gave off a vinegar smell. "Men lost their hands, caught in the machines. Or fell in, burned so badly their own mothers wouldn't have recognized them. I'd had enough."

"Are you going home?" I asked.

He nodded.

Maybe he could take my family a message. A train wheezed into the station and unloaded passengers carrying heavy sacks, their faces smudged from travel. The air turned pungent with sweat and tobacco. Many were beginning the journey that Fatty Song wanted to put to an end, and they averted their eyes from his misfortune.

"Can you tell my parents you've seen me?" I asked. "That I'm okay?"

He stared at his callused hands. "Your mother died," he said.

Ma. My first word, my first plea, my first longing.

From a relapse of the fever that had killed his sister, he explained. His beloved younger sister, for whom he'd long ago asked if I could bring back a sweet. "Your Ba collapsed and died in the fields not long after."

My father's cough had been carving away at him before I'd left home. Did it end his life? I remembered the way he stretched, his arms wide enough to embrace the sky. His hoarse laughter. His silences, sometimes days long. Before I knew of the Chairman, of revolutionary heroes, I'd only had one god: my father. He inhabited every myth, every legend: no giant as towering, no demon as ferocious. The first god I'd prayed to, yearning for the approval that I would never have again.

As if from a great distance, I heard Fatty Song say that my sister left with a traveling tailor. Gone. Everyone, gone. The noise of the train station dulled, like I'd been underwater for too long, and I needed air.

"Which sister?" I asked at last. "Which one lived? And which one died?"

"I don't know," he said. "I'd already left by then." Someone from our village, who'd later followed him to the steel mill, had told him the news.

He wrapped his arms around me until I stopped shaking. Despite my numbness over the months, I was still capable of grief. Still capable of loving my parents and my sisters. I'd harbored the hope that I might go back and see them someday. I'd tell them about you, the son they'd always wanted.

"Where have you been?" he asked.

"Traveling." We'd both lost our sisters. Both far from home, we should look after each other.

He searched the station over my shoulder, his expression sharpened with cunning. He might remember that the Party official had selected me over the other girls. I once had value. With his sister's death, maybe he'd given up thinking that he could protect anyone but himself. Who knew what he might do, in exchange for a train ticket, a warm bed, and endless meals?

I stood up. My clothes were torn, but I wasn't hunched on the ground, not like him. I told him I'd come back with more food for him. Instead, with the last of my cash, I bought a ticket for the next train leaving the station, to flee the place where I learned my family had been destroyed.

I spent a sleepless night on the train, overwhelmed by memories of my family's final days together: Ma, braiding my hair. Ba, bringing me water as I studied beneath the acacia tree. My sisters, nestled against me in bed. I don't remember the conductor, the passengers beside me, the announcements, or the landscape we passed through, only the jolt as the train arrived. Outside the station, I blinked in the sunlight, my body brittle with grief.

I didn't know where to go next, only that I had to stay away from the graves of my parents and my sister. If I never knew for certain which sister died, one could live a day and die the next, the other reborn.

THE CHAIRMAN HADN'T PUNISHED my family for my crimes, the only solace I could find in this loss. Within days, I found other reasons to blame myself. I should have been in the village, I never should have left, and I could have nursed my parents and my sister and kept them alive. I was unable to bear the sight of families, of fathers and daughters, of husbands and wives, of sisters, of their shared features, expressions, and gestures reflected and repeated. Of squabbles and slaps echoing from courtyards and apartment windows.

Sometimes, the guilt made me reckless: when I lingered at a muddy cliff's edge, when I held the blade of a sharp scythe loosely, when I ventured too close to the wheels of a wooden cart. When I waded into the deepest part of a swollen river, carrying my rucksack above my head. When my foot slipped, I pitched forward, welcoming what was to come: cold blackness, and the end.

Each time, I pulled myself back. With no reason to return home, with every reason to leave, I quickened my way to the border. The country's far southern reaches in Guangdong province were known as a land of bandits and barbarians, whose people had traveled overseas to work for more than a century. The Chairman, who'd missed his chance to study abroad, had called those who left unpatriotic, traitors for abandoning the motherland. Many rebellions originated here, but if people were rising up against the Chairman, I didn't find them. In the Pearl River Delta, the lush red earth was laced with streams, and dandelion clouds were reflected in the rice paddies. Like most everywhere I'd traveled, the locals eased my passage, feeding and sheltering me in exchange for my help with the chores.

The borders were sealed, but I learned that the determined could cross over to Hong Kong. I could try to slip past the guards and their dogs to cross the land that connected the Kowloon Peninsula to the mainland. West of Hong Kong, another route began on rocky cliffs that would take me through Shenzhen Bay. East of Hong Kong, the route through Mirs Bay was longer, and sharks were said to roam the waters.

For a month, I practiced swimming in a tributary of the Pearl River, hours a day until I became supple and strong as a beaver's tail. The Chairman used to cradle me in the pool so that I could practice my strokes and kicks. I'd been weightless in his arms. Now I'd swim farther than he'd ever dared.

The villagers must have known I wanted to escape. They didn't warn me or try to stop me, but they didn't have to: The drowned, those who didn't succeed in their quest to flee, washed up onshore, and authorities displayed their bloated, flyblown bodies and their putrid reek as a warning. I swore not to fail.

CLUTCHING A PATCHED TIRE, I arrived at sunset. The sinuous terraced lines on the rolling hills resembled the stripes of a tiger poised to leap. Pollen drifted through the air. The golden canopy of a cassia tree, glowing in the last rays of light, seemed a beacon. It was the spring of 1969, nearly three years after I'd left the Lake Palaces. Though the checkpoint, with its barbed wire fence, was on the other side of the peninsula, patrols were known to roam here, too. I waded into the channels of water that snaked through the mangroves, grasses brushing against my pants and mud sucking at my bare feet. A branch cracked and I ducked, listening and waiting. An animal, maybe. Farther into the marsh, where the air smelled of moldering, of rotten eggs, I discovered heaps of clothes, a pair of boots, tinned food, a crumpled map, a book, and other treasures the escapees pitched when they decided what was most important: this possession or their life.

I wondered if I was ready, if I should turn back. If I delayed any longer, I might lose my nerve. Blood pounding in my ears, loud as drums, I plunged into the waves. Across the bay lay Hong Kong.

The ground fell away, the salt water burning my nose and mouth. With the tire, I could rest when I needed to, and wouldn't have to swim the whole way.

I kicked and kicked until a wave slapped me in the face and I coughed and flailed, grasping at the surface, clutching at nothing. The tire slipped out of my hands. I treaded water, craning my head, but didn't see it. I'd gone too far to turn back, though. The breaststroke would sustain me longest, slow and steady through the waves.

Sometime later, I stopped again, trying to fight off the panic seeping in. I couldn't judge my direction, if I was coming or going, sinking or swimming. Was the jolt against my foot a shark nosing its way to the surface, or the tire floating back up?

The Chairman's early lessons returned to me. Stroke, stroke, stroke, stroke. Breathe. Stroke, stroke, stroke, stroke. Breathe. Stroke, stroke, stroke, stroke. Breathe. A sequence elemental as a heartbeat. As I swam toward fires burning on the far shore, I dreamed, not asleep but not quite awake, either.

I am paddling up the murky river of my ancestors. Everyone swims along with me. Ba! Ma! Your daughter has returned! And my son, my son, my son, now a toddler. We clasp hands and drift in the current flowing upstream. Silver bubbles streak behind us like comets. You let go, wanting to play in the eddies and shallows. Ahead, I recognize the grandmother I have never met, and her mother, and her mother. "Mei Xiang," they call to me. Grandfather, too, and his father, and his father: a line of lives converging. Far below, boulders are the remains of ancient cities and a flash of light is sunshine glancing off a pagoda. Fires burn and palaces appear and disappear, armies clash and race apart, and dynasties tick backward.

The Chairman waits for me. For all of us. Light streams around him, from his eyes, his fingertips, and his mouth. With cupped hands, I push back to move forward. My legs kick in time to my heartbeat, to the beginning, to a fountainhead high in the mountains, clear and pure.

CHAPTER 30

I WASHED UP ON MUDDY FLATS IN HONG KONG, WHERE EMPTY oyster shells drifted like snow.

Walking down the beach, I turned for a final look at my homeland, fuzzy green on the horizon, under skies hazy as weak tea. I squinted, and it seemed to recede. I said farewell to you and my family, to Teacher Fan and Secretary Sun. Farewell to the Chairman, and the revolutionary hero I had almost been.

At a brick church with a huge banyan tree in the courtyard, I found refuge. I received English lessons, an education, and meals in return for speaking and acting with conviction—a job I performed effortlessly, for I'd been practicing all my life. I sang the songs of miracles, of loaves and fishes, and of the dead risen.

I saved souls, lowering my eyes and softening my voice, touching my hand lightly to the wrists of strangers, whatever I could do to hold their attention. Not once did I believe. I recognized too much of the Chairman in their god, recognized my old self in the followers, praying for glory and salvation.

When the Americans put a man on the moon that summer, the world gazed up at the silvery crescent. Did the astronaut discover the moon goddess, or did she hide? Did she consider hitching a ride back to earth? Hong Kong no longer seemed far enough away from the Chairman and it was then I began thinking about more distant shores.

My escape would take a few years. To win a missionary post in America, I had to convince the pastor I could open the hearts of

Chinese immigrants. But just as I'd abandoned the revolution, the slogans and stories of heroes, I would abandon the Los Angeles church that sponsored me. I took a bus to San Francisco and found work at the Jade Dragon.

This afternoon, I've been wandering the streets of Chinatown, remembering. I stroke my mother's dowry bead in my pocket. The Chairman tried to obliterate our past, but the Chinese still revere our dead. Against his wishes, in secret, we prayed to our ancestors and asked for their blessings and protections.

I elbow past a market where produce packs the bins and turtles and frogs flop in plastic buckets, the water bubbling from a hose. The smell of scallions, earth, blood, and guts tinges the air. Disco music pumps from an apartment above the shops, and a low-slung, lime green sedan cruises the street, young men hanging out the windows.

At Portsmouth Square, the teenagers do not mourn the Chairman, gossiping instead about parties, their friends and foes. Those with a choice of idols couldn't imagine a movie star, a president, the Pope, all in one. These children would find him and his revolution backward—self-interest, not self-sacrifice, will better their lot and their families'. Their indifference would be the worst punishment of all for the Chairman.

Secretary Sun had survived his association with me—or maybe not.

After the defeat of the President, the Chairman designated the Defense Minister as his future successor. He'd proven his loyalty by creating the Little Red Book. Soon, the Chairman must have come to view him as a threat. Eventually, the Defense Minister, his wife, and son took off in a plane with half-empty fuel tanks, which crashed in Mongolia. In the newspaper, Secretary Sun was listed among those who perished, those accused of trying to assassinate the Chairman. After seeing how our country bled by its own hand, maybe he'd been desperate enough to slip secrets to the Defense Minister. How inescapable the Chairman would have seemed, as the engine sputtered and their plane spiraled out of control. How fortunate I'd been to escape the Chairman, achieving what the most powerful men in the country couldn't. If I believed in divine intervention, my survival might have seemed like the work of gods.

But I owed no one. In exchange for my freedom, I'd given up my family and my country, and lost you, a cost heavier than all the rest. Alone I survived and alone I remain.

Others made their mark on history. Not long ago at the Wong Brothers Bookstore, I came across a photo of Midnight Chang. Before her death, a young man working at the French embassy had snapped a shot of her at a rally. Her hair flowed like a banner and her expression seemed fierce as the god of war, in an image copied around the world in the days when the country remained a mystery. A face fit to lead a revolution. Although Midnight Chang had achieved what I once longed for, I had survived.

I don't know what happened to Busy Shan or to Teacher Fan. Neither of them would have liked San Francisco, a city they would have considered too small, too slow, the people muddleheaded fools who smile too easily.

After I fled, the Chairman would have had other lovers. Dozens, I suspected, for each conquest helped him deny his decline. But still, the disease would have crept through him, inexorable, incremental as the tide. As the Chairman's body failed him, his lovers would have become his nurses, his flesh meting out punishment to a man who believed himself without law and without heaven.

With his death, people here can now reach family trapped on the other side, the sons and daughters and parents they left behind in China, and return to the homeland they thought closed forever, kneel and press their foreheads to the soil.

In the newspaper box, I spot him on the front page—his fleshy cheeks, the large mole on his chin, his beneficent smile—under the headline: "Leader of Red China, Dead at 82." I suck in a sharp breath. The news that felt distant and unreal suddenly cuts me in half: before, after. The Chairman would have believed that he would face down this enemy, like all else deemed impossible to conquer. As a teenager, the most I could do was run from him, but the journey that began in my village, ascended onto Tiananmen, crossed China and an ocean, ends here.

The street steepens by the Jade Dragon, one of the neighborhood's best, where we serve meat every night, every meal, not only once a year, where the doors open to anyone who can pay, and the menu is wide enough to include a humble bowl of rice porridge and an extravagant bird's nest soup. The restaurant shares the block with a church, an herbalist, and a bakery, the air reeking of powdery herbs, incense, and pastries flaky with lard. Through the church's iron gate, a mossy angel watches. I stroke its grimy face, soot smeared like a mustache above its plump mouth, more beautiful in its imperfection, for the comfort it offers the grieving. For those who go on living.

The clank and whir of the Jade Dragon's kitchen echo in the alley. The cook is steady and kind, and his moves behind the stove fluid as a dancer's. Tonight, after clearing the dishes and flicking off the lights in the dining room, he and I will eat a midnight meal of spicy tofu and ground pork in the kitchen. It has become our nightly ritual, when my restaurant is quiet, the kitchen warm, and no one else seems awake in the neighborhood. The brightness I felt, in the best of times with the Chairman—to burn like that again is impossible. But I deserve a longer-lasting flame.

Maybe I will share my story with this honorable man. If I tell him about you, who knows what might follow?

I pass a playground where boys chase one another and girls pump their legs on the swings. They're about the age you would have turned this year, when a child's roundness sharpens and lengthens. My yearning for you returns; my yearning has never gone away. I never had a chance to discover who you were and who you would have become.

Before I met you, I viewed children as defeat, life closing in, repeating the fate of my grandmother, my mother, all the women who came before me. I didn't want to give birth to a son. I wanted to *be* the son, free of a baby strapped to my back, free to run. After I lost you, for a long time I promised myself that I'd never get pregnant again.

So much of my life in San Francisco has felt marked off, but my savings, rolled into tube socks and stuffed beneath my mattress, have been a safeguard against unknown calamities, and could provide for a future whose shape I'm beginning to see.

I duck into a store to buy a string of firecrackers. Not to celebrate the Chairman's death, but to honor your life. The Chairman drew his last breath today, minutes after midnight of the Moon Festival. It's also my birthday. When the Chairman was my age, he was still a library clerk dreaming of revolution. His glorious future was yet to come. Once I wished to be memorialized in a proverb, in a story handed down through generations, but now I just want a long life, as long as the Chairman's. Longer.

I strike a match. One, two, three, four sputter and die out in the breeze. Cupping my hand, I light what remains of the pack and toss it onto the firecrackers in the gutter. When they fail to catch, I turn to leave. Then the hissing starts. Bucking, twisting, and crack bam boom. I walk back toward the smoke and heat and light, my arms spread, ready to accept this gift.

*Y*EARS AGO, A TEASING GLIMPSE OF BLACK-AND-WHITE DOC-
umentary footage intrigued me: Chairman Mao surrounded by giggling young women in tight sweaters. As I would learn, the peasant
turned revolutionary was a fan of ballroom dancing—and young
women, who partnered with him on the dance floor and in the bedroom.

When I looked for more information about these ingenues, I
couldn't find much. In his memoir, Mao's doctor wrote, "To have
been rescued by the party was already sufficient good luck for such
young women. To be called to the Chairman was the greatest experience of their lives. For most Chinese, a mere glimpse of Mao standing
impassively atop Tiananmen was a coveted opportunity, the most up-
lifting, exciting, exhilarating experience they would know . . .
Imagine, then, what it meant for a young girl to be called into Mao's
chambers to serve his pleasure!"

I suspected—I *knew*—the relationships had to be more complicated, especially for those whom he kept on as his "confidential
clerks." Zhang Yufeng was eighteen years old when she met the
Chairman—in the liminal years between girl and woman, and so
young by comparison to Mao, then in his late sixties. In time, she
would handle and read aloud the reams of documents that the Chairman commented upon daily. Toward the end of his life, as his speech
became garbled by illness, she served an important role, interpreting
what he said.

Nothing I uncovered described the rhythm of their days: how she and the other dance partners gained his trust and maneuvered the complex politics at Zhongnanhai, the former imperial gardens turned home to the Chairman and the country's seat of power.

I believe that fiction flourishes where the official record ends, and that research should serve as the floor—and not the ceiling—of the imagination. For the first time, I grappled with the challenges of writing a historical novel. By taking a leap of empathy, I wanted to approach not only the contours but the truth of my protagonist—a truth that was emblematic of the millions of impoverished women who have shaped China in their own ways yet remain absent from the country's official narrative.

And so, I began to write about how one of these teenagers could have influenced the course of the Cultural Revolution, Mao's decade-long campaign that plunged the country into chaos. What was it like for a peasant girl to get swept into the patriotism of those times and to meet a man she'd been raised to worship as a god?

As the American-born daughter of Chinese immigrants, I've long been curious about this tumultuous chapter of my ancestral homeland, led by one of the world's most fascinating leaders. For years, I'd been under the mistaken impression that all of my relatives left in the aftermath of World War II, decades before the upheaval of the Cultural Revolution. Only as an adult did I learn that part of my extended family had suffered during the political turmoil; no one provided much detail, though. As with many who fled tragedy in search of a better life elsewhere, my elders preferred to focus on the future rather than dwell on the past—even as those hardships indelibly marked them.

I'm also a journalist who has covered Asia and the diaspora for more than two decades. San Francisco's Chinatown—the oldest in North America and still a destination for newcomers and tourists alike—became a haven for my characters in A River of Stars. For this novel, I discovered stories of those who'd survived the Cultural Revolution. An inconspicuous dim sum cook in San Francisco—once a young rabble-rouser in the Chinese countryside—would in middle age lead a workers' campaign to win back unpaid restaurant wages. Those conversations reminded me, once again, of how immigration connects the next-door to the world, and the secrets we all carry.

In 2004, on a reporting trip for the *San Francisco Chronicle* to the villages and factory towns of southern China, I met teenagers who dreamed of a bigger life, and whose strength, smarts, and courage inspired me. On another visit in 2008, I conducted interviews for my novel in villages outside of Beijing, as well as explored the Forbidden City, Tiananmen Square and the Great Hall of the People, the high red walls of Zhongnanhai, Shanghai, and Hong Kong, tracing the path that would become Mei's.

Perched on a tiny wooden stool, I interviewed grannies who'd lived through the Great Leap Forward and the Cultural Revolution.

One stared at me in disbelief when I explained that I'd come all the way from the United States. "I'm from America, but have Chinese parents," I said.

She squinted at me. "But you don't look American." I wasn't sandy-haired and hazel-eyed like my husband, who sat beside us.

In the lull that followed, he cheerfully volunteered in Mandarin, *"Wo bu dong"*—*I don't know,* one of the few phrases he can say.

She couldn't stop talking about his language prowess, but when I asked her about Mao, she grew reticent. "I don't know anything. I never learned how to read," she muttered.

I found the same evasiveness at a market where I browsed porcelain figurines depicting the Cultural Revolution. One statuette portrayed a man on his hands and knees; a Chinese friend would later translate the signboard around the statue's neck—DOWN WITH CAPITALIST ROADERS! His tormentor brandished a sword, his foot on his victim's back.

Sensing my curiosity, the shopkeeper blurted, "It's not to hurt him. It's just to show people."

It could have been what he'd been taught, or perhaps he wanted to smooth over the ugliness to a foreigner.

The political past transformed itself in other ways. In Shanghai, we stayed in a former villa of Mao's turned boutique hotel, whose grounds included a swimming pool and luxury steak house.

With the passage of enough time, could the violence of the Cultural Revolution become a joke to those who never learned much about it? While riding a train, I encountered a group of Boy Scouts who came aboard in uniform. Americans, I guessed. A teenager pulled out an English-language copy of the Little Red Book and recited from it, trying to get his friends to laugh. Yet it struck me how thin a line separated them from the young revolutionaries who had once revered those words: same age, same little scarves around their necks, same immersion in an ideology.

Some places, though, remained seemingly unchanged by time. Walking along mudflats in Hong Kong and studying the hazy green mainland across the bay, I realized it was just as I'd described it in an early draft of my book, before I'd ever stepped foot there. It felt satisfying to have nailed the detail but also eerie, as if I'd willed it into being.

In my research, I also drew from published sources, including Li Zhisui's *The Private Life of Chairman Mao;* Frank Dikötter's *The Cultural Revolution: A People's History, 1962–1976;* Yang Jisheng's *Tombstone: The Great Chinese Famine, 1958–1962;* Feng Jicai's *Voices from the Whirlwind;* Michael Schoenhals and Roderick MacFarquhar's *Mao's Last Revolution;* Alexander Pantsov and Steven I. Levine's *Mao: The Real Story;* Edgar Snow's *Red Star over China;* Xinran's *China Witness: Voices from a Silent Generation;* Lanling Xiaoxiaosheng's *Jin Ping Mei;* Shi Nai'an's *The Water Margin;* Jan Wong's *Red China Blues;* and the archives of *The New York Times.*

Many details in my book are recorded in history: Mao kept nocturnal hours, relied on sleeping pills, wrote poetry, and occasionally took to his bed, depressed. Teenage girls from cultural troupes danced with him. He also swam in the Yangtze River in July 1966, a feat heralding his return to power during the Cultural Revolution. The characters of the Madame, President, Defense Minister, and Premier are very loosely based on those in Mao's inner circle; their rivalries and alliances existed, though my novel departs in the particulars. I wanted to write a story from the perspective of someone relegated to the margins, yet who would have as much intelligence, ambition, and yearning as those leaders.

In the decade and a half or so that I spent researching and writing my book, history marched on. A half century after the Cultural Revolution, I bore witness to the Me Too Movement, the Covid-19 pandemic, and the xenophobia that stoked anti-Asian hate crimes in the United States.

While those events are anachronistic to my novel, they nonetheless influenced my thinking about power dynamics between older men and younger women, the debilitating impact of isolation and loneliness, and the consequences of demonization and demagoguery.

Mei's harrowing journey raises questions about power, manipulation, and memory that resonate then and now. The past is never as distant as it seems.

ACKNOWLEDGMENTS

*T*HE PATH TO FINISHING A BOOK TAKES MANY UNEXPECTED turns, detours, and dead ends, as I discovered while writing and revising this novel. Many times, I might have given up, but I believed in the book—and people believed in me.

Thank you, Margaret Sutherland Brown, my wise, brilliant agent—first with the incisive Emma Sweeney, and now with the hardworking team at Folio Literary Management.

My eternal gratitude goes to my editor, Susanna Porter. As with my debut novel, she dazzled me with her insight, guiding me through many drafts with passion, patience, and cheer.

The team at Random House is superlative, including Emily Hartley, Sydney Shiffman, Erin Richards, Emma Thomasch, Belina Huey, Michele Sulka, Cara DuBois, Madeline Hopkins, Toby Ernst, Angela McNally, Barbara Bachman, and others. A huge thanks to Ballantine Books president Kara Welsh, deputy publisher Kim Hovey, and publisher Jennifer Hershey for continuing to support my storytelling.

The National Endowment for the Arts provided vital support, as did my amazing writing groups. Maury Zeff, Jane Hannon Kalmes, and David Baker read countless drafts, as did Aimee Phan, Valerie Miner, and Camille T. Dungy, who helped get the novel over the finish line.

Yalitza Ferreras offered perceptive feedback, jokes, and encouragement. Dawn MacKeen remains my virtual watercooler buddy extraordinaire, and Bridget Quinn buoys me in frequent calls and texts—I wish her much pie, now and forever. And I'm grateful to Kirstin Chen and Angie Chuang, both generous, insightful readers.

When I closed my office door, Jaqueline Perez and, later, Gurneet Somal lavished loving care on my twin sons.

Many thanks to the magazines that published excerpts from earlier versions of the manuscript: "The Sea Palaces" in *At Length* and "Third Daughter" in *ZYZZYVA,* whose editors, Laura Cogan and Oscar Villalon, foster essential literary culture in the Bay Area and beyond.

My stellar professors and classmates at UC Riverside read the earliest drafts of this project, and Susan Straight, Michael Jaime-Becerra, and Chris Abani graciously served on my thesis committee. Not long after, invaluable reads by Kaitlin Solimine and Kevin Allardice helped the book evolve.

Other friends who rooted for and advised me along the way include Reese Kwon, Alicia Jo Rabins, Yang Huang, Jessica Carew Kraft, Beth Nguyen, Susan Ito, Pia Sarkar, Josué Hurtado, Ryan Kim, Irene Chan, Jason Husgen, Mary Ladd, the Pak-Stevensons, the Taylors, the Freedes, the Cooper-Jordans, the Berthaloneys, the Love Boat Crew, the Karaoke Book Club, the IBC Book Club, and the Cookbook Club.

My gratitude to the Bread Loaf Writers' Conference, the Community of Writers, Aspen Words, and Hedgebrook. It's been a great pleasure to teach and learn from students and colleagues at the Warren Wilson MFA Program for Writers, Tin House Workshop, Mendocino Coast Writers' Conference, and Sewanee Writers' Conference. A deep thanks to Anya Backlund at Blue Flower Arts. Over the years, the Writers Grotto in San Francisco has sustained me, as well as the editors and reporters at the *San Francisco Chronicle.*

I'm indebted to the libraries and booksellers who have supported and encouraged me and so many writers. And I deeply appreciate the readers who have connected with my work and shared their stories with me.

Much love to my mother, Sylvia, and my late father, Lo-Ching; my sister, Inez, and her son, Declan; my brother, Lawrence, his wife, Carenna, and their son, Jake; my in-laws, Robert and Patricia Puich; and my sister-in-law, Kristine Puich, and her partner, Jeff El-massian.

To my twins: I'm proud to be your mother. You make me laugh and inspire me daily. And to my husband, Marc, who champions me in every way: You have all my love, always.

ABOUT THE AUTHOR

VANESSA HUA is a columnist for the *San Francisco Chronicle* and the author of the novel *A River of Stars* and a story collection, *Deceit and Other Possibilities*. A National Endowment for the Arts Literature Fellow, she has also received a Rona Jaffe Foundation Writers' Award, the Asian/Pacific American Award for Literature, and a Steinbeck Fellowship in Creative Writing, as well as awards from the Society of Professional Journalists and the Asian American Journalists Association, among others. She has filed stories from China, Burma, South Korea, Panama, and Ecuador, and her work has appeared in publications including *The New York Times*, *The Washington Post*, and *The Atlantic*. She has taught most recently at the Warren Wilson MFA Program for Writers and the Sewanee Writers' Conference. The daughter of Chinese immigrants, she lives in the San Francisco Bay Area with her family.

vanessahua.com

Facebook.com/vanessahuawriter

Twitter: @vanessa_hua

ABOUT THE TYPE

This book was set in Fournier, a typeface named for Pierre-Simon Fournier (1712–68), the youngest son of a French printing family. He started out engraving woodblocks and large capitals, then moved on to fonts of type. In 1736 he began his own foundry and made several important contributions in the field of type design; he is said to have cut 147 alphabets of his own creation. Fournier is probably best remembered as the designer of St. Augustine Ordinaire, a face that served as the model for the Monotype Corporation's Fournier, which was released in 1925.